SONG

of the

DEAD

A REIGN OF THE FALLEN NOVEL

SONG
of the
DEAD

A **REIGN OF THE FALLEN** NOVEL

SARAH GLENN MARSH

RAZORBILL

RAZORBILL

An imprint of Penguin Random House LLC, New York

First published in the United States of America by Razorbill,
an imprint of Penguin Random House LLC, 2019

Visit us online at penguinrandomhouse.com

THE LIBRARY OF CONGRESS HAS CATALOGED THE HARDCOVER EDITION AS FOLLOWS:
Names: Marsh, Sarah Glenn, author.
Title: Song of the Dead / Sarah Glenn Marsh.
Description: New York, NY : Razorbill, 2019. | Sequel to: Reign of the fallen. |
Summary: Odessa and Meredy journey beyond Karthia to a land where the Dead rule
the night and dragons roam the streets, but just as they are beginning to explore the
new world a terrifying development in Karthia summons them home at once.
Identifiers: LCCN 2018026567 | ISBN 9780448494425 (hardback)
Subjects: | CYAC: Fantasy. | Dead—Fiction. | Monsters—Fiction. | Magic—Fiction.
Classification: LCC PZ7.1.M3727 So 2019 | DDC [Fic]—dc23
LC record available at https://lccn.loc.gov/2018026567

Printed in the United States of America

Paperback ISBN 9780448494432

1 3 5 7 9 10 8 6 4 2

For Lucy, for believing

SONG
of the
DEAD

I

Today, for the first time in my life, I didn't wake up in Karthia.

As a pearly dawn gives way to bright morning sun, Meredy and I, realizing that the *Paradise* has almost slowed to a stop, bound out of our narrow cabin and up to the deck to watch the remainder of our first journey into a new land. "We're almost there!" I whisper gleefully. But apparently entering the harbor and anchoring the ship is a longer process than I anticipated.

Blinking away the last traces of sleepiness, we wait at the railing and watch the dock workers milling about below. I wish I were with them. My feet itch to touch solid ground again, and judging by the way Meredy keeps stretching and pacing, so do hers.

"Welcome to Lyris," Kasmira calls across the deck of the *Paradise*, grinning at our eager expressions as her crew scrambles to drop anchor.

Lyris, the island where Kasmira has been buying cacao and coffee under cover of darkness for years while King Wylding forbade all travel to and from Karthia, doesn't look much different from the harbor in Grenwyr City. And yet, so much *is* different. For one thing, this is the first time Kasmira has been able to anchor the *Paradise* in broad daylight.

Her crew lets out a cheer, the anchor apparently secured. Some sailors slap one another's backs, and a few even dance a little. I'm tempted to join them.

We're *finally* here. It seems like we've been at sea much longer than a mere day, and as I exchange a glance with a slightly pale Meredy, I'm sure she feels the same.

Yesterday, we left Karthia trailing a swath of mist and had to skirt around a storm, everyone looking tinged with green. And while this morning brought sunny skies and calm waters, I'm worried I'm not cut out for a life at sea. Hopefully that'll change, though. After all, Lyris is only the first of many lands we plan to explore.

There's a loud thud as someone lowers the gangway.

Meredy gazes past the docks, far into the distance, and points at a collection of colorful tents that seem to stretch to the horizon. Her eyes shine, and she smiles faintly. Adventure is beckoning her, just as it used to call to Evander.

"Race you to that market," she says, nudging my shoulder.

"How do you know what it is?" I ask, but she's already barreling toward the gangway, forcing me to break into my fastest run to catch up.

We sprint past low wooden houses and inns, bound for the sprawling rainbow of tents ahead, not even stopping to take in the people and animals that fill the narrow streets.

There's a slight bite to the wind blowing off the sea, so I draw my cloak tighter as we reach the first of the tents and pause for breath at last. Wonderful smells wash over me like an embrace: perfume and pie, lavender and leather, soap and sugar. But just as I start to enjoy the market's atmosphere, a girl with long ash-blond hair hurries by, and I'm suddenly reminded of Valoria. She loves trying new things more than anyone.

"See?" Meredy pants, looking proud of herself as she takes rapid breaths of heady, sweet air. "Definitely a market." Noticing my expression, she frowns. "What's wrong? Mad that I beat you here?"

I don't have the heart to tease her and tell her that I actually beat her by two seconds. Instead, I say, "Valoria."

From the light dimming in Meredy's eyes, I don't need to explain further.

It's thanks to our new queen that we Karthians can now roam outside of our kingdom, wherever we please. Valoria, who I still think of more as my friend than as my ruler, would want to explore every inch of this place, in all its colorful, aromatic glory, in all its secrets waiting to be discovered.

"We'll take notes for her. On *everything*," Meredy assures me, stepping to one side of the nearest tent to let a man and his mule-drawn cart pass.

I nod, my throat tight. It feels like years ago, not months, that Valoria was a curious princess on her first and only trip into the Deadlands, constantly straying from my side and questioning everything around her. I'd been stuck with her while my partner in all things, Evander, walked ahead of us, forcing me to feign interest in the princess's plans to study the correlation between people's eye colors and different forms of magic, like how everyone born with blue eyes sees gateways to the spirit world and can learn to raise the dead. Learning, she'd insisted, is fun.

While I don't always agree with Valoria on the learning front, she has a point. I'm on this journey because I hope to learn something, though I'm not exactly sure what that is yet.

In a daze, I follow Meredy through the tented marketplace, trying to memorize every detail to regale Valoria with . . . someday. The people here are as varied in height, coloring, and styles of hair and clothing as Karthians, making them feel almost like acquaintances despite the unfamiliar, musical language that swirls around us everywhere we go.

A pair of blown-glass trinkets catches my eye, and immediately, my savings come out to pay for them—a brown bear for Meredy and a marigold for me. As a gentle woman carefully wraps each one, Meredy catches my eye from three stalls away, beaming as she holds up two enormous bags of coffee beans, maybe ten pounds each. "It's not a lifetime supply," she calls, "but it's a start. After all, you won our bet a while ago. We've made it more than a whole day without arguing, so . . . I figure it's time I begin fulfilling my end of the bargain."

"You remembered?" I fight back a reluctant smile, torn between regret over Valoria's absence and how happy Meredy makes me, seemingly without realizing it.

Meredy tosses her head back and laughs, momentarily warming me all over. When she meets my eyes, it's with a knowing look that tells me she caught my smile after all.

"Ooh, look at those!" she says suddenly, making a beeline toward a display of star-shaped flowers, blooms purple-red like her hair and bigger than her hands. We buy some of those, and some yellow roses, too, to spruce up our dull room on the *Paradise*. Next, we purchase thick slabs of pie laced with spices that make my mouth water in a single sniff. We buy whole dried fish for Lysander, Meredy's pet grizzly bear, and new leather gloves for Kasmira to protect her hands from the roughness of her ship's wheel. We're even tempted by a display of new fur-lined cloaks in every possible shade of a mage's eyes: from stormy gray to deep charcoal for weather workers, spring green to emerald for beast masters, hazel for healers, even hues of earthen browns for inventors.

My hand stills on the last brown cloak. There are only four types of mages represented here, not all five as I'd assumed when I saw the vibrant display.

"Huh. There's no blue." Meredy frowns, having noticed the problem, too. No sky blue to match Simeon's eyes, no dark blue like Evander's—nothing for necromancers. "Shame. They probably ran out." She shrugs, then points to a cart selling frothy pink cream in a cup. "Come on. We have to try that!"

I follow her, not wanting her to know anything is amiss. Even I can't explain why my stomach sinks as I glance over my shoulder for one last look at the cloaks.

The cream tastes like fruit—not any fruit I can name, but it's delicious all the same. Still, nothing I see or taste helps me to do what I want to more than anything else in this world—forget. Forget who I once was: a newly appointed master necromancer in love with her job and sure of her place in the world; forget the pain of losing my heart, a boy named Evander, and my mentor, Master Cymbre, within mere weeks of each other; forget the monsters I faced down with fire, monsters who had once been gentle Dead, some of whom I'd raised with my own magic; forget the living monster my former friend Prince Hadrien became when he murdered King Wylding and countless others; forget the sick, wet sound of my blade sinking into him when I ended it all so his sister, Valoria, could take the throne and lead us into a better future.

Of course, forgetting isn't easy, but I figure the more distance I put between me and Karthia, the better chance I have at finally stopping the nightmares that have plagued me since Evander's death, and gotten even worse after Hadrien's.

"Stars, it's nearly time to meet Kasmira for supper!" Meredy pulls me back to reality by shoving some of her shopping into my arms, having just returned from inspecting some patterned cloth under a big red tent. "Too bad we ruined our appetites," she adds with a guilty grin. "Say—you still thinking about Valoria? Or . . . ?"

I shake my head, not because I don't want to tell her, but because I'm not quite sure how to answer. All afternoon, this vague, nagging unease has stuck with me, as if I'm missing something, like when I was a child and I'd worry my tongue against the mushy gap where a tooth used to be without fully realizing it.

It isn't until we start walking toward the small tavern on the water where we agreed to meet Kasmira at sundown that it dawns on me: I haven't seen any Dead since we got here. Granted, I wasn't searching hard, but I should have seen at least one shrouded figure at the market. The Dead are always hungrier than the living, and the market simmered with fresh-cooked goods waiting to be devoured.

Just behind an inn to our left, I glimpse a familiar gleam of blue—a gateway to the Deadlands—and my heart leaps. There are plenty of people on the street right now. It wouldn't be difficult to sneak away from Meredy and jump into that soft blue glow for a quick look around. Just to see if there are any spirits nearby who could tell me what happened to Lyris's Dead. Mouth going dry, heart beating faster, I wait until Meredy is several paces ahead of me and duck behind the inn.

I'm a few steps from the gate when Meredy calls, "Master Necromancer?"

I freeze, not sure if I'm disappointed or glad that she immediately noticed my absence.

She hurries toward me, glancing between me and the gate—to her green eyes, only a bare patch of earth, though she knows me well enough that her face is taut with worry. "Come on. I know we aren't hungry, but we don't want to disappoint Kasmira, and you know how she feels about waiting."

I hesitate, still torn.

But when Meredy shifts all her shopping to one hand so she can grab hold of mine with the other, I let her lead me toward our destination. Partly because I'm not sure what I'll find in the Deadlands so soon after the Battle of Grenwyr City. I might see Hadrien's spirit, and I know I'm not ready to meet his arrogant, smirking face just yet. And partly because I don't want to let go of Meredy's hand.

Shortly after I take a seat across from Kasmira in the narrow tavern, sweat begins to run down my back from the press of bodies and the warmth of the fire in the hearth. I whisk off my cloak and silently scarf down the rooster pie I ordered until a funny prickling on the back of my neck forces my gaze up from my plate.

I haven't felt the sensation of being watched so strongly since a giant Shade, the largest of those rotten-looking, corpse-devouring monsters I've ever seen, stalked Evander and me through the Deadlands. Sure enough, there are several sailors casting furtive glances my way. Exchanging whispers.

"Keep your elbows off the table, Master Necromancer, before you offend everyone from here to the edge of the world," Meredy says in my ear, followed by a giggle younger than her almost seventeen years. The mead we were served has already gone to her head, turning her cheeks a glowing pink.

Kasmira sweeps her gaze around the room, unusually quiet. "Odessa, Meredy, I hope you both got enough to eat." She keeps her voice low as she sets down her fork and casually reaches under the table. I can't hear the soft hiss of her dagger being drawn, but I know the swift and practiced motion well. "Something's not right here.

When I stand, follow me outside and head to the *Paradise*. Don't look at anyone. Don't talk to anyone. Just get on the ship, sharpish."

She slinks toward the door, Meredy and I trailing in her wake, but we only get halfway across the room before our path forward disappears, blocked by bodies.

"You there, Karthian!" the man behind the bar roars from across the tavern, pointing an accusing finger at—*me*. I say nothing, startled by the recognition, and he prompts, "You speak Kanon, don't you? I caught a few words when you came in." His command of our language is stiff and slow, but clear. As I give a hesitant nod, he adds darkly, "We may not all speak your common tongue, but everyone here knows what that pin on your chest means, *necromancer*. Your kind hasn't been welcome here for over a century."

My hand flies up to cover the sapphire pin on my tunic that marks me as a master of my magic, hoping that for a room full of people this drunk, out of sight will mean out of mind. Now I understand the lack of Dead here; there aren't necromancers around to raise anyone.

A few of the people nearby look at us with disgust as they repeat the word like a warning. "Necromancer."

"Necromancers aren't welcome here?" Meredy demands, seeming upset not just for me, but for anyone on this island with blue-eyed Sight. "What is this madness? Do Lyrians not practice their magic anymore?"

"The Republic of Lyris outlawed your kind long ago, when we saw how Karthians suffered for cheating Death," the man behind the bar spits. "All our dead are buried, as it should be. And they'll stay that way, because you're leaving now."

He jerks his head toward the door, making beads of sweat fly off his brow. He's rattled by the mere sight of me, and somehow his fear cuts worse than his words or his patrons' stares. Had Hadrien not forced me to slay him, we could have exiled him here, to an island that loathes necromancers and the Dead the way he wanted Karthians to.

I try to push toward the door, but the crowd around me doesn't budge.

"Get out of my sight before I decide to call a lawman!" the barman snarls. "Your companions, too," he adds, glaring at Kasmira and Meredy beside me. "Out. Now."

"Wait!" an old woman calls from the back of the tavern, where she's polishing glasses by the hearth. The quelling look she shoots the barman is one only a mother could give. "Do you bring news from Karthia? I didn't think King Wylding allowed his people to travel, yet I see several new faces among your crew, not just the necromancer . . ."

"He didn't let us do *anything*," one of Kasmira's younger sailors blurts, the words slurred from the drinks clutched in each of his hands. Like the old woman, he sits near the hearth, his face ruddy as the coals within. "But that old bag of bones won't be handing down any more decrees, thank the stars. Gone for good now, is'n'ee?"

The whispers in the room grow steadily louder and more frantic, like the angry buzzing of hornets. I wish we'd brought Lysander to the tavern instead of giving him guard duty back on the *Paradise*.

All night, we've been surrounded by people—an entire island full of people—who had no idea, despite being Karthia's closest neighbor, of the horror that just took place so near their homes. The death of a once-great king. The rise of a new one, a man still more like a boy who believed he could change everything for the better despite not knowing what *better* looked like, who believed himself to be so much more than what he really was—mad. For all they knew until that sailor with shit for brains opened his mouth, nothing in Karthia had changed, and we had simply come here on a routine smuggling trip. Business as usual for Kasmira and her crew—apart from docking in the daylight, that is.

Kasmira levels a glare at the sailor, drawing a finger across her throat.

"What?" he asks sheepishly. "Not like it was a secret . . ."

I shake my head. It wasn't his place to share the news of King Wylding's death. He should have left that up to Valoria, when she deemed the time was right. When she and the rest of my friends were done cursing my name for leaving without saying goodbye.

"Who's in charge of Karthia now?" a woman demands. "When will we meet them?"

"Why should we believe you? Show us proof!" a man bursts out.

"Who killed the king?" someone else asks. "Tell us what happened!"

They fire off questions like a volley of arrows, one on top of the other.

With a deep breath, I push down my anger. Kasmira will disembowel her loudmouthed sailor later, I'm sure—though in his defense, none of us ever discussed how we'd handle sharing everything that happened in Karthia recently. All we can do now is give these people a good first impression of our new queen, Valoria.

"Look," I say slowly and clearly to the crowd that's still trapping me against the wall. "Karthia is under new leadership, it's true. But it's *strong* leadership, and our queen is already making preparations to help Karthia rejoin the world. You have nothing to fear from her. She's smart, and kind, and interested in learning just about everything. I'm sure she'll want to get to know Lyris very soon."

"Did *you* kill the king?" someone shouts in response. "Is that why you left Karthia?"

"Death to necromancers!" an ale-soaked voice adds.

So much for trying to have a conversation.

More tavern-goers rush to join those who have already formed a ring around us, trapping us a mere twenty paces from the door. The rancid odors of spilled ale and unwashed men claw their way down my throat, but I've smelled worse—the stench of death and the rotting flesh of Shades—too many times to count.

It seems every person here surrounds us now, with the exception of the old woman by the hearth and a pale young woman who sits with her arms folded, her scarred face half in shadow, watching the proceedings with a glimmer of interest as she twists a braid of white-blond hair through her fingers. She seems so out of place, sweating in her heavy-looking, fur-lined clothing. I can tell at once she's not a Lyrian.

Kasmira nudges my shoulder, drawing my gaze away from the strange woman. I meet my friend's deep gray eyes, which are bright with fury.

"I didn't know, Sparrow." Kasmira spits at the feet of the nearest sailor, who snaps something at her in his language. "Necromancers, illegal?" she continues, her voice taut, though she seems undaunted by the man's threats. "Of all the stupid things I've heard in my nineteen years, this one pisses me off most." She edges her way in front of me, her dagger clutched in her left hand, trying to shield me from the leering crowd.

I reach for the wrist of her free hand, trying to pull her back. "Kas, don't—"

"I won't let them touch you," she growls, shrugging out of my grasp.

"Fine," I say softly, "but you'd better not let them touch *you*, either."

Louder, I say to the barman, "You want me gone? I'd be thrilled to leave. Honestly. Just tell your friends to quit blocking the only exit."

If he answers, I don't hear it, because just then Meredy stumbles into me, shoved by a man who towers over her, his shaggy brown hair partially obscuring his green eyes.

"This fellow just called you something rude. *Four times!*" she says through gritted teeth, rubbing her shoulder and glaring at the bear of a man advancing on us. "I offered to clean out his mouth, but I don't think he's interested."

"Forget calling a lawman. I'm gonna gut you wretches like fish and toss you out back with the rest of the rubbish," the huge man grumbles. A pin of twin emeralds gleams on his leather vest—he's a beast master, like Meredy, but apparently he's not above shoving one of his own. His gaze lingering on me, he adds, "Unnatural creature."

My face floods with heat. If someone insulted a necromancer like that in Karthia, they'd be the ones filleted and tossed in a rubbish heap—or at least, they would've been, before everything that happened with Hadrien. Maybe that's not how things are anymore. Maybe necromancers aren't going to be treated like royalty the way we used to be. Either way, I'm more bothered by this man putting his grimy hands on Meredy than I am by anything he's said.

I level a glare at him. "I doubt you're so brave without all your friends behind you," I snarl. "Want to take this outside? One on one?"

"You're a disgrace to the pin you wear," Meredy adds hotly from beside me.

The man flexes his fingers, studying us coolly. "I don't need to fight you. I know I'd win. That's why you're gonna bow to me here and now, corpse-loving scum." He punches a fist into his open palm. A massive fist.

Thinking of the biting remarks Jax would throw at this man, I miss him with a sudden fierceness that hits me like a stomachache. Careful not to let the slightest sign of pain show on my face, I force myself to gaze into the man's eyes as I finger the daggers on my belt. I've lived through being ripped open by a Shade, through being blinded and left for dead—far worse ordeals than a stranger's insults. This is nothing to me. *He* is nothing.

"I'm not corpse-loving scum," I say as calmly as I can manage. "I'm Odessa of Grenwyr." I tug both my daggers free of their sheaths, one for each hand. "And I bow to no man."

He flinches, startled, but impresses me by not stepping back. He doesn't appear to have a knife on him, but he reaches for one on the nearest table. Just my luck—it's bigger than mine. I slowly lower the daggers. I don't think I'll get very far with them, not in this crowd, and much as I want to teach this ignorant man that hands aren't for shoving, I know when I'm outmatched.

I hope Kasmira doesn't try anything too crazy with her dagger, either. Cocky to the point of dangerous as she is, even she can see we're far outnumbered despite most of her crew trying to make their way toward us.

The man in front of me lowers his big knife, still glaring. Meredy flicks her hand toward the ground, the Karthian gesture to indicate trash, and clearly it translates just fine to this armed and angry man. I groan. Good thing I haven't put my daggers away yet.

From somewhere nearby comes the distinctly awful sound of two heads cracking against each other.

The man with the big knife looks away, and I follow his gaze.

Dvora, the *Paradise*'s first mate, whose raven hair is always pinned in a perfect crown on top of her head, seems to have taken the liberty of acquainting some skulls in an attempt to create a weakness in the wall of Lyrians.

Someone throws a punch at Dvora, and she catches them by the wrist before their broad knuckles can graze her face.

The punch-thrower screams.

As if in response, the crowd's noise becomes a roar, and suddenly fists, elbows, battered tin mugs, and even rooster pie are flying through the stale air.

"That's our exit," I murmur, flicking a carrot out of my hair and putting away my daggers. I grab Meredy by the arm with one hand and Kasmira with the other. They both struggle against me, especially Kasmira. She's busy arguing with an older woman who's groping for something up her sleeve. Probably the hilt of a dagger.

"Give it up, Kas!" I tug again, and she comes to her senses, reaching the door a step ahead of me.

"I'm so sorry, Sparrow," she mutters, turning to watch our backs. "In all my days coming here, I never realized—"

"Not your fault," I tell her firmly.

As we slip out into the crisp night, Meredy makes another nasty gesture at the man who wanted to gut me like a fish. He nods to a few of his friends, and they rush out of the tavern in our wake.

"You couldn't leave it alone, could you?" My heart hammers as I break into a run.

Meredy's dark green eyes flash with defiance. "Not after what he said about you, no."

"Idiot," I huff, pushing myself harder as the men pursue us down the lane to the harbor.

"Corpse-loving scum," Meredy huffs back.

We grin at each other for the briefest moment, then run until we don't have breath left to spare for words, until the melody of Kasmira's braids tapping rhythmically against her back is louder than the cadence of heavy footfalls behind us.

We round a bend in the lane, and there, at last, we're greeted by the generous bulk of the *Paradise* silhouetted against a starry sky.

Lysander softly grumbles as we clamber onto the ship, no doubt interrupting his bear-dreams of rivers hopping with fresh salmon. So much for him being on guard duty. Still breathing hard, I lean over the rail in time to watch Dvora and the other sailors from the tavern scramble aboard.

"It's a good thing you bought enough coffee to last us a year or two," I murmur as Meredy doubles over, hands on her knees, and a bag of beans falls from inside her cloak. "Okay, maybe a month or two, knowing us. But I'll have to find a new favorite snack once it's gone, because I'm never coming back here."

Meredy raises her head, studying me thoughtfully.

Squirming slightly under her gaze, I feign interest in watching two sailors haul up the anchor. I'm ready to leave this place behind, far readier than I was to leave Karthia two days ago. But some of the excitement I felt at fulfilling Evander's dream of seeing the world is already wearing off. So far, this world isn't anything like the one he used to promise me was waiting for us, the one we whispered about late at night on his rooftop.

Karthia has forbidden travel for over two hundred years. What if all the other places we land are like Lyris? What if we sail the wide world from top to bottom, only to find more fear and hatred of necromancers? I didn't feel like I belonged in Karthia after the battle, but maybe I was sensing more than that when I decided to escape to the sea.

Maybe, after everything that's changed, I don't belong anywhere at all.

II

The Shade darts toward my friends and me on all fours, drooling and snarling as it breathes the human-scented air, a rarity in the Deadlands. Bits of gray, rotten flesh fly off it as it bounds into a field of luminous flowers, gaining ground even as we run our hardest.

Valoria falls first, as the monster's bony hand wraps around her ankle and tugs. I spin around and draw my sword, but too late. Valoria's already gone, and the monster has Simeon and Jax in its fists, shaking their limp bodies as their heads loll between their shoulders.

Unhinging its jaw, the Shade grinds its razor-sharp teeth in anticipation. It pops Jax into its mouth, then Simeon, as I hack at it with my sword. The monster doesn't even seem to notice the cuts I'm making. It just keeps gulping down my friends as I sob and slash at it.

Now it's got Danial and Kasmira. I thought they'd run ahead to safety when the monster grabbed Valoria.

I shove my sword through its middle, but of course, Shades don't have hearts. Black blood leaks from the wound I created.

The Shade releases a gleeful howl, sending spikes of cold down my back. Gazing into its sightless face, I realize what's made it so happy: It's cradling Meredy's broken body, about to swallow her up.

With an anguished yell, I pull my sword free, aiming to cut off the creature's ugly head. But my sword turns to dust in my hands.

There's nothing I can do.

"Odessa!" someone calls from a distance.

But I don't look to see who spoke. Instead, I force myself to watch as the monster unhinges its jaw, splashing Meredy's pale face with drool.

Just as suddenly as it raises her to its mouth, it drops her. It grabs me by the shoulders, locking the black pits of its eyes on mine, and releases an ear-shattering cry.

"Wake up!"

I blink into the deepest darkness, breathing hard, shrugging off the lingering haze of a dream. It's Meredy's warm hands on my shoulders, not the skeletal claws of a Shade. It's Meredy accidentally sitting on my legs, shaking me awake, her breathing quick with worry.

The *Paradise* gently rocks as it glides over a swell, headed farther away from Lyris toward open seas, assuring me that I'm nowhere near the Deadlands. That the scariest thing I've really seen tonight was the crowd at that tavern.

"What are you doing?" I mumble, still trying to wake myself further. "I'm all right."

"I'm sorry," Meredy whispers, dropping her hands. "You woke me up with your muttering, and it sounded like you were having a nightmare. I wanted to help . . ." She pulls back, hastily retreating from my cot.

"Thank you," I murmur, grateful for the darkness hiding my embarrassment.

Meredy's breathing relaxes as she settles on her bed. "Do you want to talk about it? What happened in your dream?"

"No. But thanks for offering." Heat rises up my neck at the thought of Meredy hearing what I dreamed, how I couldn't protect her or anyone else even in a world that exists entirely in my mind. "If I have another nightmare tomorrow, do you think you could—?"

"I'll wake you," she promises.

Meredy falls silent after that, so I try to concentrate on the rhythm of the sea and the way the wind calls across it, first howling and then pausing, as though waiting for a response that never comes.

At last, Meredy asks in a small voice, "And if I have a bad dream?"

I nod, but realizing she can't see it, I add, "I'll do the same for you."

"Good." Rising onto her knees, Meredy fumbles with something in the darkness a moment.

Our single lantern, dangling from a beam overhead on a fraying strap, flares to life. By its ruddy light, Meredy searches for something under her bed and reemerges with a heavy book in hand. "*The Baroness's Secret Heartache*," she reads with a slight grin, cracking it open. Even from a distance, its pages smell like old clothes dragged out of a wardrobe after years of disuse. "I, er, borrowed this from Valoria's private library of stories King Wylding thought he'd burned. It's childish. The writing's clumsy at best. But it's got *everything*. Seamstresses. Kissing. Nosy relatives. A missing tea set. And of course . . ." She pauses for dramatic effect, and as I wait eagerly for her to go on, her enthusiasm chases away the last unwanted remnants of my dream. "Murder!"

"I can't imagine Valoria will miss it," I say, grinning for a moment. But thoughts of Valoria quickly become an ache I can't soothe, and soon I'm frowning again.

"If you'd like, we can take turns reading it out loud. But be warned, I make up different voices for all the characters, and I expect you to do the same." She smiles softly. "It reminds me of the plays we used to go to as a family in Noble Park—me, Elibeth, Evander, and our parents. Of course, that was a long time ago . . ."

I arch a brow. "Plays? Really? I don't much care for watching others pretend to live—why waste time doing that when you can go out and experience things for yourself?"

Meredy blinks at me, apparently horrified. "I've got to show you what you're missing!" She seems determined as she turns to the first page and takes a deep breath. It isn't until the moment of quiet that I realize hearing Evander's name on her lips didn't hurt—at least, it didn't make me miss him any more than I do already. She said his name without hesitation, as if she's comfortable using it again. Comfortable, and still so strong after everything.

As she starts to read, I say softly, "You've never explained how you do it."

She blinks, lifting up her head. "What? Sneak a book away from Valoria?"

"No." I run my finger along the worn edge of the cot's frame. "Stop missing Evander long enough to go on living."

Meredy's gaze grows distant, though she's still looking right at me. At last, she says, "I'll let you know when I figure it out. I'm still trying. Believe me, I'm trying."

She starts to read again, and this time I don't interrupt. Her voice washes over me, taking me back to the book's long-ago version of Karthia, to a time before King Wylding's rule when merchants from distant lands like Osmana and Yekar came and went freely from our kingdom, offering seeds that would one day grow into Karthian delicacies. Loving and leaving offspring who became part of the vast and varied pool of Karthian bloodlines.

It makes me wonder about the Karthia we've left behind. I doubt things could go wrong with Valoria on the throne, but then, I would have doubted that any Karthians could blindly trust Hadrien, and some did—Meredy and Evander's own mother among them.

Just imagining the challenges Valoria could be facing right now makes my breath catch in my throat. I shake my head, refocusing on Meredy's voice. Right now, the only world that exists is the one inside this cabin.

Darkness crouches all around us, but in here there's warmth and light, and Meredy's eyes meeting mine each time she pauses to turn another page, and—a small but steady spark.

"We need to have a talk," Kasmira announces the next morning as the rest of us yawn into our breakfast. Already wide awake, Kasmira has let her first mate, Dvora, take the wheel for a little while, but she's called the rest of the crew into the dining hall for some sort of meeting.

"Remind me where we're headed again?" a sailor asks. "Sorrel?"

"Sarral," Kasmira says patiently. It's a westerly kingdom one of her contacts in Lyris mapped out for us before things got heated. "And that's partly why I called you all here. See, I was just thinking—from now on, we need to have a cover story. The Lyrians never minded my, ah, trading ventures, but others might consider them . . . criminal. Besides, we don't want anyone in Sarral asking questions about who's on the throne back home. That means we'll need an excuse for why we were allowed to leave when everyone knows King Wylding forbids it. Suggestions?"

"Why do we need to treat our new queen like some big secret, anyway?" someone asks. I recognize her as a friend of the loud-mouthed sailor who let out the news of King Wylding's demise at the tavern in Lyris.

"Because we don't know how or when Valoria plans to contact other leaders," I say, trying to keep the irritation from my voice. The answer seems so obvious. "We don't know how they'll react to her rule, to the new Karthia. We need to keep things under wraps for now, to let Valoria decide how to reach out to the world on her own terms."

"What if," Meredy interjects calmly, "we tell anyone who inquires that King Wylding and his council had a meeting about updating their maps, and while he was opposed, the queen changed his mind?"

Kasmira shakes her head. "The queen hated change as much as her husband."

Grinning at Meredy, I chime in, "I know it's lame. But no one has spoken to the queen in over two centuries, so do they really have a reason not to take our word for it?"

Kasmira and a few of her sailors laugh, apparently satisfied.

But I'm not. Not quite yet. "What's our real story though, Kas? I mean . . . where do we plan to go from here? From Sarral, rather?" Given the heavy silence that follows, it's something we've all started to wonder.

"Well, speaking of maps," Kasmira says after a pause, "I'm sure the Sarralans have some. Assuming I can get them to play nice and share, we'll have our pick of destinations. I'm not particular on the *where* myself, as long as there's gold and jewels and kisses for the taking. So, how much of the world do you all want to see before we head home?"

I don't have to think about my answer for long.

"Nineteen new places," I say quickly, looking to Meredy for approval. "We can count Lyris and Sarral as two of them, so that leaves seventeen to go before we head back to Karthia. That is, if everyone else agrees."

Meredy doesn't meet my eyes, but she touches the small of my back with a shaking hand, making words impossible for a moment.

When I find my voice again, I add for the crew's benefit, "That's one place for every year Evander lived, every year he was robbed of seeing the world. How long do you suppose that will take?"

Kasmira touches her fingers to her brow in a salute—a sign of respect for Evander's memory. "Perhaps a year, or perhaps much longer. Depends how much you want to linger in any given spot."

"Not long," I say quickly, thinking of how little I liked Lyris, and what unpleasant things could await us on other shores. "Let's try to make seventeen quick stops after Sarral this year—you can choose the places, whichever ones have the shiniest jewels and the prettiest people to kiss—and then return to Karthia to share all we've seen with Valoria."

After a moment's consideration, Kasmira flashes a grin. Just like that, we have a plan.

The sea was supposed to carry me far away from my problems. From echoes of death and suffering. From nightmares. From monsters. But with the person who's becoming my biggest problem of all lying on a cot not two feet from mine, feigning sleep, the heat from our bodies stifling in this tiny room, I wonder if this trip will solve anything like I'd hoped. I wonder if King Wylding really did keep me there, sheltered behind his marble walls, for my own good. If he was right to fear the unknown.

I don't think so, somehow. In the fourteen days since Karthia's shore became a smudge of ash on the horizon, I haven't seen anything to make me scream, or even shiver—unless the tavern fight in Lyris counts. So far, the unknown is just salty, smelly, and damp. The path to Sarral seems endless.

Meredy shifts on her cot. Unable to steal a glimpse of her in the velvety darkness, I picture her lying there, restless, her hair unbound and puddling on the floor as she tries to make her lumpy pillow comfortable. It's hard *not* to think about her, even dream about her, when she's this close.

A wave jars me into greater alertness as it slaps the hull of the *Paradise*—or *My Failed Escape Plan*, as I've decided to call it—and the ship groans as the wind shudders around it. My body protests the hard tilt to the left with a shiver of nausea. I scramble upright. If the ship takes on water, I'm going down with it.

"Nightmare? Or seasick?" Meredy asks blearily, lighting our fish-oil lantern that casts deep shadows with its greasy glow. She hangs its ancient strap from a beam overhead. "Shall I fetch the bucket?"

"Nope. I'm not giving up that easily." Smiling weakly, I grip the edge of my cot as the ship creaks and rights itself. "But I suppose this is a good time to mention I don't know how to swim."

Meredy looks more alert now. "Me neither . . ."

I frown. It's not that I expect Meredy to save me if something goes wrong out here. I just tend to think of her as someone who can do everything. "Your mentor didn't give you swimming lessons when you were training to survive in the wilds as a beast master?"

She flashes a faint smile. "The lakes in Lorness aren't warm enough for that."

Funny. In our two weeks on this ship, surrounded by water, neither of us has mentioned swimming. Guess we've both had too many other things on our minds.

Another wave slams into the ship, nearly knocking us from our cots. My sword slides out from under my bed, striking the opposite wall. The bags of coffee beans Meredy bought in Lyris fly off a crooked table. And above us, the strap holding our lantern suddenly snaps, sending the heavy glass straight toward the ground.

I dive for it, flinging my hands out, and barely avoid colliding with Meredy as she does the same. If we burn up the ship, we'll have to learn to swim a whole lot sooner.

The battered wood floor scrapes my bare legs, but the lantern is safe in my shaking hands. Struggling to balance on the tilting floor, I somehow manage to climb to my feet and set the lantern gently on the ground, steadying it between the bags of coffee beans.

"Good catch." Meredy settles on her cot, legs crossed, and pats the empty space beside her. I join her, careful to keep some distance between us. The moment I sit, she locks eyes with me. "We're lucky you have such quick reflexes, Master Necromancer."

"Odessa," I correct under my breath. I've been trying to get her to use my name this whole trip, but she's still talking to me like we're sisters-in-arms. Not like two people who wake each other up from nightmares we don't want to talk about, who have nights where we read together and sometimes share memories of Evander.

Still, no matter what she calls me, I just want to chase the worry from her eyes, but it seems I don't have the magic or the words for that. All I can do is talk to her, keep her mind occupied. "The sea wasn't this rough when we went to bed. We must have sailed right into a storm. It's not like Kasmira, forgetting to check our path."

Meredy takes some coffee beans from one of the bags steadying the lantern and offers them to me. "We're farther west than she or any of the crew has ever been now, she said. I'm sure her Sight showed her this storm, but we're all eager to reach Sarral." She shrugs, but the worry doesn't leave her face. "She must think the crew can push through it."

I crunch on a handful of coffee beans, which momentarily distract me from my nerves as waves continue to pummel the ship. "She *knows* they can, or we wouldn't be here. Kasmira would never put any of us—least of all herself—in danger. Even if her confidence errs on the side of recklessness."

Saying this aloud makes me feel better for all of two seconds.

The ship leans hard to the left, trying to force Meredy and me from our seats again, and my heart attempts to claw its way out of my chest. Meredy, however, seems more bothered by my scraped knee than the fact that we might be guests at a feast for the fishes soon.

"You're bleeding." She frowns as she studies the scrape.

I hadn't noticed until she pointed it out. Apparently the floor rubbed my lower leg raw when I dove for the lantern, and I've smeared red all over Meredy's only blanket. "I'm sorr—"

"Shhh. You've nothing to be sorry for." She hurries to our water basin, the contents of which are mostly sloshed on the floor, and dampens a clean corner of the worn blanket to dab my wound. The fabric is soothingly cold. "Let me fix this."

"All right. But I owe you my blanket, at least." I start to rise, to grab the clean blanket from my cot, but Meredy begins gingerly tidying my scrape, careful never to let any bit of her skin graze mine as she works with the cool cloth.

"There," she says after what feels like an hour of silence. "How does it feel now?"

"Good as new," I assure her. "Really, thanks."

She leans closer, peering into my eyes as if trying to detect a lie, and a grin spreads across my face. I almost wish I could sink through the floor and join the fish now. This is what scares me—not how I want her body tangled up with mine, because it's surely only natural to want to kiss a girl this smart, this beautiful—but how my heart behaves around her. Sometimes, like when she's trying out a funny new voice as we read, or I catch her and Lysander stealing glances at me from around a corner while I'm practicing with my sword, I think

I want to be with her. But how can I be sure, when just weeks ago, I was willing to leave her for good?

This is what I tried to leave behind when I decided to board the *Paradise* without Meredy. This longing can never be anything more, not with Evander forever caught in the middle. Yet we're too often stuck in this cabin, where there's no escaping the current of feelings Meredy stirs in me.

"That's it. We need a distraction!" she declares, misreading my expression as fear of the storm, or perhaps boredom. "At least until we're tired enough to sleep through the rest of this mess."

She grabs *The Baroness's Secret Heartache*, flipping open to chapter twenty-six, and settles herself on the opposite end of her cot, leaving an Evander-sized space between us. I feign an interested smile, though the story has gotten less interesting with each page.

I miss the first few chapters, not because of any particular moment or character, but because I like beginnings. The endless possibilities that exist within them.

"Would you start over?" I ask. "I want to hear about when Alva meets Lunette again. They could've been great together. I mean, they *were* great, until chapter nine, when what's-his-name showed up . . ."

Meredy nods like she understands. "Of course you want to go back to the beginning. Before things get messy."

As I lean against the wall, ready to listen, another book catches my eye. Her father's journal. It must've been pushed from its spot under the bed when Meredy picked up the book we're reading.

"How's that coming?" I ask, nodding to the journal. She hasn't mentioned whether she's having any luck picking up the threads of her father's dreams to see and study the world.

"Oh, not bad." Meredy lifts the leather journal and flips to a spot about halfway through. "So far, I've filled in the names of some of the smaller islands around Lyris and such." She taps a speck southwest of Karthia, surrounded by other even smaller flecks of ink.

The mere mention of Lyris leaves a bitter taste in my mouth. From now on, whenever we finally go ashore again—which must be soon, given how our bread supply is dwindling—my master necromancer's pin will stay stashed with the coffee beans and blown-glass trinkets.

I can't really call myself a master now, anyway. I left my job behind when I left Karthia, and now I'm becoming what I once feared I would when Evander asked me to come away with him: just some girl on a ship. Strangely, with Meredy on my mind, the realization doesn't bother me quite as much as I expected. At least not right now.

"I'm taking notes on people and places, too," Meredy adds, regaining my attention. "A recipe for the fish stew they like in Lyris, and how they think the Five-Faced God is actually five gods and goddesses. I can't believe I just assumed everyone worshipped Vaia, even outside Karthia."

I think about that a moment as I run my fingers over Meredy's careful notes. "I like that there are different ways of explaining our magic," I say at last. "The world is full of more ideas and ways of doing things than I think anyone in Karthia could've imagined."

"That's what Father fell in love with." Meredy smiles. "All the potential in discovering a new place." She leans a little closer, her eyes inviting me to share in some secret. "I didn't tell Kasmira this, because I might be wrong, but . . . I think Father sailed even farther west than we are now, once. Of course, I could be getting my directions mixed up . . . and Father could've been drinking, or distracted, or completely mistaken in some other way . . ."

She's so hesitant that I smile, urging her to go on.

"He wrote about a vast land and a beast we don't have in Karthia, something like a lizard but the size of a dog, with talons. And it could breathe frost, or fire—I'm not really sure what this word is, it's too smudged . . ." Meredy trails off, biting her lower lip as if to keep from laughing at herself.

I grin back. "After everything that's happened lately, a new kind of beast sounds completely possible. Normal, even. For all we know, a giant lizard will crawl out of the sea tomorrow and eat us for breakfast."

A sharp crack sounds from overhead, harsh enough to make me wince.

The keening of the wind grows louder as it whips around the ship, seemingly from all directions. Still, it's not quite strong enough to mask the sound of someone shouting, or the current of alarm in their voice. I just wish I could make out their words.

The ship leans so violently to the right that it throws Meredy and me into the wall. Without thinking, I put my arm around her back to shield her. She clings to me, jumping into my lap as we're tossed about. A song courses through my blood as I hold her, pressing my face into her long, soft hair and breathing deeply.

The world is cruel, and it's sharpened my edges. But somehow, after everything I've witnessed and every hard thing I've done, it's still so easy to be gentle with her.

My hands shake as I run my fingers through her hair and pull her in for a kiss, but before our lips touch, shutters snap closed behind her eyes.

She turns away, sliding off my lap and out of my arms. "Ooh, it's cold in here," she declares with a small shiver, "but it'll be worse on the deck, and we need to check on Kasmira right away." She pulls on her boots and begins searching for her cloak. It's not on the peg where she usually leaves it.

"Here, take mine." My voice sounds like a stranger's, full of false warmth as I hand her my cloak. "I don't mind the cold so much." I try to search her gaze as I hold out the cloak. If she'd just tell me what she's thinking, maybe I wouldn't say or do the wrong things.

Meredy gently pushes my offering away. "I'll be fine without it, thanks." When I shoot her a questioning look, her cheeks redden. "It smells like you, Odessa, and I can never focus when I'm thinking of you!"

Well, she finally used my name.

Silence steals over the cabin, the ship's new, horrible noises filling the space between us.

At last, Meredy murmurs darkly, "You always do this. Rattle me. Push me too far. Make me say things I regret." Her hands clench at her sides. "Are you satisfied?"

For the first time since the waves jarred me awake, a bout of stomach-rolling seasickness creeps over me. "I'm not, actually. I'm not satisfied at all. I don't understand—what is it you want?"

Meredy presses her fingers to her lips and shakes her head. "We don't have time for this," she says in a small voice. To my dismay, she's put a familiar shield over her face. It's the one she used to wear around me, the one that makes it impossible to get a hint of her thoughts.

"You're right. Things sound bad out there. That crash—"

I pause, my heart beating double as more raised voices punch the air. "Moving a storm is a serious job, even for a skilled weather worker like Kasmira, and I'm sure that's what she's trying to do." I cross the few steps to the door, swaying as the ship tips left again. "I think you should try to find a healer—look for Dvora," I add, naming the first hazel-eyed person on board who comes to mind.

Still Meredy won't meet my gaze, though she nods stiffly in agreement with my plan.

For some reason, I want to put my fist through the ship's hull.

Well, maybe not that. But I'd dearly like to hit something that can't spring a leak.

"Look, I get it." I throw open the door, having pulled on my cloak and boots to cover my nightdress. "You don't like me like that, but at some point, you're going to have to speak to me again. I'm sorry, *Master Crowther.*"

Meredy lifts her head and turns toward me, but doesn't raise her eyes.

The air in the narrow room is getting much too thin to share.

"Be safe out there. Please." Her voice follows me as I head into the hallway, and I don't have to glance back to know she's making a final, frantic search for something to guard against the lashing rain before following me up the stairs.

I shake my head, more confused by her than ever. She knows me well enough to realize I have a habit of running toward danger, not away from it. And I know her well enough to detect the note of longing in her words, moments after she pushed me away.

I have a sure and sudden feeling that girl is going to be the death of me.

III

In my haste to leave the cabin, I nearly trip over Lysander. The grizzly bear fills the hallway even when he's stretched out on his belly. His amber eyes are alert, his breathing heavy, like he's just as unnerved by the storm as I am. "Don't look so worried," I murmur, patting his neck. "At least you can swim, big man."

Above deck, the wind howls like a restless Shade, distorting the sounds of the crew calling to one another. I blink rain from my eyes as fast as I can, but searching for Kasmira like this is going to take a while.

The ship leans right. I collide with the quartermaster, who curses and dashes away, leaving me to lean against the side of the ship and rub my smarting head.

"Kas!" I shout.

My voice, like the voices of the many people struggling to keep us floating, is lost to the wind, but Kasmira's lack of an answer still makes a lump of panic rise in my throat. She could be trying to divert the storm, pushing her body beyond its limits—using too much magic.

When necromancers walk into the Deadlands, we forfeit the chance for our spirits to go there when we die. Using our magic is a guarantee that someday, we just won't *be* anymore. Like Evander. But when an inventor or a weather mage pushes their magic too far, they could faint—or worse, their brains could bleed. They could die in the act of wielding their incredible power.

All magics have a price, each one terrible in its own way, but the weather mage's cost seems especially cruel just now. If we lose our fearless captain, *none* of us will make it far, let alone back to Karthia.

I can't lose anyone else. Not here. The sea was supposed to save what's left of me, not rip away the remaining pieces.

I stagger across the deck, making my way from the middle of the ship to the quarterdeck, hoping Kasmira is at the helm. The white-capped waves rear higher with each collision, sending a furious spray over the bow, making me slip far too often. I might as well have left my cloak in the room for all the good it's doing me.

This is hopeless. The wind fights me with each step forward. Not that I'm going anywhere until I know Kasmira is all right, that she has things under control.

As thunder claps, I completely lose my footing. I clutch at the nothingness around me and land hard on my back. It takes a moment to suck air back into my lungs. A passing sailor—Dvora, I realize as I blink against the gale—hauls me to my feet.

"Looking for the captain? She's that way!" The sea-hardened first mate points straight ahead, toward the mainmast, and beyond it, curtains of gray. Whatever I can or can't see, I'm sure Dvora knows what she's talking about.

When I turn to ask her how Kas is holding up so far, she's already disappeared. I guess our captain must be safe for now. With my arms out for balance, I edge slowly forward, shuffling my feet like a child taking her first steps.

"What's this?" Kasmira appears from behind the mast, gliding lithely over the slick boards like she's been doing this all her life. She probably has. "No one's drowning any sparrows on my watch." With a hand on my back to steady me, she leads me to the partially covered threshold of a door leading belowdecks, where she's been working her magic.

Once we're settled on the damp floor, I throw my arms around her. "I was so worried."

"You don't say." Kasmira pushes her dark braids over her shoulders and grins wryly, but the expression doesn't mask her pain. "I'm trying to get us out of here, Sparrow, but I've never seen a storm like this. When I checked last, the skies were clear. These clouds sprang up out of nowhere—and now they seem to be *everywhere*."

Kasmira tilts her head skyward. She gazes up until only the whites of her deep gray eyes are showing, and I know she's using her Sight to peer above the clouds. "This storm looks endless."

I shiver. "That makes no sense, Kas."

"I know." She blinks at me as if coming out of a daze, then pulls something from her pocket. A compass, its needle spinning wildly, never settling. "But we're getting close to Sarral, or we should be, anyway. Our best bet is to push through it at this point."

Familiar panic crawls across my skin as I study the thunderheads crowding over our ship. I wish there were something I could do to see us safely to shore, but this is Kasmira's fight, not mine. I command the dead. She commands the sky.

I grip her forearms. "Tell me what to do. I want to help."

Kasmira smiles softly, running a finger down my cheek. "Thanks,

Sparrow." She settles herself deeper under the shelter of the staircase's entryway. "Keep an eye on the crew for me. I'll need all my focus to blow this storm back to wherever it came from."

She sounds hollow, like a shadow of herself. "Kas, you're scaring—"

"I'll find a way to beat this," she continues, raising her voice over me and the wind. "I will. But if the only way to save my crew is to give myself to this storm, then you can help by telling my mothers how much I love them. Daddy, too, the next time he's visiting. Tell them . . ." She pauses, her voice wavering at the mention of the big, close-knit family I've always envied. "Tell them I wasn't afraid."

I hold her hand for a moment after she closes her eyes. "Be careful, danger queen. If anyone can do this, it's you."

I can't bring myself to join the crew like Kasmira asked, even though she's already slipped off to wherever her mind goes when she uses her magic. Above the clouds, most likely. Instead, I keep vigil at her side and watch her work. I'll make sure that I never have to report the worst to Kasmira's family.

She raises her right hand above her head, fingers drawn together, then drops it sharply. The winds quiet, but the ship still rocks with the force of heavy rain and waves, and thunder echoes across the swollen sea.

Kasmira brings her hands together, palms touching, the tops of her fingers level with her collarbone, then slowly draws them apart.

The rain softens, but lightning forks the sky. I hope she tackles that next.

Tucking my arms into my sodden cloak, I wish I could do something more than watch and wait as she groans under the strain of working her magic. In all the time I've known her, she's never attempted to do more than change the winds, or push away a little rain, and even that takes its toll on her after a while.

Blood trickles from her nose as the sky slowly begins to lighten, revealing the pale golden glow of early morning. Maybe only seconds are passing, but it feels like minute after minute is dragging by without Kasmira opening her eyes. I'm no good at waiting, no good at relying on someone else for rescue. The last time I felt this powerless, Evander was dangling limply in a Shade's claws.

After the rains have calmed, I peek out of our shelter, glancing up toward the quarterdeck. Dvora waves to me from the helm as she steers us toward a ribbon of calmer sea—the most beautiful sight.

"You're doing well, Kas," I whisper. "I think you can stop now."

Yet Kasmira continues to work, flinging her right arm out, then her left, shoving the darkest clouds to our backs. The last drops of rain vanish, but the bleeding from her nose worsens. My heart sinks despite her victory over the storm.

"Land ahead!" cries one of the younger sailors.

I tear my gaze from my friend to find a gray shadow looming on the horizon, far bigger than the outline of any island, and for a ridiculous, heart-swooping moment I think we've somehow steered ourselves back to Karthia. But as we speed closer, I suspect we've reached our intended destination.

Four people stand on a distant pink-sand shore, their outlines shimmering thanks to their water-resistant robes, similar to the ones Karthian weather workers wear but with different belts and adornments. The mages—as I suppose they must be weather workers, too—move their hands in an intricate dance, making gestures that echo Kasmira's, and anger flares deep in the pit of my stomach as I realize what they're doing.

They're fueling the storm. Perhaps they even made it, trying to keep us from their shore by turning wind and water against us. Maybe they're protecting gems or gold. Maybe they have a ruler who hates visitors as much as King Wylding did. Or maybe they just like killing. No matter the reason, they'd better hope their storm is enough to keep them well out of my reach.

Lightning cracks open the clearing sky, striking the *Paradise*'s foremast and splitting it in two. Sailors scramble out of the way, shouting obscenities and covering their heads as heavy chunks of wood crash against the deck, some tearing holes in the boards where they land.

We're lucky everything is so damp, or we'd have a fire to deal with, too.

The ship lists to the left, still moving forward, but not entirely under Dvora's control anymore. Her curses fill the charged air.

I grab Kasmira's shoulder and shake her. "Kas, your ship is falling apart. Your *ship*!" She always says she could never love a person as much as she loves this creaky old ship, with its many hidden compartments and the leaks it's always springing. "We have to stop these people the old-fashioned way—with our blades—or we won't have the *Paradise* to get us out of here." I shake her harder. "Death be damned! Kas, snap out of it!"

Kasmira doesn't open her eyes, but a faint line appears between her brows. She makes another hand gesture, likely trying to counter whatever the other weather workers are summoning in the clouds.

Meredy dashes up from the cabin at last, fully dressed but hastily so, her eyes widening as she spots the wreckage on deck. Lysander looms over her, rearing back on his hind legs to snarl at the unfamiliar mages.

"Let's get this mess out of everyone's way!" Meredy calls to him. The grizzly lowers himself to all fours and starts hauling large pieces of the shattered mast by clutching them between his powerful jaws.

Meredy directs him, and in the process, a flicker of fear crosses her face as her gaze passes over Kasmira. Or perhaps she's looking at something beyond Kas's makeshift shelter, wondering why we're still sailing toward shore when the people there are bent on killing us. She shakes her head, regaining focus, and grabs one end of the largest piece of split mast while Lysander takes the other.

The ship's course veers wildly, but Dvora still fights to guide us toward shore.

I hope she knows what she's getting us into.

One of the weather workers shouts up the beach to his companions. "Stand down! Don't you see, they're not—they're not from Ezora. We made a mistake. *Stand down!*"

My body stays tensed, waiting to see if the other mages will follow orders. I've never heard of Ezora, and I wonder if these people have ever heard of Karthia. They speak our language—the tavern keeper in Lyris called it a common tongue, after all—so it won't be hard for me to tell these people what a big mistake they've made when we get to shore.

They seem to realize that now, too, but the ship is drawing so near that I'm tempted to flail my way up the beach and start punching the mages on it. Then I won't just be some girl on a ship—I'll be the girl with the fists everyone should be afraid of.

The three other mages drop their hands as their leader's command registers, whispering among themselves and casting curious looks at our ship.

My shoulders relax, just barely. There's still Kasmira to worry about. I tighten my hold on her and study her face for signs of recognition. "Come on, Kas. I need to know you're all right. They aren't trying to kill us anymore."

The blood pouring from her nose thickens, spilling over her lips. She's pushing the storm farther out to sea.

Suddenly, Kasmira slumps on her side and starts to twitch, her head banging against the deck before I can catch her.

"No! Kas—I need help over here!"

Feeling utterly useless, I brush her braids away from her face, knowing, thanks to Danial's constant prattle about healing techniques, that something as simple as moving her head might lead to more harm than good. I just hope Dvora has enough healing skill to magic Kasmira's brain back to a place where it's not attacking the rest of her.

Dvora comes running at my cry, followed by Meredy. They drop to their knees beside us, Dvora immediately using her Sight to look deeper than her captain's skin and assess the damage inside. She places a hand on Kasmira's forehead, frowning in concentration.

"There's nothing you or any of the rest of us could have done," Meredy murmurs, correctly reading my stricken expression. "The storm had to be dealt with, and no one on this ship has gray-eyed Sight but Kasmira." She glances darkly at the shore. "Lysander and I have some things to say to those mages, though. I bet you do, too, Odessa."

"Nothing I want to say to them involves using actual words. I like this place even less than Lyris so far," I grumble. I don't miss the unspoken apology in her using my name, but I don't have time to appreciate it as I follow her gaze back to the pink-tinged shore.

There, standing so far down the beach from the rest of the group that I hadn't noticed her before, is a fifth weather worker. The lone mage raises her hands to the dawn sky, her fingers curling with effort. She didn't hear the message about standing down, then.

Meredy and I leap to our feet. "Stop!" she yells, frantically waving her arms.

I wave, too, calling something far less polite.

A bolt of lightning arcs over the ship in the rosy-gold dawn sky, this time striking the yards holding the sails along the mainmast—right above where Meredy and I are standing. As they start to fall, I realize the mast itself is broken. And leaning in our direction.

I have to get Meredy out of its path.

Shouts rise up from the deck, from shore, but all the noise fades to a whisper as I use the instant before the mast's descent to shove Meredy to safety.

I try to move with her, but the weight of the split mast crashes into me, stealing my breath. All sound is drowned out by a sudden ringing in my ears, and something wet coats my face, but I can't wipe it away no matter how hard I try to coax my arm and fingers into working. Agony twists my body in ways I didn't know it could move.

The ringing softens enough for me to hear Meredy swallowing a sob. Thank the stars she's alive. And, hopefully, unhurt.

I try to tell her I'll be all right, that everyone should look after Kasmira first, then try to ask if someone could spare a moment to move the fallen mast. Preferably Lysander. All that comes out is an incoherent mumble. I make up a funny remark about how bards in Karthia will soon be competing to write the best ballad about the girl who survived Shades and a mad king only to be defeated by a piece of wood, but the words get lost somewhere in the swirling black that swallows me whole.

IV

Bright light teases the edges of my eyelids, urging me toward wakefulness.

Blinking into the glow of late afternoon from a bed beside a wide window, I lean forward to peer outside, trying to make sense of my surroundings. The room I'm in overlooks a bustling street from at least one floor above ground. Men and women wearing outfits of bold-colored silks emerge from an apothecary, sunlight glinting off potion glasses in their baskets, and for the briefest moment I feel a faint and familiar yearning. Other people hurry up and down the road carrying bread, fruit, or flowers. A girl sits on an overturned basket in the shadow of an herb-seller's stall, plucking the strings of a small and handsome painted instrument I don't recognize. Red blossoms thrive between shop rows, their broad petals stretching toward the sun. I don't see anyone in a cloak, which means it must be warmer here than the weather we left behind in Karthia.

The sound of giggling drifts up from the road. Nose to the glass, I search for its source: a tiny child watching a wooden cart full of straw roll by. An older woman, her hair wrapped in a glittering red scarf, has the driver's seat. She waves to the child, then flicks the reins of—

My head throbs, white-hot all over.

I look hastily away, taking deep breaths. But when I look back, the cart is still there, though a little farther down the street. Instead of the usual horse or mule, the woman is driving a creature right out of the story Meredy told me: a dark blue-black lizard with a long snout and even longer tail, roughly the size of one of the king's beloved hunting hounds. It leaves a trail of talon marks in the street's red stone paving as it walks, but soon it can go no farther as more children flock to greet it.

Meredy has to see this. Kasmira, too. They'll tell me whether I'm dreaming.

As I turn to look for them, I suddenly remember: Kasmira's in danger. All that blood on her face, the way she was convulsing, a bolt of lightning forming in the clear morning sky . . . and there was something about a heavy piece of wood, too.

Guess that explains why my head feels like somebody used it for sparring practice.

But my pain immediately fades to background noise as I think of Kasmira. Nothing matters until I know she's all right, and the rest of the crew, too. I need to know we've all reached this mysterious land of huge lizards together.

There's a pale silk screen around my bed, but if I lean back far enough on my pillows, I can see most of the room. I sweep my gaze hopefully over white walls adorned with paintings of seascapes and flowers, a blue-and-gold patterned tile floor, and palm fronds in red clay pots scattered throughout the neat rows of beds in this large room. All the beds around mine are screen-less and empty.

I throw back my blankets and jump out of bed. I have to find Kasmira.

My head spins, and for a moment blackness creeps into the corners of my eyes, forcing me to grip the side of the bed and take a deep breath. It turns out leaping to my feet wasn't the best plan. Slowly, the darkness retreats, but it's replaced by something just as unpleasant: nausea. Swallowing hard, I grab my clothes. Someone's draped them over the back of a chair beside my bed, perhaps the same person who left a familiar book on the seat cushion. Not even *The Baroness's Secret Heartache* can make me smile right now, but it's good to know Meredy is somewhere nearby. Hopefully with Kasmira.

Just as I'm about to pull off the thin blue nightdress I don't remember putting on, a high, cheerful voice calls from out of sight, "Oh, good! I'm glad you're awake. Be right with you."

"Where's Kasmira?" I demand, not in the mood to wait.

"She's in the closed ward downstairs, where we keep the more serious cases," the voice chirps in answer. "The rest of your ship's crew are all there with her, even the bear. There's absolutely no need, as she's in excellent hands, but they're keeping vigil."

My shoulders slump with relief. I could hug that voice.

"How long was I out?" I add.

"A day and a half. You probably don't remember much since the accident, thanks to the tonics we gave you—just to keep you comfortable and still while the healers worked."

Bustling out of the shadows of a corridor leading off this large room is a girl in crisp white healer's robes that look to be two sizes too big. She carefully clutches several full potion glasses in each of her small hands.

"How's your head feeling, Master Odessa?" She pushes the silk screen aside, then perches herself on the chair holding my clothes and book without spilling any potion. Now that she's sitting, I notice the roots of her shoulder-length pale blond hair are as dark a brown as her skin and eyes.

"I'm Healer's Assistant Azelie," she adds. "Welcome to Glia Raal, the easternmost city in the great kingdom of Sarral." Her tone is brisk, almost businesslike, but a smile tugs at the corners of her mouth.

Anger crackles across my skin. This wasn't how I imagined arriving at our destination. The weather workers on the beach conjuring storm clouds is one of my last memories from before the world dissolved into blackness. "Tell me, Azelie, are you smiling because my friends and I were almost murdered by *your* friends? Or is there something else that's funny? If so, I could really use a laugh right now."

That wipes all traces of cheer from her face. "We all deeply regret our weather workers' mistake. Your crew will be given free room and board while our carpenters work to repair your ship. It's the least we can do."

"You're *sorry*? Then why attack us in the first place?"

"Your ship didn't have a yellow flag," Azelie explains quickly. "Everyone who wishes to anchor in Sarral has to fly one, to show they mean us no harm. Of course, we haven't had visitors from Karthia in over two hundred years, so how were you to know?" She laughs softly. "It's amazing. I never thought I'd meet a Karthian, yet here you are!"

I slowly shake my head, breathing hard. "We were almost *killed* for not flying a flag?"

"That's right." Balancing some of the potion bottles in her lap momentarily, Azelie dips her index finger into a magenta potion and licks it clean, making a face. "We assume any unfamiliar ship without the flag belongs to the Ezorans, and defend our shore accordingly."

"Who are they?" The name stirs something buried in my memory, but I can't seem to make it surface.

Azelie's gaze darkens. "They're a kingdom of the worst sort, hardened warriors who glory in death and destruction, taking whatever they please and leaving blood in their wake. Lately, we fear every strange ship could be from Ezora. They always arrive by sea, sometimes in ordinary vessels, and sometimes in ships decorated with the heads of their enemies."

"That's pleasant," I mutter, inwardly cringing.

Not bothering to hide a shudder of her own, Azelie continues, "They've been raiding, murdering, and generally terrorizing the borders of Sarral and many neighboring kingdoms for the past several months, trying to gain entry. So perhaps you see now why our mages tried to drown your ship before it reached us..." Her words trail away, heavy with regret, before she smiles again. "Queen Jasira takes every precaution—as would your king, if Karthia still welcomed visitors."

"Great for Queen Jasira," I murmur, feeling a little calmer as I realize my shipmates seem to be keeping to the story we agreed upon. But something is still bothering me. "You called me 'Master Odessa' when you came in. What makes you so sure I'm a mage?" Leaning against the bed for support, I prop my hands on my hips, trying to look intimidating despite the dainty nightdress. "And how do you know my name?"

Azelie tilts her head, still smiling. I decide she must be a few years younger than me to be able to smile so freely. That, or she hides her darkness well. "Your friend told us."

"Which friend?" If it sounds like a test to her, that's because it is. After Hadrien turned out to be a power-hungry killer, it's hard to trust anyone with a pleasant face.

"Meredy—the one you kept asking for in your sleep." Azelie glances down at one of her potions, missing the horror and embarrassment mingling on my face.

"Speaking of Meredy," she adds, meeting my eyes again—does this girl ever stop talking? "She said you'd want to know right away that necromancers are welcome in Sarral. Admired, even." There's a soft current of longing in her voice. It can't be easy, working in a healing house without possessing hazel Sight, not being able to do more than mix potions. She must not get a lot of admiration for her work. "It's also the law here that all necromancers, even visitors, register their names with Queen Jasira. Just so we're aware of who could be raising the dead within our borders."

Remembering the eerie absence of the Dead in Lyris, I ask, "So there are Dead in Sarral?" I don't feel the pull of any gates nearby, though maybe that's thanks to my headache.

"Of course." Finally tiring of holding so many potions, it seems, she rises to put the glasses on a table nearby. Some of the tonics give off faintly floral scents, unlike the fruit-scented ones the apothecaries make in Karthia. "But you shouldn't expect to meet them. You see, in Sarral, the day belongs to the living, and the night to the Dead."

That broken ship's mast must've split my skull open and knocked me into another world entirely, because that's one of the most ridiculous things I've ever heard. I open my mouth to say so, but then I picture Meredy looking daggers at me, warning me to be polite.

Trying to channel some of her calm, I manage, "How does that work, exactly?"

"Well, the living conduct their businesses and hold their festivals during daylight. We don't leave our homes after sundown." Glasses clink together merrily as Azelie stirs something on the table, her back to me. I wish I could read her expression, to see if she's joking. Maybe this is how Sarralans welcome their visitors, with extravagant jokes. "The Dead do all their living—for lack of a better word—by night, and return home at dawn."

My stomach twists. I can't believe what I'm hearing. All my life, I've been surrounded by death, taught to respect those souls who returned by magic to occupy their former bodies for a second or third time. From the convent where I was raised by the Sisters of Death, those who keep up the temples to our god's blue-eyed face, to my necromancer's training with Master Cymbre, the Dead have always given me purpose. Some of them even saved me. If Jax and Simeon were here, I know my fellow necromancers would be sickened, too.

"And you're . . . all right with that?" I finally grit out. Even if this girl is telling me the truth about necromancers being welcome here, I don't want to stay a moment longer.

Azelie's tone is still sunny as she turns to face me again. "I don't think about it much. It's been that way since before I was born. Our leaders thought it best, after hearing whispers of how the rule of the Dead changed Karthia." Eyes widening, she asks, "Is it true your king burned whole libraries and destroyed centuries of knowledge and progress?" When I frown instead of answering, she hurries to add, "It's just—Queen Jasira believes Karthia's people suffer under King Wylding's guidance, mixing so freely with the Dead. She worries for them."

Well, no one has to worry about Karthia's ancient ruler anymore. I bite my tongue again, wondering what Valoria would think of this Queen Jasira and her opinions.

"I suppose . . . I don't really agree with it. The Dead and the living being so separate," Azelie adds, moments later, in a whisper. "But we had a war with the Dead once, centuries ago, and it produced a great many Witherlings. People haven't forgotten."

The way her eyes widen with fear makes it easy to guess the meaning of the word *Witherling*. "Big bony things that eat corpses?"

I ask. "We call them Shades. You know you can kill them with fire, right?"

She nods. "One of the many uses of dragon's breath."

"Dra-gon?" The unfamiliar word isn't helping my headache. There's so much to take in.

"I'll show you later, once you're fully healed." She studies me closely as I blink away more blackness from the fringes of my vision. "Also, as your assistant healer, I must advise you that you really ought to sit down."

Frowning—more at the pain of taking orders from someone younger than me than the ache in my head—I sink onto the bed, rubbing my temples.

Azelie offers me a glass of magenta potion, holding it under my nose. Its aroma is sweet and a little spicy, like a flower I can't name. "This is for the pain," she murmurs. "Just until the healer on duty can fix what's left of the damage to your head."

Remembering what the blue, bitter-apple-tasting liquid that filled my days not too long ago had almost cost me, I gently push the glass away. Potion dribbles onto the bed. I'm never going back to that miserable existence, and even though this tonic looks and smells completely different, I won't risk it. "No, thanks. I'll be fine."

Azelie arches both brows as she dabs up the potion spill. "But your headache . . ."

"I've lived through worse, so unless I'm in danger of dying, I'll pass." But eyeing the many potions on the nearby table makes me wonder something. "You must have cures for lots of ailments, right?"

"For everything from coughs to helping wounds clot," Azelie confirms cheerfully.

"What about a cure for the black fever?" I ask, not bothering to disguise the hope in my voice as I think of the lethal sickness that sweeps through Grenwyr City each year. After all, the Sarralans have had so much more time to research it than Karthian healers.

"Afraid not. It's one of a handful of diseases we haven't yet solved, although luckily, cases of it here are quite rare," she answers. "We have more problems with the—"

"My ship!" The words rise through the floor, echoing around the room. *"What the blazes happened to my ship? Someone's going to pay for this in blood!"*

Recognizing Kasmira's voice, I can't help but smile. If she's feeling well enough to shout and threaten bloodshed, she's already on the mend.

Azelie snickers, setting down the potion glass. "Sounds like your friend is back on her feet. Which means she should be back with you in a moment." She flops down on the end of my bed, her grin turning conspiratorial, her dark eyes alight with curiosity. "In the meantime, tell me about Karthia. I want to know everything."

I open my mouth, but Azelie keeps going. "No. Wait. Tell me about Meredy. She was really worried about you. I had to practically shove her out of that chair by your bed to make her get some rest." Taking a breath, she grins. "And put a couple drops of sleeping potion in her drinking water."

"Where is she? Downstairs with the others?" I ask, trying to keep my expression neutral.

"She fell asleep on one of the cushions in the room where the healers usually rest." Azelie props her chin on her closed fist, smiling up at me. "So, come on. We've got time. Spill. Is there something between you two?"

I should be annoyed. I should tell this girl to quit prying and leave.

I try to summon a glare, but instead, I find myself smiling back. Her cheerfulness must be contagious, because it's making me like her against my better judgment. Besides, it's kind of nice to talk to someone who doesn't know I'm a king-slayer, a former potion addict, a girl who saw her first love die in the clutches of a Witherling.

"All right, we'll talk until the healer comes," I agree. "But why don't you tell me about *you* instead?"

For the first time, Azelie's sunny demeanor fades. "Oh, no." Her smile is back in place faster than Meredy's when she's hiding something. "Not when there's over two hundred years of gossip to catch up on."

I steer the conversation toward festivals, food, and what the weather's like in Karthia, keeping firmly away from any mention of the recent battle, the man I loved and lost, and this dangerous attraction I feel for his sister. Azelie has so many questions about growing up among the Dead in Grenwyr City, and in return, I ask her what it was like growing up in Sarral, where brown-eyed mages have always been able to invent things freely, unlike in Karthia. From the sound of it, they have so many recipes and hairstyles that I'd need to live here a year or more to try them all.

Just as I'm about to ask her what a dragon is, and whether most people in Sarral have a lizard to pull their carts, the healer on duty arrives and chases Azelie away.

"Tomorrow, we tour the city," Azelie whispers on her way out, hooking strands of her blond hair behind her ears. "You and me. And your friends, if they want to come. It's my day off, so I'll fetch you bright and—"

"Azelie!" The healer, a stern-faced older woman, groans. "It's nearly sundown, and you're not on overnight duty. Shoo!"

"Already gone!" Azelie flashes me a grin, then vanishes.

The healer lays her soft, cool hands on either side of my head, and as the pain dissolves, so does the room. Even my thoughts and worries drift away.

When I wake drenched in sweat, the nearly full moon is high in the sky, a cold and distant bystander. I must have had a nightmare, but the details are fading faster than water slipping through my fingers. Right away, I sense something wrong in the waking world, too. My head doesn't hurt anymore, so there's no question the healing worked. Still, unease clings to me, making my breath quicken.

Leaning against the window, I gaze out at the street below, where the Dead move quickly and quietly about on errands. The deep shadows of night mute the flash of their jewelry and masks and the sparkle of their eye-catching shrouds. Unlike the street during the day, there are no children giggling, no work-lizards, and no people stopping to chat. I don't like it, this separation of living and Dead, but that's not the only thing bothering me. There's something more.

As I turn away from the window to peer around the room, the moon's waxy glow reveals that only a few beds are still empty. Most are now occupied by members of the *Paradise*'s crew. Dvora tosses restlessly, while the boatswain and quartermaster compete to see who can snore the loudest. Close to Meredy's empty bed, Lysander sprawls on the floor, his bulk rising above the low bedframe. His huge claws click against the tile floor as he swipes at some invisible opponent, untroubled by his master's whereabouts.

As I take in the sight of the neatly made bed where Meredy clearly hasn't slept at all, I finally realize what feels wrong: I've gotten used to her waking me from my worst dreams.

Now wide awake and restless, I slip out of the bed and grab my sword, careful not to make a sound. I've only missed a few days' worth of practice with my blade, but even that small gap makes me feel sluggish and slow, so I might as well get a session in now. It's probably pointless—there don't seem to be any Shades around here for me to fight, and I don't need to be in shape to stay alive in the Deadlands anymore—but some stubborn part of me refuses to give up on my daily necromancer's training.

As I stride down a hallway I saw Azelie use earlier, searching for a private place to practice, I'm grateful for the dark that hides the pathetic sight of a mage working to stay fit for a fight that's never coming. For a job she no longer has.

The hallway leads me into a large sitting room. I suppose if I moved a few chairs, I could practice here, but to my left is a set of glass doors leading onto an empty balcony. Slipping outside, I listen to the hush of the Dead going about their business on the street below as I stretch to warm up my stiff muscles.

Aside from the occasional cry of a gull to remind me that we're still near the ocean, all is quiet. Too quiet. I hum a song Evander and I used to dance to as I start practicing my lunges.

"I'd hate to be on the wrong end of that blade," a voice says from the shadows.

Whirling around, my back to the railing, I find myself facing Meredy as she emerges from the spot where she was apparently leaning against the side of the building. "I was just, uh . . ." I hastily point my sword toward the ground, fumbling for an explanation.

"You're dedicated to your training, like I am to mine," Meredy says, stepping closer. "This isn't the first time I've seen you practice, remember? Nor the first time neither of us can sleep."

My shoulders relax with her understanding.

"By the way, what's that song you were humming? I like it." She smiles. "It reminds me of this play I saw one summer—"

"*The Black Violet*, right?" I shake my head at myself as she nods enthusiastically. I can't believe she's got me rattling off the names of plays. Stranger still, I even like the sound of some of them. Setting my sword down, I offer her my hand. "This is an excellent song for dancing. Shall we?"

Meredy doesn't move, her face falling slightly. "Oh, no. I can't dance."

"Can't?" I press, feeling emboldened by the dark and the quiet. "Or don't like to?"

"Don't like to," she confesses after a moment. "It's awkward. I hate it. I don't know what to do with my arms, my feet, or even where to look."

Still, I keep my hand extended. Dancing comes as naturally to me as caring for animals does to Meredy. I have sword fighting to thank for that. "You'll love it when you're with me. I promise." As she hesitates, I press, "One dance. Just one. What could it hurt?"

Slowly, like she's afraid I might bite, she reaches for my hand. I close my fingers over hers and look a question at her. When she nods, I pull her against me. Then, singing the song I was humming earlier, I guide Meredy around our balcony dance floor, sweeping her through patches of moonlight like we're on a stage. At first, her fingers are rigid where they grip my waist, but the longer we dance, the more she relaxes, even leaning into me.

"You have a beautiful voice. Have you ever thought about acting in a—?"

"Don't say it," I growl, but playfully, before picking up the tune where I left off.

Evander and I used to dance to this song all the time. Dancing to it with Meredy should feel like a betrayal, but somehow it doesn't. What would Evander say if he could see me now? That it's too soon? Over a year ago, we agreed we'd have to love again to go on living if something happened to one of us, thanks to the nature of our job. What I feel for Meredy, though, has come on swift and strong and sudden. But it feels too right for me to shy away just because I'm afraid of the things others might say. Let them talk.

As Meredy gets bolder, spinning me around with a gleam in her eyes, I realize why. We have our own rhythm. It's not the same as the one I shared with Evander, but I like it just as much—Meredy and me, making up a new dance as we go along, feeling for each other's breaths, for each slight hesitation, anticipating each other's every step so that we move as one.

For the first time, as I pull her closer, there's no one—not even Evander—standing between us. No one to keep us apart. And left to ourselves, we fit together just right.

Still, that doesn't change how stubborn she is. Too stubborn, too much like me. How many days, hours even, would go by before we had an argument where neither of us was willing to compromise? And I can't forget, her mother is locked up in the Wyldings' palace dungeon for trying to kill me. We're both essentially orphans now. What kind of life would we have together?

One where we make the rules. One where the only limitations are the ones we define. One where our family is made up entirely of people we choose.

As she smiles at me, wanting to spin me around again, the part of me that wants this—wants *her*—grows louder than my doubts. There are plenty of reasons we shouldn't work. But this spark in my chest, this thing that flares to life whenever I'm around her and keeps getting brighter, says otherwise.

I loved Evander. I still do. But being around Meredy has made me realize there's enough room in my heart for someone else without erasing him.

I want to *live*, and part of living means loving again. Maybe Meredy is the person I should give my heart to. Maybe she isn't. All I know for sure is that I want to find out. I just have to find the right words to ask if that's what she wants, too.

Meredy leans closer, laying her head on my shoulder. I forget to keep singing, but we don't break our embrace.

V

Now having realized we aren't a bunch of thieves and murderers, the people of Sarral are desperate to apologize for our less-than-warm reception to their kingdom.

And lucky for them, the fragrant, sweet waffles made by one of the weather workers who tried to kill us are so good, they almost make up for our brush with death. When Azelie drizzles some cardamom-vanilla syrup on them for me, I decide I wouldn't mind staying in Glia Raal a while if I didn't have so many other places to see.

Of course, how long we stay is entirely up to how quickly the carpenters can fix the *Paradise*. And since I've seen enough healing houses to last me a lifetime, we're moving to a nearby boarding house after breakfast.

As we crowd the healers' long dining table at the back of the house, which I'm told is usually reserved for celebrations among the staff, Lysander shoves his shaggy head between me and Kasmira. Before I can swallow the giant bite of food I just took, Lysander licks my half-eaten stack of waffles.

I laugh and start to choke as Meredy groans. "He never did this sort of thing in Lorness!"

Kasmira thumps me on the back with a fist, which only makes me laugh harder. Shaking her head at Meredy, she says, "I'm gonna guess that's because there weren't any waffles in Lorness."

"Here, Lysander." Suddenly feeling cheerful myself, I offer him the top waffle off the dwindling stack.

He accepts with an unexpected lick of my cheek.

Great. Grizzly breath.

Azelie catches my eye and waves from the end of the table. Her pale hair is wrapped in two small buns on either side of the top of her head this morning, and I get the impression she changes styles often. The variety suits her, a girl who grew up not fearing change the way we Karthians did practically from birth.

"Who's going to tour the city with me? I have the whole day planned." Azelie crooks one of her dark brows, eyeing each of the crew in turn, but they all seem to be waiting for Kasmira's answer.

"Not me, I'm afraid." Kasmira pushes away her empty breakfast plate and stands. She's wearing the clothes I remember from the night of the storm—a pale gray blouse, dark vest, and dark trousers, as well as her assortment of "cutlery," her daggers in their sheaths. She must have found a way to wash her things, as I remember a lot of blood on that blouse. "I'm off to the harbor to oversee repairs." Her expression darkens. "If they put a single nail in the wrong spot . . ."

"They'll pay for it in blood, right?" Azelie chirps.

Kasmira blinks, bemused. "That's right," she says after a moment, then sweeps her gaze over the crew. "You lot are free to do what you want until further notice." She turns to me. "Sparrow, your orders today are simple: Don't start any fights you aren't willing to finish, and don't sustain any life-threatening injuries before suppertime."

I try to hide my sheepish expression by stuffing a piece of waffle in my mouth. "Deal."

Azelie glances from me to Meredy, her smile never dimming. "Guess it's just the three—" She breaks off, interrupted by a grumble from Lysander as he sniffs the crew's abandoned plates. "Four of us," she amends as everyone else files out of the room. "First stop: my uncles' dragon nursery."

The wooden cart that pulls us out of the bustling city center is, disappointingly, driven by horses. Meredy and I take the narrow board that makes up the passengers' seat—Azelie winking at me as I slide in next to Meredy—and our tour guide herself sits up front beside the driver. Of course, not being beside us doesn't stop her from talking almost constantly as shop fronts give way to swaths of sunny fields where farmers keep watch over cows and gather produce.

"My uncles started their dragon nursery a year after they were married," Azelie says from up front, snaring my attention. "They met while working on one, so it seemed fitting. I think you'll really like it. The dragons are so cute when they're little."

Dragons, we learned over breakfast, are the cart-pulling lizards. They might be too small to ride, but they're apparently much stronger than horses. They also help farmers protect livestock from predators; guard Sarral's necromancers from Shades on the rare occasions that they visit the Deadlands; provide comfort to the sick and elderly; and—under the guidance of beast masters—run in races for sport and entertain people at festivals.

Meredy nudges my shoulder, her eyes wide, pointing at something in the distance. A jade-green dragon, smaller than the one I saw in the city, gathers apples in its mouth and drops them in a basket. Meredy looks completely smitten and seems to have forgotten some of her guilt at deciding to leave Lysander in the boarding house's backyard—which, in sharp contrast to the closet-like rooms we've each been given, is actually of generous size, complete with trees for him to nap under.

"Most people can't afford a dragon, and they're quite difficult to breed," Azelie goes on. "It's usually only beast masters who keep them as companions, but occasionally a farmer scrapes together enough savings—that's when they come see my uncles."

Raising her voice over the noisy grind of the cart's wheels, Meredy says, "I know Karthia hasn't been open to visitors, but couldn't beasts as strong as dragons swim to—?"

"Oh, no." Azelie giggles. "They're terrified of water. Now, there's a kingdom far to the west that's rumored to have much larger dragons. Ones that beast masters can't control with their powers alone, so they have to keep them in chains for fear of death and destruction." She wrinkles her nose. "But it's entirely possible my mother made that up to scare my brothers and me into behaving."

The landscape rushing past the cart turns wilder, the houses within sight of the dirt road becoming fewer, replaced by ancient, twisting trees that crowd the sides of the path ahead, making it narrower. Meredy leans into me, hiding her face against my neck as branches grasp at our hair and clothes.

"Dragons were rediscovered about two hundred and fifty years ago, which is why you've never heard of the—ah!" Azelie's words end in a yelp as she ducks to avoid a branch. "There was just one small colony left, surviving in the barren canyons far outside the village of Ithax. People always thought the noises the dragons made were the cries of angry spirits echoing out of gates to the Deadlands—until one woman was brave enough to explore and found a sick little creature too weak to do more than breathe puffs of smoke."

The trees ahead begin to thin. We've almost reached our destination.

"No other kingdom that we know of has dragons like ours anymore," Azelie continues, her words muffled as she hides her face from the branches by holding up the long skirt of her gauzy yellow dress. "That's part of the reason we're so afraid of the Ezorans. They take the most valuable things from the places they raid, and our dragons are priceless to us."

We break free of the trees at last. A man who shares Azelie's bright smile waves to us from a stable yard, and the cart grinds to a halt.

"Uncle Halmar," Azelie murmurs as she leaps from her seat and runs to greet him. "What's wrong?" Evidently, she sees something behind his smile that Meredy and I can't. "Wasn't Uncle Ino supposed to join us today, too?" she demands, seeming to shrink slightly in anticipation of the answer.

Halmar lowers his gaze. "He's not coming, dear heart. Not in the mood to see anyone, I'm afraid. The Ezorans clashed with the guards at our northern border two nights ago, and one of Ino's oldest friends was killed while on patrol—oh, no one you know," he adds hurriedly, at Azelie's horrified look. Clearing his throat, he continues, "An entire Sarralan patrol went down to a mere *handful* of Ezorans. Ino's just gotten word." He wipes his damp brow and sighs. "They're getting stronger, if that's possible. And more daring." Frowning, he finally regards Meredy and me. "I'm sorry. This is hardly a proper welcome, especially to visitors who've come from so far . . ."

"Don't worry about it," I say quickly.

"We're so sorry about your husband's friend," Meredy adds.

We exchange a look. Between us, we're so acquainted with the language of loss by now that we could probably teach others to read it.

Azelie puts a hand on her uncle's arm. "The Queen's Authority will drive them back eventually, like they have before."

"Perhaps," Halmar agrees. "But they need to drive those snakes away *for good*, not struggle through another skirmish. Of course, if the Ezorans turn away from Sarral, I bet they'll merely find another land to stain red . . ."

A chill steals over me, one that lingers despite the sun bearing down on us. From the sound of things, if these Ezoran raiders got wind of Karthia's recent change in leadership, they could devastate the kingdom in a blink. Still, if they were ever a threat in our long history, King Wylding never mentioned them. Maybe they're as unaware of Karthia as we were of them. I hope so. Karthia hasn't had an army since it finally proved long ago that no one from the outside world was allowed to enter. Now there are only handfuls of soldiers for the palace in Grenwyr, and guards for important nobles presiding over Karthia's many provinces. I can't imagine Valoria, capable as she is, has had time to recruit and train soldiers yet.

Swallowing hard, I banish the thought.

After introductions have been made, Halmar leads us around the low building to a large paddock with a wrought-iron fence that's taller than we are. Inside it, dragons are sunning themselves in short, scrubby grass partially blackened in places.

"What do you think, Karthians?" he asks, putting on a smile for us.

Exchanging a look, Meredy and I answer together, "This is amazing!"

After that, Meredy follows Halmar around, asking questions about the dragons' care while Azelie and I hang back near the paddock gate and watch a pinkish-purple dragon slurp water out of a low metal basin. The creature rolls onto its back, wallowing in a wide puddle of mud like pigs do. Its colors remind me of the flowers that grow in the sprawling garden behind the Convent of Death back in Karthia.

"Do they ever figure out ways to escape?" I ask, eyeing the sturdy metal fence.

Azelie laughs softly, though her eyes remain troubled after hearing her uncle's news. "Occasionally. That's why my uncles have a beast master who lives here with them—to keep the little scoundrels from wandering off too far."

I lean against the high fence, trusting the dragons not to burn my legs through the gaps in the metal while my back is turned, and let the warmth of the sun beat down on my face. Azelie does the same, as if the heat and light can somehow chase away the shadow the Ezorans have cast over the day.

"Seems like there are a lot of beast masters in Sarral," I murmur, breaking the silence.

"There are. Compared to other mages, at least. Beast masters are particularly celebrated here because our queen is one, so . . ." Azelie's words trail away as she follows my gaze to the far side of the paddock, where Halmar is showing Meredy how to feed the dragons something slimy from a bucket. Meredy's face glows like it does whenever she's with Lysander.

I like seeing her this way—carefree, an echo of the girl she was when we first met years ago, before too much of the world settled on her shoulders.

When I feel Azelie's gaze shift to me, it's not the sun's warmth that stings my face. Searching for a distraction to avoid more questions about Meredy, I ask, "Have you ever thought of training to be a mage yourself? I have a friend who would've loved growing up where inventors aren't forbidden. And you don't seem too happy working for the healers."

Something tightens in Azelie's face, though she's still smiling. "Inventing is the most difficult magic to work. There are only two master inventors in all of Sarral. One has spent his life working on creating a language unique to our kingdom, and he already has two apprentices. And anyway, even if I wanted to, I couldn't."

I frown. Her eyes are such a dark brown they're almost black, and the darker the hue of any iris, the stronger a person's magical ability usually is. "What do you mean? Did someone make you doubt yourself? Do masters here charge for—?"

Strong jaws clamp down on my ankle, teeth sharp as a Shade's. I scream, drawing a dagger from the sheath on my belt, and whirl toward my attacker, surprised to see the dragon with pinkish-purple scales gnawing on my ankle. It blinks its liquid violet eyes serenely as it grinds its teeth. Sweat drenches my brow as I hold back another scream.

Lowering my blade, I yell, "Death be damned, get this filthy beast off me!"

Meredy and Halmar have already closed half the distance between us, having come running at my screams with wide eyes.

"As your assistant healer, it's my duty to advise you that this dragon is female. And the females, in addition to breathing fire, have mildly poisonous teeth," Azelie says cheerfully as she tries to pry the dragon's jaws open. "We think it has something to do with protecting their young, but we're still learning about them. We don't even know what most of their powers are yet."

"Powers?" I grit out. "You mean this thing could kill me with magic, too?"

Azelie shrugs, her expression turning thoughtful. "According to legend, all dragons have certain magical abilities that they can only use once they've reached adulthood. I suppose it could just be an old rumor, though I like to think it's true."

Finally, after what seems an eternity of heat creeping up my leg—it must be an effect of the poison—Azelie manages to get the blasted creature off me. "You're lucky. It's just a little love nip," she declares cheerily as she inspects the wound.

"Stupid nipper," I growl at the beast, who wags her long tail like a dog in response.

I hastily count thirty or so tooth marks. They ooze with a mixture of blood and something sickly yellow, making me cringe. Looks like I've already broken Kasmira's order about not doing anything that leads to life-threatening injuries, and it's not yet noon.

Meredy reaches us, putting an arm around me for support. I slump against her, glad to take weight off my rapidly swelling leg.

"What happens when this poison reaches my heart?" I gasp, wiping sweat off my brow. More sweat pools beneath my arms and trickles down my spine.

"It won't!" Meredy says firmly. "We both know Kasmira would kill me if I let anything happen to you."

"Dragon's poison isn't fatal," Azelie says soothingly, inspecting my leg while her uncle admonishes the dragon. "It just burns like you've swallowed fire for a few hours. But there's a healer just down the road. I'll go fetch him . . ."

I'm ready to leave even before the kind young healer mends my leg as a favor to Azelie's uncles, but I'm glad we stay for lunch in the house up the hill from the paddock. Watching Azelie and Halmar, I dip my bread in my soup, soaking up the extra broth. The two of them talk quietly, catching up on Azelie's life in the city—Halmar worries about her, being only fifteen and already living on her own above a tailor's shop—while Meredy talks in a low murmur with the resident beast master who's just come in from cleaning the stables.

I barely listen as they talk about bonding with their animals. I'm ready to get back to the city, away from things with too many teeth and fiery breath.

But when I open the door to walk back to our cart and patiently waiting driver, who's immersed in a book, the sight of a familiar pinkish-purple beast the size of a hound stops me from stepping out the door.

"What's Nipper doing here?" I ask Azelie over my shoulder, not daring to take my eyes from the beast's long snout in case she's thinking of using her teeth again.

"Ooh, you've named her," Azelie coos, completely missing the point. "I love it."

The dragon ambles forward, flaring the glistening purple webbing around her head and neck. I take a step back, retreating into the house. Her scales seem to turn more pink than purple as she hurries toward me. I reach for the door, about to slam it shut when Meredy stops me with a hand firmly placed over mine.

"She likes you, Master Necromancer," Meredy says slowly, apparently reading the dragon's emotions with her Sight. "A *lot*. She's afraid—probably that you're leaving. I'm not entirely sure, but I think she wants to come with you."

I shake my head. "Oh, no. What in Vaia's name makes you think we need another creature to look after?"

But Meredy doesn't appear to hear me as she looks thoughtfully toward Halmar. "I don't suppose . . ." she begins.

"She can accompany you," Halmar says gently, giving us the first true smile I think we've seen from him. I'm surprised, but when he says, "Karthia and Sarral were once great allies. Perhaps Karthia has forgotten, but Sarral's memory remains as sharp as ever," I start to understand. "Normally," he continues, "we'd never dream of letting a visitor leave with one of our babies, but . . ." He gazes solemnly between me and Meredy. "You're no ordinary visitors, are you? You're the first Karthian cartographers—no, the first Karthian *ambassadors* of King Wylding's long reign!"

He says it with such admiration that my insides squirm guiltily at our deception. I hate lying to someone who's been so good to us, but we have to do what we can to keep Valoria's rule a secret until she's ready to tell the world herself.

"Besides," Halmar continues, unaware of the guilt now souring my mood, "we've tried to breed this particular dragon a couple times, but she wasn't interested in a mate. We were planning to sell her to a farm nearby—"

"As you should!" I agree, breathless, as Nipper rubs her scaly head against my legs. I'm just waiting for her teeth to come back out.

"A female dragon's bite can sometimes be a sign that she's chosen a mate," Halmar adds with a barely suppressed chuckle, now collecting the dirty lunch bowls. "I don't think she'd be happy with the farmer now that she's met you."

Taking a deep breath, I crouch face-to-face with the dragon, hoping I'm not about to be hit with a cloud of fire. "Go away," I say firmly. "And I'm hopeless at taking care of anything more complicated than a daisy. The last person who followed me around died at the hands of a monster, so really, I'm doing you a favor. Now go."

The dragon rears back on its hind legs. I almost lose my footing in my haste to move out of its reach. The dragon lunges forward, laying its clawed front feet on either side of my neck. She flicks her forked tongue across my cheek.

"I hate you," I mutter. But as I stroke Nipper's long nose, and find her scales surprisingly soft—more like fur than snakeskin—my resolve slips away. My love of all living creatures apparently extends even to ones that bite me by way of hello.

"I'll send word to the queen today and let her know this little one is under new ownership," Halmar declares. "And we hope you'll tell King Wylding where you got her, so that he might look upon Sarral with fondness, and perhaps . . . if it isn't asking too much . . ." He meets my eyes as his voice breaks over his next words. "Perhaps this great gift will encourage him to consider sending aid to Sarral in honor of our old alliance, should our borders fall to the Ezorans."

When I answer, holding Halmar's gaze, my words are heavy with the weight of a promise that's the least I can do for people who have shown us so much kindness in a short time. "I'll make sure the Wyldings know that Sarral would welcome an ally in Karthia once again."

"You promise?" Azelie asks, her eyes round with hope.

"I give you my word," I say, shaking her hand, then Halmar's. This kingdom clearly needs allies if a few Ezoran warriors can destroy an entire Sarralan patrol.

And if Karthia were in trouble again, I'd want the whole world to rush to its aid.

VI

Music fills the night air, a loud song with a fast, pulsing beat unlike anything I've heard in Karthia. Tired from our tour of the city, Meredy and I share a blanket on a hillside behind the healers' house. On another blanket nearby, Azelie's friends talk quietly while we wait for a fireworks show to start. Occasionally, one of us shivers in the sea breeze.

"Any minute now," Azelie whispers, casting an eager glance at the sky.

I think she hopes the fireworks will drive news of the Ezorans' latest attack from everyone's minds, but I doubt all the wine in Karthia could do that. Not when it seems a war is brewing on Sarral's doorstep.

One of Azelie's friends murmurs something too soft for me to hear over the music the Dead are playing, well aware that if we're caught outdoors at night, we'll be in trouble with the Queen's Authority.

Still, when Azelie showed up at the inn just before sundown, Meredy and I agreed we could hardly refuse her offer to see the Dead hold their Festival of Rella, the blue-eyed death goddess they share with the island of Lyris. After locking Lysander in Meredy's room, and Nipper in mine, we snuck out.

Azelie led us with confidence around the few living soldiers patrolling the streets, giving the impression she's done this many times before. Our only light came from the stars as we climbed the hill to meet her friends. Clouds cloaked the nearly full moon, and still do, as we wait for the fireworks to begin.

I gaze down the hill at a glimmer of blue visible only through gaps in an expanse of trees, my first glimpse of a gate to the Deadlands since arriving here. The glow calls to something deep inside me, and my feet itch to march into that light. Maybe the spirits would have some news from Karthia for me. I need to know what's happening there.

Funny. I was so desperate to escape it, yet with each day that passes, I crave word from Karthia more and more.

Beside me, Meredy murmurs, "I wish they'd hurry up with the show. I don't want to get Azelie in any trouble."

I frown, more worried about the Dead than Azelie. "Doesn't this bother you?" I make a sweeping gesture toward the field below where the Dead are preparing their festivities to the lively beat of drums and some other instrument I can't name. "The living and the Dead, trying to ignore each other's existence?"

"Of course," Meredy says at once. "But we just barely survived one battle . . . I don't think we're ready to start another. Besides, maybe the Dead here are happy. We haven't exactly asked them."

"I guess you're right." But that doesn't stop me wondering whether any semblance of equality here is an illusion, even though Karthia's new stance on the Dead keeps them so far removed from the living that they can't even enter our kingdom anymore. Of course, they have their own world where they can thrive. I'd just love to ask a Sarralan necromancer why they bother bringing the Dead back at all when they don't seem to really want them around.

The first firework soars into the air, startling me with a high-pitched whine. It explodes in a shower of red and gold sparks that loosely form the shape of a flower.

Meredy leans forward as she admires the sight, pulling out a small silver flask from the bag she brought and handing it to me. "No questions," she whispers, offering it to me. "Just drink this."

I tip the flask against my lips. The liquid inside tastes just like coffee beans, and I close my eyes as it lingers on my tongue.

"I saw someone in the city drinking this earlier and thought you'd like to try it," Meredy says, sounding pleased by my reaction. Suddenly, I have the urge to say all the things I've been holding back since we danced last night.

"Meredy, I . . ." My heart clamors in my ears as she leans closer to hear above the noise of a second firework shooting skyward.

She studies me as I hesitate. Tucking a thick strand of hair behind my ear, she grazes my cheek with her fingertips, and just like that I'm stunned into silence.

"If you're trying to thank me, don't worry about it. I'm the one who should be thanking you," she says firmly. "You keep saving my life, you try to do all the characters' voices when we're reading, just for me, and now you've shown me that dancing isn't so bad. I'm beginning to think I'll be forever in your debt." She flashes a smile, and while I know she's joking, I can't return the gesture.

Despite my mouth being dry as bone, I somehow get my tongue working. "Don't worry. I'm not keeping score." Deep breaths. "Meredy, I like you. I don't even think *like* begins to cover it, but that's what I want to find out."

This time, I smile, but her face is a blank canvas until splashes of blue, green, and gold wash over it from the fireworks. My smile fades, but my pride must be as broken as the rest of me, because I still continue, "I want you to know, I'm done fighting it—whatever this is between us. Ever since we lost Evander, everything I do feels like a battle. Getting up in the morning. Eating toast. Talking to people. But when I'm with you, I don't have to wear my armor. Being around you is easy, and it makes me want so much more. Will you be my girlfriend?"

She says nothing. Her eyes shine unnaturally bright as the moon peeks out from behind the clouds.

"You don't have to answer right now," I add quickly, feeling sick and slightly shaky since the words have left my mouth. Maybe I asked her too soon. "I won't wait forever—I don't *have* forever—but I'm willing to wait an unreasonably long time when it comes to you."

Meredy turns away from the fireworks as bursts of color form the shape of a dragon. Now that her face is half in shadow, it's unreadable. The way she likes.

"Say something, please. Just let me know you heard me," I urge her quietly, unnerved by her silence. "After last night, you can't pretend you haven't thought about us—"

"Aren't they something?" Azelie interrupts, leaning toward our blanket and gesturing skyward, seemingly oblivious to what's taking place beside her. In a way, I welcome the interruption. I'm able to smooth my face into a mask of not caring.

"So here's the deal," Azelie continues. "I have to go to Skria Flor—the capital—in a few days for a special flower they don't sell at the markets here. I always get a better price when I go in person, so the healers send me every few moons, but given recent events . . ." Her grimace leaves no doubt as to what she means: the attack on Sarral's border. "The boss is insisting I take someone with me. Do you two want to come? It'd be a good way to see more of the countryside . . . and I could use someone to talk to on the road," she admits with a grin. "I promise, no matter what the boss says, I can rescue myself if there's trouble."

I shake my head, trying to catch Meredy's eye, but it's not working. "Thanks, but I'm not in the mood for a trip."

"You should go," Meredy says suddenly, without looking at me. "I'll mind Nipper for you. There are some things I want to do here. Kasmira said the repairs are going to take several days yet, so you've got time."

I turn away from her, suddenly finding it hard to breathe. I thought I could be myself with her, but not wearing my armor only got me hurt again. Faking a smile as fireworks flash and sizzle overhead, I say, "Sure. It'll be . . . fun."

Azelie whoops with delight, shifting over to our blanket and linking her arm through mine. "We'll have the best time," she promises. Something in her voice makes me think she overheard more than she initially let on, and I feel a rush of gratitude for the perpetually cheerful healer's assistant. I need a little more happiness in my life.

Besides, should there be trouble of any sort, I can protect Azelie with my blades—a small step toward repaying her and her uncles for my dragon companion. But it would be a start.

With Meredy not willing to meet my eyes, the thought of going somewhere new with a girl I've only just met suddenly sounds wildly appealing.

Three days later, as our cart nears the sprawling outskirts of the city of Skria Flor, Nipper—who insisted on coming—strains against the heavy leather collar attached to the lead in my hands. I pull hard on the lead, and Nipper sheepishly settles in my lap. When she cranes her neck up to study me, her eyes flash with different colors, as if concerned by the pain she sees in mine. She nudges my hand until I start petting her cool, scaly back. At least she gives me something to focus on besides Meredy.

Given the way she's been avoiding me ever since the fireworks show, I'm pretty sure our relationship ended before it even really started. Thanks to her silence and near-constant absence, I've been lying in bed alone every night at the boarding house in my tiny room, my hand between my legs as I think of her, trying to feel anything besides empty. I thought seeing the world would heal my mind as quickly as healers' magic mends a broken bone, but all it's done—all *she's* done—is open new wounds and pick at old ones until they're raw.

Our cart hits a bump so hard it rattles my teeth, forcing my attention back to the road as it forks ahead of us. Instead of taking the wider, flatter path that leads into the city, Azelie steers us onto the narrower, overgrown path *around* it, heading north.

"What are you doing?" I demand, leaning forward to study Azelie's expression. But while she's in the driver's seat, it's hard to see her face. "What about the market?"

"We'll head there shortly," she promises. Her voice sounds different all of a sudden—older, and distant—and it sets me on edge. "This will only take an hour or so."

"Where are we going?" I touch my free hand to one of the daggers on my belt, seeking its silent reassurance. Or maybe I'm just in the mood for a fight—anything to take my mind off Meredy.

"To see if the rumors are true," she answers calmly. "To see what the Ezorans are truly capable of."

Neither of us utters another word as the scenery changes. The houses on the city's outskirts are soon at our backs. We abandon them for wilder land where everything flanking the path is green and growing at first, but as we travel farther north, the riot of color usually found in forests and meadows gives way to barren land. It's as if someone has leached the color from every flower and tree, and even from the sky. When I run my fingers over a low-hanging branch and they come away coated in fine gray powder, I realize it's ash. The Ezorans carelessly set fire to so much here, all they left is a memory of a place, an echo of the life that used to color this now-muted land.

The road ends just after we crest a large hill. There's a smaller footpath from here onward, leading down the hill into a valley where a great many soldiers—more armed men and women than I've ever seen—march in small groups toward what must be the kingdom's northern border, hidden by more hills. Other soldiers remain in the valley, bustling in and out of tents that have been propped up amidst the blackened foundations of farmers' cabins, perhaps tending to their wounded.

Deeper gray stains the horizon as far as I can see. If I didn't know it was morning, I wouldn't be able to tell. Day and night don't seem to exist in this place anymore.

Azelie climbs down from the driver's seat, and I follow her out of the cart with Nipper.

She makes no movement toward the footpath—I doubt civilians are allowed to be as close as we are—but instead stands in silence looking down into the valley, her arms crossed, her hardened expression never wavering.

"So many dead," she whispers at last. "And all the poor flowers and orchards . . . who knows if they'll recover?"

Her words pull me back to another valley, one scarred by fire and blood, where Meredy and I witnessed the aftermath of a Shade attack.

The devastation here is just as bad—perhaps worse, knowing who the culprits were. I expect senseless cruelty and violence from Shades, after all. That's what monsters do. So when humans inflict just as much damage . . . I guess that makes them monsters, too. The grim sight before us proves the Ezorans are a force to be feared, to be met with blades. *Not* creatures to be reasoned with.

VII

"So, what do you think?" Azelie's eyes gleam in the early afternoon sun as she slows the horses in front of a stable across from one end of the market. Ever since we returned to the city's outskirts, she's been her usual, bubbly self. "This place claims to be the world's largest flower market. I don't know if it's true, but it has plenty of rare plants."

While Azelie talks to the stable girl, I lead Nipper out of the cart, onto the worn stone street, and take my first good look around.

The market occupies several city blocks, stretching south from the stable as far as I can see. Vendors are arranged under tents with colorful roofs and open siding to better allow the throngs of basket-carrying shoppers to move about. Flowers of every shape, size, and color, many that I don't recognize, hang from baskets and cover display tables. There are plenty of herbs and even some vegetables for sale, too.

As the breeze shifts, the scent of the place finally hits me: like diving nose-first into a fragrant rosebush. Sure, there's a faint undercurrent of hay and musk from the stable, and a hint of whatever Nipper smells like—which definitely isn't flowers—but there's no question that people come here to be immersed in a giant garden that's all for sale.

Meredy would love this place. If she were with us, she'd already be across the street, filling up a basket, buying flower crowns, and petting every cat and dog in sight.

Turning away from Azelie so she can't see the hurt in my eyes, I spot several flyers tacked to the side of the stable and hurry over for a closer look.

IF YOU SEE ME, CONTACT THE QUEEN'S AUTHORITY AT ONCE! The four flyers say the same thing, but the pictures drawn above the words are different. The faces of the men and women in them are all as pale as Valoria, as if they come from somewhere with little sun, though it's hard to tell at first because of the smudgy charcoal symbols drawn on some of their cheeks and foreheads. I think the smudges are supposed to be *blood*.

Something about them is vaguely familiar. Their pale hair, their scars, and their fur-lined clothing tugs at the corners of my memory. One of the drawings shows a hard-eyed woman with small, intricate white-blond braids running along the sides of her head.

Suddenly, I remember that night at the tavern in Lyris as clearly as if I were standing there again. I only saw her for a moment then, but I'm sure that the woman who lingered in the shadows, watching us face down the crowd with interest, had the same hairstyle, the same fur clothes, and as many scars as her fellow warriors on the flyers.

My stomach drops. We've seen an Ezoran without realizing it. Though what she was doing in Lyris, apart from her kin, I can't say. If she was a scout, she should have realized pretty quickly that Lyris is too tiny and too poor to be worth conquering.

Karthia, on the other hand, with its new queen still figuring things out . . .

"Awful, aren't they?" Azelie appears at my side and links her arm through mine, apparently ready to leave the stable.

I shrug. "They don't look so tough, those four." Aside from their many scars, their sneers, and the hungry looks in their eyes, that is. Mind still reeling at how close we came to one of them, I mutter, "Bet I could handle them."

"Not me!" Azelie declares, guiding us toward the market at a steady pace. "Even their portraits scare me. People were handing out those same flyers everywhere last month, because a couple of Ezorans somehow snuck past the border—we think they wanted to kill Queen Jasira. The soldiers who chased them back couldn't even *capture* them." She shivers. "Everyone says they fight better than us, even though they aren't used to the heat here. That they're as clever as they are cruel." Lowering her voice to a whisper, she adds, "I've even heard they like to experiment with magic. *Dark* magic. That they push the boundaries of mages' powers to do terrible things."

I have so many questions on the tip of my tongue—namely, what sorts of magic the Ezorans could possibly be doing when I only know of five types—but Azelie's expression encourages me to change the subject instead.

"So, what kind of flower are we looking for?" I ask, shortening Nipper's lead as a woman and her child stop in their tracks to stare at our passing. "And what's gotten into them?" I nod to the onlookers.

Azelie grins, flicking her high ponytail over her shoulder. "Most people here have what I call 'dragon fever.'" She shrugs, steering us along the walking path opposite the market, where there are fewer people. "The fever's never gotten me, since my uncles have the dragon nursery and I can see them anytime I want. But most people are fascinated. You'll find all kinds of touristy stuff when we get inside the tents—speaking of which, you and Nipper should do some exploring. I need spirit orchids, and there's only one vendor, but it's going to take me until sunset to wear him down to the sort of price I'm comfortable with."

We step through the rolled-up side of a long blue tent. The woman nearest the opening waves, trying to draw our gazes to her display, and I can't help but take the bait. Silver dragon brooches, earrings, and necklaces glitter on her table.

"You'd be a tough sell," the woman murmurs, her wide brown eyes on Nipper. "Seeing as you have the real thing." Feeling suddenly protective, I step in front of my little dragon, shielding her from the woman's view.

"I'll meet you back at the stable at sunset. Oh, and don't spend all your gold in one place." Azelie winks and disappears into the fray, leaving me and Nipper alone among the curious shoppers.

Shortening Nipper's lead, I move through the tables with my head bowed to avoid the notice of overeager vendors. When a not-so-lovely-smelling flower wafts in my face, I sneeze, and a few tables down, I wince when the scent of fresh vanilla pods tricks my senses into thinking that Meredy is nearby.

I lead Nipper toward the far end of the market, drawn to the smaller crowds and a sense of quiet. Clouds of dust and pollen dance lazily in beams of sunlight streaming in through the sides of the last few tents, and Nipper flicks her tongue at them.

"You there." The gentle rasp of an older man's voice forces me to look up. His shoulders are hunched, perhaps from the weight of carrying so many years, and his dark clothing covers everything but his head and his gnarled, waxy hands.

I pull Nipper to a stop—she's more interested in the roses

behind me than this old man's display of carved stones, copper dragon statues, and jewelry boxes.

"Can I help you?" I ask, my free hand trailing over my heart as I check to make sure my master necromancer's pin is still stashed with my things at the boarding house.

The old man's smile is gentle. "I believe *I* can help *you*." He reaches toward a small cabinet on one end of his table, turning it so its glass front faces outward. Inside is a large chunk of pale blue crystal, a little bigger than my fist. Nodding to Nipper, he adds, "You look like a lady who's interested in the rarer things in life. Dare I say—the priceless things?"

I fight the urge to roll my eyes. This guy wants all my gold for some stone? "Sorry, but no thanks. You picked the wrong girl to swindle today." I turn to leave.

"I see. So you've never lost anyone?" The man doesn't raise his voice, but it somehow carries.

I glare at him, thinking of Evander, Master Cymbre, and Master Nicanor. I'm even afraid I've lost Meredy, in a way, but he doesn't need to know any of that.

He continues to press. "There's no beloved spirit you wish you could speak to without ever having to set foot in the Deadlands? No absent voice you've been longing to hear?"

I pause and turn back to him, shivering despite the sunlight pouring into the tent. We seem to be alone in here now, except for Nipper and two other vendors who have already started packing up for the day.

Thinking of Evander, Master Cymbre, and Master Nicanor, whose spirits would have simply disappeared after their untimely deaths, I say firmly, "No. No one I love is in the Deadlands, and that's the truth."

"You've lost someone with blue eyes, then," the man says quickly. "Someone whose spirit you've feared you could never reach. Well, with this, you can."

As I watch from the corner of my eye, he picks up the pale blue crystal. "This was stolen—not by me, of course—from the Temple of Rella, and infused with the magic of one of her priestesses." He cradles the crystal against his chest almost reverently. "It will allow you to talk to any spirit, even those who don't move on to the Deadlands after their body dies, and hear their voice as clearly as if they were standing beside you . . ." He lets the words trail away, no doubt for effect, then adds, "If you can afford it, that is."

I stare at the crystal, trying to keep my face blank. It's probably just a hoax. Some junk this man sells to tourists, drawing them in with his little story about Sarral's death goddess. But I'd give up all my gold and more for the slightest chance to talk to Evander, even one last time. For another chance to memorize his laugh, and to hear that he still loves me, too, after everything I've done.

"How much?" I say, feigning boredom by picking dirt from under my thumbnail.

The old man looks hopefully at Nipper.

"Not a chance." I pull the dragon closer. For the first time, I realize just what having Nipper beside me means: I have a companion again, one I can rely on, and that's even more important now that Meredy seems content to pretend I don't exist. "You can't sell me anything that's worth a life."

The old man's eyes harden. "Fine," he grumbles, clinging to the crystal as though he thinks I'll snatch it away without paying. "Make me another offer, then."

When all is argued and negotiated, I've barely got enough money left to buy a couple of cheese-covered snacks to share with Nipper.

As we amble back toward the busier part of the market, a hot feeling of shame spreads up my neck and face. I just spent a good portion of my savings on a lame stone. I don't even know if it does anything, let alone what the old man swore it could. Glad it's hidden in a bag, I vow not to tell anyone what I've done.

There's no way the crystal works, besides. If there was some chance I could talk to Evander, I'd have heard of it before now. Or would I? I hadn't heard of dragons until we landed in Sarral. Still, if it really worked, wouldn't this old man be rich by now, not haggling in the back of a market with people who might not have a copper to their name?

By the time I hurry back to the opposite end of the market to return the blasted thing, the old man is gone, along with all his wares.

I slam my fist on the empty table.

He's probably at a tavern right now, raising a glass to the foolish girl who just paid his wages for the next few years.

I'm not the only one who stays quiet on the ride back to the coast the next day. Azelie's silence is much stranger than mine, as she normally never shuts up, but today she just sits in the back of the cart beside Nipper, looking thoughtfully down at her milk-white spirit orchids wrapped in paper. I suspect the gray sky, which reminds me of the ruined valley, has something to do with her mood—unless she, like me, was an idiot and spent all her money on a crystal that came with a good story.

"Kasmira said she wants to leave Sarral as soon as you're back, provided the repairs are finished," Azelie murmurs as the city of Skria Flor becomes a blur on the horizon behind us, still gazing down at her flowers. "That could be as soon as tomorrow."

The reminder makes my shoulders tense. "I'm not surprised" is all I manage to say. Kasmira always gets restless quickly, but I like it here. I don't want to think about leaving right now. I especially don't want to think about facing Meredy and her sudden coolness toward me again so soon. What will sharing our too-small cabin on the ship be like when she's so determined to ignore me?

"I'm going to miss you," Azelie adds, drawing my attention back to her. "The older healers never talk to me this much. And your life is *so* interesting." A shadow of a grin crosses her face. "Assuming it's still standing after the Ezorans have their way with it, do you think you'll ever come back to—?"

She chokes back a shout of alarm as I pull hard on the horses' reins.

A large fallen tree blocks the narrow road. As the horses stop, I turn in the driver's seat to gaze in all directions. There's no one around trying to remove the tree, no houses or farms within view, and no noise of other carts rumbling down the road in either direction. For a moment, I consider just guiding the horses around it. But the ground here is swamp-like, with more mud and puddles of standing water than dirt, and I'm afraid we'll get stuck.

I smile reassuringly at Azelie. "I'm sure someone will be along to help soon. At least this one didn't fall and hit me in the head, right?"

A faint crease appears between her brows. "Someone will come eventually. But we can't be sure when, since this isn't a main road. I—I took a shortcut before we switched seats, and . . . this is wild land, where the wolves hunt."

"Wish you'd mentioned that *before* we started down it," I say through gritted teeth, jumping down from the driver's seat into a puddle. Nipper coos, blowing smoke at me as I splash mud everywhere.

I start toward the tree. "If this thing's dry enough, maybe I can have Nipper burn it with her fire breath."

Nipper coos again, louder this time.

The baying of something wild answers.

Branches crack and rustle in the distance to our right, somewhere beyond a thicket of trees too dense to see into.

"Death be damned," I groan, gooseflesh rising on my arms at the sound.

"Get in the cart, and get your daggers ready just in case this doesn't work," Azelie mutters tersely as she jumps down beside me. "Hurry. Get in the—"

"What are you going to do?" I blink at her, completely at a loss as to how a girl of her size could move a tree that big before whatever's crashing through those trees comes out. "I'm strong, let me help—"

Another howl cuts me off, louder this time, as Azelie's eyes flash a warning.

"I have to do this alone. Just trust me!" she calls as she runs toward the fallen tree just a few paces away. Crouching beside it, she lays her hands on the trunk.

Climbing back into the driver's seat, torn between training my gaze on the rustling trees and watching Azelie work, I pull out my daggers. Hopefully I won't need them. After all, I've got a dragon on my side now—a fire-breathing, poisonous, biting dragon. Wild bears or wolves should run from *her*.

The fallen tree groans, rolling to the left. Azelie rubs her forehead with one hand but keeps the other on the bark. There's no way she has enough strength to push it, but somehow, the tree keeps rolling until it's almost completely off the road, giving us enough space to pass. Azelie looks ready to collapse. Either she's way stronger than she looks, or I just witnessed something like magic.

As Azelie staggers back to the cart, Nipper imitates the howling, and the wolves—definitely wolves, I can't mistake their calls now that they're so close—answer. Nipper's scaly tail swishes from side to side as the sounds of unbridled hunger shiver past our ears. I think she likes them.

So much for having the dragon on our side in a fight.

Gathering the horses' reins in one hand, I take aim with one of my daggers in the other, my gaze trained on the thicket. "Whatever it was you just did to that tree—thank you," I murmur shakily as Azelie jumps in beside Nipper.

I flick the reins, and the horses charge forward just as the first sleek, dark body bursts from the trees. The wolf snarls, stumbling in a deep pool of mud.

The dagger still in my other hand, I hesitate. The last life I took was Hadrien's, and I hadn't really wanted to kill him. He forced my hand, but he had a choice. This poor beast is acting out of necessity. I can't bring myself to end its life just because it's doing what all wolves do. I can't even bring myself to wound it, knowing the only help it might receive from a passerby is a swift end. I drop the dagger and urge the horses faster, until white foamy sweat flies from their hides and the wolf and his friends are far behind.

Only once the horses have slowed, and there's no more distant baying, do I turn to look at Azelie over my shoulder.

The fallen tree seemed to move of its own accord, and it reminds me of a story Meredy told me once, about a man with amber eyes who could change his shape. But Azelie's eyes are the darkest brown. According to the rules of Vaia, the Five-Faced God, her gift *should be* inventing, like all brown-eyed mages. Yet . . .

"What exactly did you do back there?" I ask softly.

As she raises her gaze to mine, an errant ray of light breaking through the clouds spills into her eyes. For the first time, I notice that while one of them is blackish-brown, the other is a green so deep it's almost black, too.

"Now you know," she murmurs, seeming to brighten with the sun's touch. "I see colors around plants. I figured out when I was little that I could make them do whatever I wanted, if I touched them and spoke just the right way. I made flowers dance in my mom's garden. I made carrots grow faster. I made night-blooming jasmine open in daylight. It scared the few friends I showed, and even my family." She bows her head. "It's why my parents never liked me as much as my brothers. They taught me to hide what I can do, because there's no one to teach me how to control it. If anything, I—I'd wind up as an experiment or something, studied to see how my gift works. And of course I wouldn't want—"

"Azelie!" I take a quick glance at the road, just to make sure there aren't more obstacles in our path, then turn back to her. There was a time when witnessing a strange new gift would have terrified me— after all, my entire life, everything new and different was forbidden in Karthia—but the part of me that was paralyzed by newness died about the same time King Wylding did, taking his fear and hatred of change with him. "Calm down. I'm not afraid of you, and I'm not going to tell anyone about your gift, all right?"

Taking a deep breath, she nods. "All right. And, Odessa?" Her smile finally returns. "My friends call me Zee."

Relaxing against the driver's seat board at my back, I nod, an idea quickly forming in my mind. "You know . . . my friend Valoria is starting a school for mages of all sorts back in Karthia. I have a feeling you'd fit right in—that is, if you don't mind a bit of seasickness and a yearlong detour to get there. If that doesn't deter you, you're welcome to come along."

Azelie leans forward, her eyes widening. "Seriously? You're talking about a chance to see the world *and* attend a . . . a school for mages? That's a real thing?"

"I wouldn't joke about something like that." Holding her gaze, I take a deep breath and plunge ahead. "Founding the school was one of the first things Valoria wanted to do as the new queen of Karthia."

Azelie grips the seat of the cart like it's all that's keeping her from falling over. *"Queen?"*

"That's right. If you're going to consider coming to Karthia, there's a lot you should know. Kasmira's not a court-appointed cartographer. None of us are . . ."

I hesitate on the verge of saying more. She's given me no reason to doubt her, but then, I'd have said the same of Hadrien not too long ago. I trusted Meredy, too—with my heart, of all things—and look how that's turned out. But as Azelie smiles at me, her face warm and open, my resolve to keep to myself weakens. I guess I'll never learn.

After swearing her to secrecy, as we ride through lonely stretches of swamp and fields, I explain everything that happened before we came to Sarral—starting with the day Evander and I watched Master Nicanor die at our feet.

VIII

We don't reach Glia Raal until late evening, missing the curfew for the living along with supper, but I'm not hungry after so much discussion of Karthia and all that recently happened there.

By the time we part ways at the boarding house, after asking a million and one questions, Azelie has decided to join us on the *Paradise* to see the world and attend Valoria's mage school. She dashes off, almost colliding with a Dead woman in the street, promising she'll be at the harbor tomorrow.

When I trudge up to my room at the boarding house, leaving Nipper to frolic in the backyard for a bit, Kasmira greets me at the top of the stairs.

"My old girl is seaworthy again, Sparrow," she declares with an air of long suffering. "Finally. Being stuck on land makes me itchy after a while." She follows me into the cramped, daffodil-colored room where I've spent my sleepless nights, and sits on the bed.

"That's good news, Kas." I try to smile, but find I can't, as I look down the hallway and see no sign of Meredy.

"Yeah?" Kasmira tilts her head, deep gray eyes searching my face. "Doesn't sound that way, and here I thought you wanted to see seventeen new places this year . . ."

"It's not anything you said." Turning away, I bury the leather bag holding the stupid crystal at the bottom of my pile of belongings. "Look. I'm packed already. Wouldn't want to miss another chance to be, I don't know, locked up forever just for being a necromancer, would I?" I force a smile. "We leave tomorrow, first thing?"

Kasmira's still looking a bit too closely at me when I turn back to her. "I don't know about first thing. More like afternoon. Dvora and I are meeting a few of the others at a tavern for one last night of drinking and depravity." She grins. "I know this city has a curfew and all, but we've found a fine establishment that'll serve you at any hour whether you're living or Dead, long as you can pay. You're welcome to come, but . . ." Her expression softens, and there's no mistaking the concern in her gaze. "I imagine you want to spend your time saying your goodbyes here. Unless, of course, you want to stay, too."

"Stay? What do you mean? Who—? Oh." Understanding dawns before Kasmira can elaborate, and my heartbeat quickens. "Meredy's staying here? What? Why? When did she decide—?"

"It's not my place to say." Kasmira climbs to her feet and throws her arms around me. She pulls me in for a hug with immense strength.

"Kas, I need to breathe."

"Oh! Sorry." Kasmira sighs against my hair, but she doesn't let go just yet, and neither do I.

"Why is she staying?" My voice comes out slightly cracked.

"You should go talk to her." At last, Kasmira steps back, but she raises my chin with her fingers. "She was outside last I saw, in the yard with the others."

I don't stop to ask who these *others* are. I'll find out soon enough. Nearly tripping over my own feet in my haste, I somehow manage to get down the stairs and out into the large fenced yard where I left Nipper to play. The sky outside is black and starless, but thanks to the firelight spilling from the boarding house windows, I can see well enough.

Beneath the shelter of a large tree, Meredy and three strangers— a girl with raven hair and twin boys with emerald pins on their tunics—sit in a circle, their hands in their laps and their eyes closed as if in a collective trance. None look up at my approach, and as I glance toward the far end of the yard, through an open gate and up a hill, I understand why.

The strangest group of beasts I've ever seen are running through the night together, barking, growling, and nipping playfully at one another whenever they get close enough: Lysander the grizzly, a black dog with long, glossy fur, and a pair of giant cats with identical spotted coats. The animals' eyes all glow an unnaturally bright green as their masters share their minds—all except the eyes of the small pink dragon who rolls herself into a ball and collides with one of the big cats, causing them both to tumble downhill.

"Nipper," I groan, shaking my head. Any other time, her antics would make me laugh.

Slowly, the glow fades from all the beasts' eyes, and the people beneath the tree begin to stir. My heart quickens as I hurry to Meredy's side. Sometimes, she needs help remembering who she is after occupying Lysander's mind. I've seen it happen before. All beast masters are a little more like their animals after using their magic; it's the cost of their gift. The longer they stay inside a creature's mind, the more feral they tend to become. And if they push too far, they can lose themselves entirely, stuck inside a creature's mind forever.

But as I help Meredy climb to her feet, there's instant recognition and alertness in her eyes. "Welcome back," she says softly. Her face radiates happiness, her cheeks glowing pink as though she, not Lysander, just enjoyed a run through the night air.

"Meredy," I say in a low voice as her friends talk among themselves. "Why aren't you—you know . . . ?"

"On all fours, trying to catch a squirrel for supper?" she finishes for me, grinning. "My new friends have been teaching me how to control my magic better." She stands a little taller, seeming proud as she explains, "That's why I couldn't come with you and Azelie. I just didn't want to say anything in case things didn't go well. But as you saw, they did!" Her face falling slightly, she adds, "I still have a lot to learn, though. So much that I've decided to stay a while and work on my bond with Lysander."

Suddenly, every angry word I wanted to shout, every question I wanted to throw at her about staying dissolves on my tongue. She looks more alive in this place, more at ease than she ever did in Karthia.

Her desire to stay has nothing to do with me. She deserves this. Sure, I'll miss her every second of every day, but who would I be if I couldn't see how she's slipped right into this world that celebrates her magic as though it's where she's always belonged? Seeing her like this, I realize her happiness matters far more than what I want. Not only that, but if she gets an even better grasp of her magic here, she'll be far less likely to descend into Lysander's mind for good. She'll be safe. She'll always be the person I've come to care about more than I would have imagined possible.

"I'm sorry about earlier—at the fireworks," she continues, seeming hesitant when I'm the one who's silent for once. She's so focused on me that she doesn't even wave as her friends and their animal companions depart. "But I needed to make this decision on my own, and I couldn't let you factor into it. That's why I kept my distance, even before your trip with Azelie. Besides, I thought if we spent more time apart, my staying here might hurt less." She bows her head. "You don't deserve to hurt anymore."

She extends both her arms, beckoning me closer. I hesitate a moment, but I can't seem to resist her pull, the tide to her moon, and I let her draw me into an embrace.

"You could stay, too," she whispers, her lips brushing my ear. "And if the chance to be your girlfriend is still—"

"We both know I don't belong here. I don't know *where* I belong," I interrupt, not wanting to hear the rest of what she was going to say. It would hurt too much. "But I've never seen you like this. You deserve to be where you're happiest, and that's why you have to stay, no matter how you feel about me."

Meredy's eyes shimmer, forcing her to blink hard to clear them. "Will you take my father's journal, then, and fill out more of the maps he started before he died? And keep Evander's dream of seeing the world alive? I mean, the way you came up with nineteen places . . . you were more than worthy of his love. I don't know that I'd have thought of it."

I nod, my throat too tight for words.

If I could, I'd tell her that I meant what I said about waiting a long time for her. I'd tell her I'll miss keeping each other company through the deepest, longest stretches of night. I'd tell her this wasn't how I wanted our story to end.

Her voice unnaturally high, Meredy says, "I guess this is goodbye, Master Necromancer."

Drawing a breath, I manage to whisper, "Goodbye, Master Crowther." I turn to go.

Meredy puts a hand on my shoulder, pulling me back. "Odessa. Wait."

Her lips are so close to mine as she tries to kiss me. I turn my head so her kiss grazes my cheek, cool and dry.

As I stride back to the inn without another word, something inside me cracks. Just a hairline fracture at first, becoming a full-blown break by the time I'm at the staircase, the pain intensifying with every step I take away from Meredy.

I'm happy for her.

"I am," I insist as I try to drink a cup of tea in the boarding house's small parlor, watched over by Nipper. "So happy. See?" I attempt a smile.

Nipper yelps and scoots backward, her long tail nearly swiping a lamp off a table. I guess my smile isn't exactly convincing.

As I raise the delicate teacup to my lips, Nipper scampers off, only to return moments later with something between her teeth. She drops a drool-covered sock in my lap and swishes her tail from side to side again, clearly proud of herself.

"Thanks," I tell her weakly, rubbing her head.

She disappears again, this time returning with a torn-up book.

A dirty glove.

A knit hat with holes in it.

An apple core.

Before I've even finished my tea, I've accumulated the contents of a rubbish heap on my lap. I can't help it—I laugh. "You're not so bad to have around, you know," I tell Nipper as I throw my arms around her neck. I let her chew affectionately on my hair for a moment. "Is this one of your magical powers Azelie was telling me about? Making me laugh when I'm miserable? It's pretty impressive."

Later, after tucking Nipper into my bed—someone might as well use it—I stagger bleary-eyed into the tavern where Kasmira, Dvora, and the rest of the crew are already deep in their cups. Just for tonight, I'm going to wallow. I'm going to mourn the loss of a future with Meredy that never got started, and tomorrow, I'll be stronger.

While Kasmira and her crew play a game of darts that involves drinking and losing various items of clothing when they miss the board—Dvora is already without her blouse—I stride to the bar. I want to try something new, something strong and bewildering enough to make me forget Meredy.

Nearby, a woman with battle scars on her cheeks and hands— I'd recognize the mark of a blade anywhere—lifts a slender glass of crimson liquid studded with berries and topped with a pink blossom. As I lean in to ask what it is, her conversation with the man on her other side becomes clearer, and I pause to decide whether I should interrupt after all.

"Still doesn't feel real that the commander sent me home." The woman sighs, lifting the crimson drink to her lips. "Three days ago, I was fighting the Ezorans, and then I took a blade to the leg that forced me off the battlefield for who knows how long . . ." She shrugs. "Not that I'm complaining. This way, I'll be home with my wife and son on their birthdays. Of course, I hate to think of what new, painful tactics the Ezorans will devise while I'm away."

The soldier's companion swears creatively, then grunts. "No sense worrying about them for now. Enjoy your holiday." He takes a sip of his ale, then peeks at Kasmira and the crew over his shoulder, his expression turning thoughtful. "Say, here's something to distract you: Have you heard the latest news from Karthia? About the rebellion?"

I grip the edge of the bar as my heart falters.

"Apparently King Wylding is dead," he continues, his voice softening with awe. "There's a young queen on the throne now, and her citizens aren't happy. A couple Shade-baiters—that's what Karthians call rogue necromancers—created a Witherling on purpose and set it loose on her. She'd barely recovered from that when a weather worker turned traitor and struck her with lightning. And it's not just the attempts on her life—the unhappy people are organizing, she claims, building a force to oppose her guards . . ."

For a moment, the man's voice becomes too soft to hear. There's a faint ringing in my ears as I imagine Valoria on the brink of death. Valoria, hurt and scared in the face of a Shade's unrelenting hunger, the way Evander once was.

Digging my nails into my palm, I force myself to refocus on the conversation.

". . . the details aren't exactly clear, mind, as I heard all this from my second cousin who works as a lady-in-waiting for Queen Jasira," the man says proudly, his chest swelling a bit. "Karthia's new queen sent ours a message just yesterday, asking for help in sending a distress call to her missing friends. But the best part is *how* she sent the message. Want to know?"

His soldier friend nods, looking stunned. "I . . . suppose . . ."

"A metal bird with working wings that took it all the way across the sea!" The man grins. "I just hope this new Karthian queen lives long enough to make an appearance over here. I'd like to shake the hand of anyone who can make metal creatures strong enough to fly over the sea. That's a fine mind."

"Not likely." The soldier scoffs, shaking her head. "You know what they say . . ." She lowers her voice to a whisper after casting a furtive glance at Kasmira and the crew. "Getting a Karthian to change is harder than teaching rocks to dance. This new queen isn't the leader they're used to, which means she doesn't stand a chance at living out the year."

I dig my nails harder into my palms, fighting the urge to scream *shut up shut up shut up* as more images of a bloodied Valoria clutched in a Shade's claws flash through my mind. She must really be in danger to have sent a distress call—I doubt that's how she wanted to introduce herself to the world.

"Karthians are impossible," the soldier's companion agrees in hushed tones, disappearing momentarily into his ale. "This queen had better hope the Ezorans don't get wind of her troubles, or soon she'll be fighting them off along with her own people. What a mess."

A chill sweeps through me. The man is right. The Ezorans getting wind of Karthia's new queen could mean trouble, and they *definitely* know, thanks to that loudmouthed sailor from the *Paradise* gossiping at the tavern in Lyris. The Ezoran woman who was there that night, watching from the shadows, even heard me confirm it.

The man pushes away his glass and stands. "Queen Jasira's delegate should be contacting the Karthian ship captain with the message tomorrow, but since she's here, and I'm here . . ." He shrugs. "Might as well pass along the news myself, right?"

"Don't bother," I tell the man swiftly as I stride past him. "I heard everything."

Rushing toward Kasmira, I kick someone's discarded trousers out of my way in my haste to reach her. We have to go to Valoria. Now. We can worry about the possibility of the Ezorans setting their sights on Karthia later.

If there are mages working against our queen, aiding in a brewing rebellion, she needs the strongest and best at her side to stop them. Ordinary guards will only suffice against ordinary dangers. I was King Wylding's prized necromancer, and while Jax and Simeon are smart and strong as can be, I'm the only necromancer close to Valoria who's killed a Shade. Make that several. And Kasmira . . . I used to think she was the strongest weather worker in Grenwyr, but after seeing her handle a storm created by several of her fellow mages, I'm sure of it. She might be the strongest in all of Karthia. Valoria already has the best healer at her side—our friend Danial—but she needs more than that. She needs her most capable mages to fight for her with the power and control we've worked so hard to master.

"Sparrow!" Swaying like we're back in rough seas, Kasmira throws an arm around my shoulders and pulls me close. "Dvora and I have a bet going. Suppose I can—?"

"Valoria's been attacked by a Shade!" I cut across her, my mouth going dry. "Shade-baiters did it on purpose, just like—just like before." I swallow hard, thinking of the massacre Hadrien and his pet necromancer Vane caused in a similar fashion. "She was hurt badly, from the sound of things, and worse, there's a rebellion forming against her. We have to go—" My tongue sticks on the word *home*, so I amend, "To Karthia."

My words seem to have a sobering effect on the entire crew. Just like that, Evander's dreams—and Evander himself—seem a little dimmer, a little more out of reach. But Valoria, my dear friend, comes first.

A stillness hangs over us, the air turning so heavy it's as if we're at a funeral, not in a tavern where some of us are half-undressed with drinks and darts in our hands.

"Of course we do!" Kasmira declares at last, sounding ready to go to battle on the spot. "If Valoria needs us, we're as good as there."

Dvora nods in agreement. "Anyone who tries to hurt our queen is going to regret it." She clenches her fists at her sides, somehow looking fierce even without her blouse. "If they're still alive when we're through with them, that is."

I nod my agreement, lost for words. It's a sickening feeling, imagining that one of the people we fought for—who *Valoria* fought for—could be angry enough to kill her when she's only been on the throne for weeks, not even months yet. There's no change she could be making, no law she could be passing to justify these attempts on her life.

"Go grab your bags, everyone," Kasmira says, clapping her hands to startle the weariest of her crew into greater alertness. Eyes flashing as she sweeps her gaze over us, she says firmly, "The moment you're all on board, we sail."

Paying no heed to the guards roaming the nighttime streets, I rush to tell Azelie what I've learned. To my surprise, the suggestion that she stay here in Sarral, where there aren't any rebellions to fear, makes her eyes shine hard as glass.

"Oh, no." She crosses her arms, frowning. "You can't offer me a chance to finally belong somewhere and then just take it back." Opening my mouth, I start to say the offer still stands, but she raises her voice over mine. "I've been waiting my whole life for something like this! *Fifteen years!* I'm not waiting any longer. I'm getting on that ship with you."

After agreeing to meet her on board, I hurry to grab my bag from the bedroom where I've hardly slept at all. As I sling the bag over my shoulder, I notice Meredy's father's journal waiting on the bed. She even turned down my blankets.

I want to hit something, but since this isn't my room to destroy, I settle for ripping the blankets off the bed and throwing the pillow as hard as I can against the far wall. Breathing hard, I pull a crinkled piece of paper from my bag. It's the drawing of me, Meredy, and Valoria that our new queen did before any of us knew how bad things were going to get. Before Meredy and I witnessed a massacre and realized Hadrien was behind it.

Opening my door, I tiptoe down the hall to Meredy's room, the drawing in hand. Unlike when I hesitated to say a final farewell to her back in Karthia, there's light seeping through the cracks around her closed door, leaving no question that she's inside.

That's when it hits me: She has no idea what's happened to her friend. *Our* friend. If she did, she'd surely want to come back and protect her with us—and that's exactly why I can't tell her what I just learned. This is her chance to be happy, after all.

I drop the crumpled paper—tears, smudged ink, and all—right in front of her door, just in case she's the least bit scared or regretful when she realizes we're gone. Just to let her know I'll still be waiting.

IX

Starlight gilds the *Paradise* as I step on board, struggling with a dragon who seems to love straining against her lead. The boat looks good as new—possibly better, though I won't tell Kasmira that—as it bobs in the harbor's moonlit water.

I suppose I could have taken a sip from the flask Kasmira offered me before I rushed out of the boarding house ahead of her, just to dull the pain of leaving Meredy behind, but this is what I'm learning to do: take the losses and keep going, keep running toward danger while there are people I love left to fight for. Still, there's an aching, hollow feeling in my stomach as the crew darts around me, preparing to leave.

After leading Nipper down to a damp section of the cargo hold where she can't possibly set anything on fire and tossing her a couple pieces of Lysander's leftover fish jerky, I make my way slowly to the tiny cabin I shared with Meredy. With only one bag to my name, unpacking goes quickly, even as I take extra care to avoid looking at Meredy's cot. Some coffee beans are scattered across the floor, no doubt having spilled during the storm. I pick them up, blow the dust off them, and pop them in my mouth.

I hope the crew makes quick work of setting sail. We need to reach Valoria before any more attempts on her life are made, if that's even possible. We know nothing about the extent of the rebels' plans, and the not knowing is what frightens me most.

As I start to shove my bag under my cot, I realize it's a bit too heavy to be completely empty. Reaching inside, I grab the fist-sized blue crystal and remove it from its leather wrapping. I'd forgotten about this thing already. I guess my mind was trying to spare me the embarrassment of recalling how much I paid for a piece of junk with powers too good to be true.

But since I'm alone in here, at least until Azelie brings her bags down, I might as well see if it does anything while no one is around to witness my humiliation.

Sitting cross-legged on my cot, I cradle the crystal in my cupped palms as the old man instructed. Nothing happens. I think he said something about closing my eyes and focusing on the person I want to contact, so I try that, too.

"Master Cymbre," I whisper. "Can you hear me?"

Still nothing. Of course.

This is dumber than the only time it snowed in Grenwyr City, when Evander, Jax, and Simeon tried to build an icy cave to sleep in, and it fell in on their heads.

One more try. That's all I'm giving this rock before I toss it into the harbor.

Keeping my eyes closed, I let the image of Evander fill the darkness behind my eyelids. His cropped brown hair, eyes of the darkest blue so stark against his pale skin, and the smile that won me over the first time we met as apprentices still awaiting growth spurts. Seeing him this clearly makes the rest of the world melt away. I forget where I am. I forget why I feel like I don't belong anywhere anymore.

"Van," I murmur in a choked voice. "I wish you were here."

The crystal seems to shake slightly between my palms. It flares with a sudden warmth, startling me into opening my eyes. The rough-cut surface of the crystal glows from every angle as if lit from within. It's almost uncomfortable to hold, like touching the door of a stove with bare hands, but I cling to it and hastily shut my eyes again.

"Evander?" I ask hopefully, my heart working overtime.

"I've missed you, Sparrow." The achingly familiar voice echoes softly in my ears.

I gasp, amazed, not quite trusting what I just heard. "Van . . ." A sob catches in my throat as I try to speak. "Where are you?"

The answer takes a moment to arrive. "The island."

"What island?" I demand, no longer whispering. I don't care who hears. I don't even care that the crystal is so hot, it's probably leaving red marks on my palms. "The one your father used to talk about?" I shake my head, trying to rid myself of the fog of shock so I can focus on what matters: making up for lost time. "I can't believe it's you! I've missed you *so much*. I'll come to you, I—"

"I can't say where I am," he answers slowly, the words tinged with sadness. "I'm afraid we can only talk here. So tell me: What's bothering you, Sparrow?"

Tears sting my eyes, blazing trails down my cheeks when they finally spill over.

He could always tell when something was upsetting me, even when I tried to hide it. *Can* always tell, that is. Because apparently, his spirit is out there somewhere. Still, I can't believe I'm finally hearing him again. I need to hear more, so the doubting voice in the back of my head will shut up.

"This is probably going to be a bit of a shock . . ." I begin. I hadn't forgotten how easy it is to talk to him, but I'd buried the knowledge somewhere deep, so I could carry on with the business of living. "King Wylding is dead, thanks to Hadrien, that traitorous little worm. I had to kill him. Valoria took the throne, and now someone has tried to kill her—is still trying, from the sound of things. There are Karthians who want her dead, and there are rogue mages among them . . ."

The cabin door creaks open. I throw the crystal under my bed, dabbing my sweaty palms on my worn black trousers.

"Azelie, now's not really a good time," I groan, hastily wiping my face and turning to her as she sweeps inside and shuts the door.

Blinking, I try to understand what I'm seeing.

It's not Azelie at all.

Meredy gently sets her bags—one for her, one for Lysander—off to the side of the door. Straightening, she absently rubs the long scar on her cheek as she studies me, looking more nervous than she did the time we were facing down a whole group of Shade-baiters in the Deadlands.

She clears her throat.

I can't tell if my heart is beating out of control because I just talked to Evander or because I'm so glad to see the girl standing in front of me.

"Hi, Odessa," Meredy says softly, crossing to where I sit. She drops down beside me, taking my still-burning hands in her pleasantly cold ones. "Kasmira told me everything when I bumped into her at the boarding house—on my way to see you." I'm momentarily stunned into silence as she continues, "I can't believe I almost walked away from you again. I'm coming with you—to protect Valoria, of course, but also because I—I'm done fighting this, too. That's what I was on my way to tell you."

It's only after nudging the crystal deeper under the bed with my foot—I don't want Meredy to see it—that I find my voice. "Fighting...us? I'm glad, don't get me wrong." I pause, gazing steadily into her eyes, hoping she can see that I mean what I'm saying. "But I know how happy you are in Sarral. I saw it. And I know what you'll be losing in skill if you don't keep training with the beast masters here. I'd never want you to risk your happiness, let alone your safety. That's why I didn't tell you the news about Valoria."

"What do you know about a beast master's skill?" Gently, but firmly, Meredy adds, "I've learned plenty of new techniques already, and I'm confident in the progress I'm making. Besides, I know what you *thought* you saw when you looked at me in Sarral. But you're mistaken." For reasons completely unknown to me, she smiles faintly as she rubs her thumb against my palm. "When Firiel died, and then Evander, too, I knew part of me was missing." She leans closer, her breath spilling over my lips, making my own breathing quicken. "I found that part of myself again when I saw you at the palace in Grenwyr. Earlier tonight, you told me I deserve to be where I'm happiest, and—this is it. I'm only sorry that it took you almost leaving for me to realize it, but I'm happiest with *you*. You're my heart, Odessa."

I put a finger to her lips as she tries to close the narrow space between us. I want her in my arms right now more than I've ever wanted anything, but there's something I have to say first. "This is your one chance, so don't be reckless. It's just . . . if you're even the least bit unsure, I'd rather you leave now, because my heart can't take much more."

Meredy gently lowers my hand, tangling her fingers with mine, and kisses me hard enough to steal my breath, erasing my thoughts of everything but her. "I had a chance to live in a place that celebrates beast masters, a place where I could have learned so much. But my heart chose *you*, and I want to be by your side every day. So, since I'll not be giving you up anytime soon, you should probably know that once I've made up my mind about something . . . well, Evander would have said I was stubborn." She gives me a rueful smile. "I like to say I'm steadfast."

"Do I get a few days to think it over?" I tease, struck by a rush of giddiness as she gently pushes me onto the bed, pinning my shoulders and hovering over me in response. "All right," I gasp. "I accept!"

This is better than any late-night fantasy, the real Meredy on my bed, holding my gaze, her smile so open and inviting.

She traces a finger along the inside of my lower lip. That tiny gesture makes all the right places ache in new ways. "My girlfriend is so beautiful," she murmurs. I push her hand away, impatient to join our lips again.

After all, we'll be back in Karthia soon, and kissing Meredy gives me strength. I have a feeling I'll need it, especially if Grenwyr City is restless and violent enough to attack its own queen with a Shade after experiencing firsthand how uncontrollable the monsters are.

Pushing back thoughts of what's to come, I deepen our next kiss, my hands in her hair. "*My* girlfriend," I say aloud, thrilled by the sound of those words.

Between kisses, I help Meredy pull off her blouse and her white cloth breastband, impatient to be joined with her body the way our hearts and minds are already bound. She pulls off my tunic and breastband next, throwing them down beside hers to make colorful puddles on the floor. I kiss the scar on her cheek in response, then run a finger along the jagged white line, memorizing its path from beneath her eye toward her jawline. My hands shake slightly as I touch her, like I can't quite convince myself this is real, like I'm scared I'll wake up any moment, alone and grasping at air.

"I've thought about this every night for a while now," she whispers against my neck, grazing the tender skin there with her teeth and then kissing away the sting. The longer she talks, the more she touches me, the more I'm sure this is real.

"Me too," I mutter, running my hands over every part of her—her back, her breasts, her stomach—learning by the quickening of her breath what she likes most. "But . . ." I hesitate, but then she kisses a particularly tender spot on my collarbone, and I know I'll regret it if I don't say something now. "I've never been with a girl before."

My face radiates heat at the admission.

Meredy swiftly kisses each of the sparrows tattooed on the backs of my arms, then gives me a blazing smile. "That doesn't scare me in the slightest. But if you want to stop, just say the word." Her hand moves up my thigh, and unlike that night on the ship when she avoided my kiss, today she doesn't shy away from what she really wants.

I arch my back, gasping against her lips as she kisses me while moving her hand higher, her fingers brushing inward.

"Take them off," I demand, tugging at the buttons on my trousers.

She unfastens them at an agonizing pace, like she enjoys watching me writhe under her touch. And judging by the pink in her cheeks, she does. She leaves a trail of kisses down my stomach as she starts to slide my trousers maddeningly slowly down my hips.

"Meredy," I growl, impatient and on fire. Even her name tastes sweet.

The cabin door flies open.

"Sparrow, I'm going to—whoa!" Kasmira shouts as Meredy and I pull a rumpled blanket up to hide our various stages of undress, both of us still breathing hard.

"What? Is Azelie pestering the crew or something?" I'm so out of it, still half in another world where only Meredy and I exist, that I don't even know where my daggers are right now. On the floor, but hidden under my tunic, maybe. It's all a blur.

The lantern on the floor rattles softly, and for the first time, I notice the faint, now-familiar motion of the *Paradise* cutting through calm waters as it heads back to sea.

"Of course she is." Kasmira looks worn already, which doesn't bode well for the trip ahead. "But that's not why I came down here. I'm about to speed our trip along with a bit of magic, and I need your help with something."

"How soon can you get us there?" I ask. By my count, it took fourteen days to get from Karthia to Sarral, but that was with storms and our regrettable stop in Lyris.

Kasmira is silent a moment, only the whites of her eyes showing as she uses her Sight to check for storms in the day's path. "Assuming nothing changes . . ." She pauses, opening her eyes again and holding my gaze. "We'll reach Karthia in twelve days. *Maybe* eleven, if I never rest. That's where you come in. If either of you see me pushing myself too hard, I need you to bring me back to the ground, so to speak. I've got to save some strength to help Valoria."

"We've got your back. Promise." I poke a hand out from the blanket to salute her. "Make the weather work for us, Captain."

If there was ever a time to push the boundaries of our magic, it's now, when Valoria needs us. If Shade-baiters aren't afraid to make new monsters, they'll have to answer to my blade and my dragon's fiery breath right along with the Shades themselves.

"Already on it," Kasmira says, raising one hand with her palm turned skyward. She flashes us a grin, but it falters as her hand starts to tremble. She mutters a curse, shoving the hand into one of her vest pockets, but too late.

Meredy and I exchange a worried look.

"It's been like that ever since I woke up at the healing house in Sarral," Kasmira says quietly, before either of us can ask. "The shaking comes and goes. It doesn't seem to be getting any worse, though, so I'm not worrying about it—*and neither should you two*. Just don't let me keep my head in the sky too long, all right?"

I press my lips together, hoping I have enough self-control to respect her wishes.

A distant call echoes down to us, and Kasmira's shoulders slump in relief. "I'd better get back up there," she says quickly, turning to go. "And I'm sorry for walking in on your it's-about-damn-time."

As she shuts the door, Meredy bites her lip and grins. "Where were we?"

I throw the blanket over both of our heads in answer.

In the first ten days of our hasty journey back to Karthia, the only other ship we see is a small Lyrian fishing vessel cutting through choppy seas the day after a storm.

Still, I'm so worried about Kasmira and her shaking hand that some days, like today, I keep her company at the helm—even though my girlfriend is waiting for me belowdecks, fletching arrows in the double bed we made from our cots.

She's promised to do unspeakable things with me later tonight, and she readily reminds me of those things when I see her at supper, as most of the crew crowds around the table to fight over a bowl of boiled potatoes.

She doesn't say anything out loud. She doesn't need to. Our eyes meet across the table, and the look she gives me is so deep, it's as if her hands are all over me right here, in front of everyone.

The moment is broken when Nipper shoves her scaly head into my lap, smoke curling from her mouth as she begs for scraps.

Meredy shakes her head at the dragon's antics, then begins telling a story about a pet she had when she and Evander were little. She feels his absence each day just like I do, and we remember him together.

The days at sea, which once felt long, fly by as I practice with my sword, as Meredy tells me silly stories about the pets of Noble Park and their owners to keep us both from worrying about Valoria, as we dance and keep Evander's memory alive.

"Two days to go," Kasmira sighs over the sounds of Azelie's animated conversation with the boatswain at supper one night. "One, if I can help it . . ."

"Don't push it," I insist. A pang of guilt jabs my insides as I say it, because the words aren't just for Kasmira's sake. Even knowing full well that Valoria needs us now, I'm dreading the moment we arrive in Grenwyr Harbor.

Meredy pulls something from her pocket, leaning over the remains of her supper—boiled potatoes, and a more meager portion than yesterday at that—to hand it to me. "We're going home, my Sparrow," she says, smiling as she watches me hold up my newly polished master necromancer's pin in the dim light of the mess hall. She fastens it to my tunic in a spot right over my heart, a reminder that once, I was someone who mattered. "I have a feeling you're going to need this."

"Thank you," I say as warmly as I can manage while my insides turn cold.

We've been gone less than two months, yet when I left Karthia, I already felt like a stranger on its misty shore.

I don't want to think of what else might have changed there in our brief time away.

Of course, some changes—as Meredy reminds me every day—are good ones. So maybe it's not what's changed in Karthia that scares me.

Maybe I'm afraid of what remains the same.

X

It's quiet in the city. A restless, uneasy quiet that reminds me of the aftermath of Hadrien's Shades running loose through the streets. Even in the markets, usually bustling places for meeting, only a few people linger. Most of them barely look up as Meredy and I pass by with our beastly companions, having left Azelie, Kasmira, and the rest of the crew to secure the ship and tend to business at the harbor. The odd person who does bother to give us more than a glance looks for too long—as though they suspect us of something. Palace guards stand at the four corners of every square, armed with more than just their spears. Each one holds a crossbow, and I have a feeling the satchels at their sides must be full of the flammable potions I've used to kill Shades in the past.

Valoria has equipped them far better than King Wylding ever did.

The guards nod stiffly to us, and a few mutter a greeting, but somehow I'd feel safer if they were gone and I could hear laughter, or even an argument over the price of bread.

We pass buildings destroyed in the Battle of Grenwyr City,

many of which bear evidence of attempted repairs—abandoned tools, mostly—but also signs of anger and further destruction: new windows shattered by rocks, the broken glass still framed by freshly painted sills. New murals of Vaia's faces—including Change—marred by scorch marks and curse words. There are even the beginnings of foundations for new buildings, places where the land has been cleared and a few stones laid, but no sign of any crews working.

Most baffling of all are the iron rods placed at regular intervals along the main road through the city, which don't seem to serve a purpose.

The Wyldings' palace awaits us at the top of the cliffs overlooking the sea, its white marble walls dripping with red light as the sun sets. When the wind blows, it carries the scent of the palace itself toward us—sweet, with a hint of spice, like the bergamot and lemon trees hidden within its courtyards.

But beneath the sweetness lies something bitter that brings me back to the Battle of Grenwyr City with a single whiff. Ash and sorrow rest heavy on my tongue, becoming more cloying with every breath.

For the first time in memory, guards outnumber the wildflowers on the palace hill.

The very air feels wrong once we're inside those marble walls—wrong as a splinter I want to rip out, if only I could find its edges.

As Meredy and I lead a hurried procession of a dragon and a grizzly bear down the hall to the throne room, our footsteps make lonely echoes off the polished marble. Just like on the hill, there are more guards than usual stationed throughout the warren of halls, but there are no masked and shrouded figures flitting through any of them. No dry, rattling conversations and laughter of the Dead filling these halls the way they always have.

And that, I realize, is what's bothering me.

All the rooms once belonging to the Dead are empty, together composing dusty chambers of a hollow, lifeless heart. A heart whose rhythms were as familiar to me as those of my own. I've lost something else I can't replace, and suddenly, as we walk over a large scorch mark darkening the hallway, I have the urge to grab Meredy's hand.

"It feels odd being home, doesn't it?" she whispers, squeezing my hand as if the absence of the Dead has her on edge, too.

"This is Karthia," I answer, the words sticking in my throat, "but it isn't home."

Meredy arches a brow. When I don't offer any explanation, she leans in to kiss my cheek, making me feel as though I've just swallowed a cup of hot, strong tea.

With her by my side, it's easier to square my shoulders and hasten toward the throne room doors as two guards draw them open. They bow low as I pass, whispering, "Welcome home, Sparrow," and I somehow find a smile for them.

They stare openly at Nipper, exchanging guesses as to what she might be—"Is that a wild cat?" "A sort of boar?"—as her tail slithers over their feet on our way past. It's clear they're hungry for any distraction from the palace's pervasive air of misery.

Their curious chatter fades into the background as I take in the sight before me. It's amazing how much someone can change something in a short time, if they're determined enough. The last time I was in this room, I killed a man I once trusted. A man I once called a friend. The blood has long been wiped from the glistening marble floor, of course. But now, on the raised dais where the throne was proudly displayed—a seat occupied by Valoria's ancestors for countless centuries, and coveted by many—there's a new chair, more comfortable and less imposing-looking, decorated with gems, its arms painted a warm rose gold.

Valoria sits on its wide, black velvet-cushioned seat, flanked by girls I don't recognize, girls who must be her ladies-in-waiting. Just as I've often pictured her while we've been gone, her head is bent over the notebook where she maps out her inventions and plans, and a stick of charcoal rests between her fingers. My heart aches at the familiar sight, and I suppress the sudden urge to throw my arms around her.

Instead, I mount the steps to the new throne and kneel stiffly before her while Meredy lingers at the bottom of the steps to lecture Nipper for trying to bite one of the guards stationed around the dais.

"Valoria. Thank the stars you're all right. We came as soon as we got your message—or rather, overheard it," I say quickly, before the lump in my throat gets any worse. There's a small scar on her collarbone, almost hidden by the high collar of her inventor's jacket, and beside her rests a long, polished piece of black wood with a wolf's head carved into its handle. A cane. "Valoria, *please* say something. I want to know everything."

Snapping her notebook shut, Valoria lifts her head. Perhaps it's a trick of the scant light cast by one of the many chandeliers she's installed in here, but her deep brown eyes seem to shine harder than the glittering stones of sapphire, emerald, jasper, smoky quartz, and turquoise set in her tall golden crown.

"You're later than I expected," she sniffs.

Smudges of charcoal decorate her face and neck, but her inventor's jacket, with its stiff shoulders and glittering gold threads, still looks immaculate.

Gathering the loose fabric at the end of my shirtsleeve, I reach to dab the biggest charcoal stain beneath her eye. "It's so good to see you." I don't add *alive*, though I think it. "You've got a little something—"

She raises a hand as if to slap me, making the rest of my words stick in my throat. I gaze deep into her eyes, daring her to go through with it, but her lower lip trembles and she drops the hand as swiftly as she raised it.

"Death be damned, Your Majesty," I mutter under my breath as I leap to my feet. "If you need a punching bag, I'm right here, *friend*. But give me some warning first."

Valoria staggers to her feet, aided by the two girls on either side of her. One of them offers out the cane, but she shakes her head, refusing it.

"*Friends* don't call each other by their titles!" she snaps, leaning so close I can smell her perfume of daffodils and rosewater. "Friends don't bow to each other." Her eyes are shining so bright, I realize, with the effort of holding back tears as everyone else in the room looks on in quiet awe. Valoria has certainly found her leader's voice. "Oh, and friends don't vanish from each other's lives in the middle of the night without a word like they never really mattered to each other at all, especially not when one of them just took over running a kingdom." She takes a deep breath and adds with a hint of pride I've missed, "It's good to know my little winged messenger made the journey to Sarral, at any rate. Did you see it? What did you think of the design?"

When I shake my head sadly, she nods and drops back onto the throne, as if the effort of standing without the aid of her cane cost her something. I note the old, familiar gleam of curiosity in her eyes as Nipper peers up at her, but she doesn't ask about the dragon.

"Where are the Shade-baiters who attacked you?" I demand, trying to forgive the way she nearly slapped me. I deserved it, but it's not like the Valoria I know to hold on to so much anger.

"Rotting in the dungeons, along with Lyda Crowther and the other traitors loyal to my departed brother. Danial made sure the would-be murderers never see daylight again," Valoria answers coolly. "And in case you're keeping count of everyone who's tried to kill me, that's: Count Rykiel, Duchess Nyx, Baroness Crowther—she's a snake even from her cell—and three rogue mages from Grenwyr City. We've had an assassin sent from as far as the Idrany Islands, too, so add another to the tally."

"Seven?" I shake my head, stunned. "And the Shade—was there really a Shade?"

Valoria nods grimly. "Jax and Simeon took care of it. My only loyal weather mage put out the resulting fire."

That explains the scorch mark in the hallway. Once again, I have to fight the urge to put my arms around Valoria. If Danial couldn't heal her limp, she must have truly brushed death. I just want to shelter her from this place that's turned against her.

"Of course, now that my most experienced necromancer has answered my summons, I have work for you to do," Valoria continues, her tone much too formal for my liking. "You're to guard my back from Shades and anyone dangerous enough to create them. You'll also need to keep a close eye on the gates in the city—there are usually only a handful at a time, as I'm sure you recall. You'll also assist Jax and Simeon in watching the cemeteries so no one goes disturbing the dead. Oh, and have Kasmira come see me as soon as she's finished with her usual business at the harbor. I have work for her and the crew, too. Understood?"

"Of course. Anything you need, I'm here. I was so scared when I heard what had happened." I kneel again so she's forced to meet my eyes. "Everyone was. Kasmira used so much of her magic trying to get us here, I'm afraid her hand might be damaged for good." Taking a deep breath, I add, "Valoria, leaving was never about hurting you. It was . . ." My voice trails away as I struggle to put into words all the wounds I was trying to mend after the battle. "It doesn't matter what it was. I'm sorry I wasn't here before, but I'm here now, and if anyone else tries to send a Shade after you, they'll have to answer to me. But how did a Shade get inside the palace in the first place?"

"I fear you'd have to ask my council about that," Valoria says coldly.

I follow her gaze past the swarm of guards around the dais to the empty chairs that are usually occupied by the royal family's advisors. The usual offerings of fruits and cakes on the table nearest their seats are untouched.

"What?" I look around some more, confused. "Where are they?"

"They've all retired for the evening. They still do things on Eldest Grandfather's schedule, even though they all claim to support me," Valoria says, a hint of sourness in her voice.

"But surely they wouldn't try to—?"

I don't even finish the question before Valoria cuts in, "Oh, no, I don't suspect any of them of being a Shade-baiter." She gestures to her leg, and though it looks ordinary beneath her crisply pressed trousers, it must be the reason she needs the cane. "However, I believe that at least one of them got drunk enough to let slip to someone in the city about the inventions and new laws I've been working on." She sighs. "Or perhaps it was someone else who's frustrated with me for any number of reasons—a worker who can't do the job I hired them for because no one wants me to rebuild the city my way, or someone who's afraid of my fireposts—the rods you saw on your way here. For lighting the road at night," she adds at my confused look.

Peering more closely at her, I wonder when she last slept, truly slept. Given the storm brewing behind her sharp eyes, I don't dare ask.

"I just want to improve people's lives, but they destroy every project I start," Valoria says, taking a shaky breath. Perhaps she's closer to unraveling than I thought. "I'm trying to give them a safer city, and jobs, and fight poverty in seven provinces! Yet Karthians are so focused on how much they miss their Dead, and they blame me for sending them away. Somehow, on top of everything else, I've got to make people understand that the Dead being in their own world is for the best."

"That's why you have me, and Jax, and Simeon. Plus, Kasmira and her crew are well known in the city. They have some influence there, too. We'll help the people see things your way."

"I'm counting on it," Valoria says firmly. "That's why I need to speak to Kasmira as soon as possible."

I nod. "As for your council—you need to talk with them about building a proper Karthian army, if you haven't already."

I can't help but picture the scorched Sarralan valley as I say it.

Valoria blinks a question at me, and with help from Meredy, we explain everything we know about the vicious warriors with a rumored penchant for dark magic. We talk for so long that Valoria's ladies-in-waiting, yawning, ply us with bread and cheese and juice.

Lysander swipes a block of cheese for his enjoyment, which only lasts a few seconds before Nipper starts trying to pull it out of his mouth.

"If a bunch of strangers want to kill me," Valoria says after a pause, drawing my attention away from the beasts, "they'll have to get in line. However, most of the other rulers I've written to so far have had the decency to at least acknowledge my claim to the throne." The shadows on her face deepen as she adds, "It's the people of Karthia who *hate* me. If they aren't blaming me for King Wylding's death, they're claiming I sympathized with Hadrien because I'm restoring the Temples of Change, or else they hate my plans to strengthen the city's layout. There aren't many who'd fight in my name."

"Shouldn't you let the head of your guard try to fix that?" a familiar, silky voice asks from the doorway.

Danial Swancott, master healer and—judging by the gleaming new pin on his chest—captain of Valoria's personal guard, leans against one side of the entryway. His kohl-lined hazel eyes dazzle everyone in whatever room he's in, but they're especially bright as they sweep over Meredy and me.

"I'd come in and give you both a hug," he adds, glancing at the dragon half-hidden by Lysander's furry bulk, "but your giant lizard is smoking at the mouth." He wipes his palms on his crisp healer's whites. "Just watching it is making me sweat."

"Danial!" I rush down the dais steps and crash into his open arms. *This* is what I missed the most. My friends.

"Let me get a look at you, Sparrow," he says, sounding relieved to see me in one piece.

"Where are Jax and Simeon?" I ask as Danial draws back slightly and sweeps my hair away from my face.

"Simeon's at the school," he answers vaguely, scrutinizing the tiny scar on my forehead left over after the healers in Sarral saved me. "You should go see him as soon as you can. There's something we want to tell you, but Si will kill me if I ruin the surprise . . ."

Noting the silver band on his right ring finger for the first time—a sign of another ring soon to join on the left—I grin. "You two were busy while I was gone. Will Jax be acting as Witness for the ceremony?" I peer into the back of the room, half expecting to see him. I would have thought, given his skill with a blade, Valoria might encourage him to stay close. "Where is Jax, anyway?"

"I can fix this, if you like," Danial murmurs, distracted from my question as he rubs a thumb over the little scar on my head. Mild amusement coloring his voice, he drops it to a whisper to add, "Unless your lady finds you more fanciable this way, of course."

Shaking my head at him, I step back while Meredy gives him a hug. They spent much of the battle together, which seems to have forged a bond between them.

Up on the dais, Valoria and her two ladies-in-waiting have their heads bent close together.

As if sensing my gaze, the girls draw back and study me with unfathomable expressions. The one on Valoria's left, a petite girl with freckles in many shades of brown sprinkled across her face, sweeps her long raven hair over her shoulders as she meets my eyes.

A shiver runs through me: Her irises are a rich shade of amber, a color so rare, it isn't present in any of Vaia's five faces. I've never seen the like, not even in Sarral.

As we stare each other down, the edges of her figure start to blur. For a moment, I wonder if I'm going to pass out. But nothing's wrong with me. Danial would have noticed.

The freckled girl's body contorts, her ears lengthening and her fingernails becoming claws as she hunches over on the marble floor. She tugs at her lavender robe, loosening it, as her bones poke out at odd angles and her skin stretches to accommodate them. A quiet groan escapes her as her mouth reshapes itself into a whiskered snout. Suddenly, in her place is a silvery, black-spotted cat with shaggy fur, bigger than any I've seen before. It flicks its long tail, shoving away the discarded robe, still staring me down with the girl's amber eyes.

Behind me, Meredy whistles long and low. She's impressed. "Is she a beast master?" she asks Valoria, nodding to the big cat. "She's got to teach me how to do that."

Valoria frowns as she answers Meredy. Apparently I'm not the only one who's earned her anger for leaving. "Bryn is her own sort of mage. She doesn't have a name for her magic—yet." She strokes the cat's speckled fur absently. "She came here to attend the new mage school, in the hope of meeting others like herself, or at least drawing them out of hiding."

I arch a brow, and at my curious look, Valoria adds, "The cat she changes into is called a lynx. I'd never seen one before I met Bryn. Nobles in their home province of Oslea have hunted them almost to the point of extinction—something I intend to challenge them on, if they ever deign to meet with me in person."

Meredy gives a nod of approval at that.

While she's talking, Bryn turns back into a girl. Her bare shoulders have a multitude of freckles, too, I notice. I quickly raise my eyes to her face as she wraps herself back in her lavender robe without the slightest hint of shame.

"I'm Sarika, by the way," the other girl at Valoria's side adds without prompting. Her eyes are just as unusual as Bryn's. They shift through hues of blue and gray, then brown and hazel, then green as she takes a step closer, her irises seeming unable to settle on just one of the five usual colors. She winks, and as she twists a heavy-looking silver locket on a chain around her neck, her wavy dark brown hair lengthens from her shoulders to her waist and turns as blue-green as the sea.

Valoria blinks a question at her, and she smiles sheepishly. "What? Bryn was showing off, so I thought I might as well, too." The blue-haired girl beams at me as her hair darkens back to brown. I wonder if that's its real color, though. "There's no name for what I do, either, but I call myself a mimic. I can make myself look like anyone I've seen." With a wink at Bryn, she adds, "Changing into a big cat would be way more interesting, but I can only impersonate other humans."

"She's an excellent spy for me," Valoria says, frowning again. "Not that I ever wanted to have to resort to that. She's even been brave enough to attend a meeting with some hostile southern nobles while impersonating me."

She puts her arms around Bryn's and Sarika's shoulders. They seem to be more than just her ladies-in-waiting—they're her replacement friends.

"Look, it's great to meet you, Freckles." I nod to Bryn, a sour taste in my mouth. "Sunshine." I nod curtly to Sarika. "But we need to get back to that pesky little matter of Karthia's safety, Valoria. I know the city is restless—more than—but won't you at least consider raising an army? Talk it over with your council, just in case the Ezorans ever decide to look our way?" As she purses her lips, I add, "Please. I understand that you're mad we left, but you know me. You know I wouldn't lie."

"All right. I'll do it," she says at last, holding my gaze, and my shoulders relax. It's nice to know there's still trust hidden beneath all her hurt and anger. "But my people's needs still come first. It would be hard, if not impossible, to fight an outside enemy while we're divided from within."

"We should start right away, as Odessa suggested," Danial says in his gentle manner, somehow managing not to sound like he's questioning his queen's choices. "This is a new Karthia, as you often say, and we need to protect ourselves like the rest of the world."

Valoria grabs her cane and slowly descends the dais until she's face-to-face with Danial and me. "Then how do you propose I inspire anyone to fight for me?"

"*Everyone* should want to learn how to fight, so they can protect their homes and their families. You'll be doing them a favor by training them," Meredy says firmly, moving to my other side and propping a hand on her hip. She's so cute when she's trying to look stern.

"You're assuming we can convince them of the need for an army in the first place," Valoria counters, pushing up her glasses like she's thinking hard about something. "Besides, they won't fight well enough to win, if it ever comes to that. Not for a queen they don't believe in." The shadows on her face are deep and dark as bruises, especially around her eyes, as she seems to struggle to stay standing even with the help of her cane.

Bryn and Sarika rush to grab her elbows and support her, but she gently shakes them off and squares her shoulders. That's the Valoria I know.

In a calm, clear voice, she says, "Still, we'll try it." She looks to the mimic. "Sarika, please head to the rookery and tell Scribe Oren to send ravens to every province, asking for volunteer soldiers."

As Sarika slips away, Danial asks, "And who's going to train these brave volunteers?"

Valoria actually grins. "You are, of course . . . General."

Danial's brows shoot up. "What did you—?"

"You heard me," Valoria cuts in. "In light of the recent uprisings and what Odessa and Meredy have told us, you're being promoted, General Swancott. The Karthian army"—she pauses, making a sour face—"pathetic as it will be, is yours to command."

Bowing low, Danial murmurs, "I . . . well then. I won't let you down, Majesty."

Valoria squeezes his shoulder, encouraging him to rise. His eyes glisten slightly as they meet hers, and he stands taller than before—not weighed down by this new title, but rising to embrace it.

"Now that's settled," Valoria says briskly, looking from me to Nipper, "I want to hear everything about your new companion. But first . . ." She reaches for my hand, then, after setting down her cane, takes Meredy's with her other. Her touch is cold, as is usual for her. "I know I didn't give you two the warmest welcome," she says, "but I hope you still consider me a friend."

"Always," Meredy and I answer, almost in unison.

"Good." Valoria smiles, and that simple gesture seems to take years off her face, turning her back into the enthusiastic inventor I know and love. "Odessa, when the first volunteers arrive, I want you to train them on how to wield a blade. Meredy, if you could teach them archery? I understand you're a decent shot."

That understatement earns a grin from Meredy.

"There's one last thing," Valoria says, her eyes narrowed in thought. "Odessa, I'd like you to meet me at the Temple of Change tomorrow after breakfast. That's where the mage trainees have been living and studying for the past few weeks. There are a handful now. Maybe they can help us think of another way to defend Karthia from any future threats—wherever they might come from. Besides," she adds with a wan smile, "I think some of them could learn a lot from you."

We agree to meet there tomorrow, first thing. I know Azelie is more than ready to see the reason she came here.

"Just promise me you'll get some rest tonight, Valoria," I say in a stern voice, or as stern as I can manage when I don't think I'm in a position to lecture anyone on their sleeping habits. "You're as pale as something from the Deadlands."

"Whether you like it or not—whether *anyone* likes it or not— we *all* need you," Meredy adds, letting the concern in her gaze shine through.

"And while you're at it . . ." I drop my voice. "Promise us you won't start taking any potions." As I take a breath, fighting not to sink into memories of the bitter blue liquid and the pain it helped me escape,

Meredy lightly touches the small of my back. Finding my voice again, I continue, "Nothing stronger than tea leaves, all right?"

"Promise," Valoria echoes softly. She stands taller and adjusts her glasses as a hint of mischief flickers in her eyes. "That is, if you promise me you'll both help me test out my new air balloon design whenever I get back to it."

Exchanging a grin, Meredy and I agree. For the moment, at least, things feel normal between the three of us.

"Now that's settled," Danial says, craning his neck to get another glimpse of Nipper, who's apparently still being chased by Lysander over the cheese. "Would anyone care to explain what that giant lizard is and where it came from?"

XI

We barely come within sight of the Temple of Change when shouts erupt from inside.

Recognizing at least one of the voices—there's no mistaking Jax's deep growl for anyone else's—I run toward the large white stone building that, after centuries, is finally being scrubbed of crude drawings and random phrases. Its crumbling columns are in the early stages of being restored, the boards have been stripped from its once-sightless windows, and the creeping vines that covered it have been partially hacked away, allowing the harsh morning sun to pierce the building's shadowed heart.

A crash echoes in my ears, a brittle sound like breaking porcelain, quickly followed by more voices joining in the shouting. I quicken my pace, breathing hard as I come within reach of the door, trusting Azelie and Valoria will catch up eventually—even if it takes a little longer for Valoria with her cane.

The guards stationed around the temple nod a greeting, but despite recognizing a few of them, I don't stop to say hello.

As I grab the gilded door handle that resembles Change's wizened face and push my way inside, a strange sight greets me: On an ornate carpet, surrounded by dusty bookshelves and the shattered remains of an ancient vase, Jax and another young man about his age sit across from each other, breathing hard. The stranger's nose is bleeding, and Jax has a split lip, making his expression when he sees me look more sinister than welcoming.

Still, I run to him, past the curious stares of several boys and girls I don't recognize, and a few adults as well. Dropping down beside Jax, I throw my arms around his work-hardened shoulders, wincing slightly as the dark stubble coating his copper skin brushes my cheek. My breath catches in my throat as he stiffens at my touch, and I draw back.

It seems I left a lot of damage in my wake when I went to sea.

"I've missed you," I say anyway, catching Jax's crystal-blue eyes with mine so he'll know I mean it. He nods but doesn't return my embrace, and my chest aches as I remember the way I used to fit in his arms at night—never quite perfectly, but close enough that I could pretend it was right and sink into him.

Movement out of the corner of my eye draws my gaze. A boy is helping the student with the bloody nose to his feet. "It's not so bad, Karston," the boy assures him. Touching his own face and grinning slightly, he adds, "Although, that shiner on your eye is even bigger than the one from when you went sleepwalking into the kitchen and got attacked by the frying pans last week."

Karston turns his back on the boy, ignoring him, which is a lot kinder than what I'd do if someone was loudly telling embarrassing stories about me to a busy room. When Karston moves past a window, no doubt on his way to clean up his face, the sunlight catches on more blood glistening almost darker than his black skin. Just below one of his blue eyes is another injury sustained from a heavy fist.

I glance back to Jax in alarm, inhaling the musty scent of books from centuries past. "What did he do to you, anyway?"

Jax shakes his head, apparently lost for words.

It's Simeon who answers as he hastily strides into view from around a bookcase. "Nothing that merited an old-fashioned ass-kicking from his teacher, that's for sure."

"Teacher?" I blink, more stunned than I was the first time I saw a dragon. If there's one thing Jax loathes, it's being responsible for other people. "Jax? You're a—really?"

Simeon quickly closes the distance between us and kneels, pulling me into a fierce hug. He murmurs an explanation, keeping his voice soft despite all the commotion happening around us. "Since raising the dead is forbidden now, Jax and I are teachers here. Or, we're supposed to be . . ." He sighs. "Valoria asked us to instruct people in the noble art of necromancy. Any age, so long as they have the desire to learn. We don't have many students yet—"

"Of course not. This school isn't exactly popular right now," Jax interrupts, disgust for this view evident in his tone. "Why should anyone want to join our ranks when we represent the thing everyone fears most?"

He glances upward, toward the mural of Change that decorates the high domed ceiling.

"Karston joined, though. He's one of us." Simeon sighs, giving me a pained look as he ends our embrace and offers Jax a hand to climb to his feet. "So you can't punch him in the face just because he's getting on your nerves. You're supposed to *teach* him, not pummel him."

"He doesn't respect me!" Jax snarls, standing up unassisted and wiping the blood from his mouth with the edge of his black shirt-sleeve. "Learning can't happen without some respect between student and teacher. I'm sure Master Nicanor would've agreed."

Simeon crosses his arms. "Your problem isn't Karston. Your problem is that you don't want to be here."

"Damn right I don't!" Jax turns as if to leave.

Simeon rubs his temples, like they've had this argument before and he isn't in the mood to relive it. I stop Jax instead, roughly grabbing his shoulder. I don't like the hurt look he's put on Simeon's face.

"Why not? Why don't you want to be here?" I demand, though I think I know the answer. Jax must feel as lost as I do now that necromancers are no longer needed the way they used to be, and this place is a glaring reminder of that. When Jax says nothing, I lean into his space, my chest pressed against his. "Talk to me. Then you can storm off."

"Fine, Sparrow." Jax shakes his head, mutters a curse, then says, "I don't know about you—actually, I do, and I'm sure you feel the same." He leans closer, bowing his head so we're almost nose-to-nose, like he doesn't want anyone in the busy room overhearing us. "I can't do the job I was born for, the job I trained half my life for. I couldn't even protect Valoria from those Shade-baiters and the monster they set loose, not until we'd almost lost her. Lately, it's like I'm completely useless."

I wrinkle my nose. I'm still not happy with him for upsetting Simeon, but I understand what it's like to feel helpless and lost. Unmoored. "I see your point. But there's still work for you to do, like preventing any more Shades from being made by patrolling the gates and cemeteries—"

"I know," Jax interrupts, his handsome, narrow face tightening in a grimace. "And that beats being stuck in here. In fact, I wouldn't come here at all if we didn't owe Valoria a favor for letting us keep our rooms at the palace and everything." He runs a hand through his dark curls, suddenly looking uncomfortable. "Anyway, I don't know why I even bother showing up when Simeon handles this place just fine on his own. I'm off to patrol."

With that, he twists out of my grasp and storms toward the door. I'm not surprised. It's exactly what I would do. I'd run after him right this minute if I didn't realize that, like me, he'll want to be alone for a while to clear his head.

The students scatter to either side, creating a path for him. Azelie nearly collides with him by the door, looking slightly winded, her cloak's hood still drawn up.

Something else stops Jax's hasty exit when he reaches the threshold. Over his shoulder, I catch a glimpse of blond hair in the sun. Valoria. Shifting slightly for a better view, I watch her talk to him, one of her hands resting squarely on his chest as if to hold him in place, the other on her cane. Her voice is so low, I can't make out what she's saying, but something in her seems to calm him. After a while, Jax's shoulders relax.

Valoria finally steps aside, her expression pained as Jax walks past, although his stride is much less hasty and his posture less rigid than before.

"All right, everyone," Valoria says in a purposeful voice, clapping her hands to draw all the students' eyes her way. "Gather round. I have a favor to ask you. Karthia is in need of new defenses against any outside forces that might seek to threaten us in the future, and I want to hear your ideas . . ."

"There's a lot we need to catch up on, sister dear," Simeon says, his voice soft in my ear as he draws my gaze away from Valoria. Holding up his right hand to show off the shiny band on his ring finger, he adds, "So much changed while you were gone."

I smile, partly at the sight of that ring and the promise it holds, but more because of the way at least one of my friends is welcoming me back without hesitation or judgment.

"When's the wedding?" I ask, allowing Simeon to drape an arm around my shoulders and steer me through the library and out a set of glass doors that lead to a central courtyard. It's open to the sky but sheltered on all sides by the circular building's walls.

"The sooner the better, now that we'll have an army to train. Think they'll all expect invitations to the feast after our ceremony?" He winces at the thought, then brightens. "I don't mind, I suppose, as long as they bring us really expensive gifts."

Simeon's attempt at humor brings a reluctant smile to my lips. "Danial told you what we discussed in the throne room last night, then?"

He nods. "He's in the city right now, trying to drum up volunteers so we can start training. It was on his mind well before you convinced Valoria, as he keeps reminding me. But with citizens giving speeches against Valoria almost daily, I don't know if he'll have any luck getting people to join our cause." He gestures to a stone bench beside a small pond.

The courtyard's carefully tended shade trees hanging over both bench and pond make it a tempting spot to linger. "As you know, Valoria seems to think the students here can help with Karthia's defenses, too."

The skepticism in my voice must be obvious, because Simeon says, "You'd be surprised what some of them can do, and I bet they'll soon surprise themselves. Like Noranna there. I can't wait to see what she'll invent." He takes a seat on the bench and points to the glass doors we came through to get here.

Just on the other side of the glass, Azelie talks animatedly to a girl with tight brown curls and soft, dark eyes who must be Noranna.

After a moment's hesitation, the girl slips her metallic right arm through Azelie's, whisking her away somewhere. Remembering the mechanical leg Valoria designed for her father, I smile, recognizing her handiwork in the girl's arm.

That's Valoria for you—still finding ways to help her people, even when many of them are calling for her death.

Glad to see Azelie settling in here so quickly, I sit on the bench and take a closer look at my brother in every way but by blood. Aside from the Sisters of Death, who found me as a baby, I've known Simeon longer than anyone, since before we could talk in complete sentences.

At first glance, he looks much the same as when I saw him last— like he doesn't get enough sleep anymore. Who does, nowadays? But the longer I study him, the more I notice little lines on his face that definitely weren't there before, etched by some worry or another, and wonder how many more he'll have before his twentieth birthday.

"How do you really like it here?" I ask, still reeling from Jax's abrupt exit.

Simeon runs a hand through his sandy blond hair. "It's not bad. We've gotten ten students since Valoria reopened this place as a school, and your friend Zee makes eleven. Their studies seem to be going well so far."

I arch a brow. "And just what is it they study? No one's been clear on that."

"Magic. If they already know their power, they're supposed to delve deep into it. Push the boundaries, but also learn control," he explains. A hint of pride for the students glimmers in his sky-blue eyes. "Valoria encourages every exploration, which is why—"

"She's gotten so many death threats, and worse," I finish for him. A phrase I heard in Sarral pops into my mind, and I add, "You know what they say—getting a Karthian to change is harder than teaching rocks to dance."

Simeon snorts. "Where'd you hear that?" He shakes his head. "*I'm* the one who's supposed to make *you* laugh, remember? Or did you forget how this whole sibling thing works while you were gone?"

I reach a hand up, about to ruffle Simeon's hair until it sticks out in all directions, when his expression turns solemn. I drop my hand as he takes a deep breath, seeming to decide something. "Can I count on you to help with the wedding planning, then? Or will you be gone before the big day? I understand if you need to leave again, of course," he adds hastily. "But if I'd known you were hurting so much in the first place—"

"We all were. And there's nothing you could have said or done to make me stay. I wanted to leave. I needed to," I explain, my throat suddenly tight.

"I know. I know *you*. Which is why"—Simeon pauses, a hint of a smile touching his face—"I'm trying to say that I wouldn't try to stop you if you needed to leave again. A little warning next time would be nice, is all. Because it hurts when you're gone."

"I'll be here for your wedding, Si," I say firmly.

"Promise me the usual way. Our way," he says at last, with no hint of teasing.

Just like we've done since we could talk, we spit into our palms and shake hands. It's disgusting, but being Simeon, he somehow makes me laugh. I think it's the way he nearly gags as our hands slide together that I find so entertaining.

"This is what you asked for!" I remind him as we hastily wipe our hands on our pants.

"True," he sighs. Glancing sideways at me, he adds, "It's good to see you like this. Happy again." He squeezes my shoulder. "I believe I have a certain stubborn redhead to thank for that?"

My lips twitch upward. "Maybe."

He's right. One mention of Meredy, and I'm already thinking about the next time I'll get to see her. The smile is because I know how good it feels just being around her.

The morning breeze ruffles my hair as Simeon and I lapse into an easy silence. I rest my head on his shoulder, watching a rainbow of fish scurry around the pond near our feet. If only the peaceful morning could make me forget the rebellion brewing in the city.

Simeon hums something, a catchy tune, so soft at first that I almost miss it over the breeze rattling branches overhead. After a moment, he adds words to the melody under his breath:

> *"Should've stuck to dancing*
> *And combing his hair*
> *All the ladies used to find him quite fair*
> *Our king for a day."*

I blink at him as I try to process what I'm hearing. There's a song about Hadrien already? It's catchy, like one of Kasmira's sea chanteys, the kind sailors howl in off-key voices when they've ventured too deep into their pints, though Simeon can actually carry a decent tune.

Seemingly oblivious to my incredulous stare, he continues to sing:

> *"He had a silver tongue*
> *And a golden spoon*
> *He gave us death when he promised the moon*
> *Our bloody king for a day."*

Someone sniggers under their breath. I glance sharply in the direction of the sound, toward the glass courtyard doors. The tall, broad-shouldered boy leaning against them—Karston, the one who fought with Jax—covers his mouth with his hands in a poor attempt to stifle his laughter. The cut beneath his left eye seems shallower now that he's washed the blood away. There's another cut on his slightly crooked nose, though it looks older—perhaps a scar. He's brushed the carpet fuzz and dust from his close-cropped dark hair, too, I see. The sight of his simple black necromancer's uniform makes me miss Evander in a swift, painful rush, the strongest one I've had in days.

Karston doesn't seem to notice me staring, all his attention on Simeon's song. I focus on my friend's voice again as another verse begins:

> *"With a head far too big*
> *To fit in his crown*
> *He—"*

The rich sound of laughter gets louder, drowning out the words. Simeon falls silent. A faint flush creeps into his face as he takes note of his growing audience.

"Forgive me, Master Simeon," Karston says, squaring his shoulders and moving toward our bench with long, purposeful strides. "But after what happened with Master Jax in there, I needed a laugh. I came out here to get some air, and heard—" Swallowing another bout of laughter, he grins and shakes his head. "Sorry. Again. What's that song called? It's brilliant."

Simeon's face and neck glow red as he answers, "'King for a Day.'"

"It's great. I'm surprised I haven't heard it before."

"You couldn't have." In almost a whisper, Simeon confesses, "I made it up."

Karston gives a low whistle, impressed.

"Forget teaching. I think you have a future as a bard," I add, mustering a smile to show Simeon how much I enjoyed the melody despite the reminder of Hadrien. "Have you thought of writing Danial a song for—?"

"Whoa!" Karston's yelp of surprise cuts across me. He blinks a few times, and when he speaks again, it's with a hint of a slight drawl whose province of origin I can't place. "You're her. Sparrow. The king-slayer!"

I wince at that name and hastily roll my sleeve down to my wrist. "Please, don't call me that." I wish I could sink to the bottom of the fish pond here and now.

"Karston," Simeon says quickly, shooting me a look of mild concern. "I don't think she wants—"

"I saw one of your tattoos. Part of it, anyway. You're a legend," Karston says quietly, rubbing a hand along the stubble lightly covering his sharp jaw. "You were the reason I came to Grenwyr City, to the new school, even though my father disowned me for it." He kneels before me like a warrior about to be honored by his leader. "You're a hero to a lot of people around here." He gestures to the temple walls, then flashes a triumphant grin. "I *knew* you'd come back. The others said you wouldn't. But I never doubted."

As he holds my gaze, I now understand why he sought out Valoria's school—beyond his thought that I would be involved, apparently: His eyes aren't blue, like I thought when I first saw him. They're a rich violet color that only looks blue in certain lights, like when the sun peeks through gaps in the shade and washes them out.

"What does your Sight show you?" I ask, my curiosity warring with my discomfort over being called a hero.

"Gates to the Deadlands, like you," he says with a touch of pride.

I exchange a glance with Simeon, who raises his brows. Everyone else I've met with an unusual eye color has a unique magical ability, a power other than one of Vaia's five gifts, so there must be more to Karston's skill.

"Thanks to Jax and me, Karston knows everything about being a necromancer that you can put on paper," Simeon adds. "We trained him, because as far as we can tell, he's one of us."

"But with no dead to raise, what's the point?" I sound just like Jax.

Simeon shrugs, his expression neutral. "Valoria seems to think our magic might still be needed someday. She doesn't want to lose what we've learned about raising the dead the way King Wylding lost so much other knowledge."

I glance back at Karston, who's still kneeling. Sliding closer to Simeon, I make room on the bench, but Karston doesn't rise.

"Get up," I urge. "I'm nobody's hero."

Completely ignoring my words, he says in a rush, "Master Odessa, would you ever consider taking me on as your partner?" Running a hand over his close-shaven dark hair, he amends, "I know no one could ever replace Evander. I'm not half the swordsman he was. But now that you're back, you might need to go to the Deadlands someday, and according to the rules . . . no one should ever go alone."

I cross my arms. "No way. I don't need a partner, and *no one* needs to go to the Deadlands anymore. We can stop potential Shade-baiters before they ever reach the spirit world. You can help us patrol the cemeteries around the city—without a partner." I'm not sure why I feel a pang of guilt as Karston's face falls, though he quickly hides it. "Besides, I'm . . ." My voice trails away as I think. What am I, now that

I don't raise the dead? I go with the first thing that comes to mind. "A fighter. I have to keep Valoria safe as she tries to make peace with the rebels *and* train up an army."

"I understand," Karston says solemnly, climbing to his feet at last. "But if you decide you need a hand with matters of death in the future, I hope you'll consider me." There's something about the way he carries himself, a certain confidence that I like. Maybe even respect.

"I'm a terrible partner, anyway. I'm unreliable," I add hastily, more to myself than Karston, ignoring Simeon's muttered protest. "I'm selfish and short-tempered. I make bad decisions, because sometimes I think with my fists instead of my head, and—"

"Me too," Karston cuts in, grinning sheepishly as he touches the swollen spot beneath his eye. "From what I've heard, we've got a lot in common."

Just like when Nipper wagged her tail at me back at the dragon farm in Sarral, I can feel my resolve slipping faster than water through my fingers.

"How much do you know about raising the dead, anyway?" I press.

"Everything—at least, in theory," Karston says firmly, echoing Simeon. "I know you have to anoint the dead person's body with milk, then take one of their kin into the Deadlands with you in search of the spirit you want to return to our world. You call the spirits to you by spilling blood, and you keep your wits about you by eating honey."

I frown. "Any child in Grenwyr City could tell me as much."

He's reminded me of an old rhyme, one the Sisters of Death taught me as I worked alongside them in their kitchen making sticky buns. *Milk to wake them, blood to sate them. Honey to steady, sword at the ready.*

Karston gives me a long, considering look. "I know it's a good idea to always carry liquid fire with your blood and honey, too. One well-aimed vial could take down a hungry Shade just waiting to gobble up you, the spirit you came for, or both."

I nod, resigning myself to the inevitable. He has knowledge but not experience. Of course, he can't get that without traveling to the Deadlands . . . with a partner. And while there's no need to go there now, I don't know what the future holds. If there's one thing I know, it's that I can't count on anything forever.

"People who hang around me tend to get hurt," I snap, but the bite I mean for the words to hold isn't quite there. "Sometimes fatally."

Karston nods, his brows drawn together in thought. "So I've heard."

"And?" I prompt, though I already suspect what he's going to say, because it's just what I would.

"I'm not afraid."

"Then, if you're serious about this, I suppose we can try it out sometime, should the need arise . . ." Leaping up from the bench, I offer Karston my hand. As he takes it, I add, "But so we're clear: You could never replace Evander, and it may be years—if ever—before I need to return to the Deadlands. Which means the most we'll be doing for the foreseeable future is trading off patrol shifts a few times a day to keep Shade-baiters from doing anything stupid."

Karston's grip is warm and strong as we shake on it. "If there's one thing I understand about the world after eighteen years," he says, "it's that I have to take whatever I can get, whenever I can get it."

XII

That night, after patrolling two cemeteries and chasing away a fleet-footed shadow from a Deadlands gate, I try and fail to fall asleep without Meredy beside me for the first time in days. It makes sense that Meredy would return home to Crowther Manor, the huge house in Noble Park that her older sister inherited, to spend some time catching up with Elibeth. I've always liked the eldest Crowther sibling, another beast master, and the pack of tall, skinny greyhounds that follows her everywhere. I certainly shouldn't envy her, not after I spent most of my day with Simeon, yet I wish Meredy were here with me instead.

As I push back the blankets on the large bed, Nipper hisses a puff of smoke, startling awake. She uncurls herself from her spot on top of my feet, wagging her tail and looking at me expectantly like she's ready for an adventure.

"Don't get your hopes up," I tell her. It's nice having someone to talk to when the world is silent and still, even if the dragon can't answer. "I just figured we might as well unpack."

The wood floor is cold against my bare feet as I climb out of the four-poster canopy bed that used to belong to one of Valoria's Dead aunts. I chose her room, close to the bustle and warmth of the kitchens, instead of my old one because it more comfortably fits two. That, and going back to my old room felt wrong somehow. When I stepped inside, nothing was quite as I remembered it, or quite so welcoming despite someone having spruced it up, like I was trying to fit myself into a space meant for some other girl.

After lighting the lantern on my bedside table, I sweep across the room to the wardrobe. My lone bag sits beside it, waiting. I pull out rumpled tunics and trousers and the one dress I kept from my days of near-constant parties at the palace. As I sort things into piles, I wonder if Valoria has kept up her Eldest Grandfather's tradition of celebrating every single festival on the Karthian calendar, resulting in three or four parties a week.

Finally, after unpacking and eating some of my coffee beans, there's only one leather-wrapped parcel left at the bottom of my otherwise empty bag.

The crystal. The one that let me talk to Evander. With a stab of guilt, I realize I haven't even thought about it since before we stepped off the ship. How could it be that I feel closer to Evander when I'm remembering him with Meredy than I did when the crystal allowed his voice to surround me?

Perhaps it was the way the crystal burned my hands, which made me wonder if I could trust it. Or perhaps it's that I know Evander, and if I was suddenly talking to him—actually connecting with his spirit—doubt wouldn't linger in me. The crystal brought back the pain of missing him, of that much I'm sure. But even if it's nothing more than a clever bit of magic, I really want to hear his voice again.

I should probably wait until Meredy is with me, though. I know it's going to hurt, but this feels like something we should do together.

The bedroom door creaks open. Nipper barks once, not a warning but a greeting, and I have a feeling I know who's on the other side before she enters.

The half-wrapped crystal falls from my hands in my haste to welcome Meredy in the best way I know how. Lysander follows her into the room, and for a moment, all I can do is smile against her lips. That is, until I draw back from the heat of our long kiss to take a breath and get a look at the trouble lurking behind her eyes.

"I thought you were staying with Elibeth tonight," I say as I sink onto the edge of the bed and try to focus on reading Meredy's expression. One kiss from her is enough to make my body want something more, but now isn't the time.

"I changed my mind. I love my sister, but her snoring is worse than Lysander's, it was hard to sleep without you, and the manor holds too many memories for me to want to be there long. Besides, I couldn't stop thinking about my . . ." Meredy's voice fades. She frowns as she moves closer, studying my face. "It seems I'm not the only one who's upset. Tell me what's bothering you."

"Nothing," I say, wanting to solve her problem first. But she levels a look at me that makes me want to spill all my secrets, and it's clear she won't talk until I do. "Fine. Since we came back, very few things feel right about this place anymore." When she sits beside me, I hook my fingers around her waist and pull her against me, kissing along her cheek until I reach her mouth. I smile as she bites her lip, her breath stilling. "You're one of them, though."

"Dessa," she murmurs—a new nickname I don't mind, because it came from her. "Nice try, but you won't distract me. Talk to me." She draws back slightly, moving across the bed out of kissing distance, and gives me a serious look.

"All right," I sigh. "It hurts to watch Valoria limping around the palace, I feel rotten that I wasn't there to protect her, and Simeon wasn't sure whether I'd stick around to see him and Danial get married. Oh, and I hate Valoria's replacement friends." I pause as Meredy's lips quirk in mild amusement and frown at her. "I'm serious. Valoria said there are a lot of people out for blood—what makes her so sure she can trust those two?"

Meredy takes my hand, rubbing her thumb across my palm. "Don't you trust Valoria?"

My frown deepens. "Of course."

"Then you have to trust her judgment about others, too."

"I guess. But if I'm right and they're secretly trying to overthrow her?"

Meredy takes a long moment to answer. "Valoria will survive whatever comes her way next. We all will."

"What makes you so sure?"

"Because we've got you." She squeezes my hand, but far from feeling reassured, I ache with a sudden emptiness, wishing I had half the confidence in me that she does.

Resting my head on her shoulder, I tell her about my potential partner in necromancy, Karston, as the lantern on the bedside table sputters and dies. Meredy reassures me that I'm not going to get that violet-eyed boy killed if I ever bring him to the Deadlands, untested as he is, and that Evander wouldn't resent me for entertaining the idea of a new partner.

"Now it's your turn. What's bothering you?" I ask quietly. Nipper and Lysander are curled up back-to-back on the other side of the room, softly snoring, and I don't want to wake them.

Meredy doesn't answer, but she pulls me closer. Her touch wakes me like nothing else, so even though it's late, I'm not tired in the slightest.

As we hold each other, the world grows a lot smaller. A lot safer.

"Lyda. I went to see her today," she says at last, dropping her gaze. "So, go ahead and tell me why it's a stupid, horrible decision, like Elibeth did."

I gently touch below her chin, lifting her head and returning her eyes to mine. "I'm not here to judge you. I'm here to listen. I'm here to punch people for you when you don't have the strength. I'm here to help you with whatever you need to figure out, but only if you want me to." Lacing my fingers through hers, I murmur, "I'm here to help you get what you want, because I like it when you smile."

Her eyes well up again before I've finished speaking. Not long ago, she never would have let me see her like this. Unguarded. I wonder if she knows she looks even more beautiful this way, with all her emotions written across her face.

"I went because I thought I missed her," she says in a hushed voice. "I missed having a mom, someone who'd share in my happiness when I told them about you. Someone who'd remember to get Lysander a fresh deer carcass for his birthday and that sort of thing. But when I got there, I realized she's never been that person, and she's not about to start now. It just made me so sad, but I'm going to speak to her again. I need to keep trying. I have to have..."

As her voice fades, I search for the right word for her. "Hope. You have to hope. I understand." I press my cheek to hers, wishing I knew some better way to comfort her. But never having had a mother myself, I'm at a loss. Absently, I begin to hum the song that's stuck in my head to fill the silence.

"What's that?" Meredy asks after listening a while, a smile in her voice. "Something new for us to dance to?"

I blink, surprised at myself. Simeon's song has been drifting through my mind all day, but with so much else to occupy me, I hadn't really noticed.

"*Should've stuck to dancing, and combing his hair*," I sing for her.

I don't remember all the words, but the few that I do, combined with the catchy melody, earn a peal of laughter from Meredy. The sound warms me all over.

"I've always thought Simeon would be an excellent musician," Meredy says, shaking her head and smiling. "He should try his hand as a playwright, while he's—"

"Do you want to stay here with me?" I blurt, unable to hold the words in any longer. "I mean, live here, and share this space every day? Maybe it's too soon for me to be asking. It's not like we've been dating that long. You can say no," I add quickly, over the sound of my heart clamoring in my ears. "It won't change how I feel about you. I promise."

She answers me with a kiss. And that's enough.

A sharp knock wakes us just before sunup, after only a few hours' sleep.

At first, I assume I've somehow overslept and missed a patrol shift and that Jax has come to find me, but I quickly realize the knocker isn't nearly as heavy-handed as him.

Blinking grit from my eyes, I hurry to the door before Lysander's growling chases the poor visitor away. I only open it a crack, but I still have to push Nipper back as she tries to shove her scaly head through my legs to lick the guard waiting outside.

"Her Majesty requests your presence on the training grounds in an hour," the guard says, her green eyes widening as she gazes down at the dragon struggling to get past me. "The first volunteers for our new army have arrived."

Yawning, I nod. As soon as the guard is out of sight though, I grumble, "Someone should really tell Valoria that even an army needs time to do ordinary things like *sleep*."

Still, knowing the Ezorans are out there, and who knows how many other armies like theirs, starting to train our own forces now could be the difference between life and death.

After a hasty breakfast, Meredy and I make our way to the expansive grounds behind the palace, where archery targets, straw dummies, and weapons sheds loom like menacing shadows in the morning mist.

"I'm going to take it as a bad sign that we're the first ones here."

I've barely finished speaking when Valoria appears, mist swirling around her ankles like a devoted pet. She's followed by Danial, her two ladies-in-waiting, and about forty people. They range from one who's still losing her baby teeth to a gray-haired man with a ruddy, almost purplish complexion warning of imminent sickness.

I vow to avoid him on the very slim chance he's carrying the black fever. It's nearly outbreak season for the one illness healers can't cure.

"These are the first volunteers, all from Grenwyr," Valoria says cheerfully, like she's been awake for hours already. "Of course, many more will be joining them soon, both from our province and others."

"Seems we've got our work cut out for us this morning," Danial whispers to me. "Valoria especially—she won't admit it, but she's in constant pain."

"The Shade that attacked her—?" I ask.

"Tore her leg off just below the knee when she tried to escape," he says grimly. Softer, he adds, "Even though I was able to reattach it and heal her, the scar seems to go much deeper than her skin—for one, there's the pain. The limping. And something more, too."

I know what that's like. Danial must be thinking along the same lines, as he reaches over and squeezes my hand.

Not wanting to slip into my darkest memories, I take a moment to look over each volunteer in turn. With the exception of a couple farmers who bear the marks of years of hard labor, none of them strike me as naturally inclined fighters, especially compared to the strength and skill of the Ezorans.

I really hope Valoria wasn't just wishing aloud when she said more volunteers are coming soon.

Meredy and I exchange a glance, and it's clear from the crease between her brows that she doesn't want to hand any of these hesitant-looking people a weapon, even a wooden one designed for practice.

"Well, no point standing around all morning," Danial whispers to Meredy and me. "If I can learn to wield a blade while scared for my life, these fine citizens can learn in a safe, controlled situation." Taking a deep breath, he claps his hands together, and everyone else's chatter ceases.

After making introductions, Danial calls them forward to assess them one by one, deciding who he thinks can handle close combat. Meredy moves alongside him, confident and focused as she chooses people to train with a bow and arrow. I could watch her work all day, if there wasn't someone nearby who I've really missed talking to: Valoria.

As I wait for Danial to bring over the volunteers he's selecting and splitting into groups for the two of us to train, I pull my friend away from her ladies-in-waiting, Freckles and Sunshine.

"Where's your crown?" I ask, putting a steadying hand on her shoulder. She's leaning on her cane less than usual, but she still looks like she could use the extra support. "And why are you wearing *that*? Surely your maids didn't pick it out for you." I nod to her tattered trousers and her rose-patterned blouse with several moth holes in it, offering her a slight, teasing smile.

Valoria shrugs away my touch, then pulls off her glasses and folds them up without a hint of hesitation. "I'm here to learn how to fight, too." Holding her cane slightly off the ground, she musters a grin and adds, "Since the damage the Shade did to my leg seems to be permanent, I might as well learn how to wield this baby in self-defense, no?"

"Majesty, you can't—" one of the ladies-in-waiting says fretfully, biting her lip and glancing at Valoria's injured leg.

"Actually, I've found there's surprisingly little I *can't* do," Valoria says, raising her chin and turning her back on her lady-in-waiting to meet my gaze with eyes sharp as cut glass. "Now, Sparrow, don't go easy on me just because you know me, or because you feel sorry for me."

"I'd never," I say quickly.

"Good," Valoria says, visibly relaxing. "There's nothing to be sorry about, anyway. I'm lucky—unlike many in Karthia, I'm still alive. And grateful for every breath." She taps her cane against the ground. "I'm still me. Just in a slightly different form."

"You look like you're in fine fighting shape," I assure her. "I'll challenge you accordingly."

"Not before I do!" a familiar voice shouts. "I want you to give me the beating of my life . . . if you think your fists can take it."

Striding through the mist, Jax's hulking shadow comes into view.

He whistles Simeon's song under his breath and flashes a wolfish grin as he approaches. His mood seems lighter this morning. Too light. I wouldn't trust the change if I didn't know him so well. Fighting is something he's good at, and without his old job to occupy him, this is probably the first chance he's had to burn off some of his restless energy since we said farewell to the Dead, or at least since he fought the Shade that someone turned loose at the palace.

"You and me. Let's do this. Hand-to-hand combat, for those fun times when swords aren't an option," he says, wiping a trace of sweat from his brow and locking eyes with Valoria. "If you really want to learn, I'll teach you how to take down someone twice your size," he says, a current of pride—and perhaps something else, though I'm not sure what—running through his voice. "Bring your cane. It'll make a sweet staff." He nods to the black polished wood with the wolf's head for a handle. "And I won't go easy on you. Promise."

He extends a hand to Valoria, who takes it after a moment's slight hesitation. Hand in hand, they disappear into a stretch of grass behind one of the weapons sheds.

Wondering if they're finally about to act on what I've sensed between them for a while now, I watch as Meredy patiently organizes a small group of would-be archers. Nearby, Freckles, Sunshine, and a couple of the larger men test out wooden practice swords under Danial's careful supervision.

With the sun now burning off the mist, the beginnings of our volunteer army don't look as bad as they did at first glance.

Hurrying over to help Danial with his trainees, I take a moment to study Valoria's two favorite ladies-in-waiting as they watch others sparring. Both girls are holding their practice swords at angles that suggest they have no idea what to do with them. I'm not sure why Freckles, the one who turned into a big cat in the throne room, would even want to learn swordplay when she can transform into something that kills with a swipe of its claws. And as for Sunshine, her appearance-changing magic seems to make her better suited to spying than any type of fighting.

As if to confirm my suspicion, Sunshine waves her short wooden sword in a greeting at my approach. The blade smacks Freckles square in the face, and she cries out, more in surprise than pain. Still, Danial rushes to check on her.

They're hopeless at this.

I rub my temples, wishing I'd brought some coffee beans out here with me.

I've just started explaining how to block an opponent's blow to the rest of the trainees when Simeon calls breathlessly, "Wait for us!" When he strides into view, leading most of the crew of the *Paradise*, he pants, "Sorry we're late, but this lot would've missed the morning summons if I hadn't gone to fetch them." In an exaggerated whisper, he jerks a thumb at Kasmira and adds, "Too much fun last night."

"By *fun*, he means we got into a scrape with some of those who oppose Valoria's reign last night," Kasmira says to me and Danial, ignoring Simeon's jibe completely. "So forgive us if we're moving a bit slowly this morning, but we figure now's as good a time as any to learn some, ah, proper killing techniques." She wiggles her fingers and makes me laugh for a moment—that is, until I notice the bruises on her face and arms.

Frowning, I reach absently to rub the spot where my master necromancer's pin used to be—the one I no longer wear despite Meredy's encouragement—and I get to work at last.

The volunteers might be a bit hapless, but they're eager to learn. Watching a young boy demonstrate some decent footwork, teaching

Freckles the proper technique for blocking, and helping Kasmira with her stance raises my spirits slightly.

A while later, Jax and Valoria emerge from behind the weapons shed, bruised and muddy but both grinning.

Jax looks my way and calls, "Your turn next, Sparrow!"

I don't know what this means—if this is him forgiving me for leaving without saying goodbye—but my toes practically skim the grass on my way over to him. I link arms with Simeon, dragging him away from his sparring partner to join Jax and me in a little hand-to-hand demonstration for the volunteers.

If only Evander were here, it would be just like old times. But if Evander were here, I wouldn't be with the girl who gives me the best dreams. I can't wish Evander back to life. It seems to be a habit, but I've got to stop trying. Evander would want me to be happy, and in the moments when I'm not worried about what he would say or think if he were still here, I finally am. Happy, with Meredy. And we can't move forward if I stay stuck in the past with a phantom.

Our mock battle begins, demanding my attention.

As I swing my fist toward Jax, someone screams.

XIII

I drop my hand at the sound that startled me, a hot, prickling feeling washing over me as I look for the screamer. "Relax," I growl at the crowd, still breathing hard from the half demonstration we managed. I wink at Jax. "I'm not gonna do anything that'll permanently damage that pretty face of his."

Jax doesn't laugh like I expected. Instead, he nudges me in the ribs and points at something in the distance, toward the front of the palace.

A plume of smoke rises into the clear sky like a sinister, twisting serpent. Grabbing my sword—the real one I'd set out of reach before practice—I race toward the palace's front gates with Jax and Simeon running alongside me, Kasmira and Meredy not far behind.

As we draw nearer, a buzzing like angry hornets fills my ears. It's a good thing we've started training. Our volunteers are about to see firsthand why there's a need.

Rounding a final corner and emerging onto the palace's front lawn, the source of the smoke and the shouting becomes clear:

Beyond the wrought-iron gates and the line of guards protecting them—guards who must have been forced to retreat up the hill—a figure burns high on the hillside while a crowd looks on. Some watch in horror, but a few have a certain gleam in their eyes that tells me exactly who started the fire. Others break away from the crowd, running to fetch buckets, I'll wager.

But somehow, given the distance to their homes, I don't think they'll be fast enough.

The burning figure is about three times the size of a normal person, with an old man's gnarled face and a stack of books clutched to his chest, made entirely of straw. A hastily and poorly constructed statue of Change.

Monsters I can handle, but I have no idea what to do about unhappy people.

As the figure continues to smolder, its legs, thick as tree trunks, give way. It collapses facedown on the hill in the direction of the palace, setting the grass ablaze in the same place where Hadrien turned a beloved king into a soulless monster.

Though I should be hot from running here, the sweat that clings to my skin is cold as winter rain.

Jax, pushing his way through the guards, bangs a fist against the iron bars of the gate and shouts an obscenity at the crowd. Of course, that only riles those who started the fire further. Even among those who didn't, there are some who join in the chanting with a certain note of desperation that rattles my bones.

"The inventor queen is mad!"

"Bring back our Dead!"

Following the path Jax created, I push my face up against the gate as the crowd grows, so many expressionless faces turned toward the fingers of flame reaching toward the palace. Unlike our meager volunteer army of forty, there are hundreds of unhappy Karthians. Some even climbed the hill to swell their ranks despite bearing signs of pox and other illnesses.

The first few who left now come running back up the hillside with buckets, sloshing water everywhere, but the fire is spreading toward the bountiful palace gardens too quickly for them to do much good. If they don't stop it in time, we could lose everything from ancient strains of flowers to our precious citrus trees.

"Now isn't the time for this!" I yell through the gate at the angry and worried people alike, even though there's no way they can hear me over their own shouts. "You're all impossible!"

These people, the same people who helped stop Hadrien and killed Shades to save the city, seem to think Valoria is no different from her brother, hungry for progress at any cost. I have to help them see that the only changes she wants are ones for the better, because right now, all they're doing is hurting the person who wants to protect them most. Yet while defending Valoria against threats involving the Dead comes easily to me, I don't know how to begin changing people's hearts and minds. Spirits are simple. The living perplex me.

Someone touches my shoulder—Valoria, having limped her way here at last—and I extend an arm, inviting her to lean against me for a moment before I join the palace guards and our volunteers rushing to put out the flames now licking at the garden's edge.

She shakes her head, smiling regretfully, then steps forward to address the crowd. "Who did this?" she demands, her voice ringing out like a battle cry. "Whose idea was it? Please, I'm not going to shoot you." She motions to her closest bodyguards to lower their weapons. "We're too much at odds already. In Vaia's name, I just want to *talk*."

"How about you listen instead?" someone challenges. "Or do we need to keep destroying your creations?"

I pass a bucket off to an older man and decide to linger at Valoria's side a while longer. I want to see who spoke, and with some of the crowd now joining the guards in attempting to douse the fire, I'm not needed as urgently.

There's a small stir as a tall, blond young man breaks free from the crowd and lopes up to the gate. His big hazel eyes gaze steadily at Valoria as he approaches, his hands raised to show he has no weapons. "Tell me: What else will we have to burn, *Majesty*, before there's no more change in Karthia? Before you honor King Wylding's ways? Our demands are simple: Rebuild Grenwyr City as it was, not how you want it to be. Uphold the laws we've always had instead of writing new ones. And most importantly, have your necromancers return all the Dead you sent away."

Valoria and I exchange a glance. "At least he's not trying to murder anyone," I mouth to her before directing a glare at youngish man's angular, lightly bearded face. I like that he's direct, but I don't like the threat he poses to my friend.

Squaring her shoulders, Valoria meets the man's eyes. "Assuming you don't want to set any Shades loose within my walls, would you consider sitting down and speaking with me further about these demands over tea, sir—?"

"Devran," he supplies at her prompting. Narrowing his eyes, he adds, "And my people didn't have anything to do with the Shade. We understand how dangerous they are. We didn't know the weather mage who attacked you, either. We don't want you gone or hurt or anything like that—I mean, at least you're a Wylding—but until our demands are met, we'll keep destroying whatever you try to create. We didn't mean for the fire to spread like this, only to send a signal you couldn't ignore."

"Death to the queen!" someone shouts over the end of Devran's words.

"That's not the way!" he yells back. Shaking his head, he mutters more to himself than to Valoria, "There are weirdos in every rebellion."

"Very well, Devran. I'd like to hear your concerns." Raising her voice, Valoria adds, "I want to hear *all* of your concerns! I want everyone to be happy, but in order to work toward that, we've got to start talking. There's so much I want you to know—and so much for you to say to me, I'd imagine. At least give me a chance to hear you and see if I can meet your needs before you continue scaring away my work crews and wrecking everything I'm trying to build."

Devran smiles thinly, his gaze cool and calculating.

For a long time, they just stare at each other. Either he's trying to read her mind or trying to make her lose her temper. But Valoria is unwavering, hardly even blinking.

At last, Devran says, "I'll need your word that I'll come out alive."

Terms negotiated, the palace guards open the gates to allow Devran and his right-hand woman inside as the few wisps of clouds in the blue sky swiftly turn black, drawing together into one fearsome thunderhead.

I don't have to look to know that somewhere nearby, Kasmira is working her magic despite her weakened hands, wrenching water from the sky to vanquish the remnants of the fire before any more harm can come to the garden.

Raindrops mix with the tears on my cheeks, diluting their salty taste, erasing any trace of my longing for the Karthia I used to love. As for this new Karthia, the one that now seems to be resting on the shoulders of Valoria and a young man with a jaunty walk I don't like, I'm not sure what to make of it. Only time will tell.

* * *

With the fire reduced to a few smoldering remains, we all go our separate ways: Kasmira and her crew back to the *Paradise*, Jax and Simeon to the school to check on the students, and Valoria to talk alone with the rebel leader, leaving Meredy and me to return to our room. It takes all our self-control not to eavesdrop outside the throne room instead.

"I need to unpack, anyway," Meredy announces as we reach the door and let our beasts enter before us—Nipper in the lead, of course, followed by her giant grizzly friend. "Dessa, if you help me, I'll make it worth your while . . ."

"Is that a promise?" I ask, my heart beating a little faster.

But all thoughts of what we might do on top of Meredy's clothes vanish as Nipper bats something across the floor under Lysander's nose, inviting him to play. The crystal rolls across the boards, leaving a trail of chalky marks.

"What's that?" Meredy asks, swiping the crystal away from Nipper. The dragon bares her teeth warningly, but Meredy, knowing the little pink creature is more smoke than fire, ignores her. She sits cross-legged on the bed, cradling the rough blue stone and watching me, evidently waiting for an explanation.

It takes a moment to get my mouth to work, but when it does, I sit beside her and tell her how I found the crystal, and what happened the one time I used it. I can barely look at Meredy as I fumble my way through the story, but when she forces my chin up so she can study my face, there's no judgment in her gaze whatsoever.

Only curiosity and, I think, a bit of hope.

"We have to try it. Right now," Meredy says, her eyes bright and eager.

"But it's . . . it might not work again," I insist, less confident now that she looks so hopeful. "Fine. We'll try it."

When she and I each have a hand on the crystal, just as the old man instructed, she asks, "Ready?"

I nod, even though I'm not. It's like every time I decide I'm ready to move forward without Evander, something drags me back to the painful place where all I do is miss him and relive the worst days when his absence was fresh and raw.

I count my breaths until they're slow and even, letting every thought that's not of Evander slip away. The crystal twitches, sending a tremor up my arm.

Heat sears my palm. Gritting my teeth, I tighten my grip on it despite the pain and finally open my eyes.

"Evander?" I ask hesitantly as the crystal begins to glow. I feel silly. Maybe I only imagined the voice on the ship. After all, I was feeling at my lowest then.

Nipper chirps curiously, jumping onto the bed and trying to force her way between me and Meredy, but I ignore her.

"Hey, Sparrow. Hey, Mer-bear." A warm voice, a voice that sounds very much alive, fills my ears. "I was beginning to think you two had forgotten me."

It's a good thing I'm sitting down, or I might fall over at the sound. "Never!" I declare, shame burning my face as I wonder whether I've been selfishly keeping Evander, the real Evander, from talking to Meredy—and me—for days.

Meredy gives me an awed glance, her eyes filling with tears.

"Tell me everything I've missed," Evander prompts in the silence. His voice is like an embrace, more than making up for the pain in my hand from holding the hot crystal.

I shake my head at Meredy. A little voice in the back of my mind still isn't buying this for some reason. I open my mouth to ask him a question, something that will prove beyond a shadow of a doubt that the little voice is wrong, and he's really speaking to us. But what comes out is "Van, there's something you should know. Meredy is my girlfriend now."

For a moment, silence hangs over us.

Then Evander's voice says softly, "Moved on a little quickly, didn't you, Sparrow? I . . . I don't know what to say. Don't get me wrong, I'm glad you're doing well, and I know we agreed we'd have to love again to go on living if something happened to one of us—nature of the job and all. It's just . . . so swift and sudden, I suppose. I'm sure our friends feel the same. Have you noticed them whispering without you?"

Meredy's eyes are wide, and when she blinks, tears fall onto her cheeks.

I pull the crystal out of her hand and throw it across the room as hard as I can, breaking our connection to the magic.

Tears fill my eyes, but not because of what Evander said. Meredy takes my hands, both of us wincing at the rawness of our burns, but we don't let go, not even to stop Nipper from batting the crystal around in another attempt to get Lysander to play.

It's only after I've been holding on to Meredy for a while that I can speak. "That *thing* in the crystal . . . whatever it is . . . it's not Evander. I'm sure of it. It was just echoing thoughts I once had, but in his voice. Not that I still have any doubts about us. Not at all," I add quickly, as Meredy winces.

The magic in the crystal was only repeating the doubts I'd had before I realized that what I felt for Meredy had nothing to do with Evander. Before we danced on a rooftop and fit together just right. The crystal reflected my worries almost word for word, like it was just reading my thoughts in Evander's voice.

"Oh, and another thing. Evander never would've said, 'I suppose,' in that snooty tone," I add, trying to make Meredy smile with my impression.

She still hasn't said anything, although her eyes are now dry.

"It isn't him," I insist.

"Evander didn't use that phrase, not that I can remember," she says at last, nodding in agreement with me. "Still . . ." She swallows. "It was nice to hear his voice again, wasn't it?"

"Of course it was." I squeeze her hands. "But we have to get rid of that thing. Evander wouldn't want us holding on to something that only hurts us." I nod to the crystal as Nipper swats it with her tail. It sails dangerously close to the lantern on the bedside table and strikes the wall. Good riddance. "Nipper will bury it somewhere for us, won't you, girl? And not destroy anything in the process?"

The dragon chirps dutifully and grabs the stone between her teeth.

I smile at her but only briefly. Something Meredy said is bothering me: Even knowing I was only talking to a clever enchantment, it was still intoxicating to hear him. To feel the rush of memories his voice conjures. With the crystal, I could do that every day. Just like when I was taking the potions that let me see his face, even when I knew it was only an illusion, I could cling to the magic's deceptive voice. Live for that voice.

But I'd only be living for a memory. And in the process, I'd be hurting myself and everyone around me. I can't do that again. I can't get consumed by memories of Evander, losing everything and everyone else that I love.

Never again.

Leaping off the bed, I open the door for Nipper. "Get that awful thing out of my sight," I tell her firmly. "Bury it in an empty grave. Or throw it off the cliffs if you have to."

She scampers off, her friend Lysander close behind.

When I turn back to Meredy, who still looks shaken, she carefully wipes the tears from my soaking face. I can't explain why I'm crying, exactly. I feel better than I have in as long as I can remember—sure of who loves me, sure that the crystal lied, and sure of my future. It's here, with the youngest beast master in a century, who finally cracks a smile when I get her to join me in a chorus of "King for a Day" as we unpack her bags in the room we now share, and who eagerly follows me down to the throne room to see if we can eavesdrop at last.

Of course, by the time we get there, the talk is over. It was, Valoria insists, just that—a few tense hours of talking. But by the focus in her eyes and the way she sends her ladies-in-waiting to summon the council, I sense that it was more than that.

Not just a talk, but a beginning.

XIV

For taking care of the crystal, I give Nipper extra treats—sweet rolls and bacon—over the next several days. I definitely don't miss its presence and the false hope it provides. The burns on my hand begin to heal, helped along by a salve Meredy mixed herself.

Lately, she's been gone for hours at a time—to see Lyda again, I'm sure—but I don't press her for details. She's lost enough without losing her mother completely, too. Besides, it's not like she expects me to report to her whenever I leave for or return from patrolling for Shade-baiters—although I do, just so she won't worry.

Only about thirty new volunteers arrive to join Valoria's army, not even enough to double our ranks, despite Valoria having sent ravens with requests for help to every wealthy noble in Karthia. People who still owe favors to her Eldest Grandfather.

We all gather in the dining hall before our usual morning training session—Valoria and her ladies-in-waiting, Danial and the ragtag volunteers, Kasmira and her crew, and me. There's no sign of Jax, which I hope means he's at the school with Simeon. Nor of Meredy, who said she had to help her sister with something bright and early and wasn't sure when she'd be back.

I miss her, but I'm glad she's spending more time with Elibeth instead of Lyda.

Just as we're about to tuck into breakfast, a girl I vaguely recognize as one of the students from the mage school scurries to Valoria's side with a message.

Whatever the girl whispers, it makes Valoria drop her fork. "Odessa, grab your breakfast and follow me. We need to get to the temple right away." I don't have to ask which temple she means—the school. She's breathless with excitement. "Danial can handle the training just fine on his own today. It's not like we have a big crowd yet."

"I'm ready to go," Freckles announces, rising from her seat.

Valoria smiles, then shakes her head. "Thank you, Bryn, but I want you and Sarika to stay here. I'll be fine with this one." She nods to me with a small smile. "Even Shades should have the sense to run when they see her coming."

With that, the two of us set off for the Temple of Change, less than a mile's walk from the palace.

"Simeon said one of the students—Noranna, our inventor—has something to show us," Valoria explains as we make our way down the deserted hill, where the ground still bears the scorch marks of a restless, unhappy kingdom. At least someone removed the blackened remains of Change's straw figure. "Something she says would shock even the most hardened warrior. Some sort of weapon, I expect."

We take a longer route to the temple, avoiding the main path in favor of dirt tracks through gardens and, sometimes, no path at all through groves of unkempt trees. But with the fire still fresh in our minds, I'm uneasy about Valoria venturing out of the palace no matter how well she insists her talk with the rebel leader, Devran, went. They haven't been able to agree on anything yet, not with Valoria so set on the idea of building her Dream City and most of her council as unwilling to bring back the Dead as she is. And while she and Devran have scheduled a second meeting to discuss a temporary halt on all building projects, I can't stop thinking about something Devran said earlier: The Shade-baiters seem to have acted alone against Valoria, which means she has other enemies to worry about besides his people. Especially if, as they said, they only plan to destroy Valoria's inventions and palace property when their demands aren't met. Destroying lives is different.

Hopefully Kasmira and her crew will be able to figure out who Valoria's most sinister enemies are as they make their usual rounds at the city's taverns and other meeting places, keeping their ears open just as their queen ordered them to—whenever they aren't training with the volunteers, that is.

Ten of the mage students—all but one of them, if memory serves—greet us in the library that only holds a few books. While they keep a respectful distance from Valoria, they welcome us enthusiastically, all talking at once.

"Noranna's really excited to show you what she came up with," Karston tells me, raising his voice over the others. A slight frown crossing his face, he adds, "I thought she might show me first, but she wouldn't let anyone see until Her Majesty arrived."

"Knowing Noranna," Azelie adds from her seat near the window, where she's making a flower do cartwheels along her forearm, "it'll be *good*. She designs the neatest things—like a greenhouse where I can work with all sorts of plants, all year round."

Seeing anyone do a trick like that with a flower would've startled me once, if not shocked me. But now I only feel the barest shiver of wonder as the milky-white orchid on Azelie's arm takes a bow.

"You're only excited about that greenhouse because we haven't started building it yet," Karston says to Azelie, shaking his head. "Wait till you've spent a few days swinging a hammer, and you'll start dreading the work as much as the rest of us."

Listening to their easy banter makes me think of the way Jax, Simeon, Evander, and I used to joke when we weren't training.

"Have you seen Jax lately?" I ask Karston in a low voice.

Jax missed our last two practice sessions with the volunteer army, and I haven't had a chance to really talk to him since the day of the protest on the palace lawn. Before that, it seemed like things between us were on the mend. I hope they still are.

"He's probably at the Rotten Rose." Karston shrugs, seemingly unaware of how troublesome that news is. "That's where he said he planned to head after his patrol shift yesterday. Usually, when he goes there, he doesn't come back for a while."

A flicker of alarm crosses Valoria's face as she overhears, and I nod grimly. I've never been inside the Rotten Rose, a pub deep in the Ashes, but I've heard the name in passing. It's the only place in the city where Kasmira and her crew won't go for a drink.

"So," Karston says, drawing my attention again with a smile and a look. "Any chance the students here can enlist in the army you're training?"

It's not a bad idea. Since people are afraid of the change that the students at the school represent, they might eventually take out that fear on one of them. They'll stand a better chance if they know how to fight.

As if sensing my thoughts, Azelie leans forward and, in her usual bubbly voice, says, "Don't look so worried. We're working on creating our own defenses for this place, and for the palace as well. You'll see soon enough, I think." Grinning at me, she adds, "But it'll be worth coming to training just to see you kick some ass."

Shaking my head, I mutter, "Thanks, Zee."

She makes her flower walk from her arm to mine, using its drooping leaves like a pair of legs. It climbs up to my shoulder and kisses my cheek with its petals to applause from everyone watching us.

Someone nearby chuckles softly, a good-natured sort of laugh. Glancing toward the sound, I meet Valoria's eyes for the briefest moment. It's good to hear her laugh again.

As I excuse myself from Karston to make my way to her side, Simeon emerges from another room, his arm around the shoulders of the curly-haired girl who showed Azelie around on her first day here. Noranna.

She keeps her doe-brown eyes trained on Valoria as she moves away from Simeon to give the queen a bow, then clears her throat. Everyone goes quiet.

"Before you gave me my super-arm," Noranna begins in a soft and steady voice, gesturing to the metallic lower half of her right arm, "I got by just fine. I wasn't always happy, but I did things my way, and most days, that was okay." She swallows. "But when you gave me this"—she taps her fingers against the metal with a hint of pride— "I felt complete. Not at first, but after a while, I realized I could do things better than before." Gazing around at the other students, her lips twitch into a slight smile as she says, "Maybe even better than some of my friends here."

I sneak a glance at Valoria, whose eyes glisten with admiration as she puts both hands on the wolf's head that tops her cane.

"So anyway," Noranna continues, excitement making her words come out in a rush, "when you asked us for help building a defense for

Karthia, I thought: What if we had soldiers that were as strong as my super-arm? No amount of skill would stand a chance against them. I was already building mechanical people to serve as butlers, so I just had to tweak the design a bit, and now I'm proud to present . . ."

Her voice trails away as she runs back into the small side room she and Simeon came from earlier.

"Your very own indestructible soldiers!" she shouts from out of sight.

There's a creaking, like rusty door hinges but louder, and clanging, like the cooks throwing pots around in the palace kitchens, as three figures march stiffly into the library. Sunlight gleams off their iron bodies and the spears clutched in their hands as they shuffle deeper into the room, cutting a path through the students.

I step back, almost bumping into Karston as the soldiers draw near. He steadies me with a hand on my elbow, though his awed gaze stays fixed on the three metal figures marching.

Noranna reappears in time to hear Valoria declare, "They're fantastic! But how do you get them to move? I must know." In a lower voice, she adds more to herself than anyone else, "Amazing. Dreaming up things and seeing them become reality. *This* is the future I want for Karthia."

"So, there are two cords in the back that you pull," Noranna says, missing Valoria's softly muttered words in the excitement of her big moment. "One to make them walk, and one that makes them use the spears. Their hands have every joint a real one does, since I followed the design you used for my arm, but then I added—"

The rest of her words are drowned out as the soldier in front walks into a bookcase, causing not only the books but the large wooden shelf to come crashing down on top of it. There's a screeching of metal that makes everyone cringe as the other two soldiers collide with each other and the mess. Down they go, their spears flying from their hands.

I duck, pulling Azelie down with me and muttering a curse under my breath.

Everyone else shouts and scatters, too. Except Noranna.

"I . . ." She stammers, standing frozen amidst the wreckage. "I guess they need some work still." Her eyes shimmer as she crouches beside the mess and lifts a book, its cover now torn off, from the rubble.

The metal soldiers stare up at her with empty, dark eye holes, the only step she took toward giving them a proper face.

I shiver, wishing Meredy hadn't had to visit Elibeth today, so she could see this with me.

Karston is by Noranna's side in an instant, and I hurry to help him lift the bookcase off the soldiers while Azelie collects the spears. Valoria gathers up books, while Simeon shepherds the other students into the courtyard to give Noranna some space.

"This was such a stupid idea," she groans as she tries to pull one of the soldiers upright. "So stupid. Majesty, I'm sorry for wasting your time this morning. These are going straight in a rubbish heap—"

"Don't say that, Nora," Karston cuts in sharply. "You've come closer than any of us to thinking up something useful." His violet eyes are full of concern for Noranna, and perhaps something more, too. He looks at her the way Valoria sometimes looks at Jax.

"It's all right, Karston," she says, clearly not all right herself as she pats a metal soldier's arm and swallows hard. "I failed. It happens."

"You didn't fail." Valoria takes Noranna's hands, drawing her away from the mess while Karston and I continue putting things back. "You're experimenting, just like I do. Did, rather, when I still had the time. My point is, do you think I'd have invented anything useful if I tossed every past attempt in the rubbish? You're not giving up." Perhaps sensing a protest brewing in the younger inventor's gaze, she adds firmly, "That's an order."

As I help drag the three metal soldiers back to the workshop they came from, staring at their blank, eerie faces, I'm more determined than ever to make our volunteer army into the fighters they never knew they could be.

Because no matter how brilliant an inventor Noranna is, she'll never be able to design what her metal soldiers would need in order to fight a human opponent: brains.

Strong as they are, unless these things can think for themselves—know where to go, anticipate their enemy's next move, understand when to strike and when to defend—they'll be completely and utterly useless in any battle to come.

At the next morning's training session, I push everyone harder than ever, even the students from the mage school who decided to join us.

Jax and I are leading hand-to-hand practice today while Danial helps a small group with their wooden swords. At least, that's the idea. There hasn't been any sign of Jax yet, Valoria needs to prepare for her next talk with the rebel leader, and Meredy said something about helping Elibeth pick out a new dress for a very important first date. So for now, I have the whole group to myself to command.

"Seen Maxon this morning?" a woman grunts to her sparring partner as she blocks his fingers from jabbing her in the throat.

"Nah. He stayed in bed today," the man replies, groaning as the woman knocks his feet out from under him. "Good thing, too," he pants from the ground. "He couldn't stop coughing last night. Kept me up for hours."

"Typical Maxon," the woman laughs as she offers the man a hand up. "Have you considered introducing him to soap? If his hands weren't so dirty all the time, maybe he wouldn't catch every little sniffle that goes around."

"It's more the company he keeps, if you ask me," the man chuckles as they get ready to go again. "Always going into the Ashes for something."

"Less talking, more punching!" I shout, even as I try to remember if I've gotten anywhere near the absent man in question during our recent practices.

A cold wind rushes past us, whispering promises of winter, of endless gray days coming soon. It dries my damp forehead and covers the musk of sweaty bodies by carrying over the sweet, lightly tart scent of bergamot trees from the courtyard and gardens.

I take a deep breath, filling my lungs with sweet air, and gag.

There's something sour in the wind all of a sudden, something that reeks of strong whiskey, poor bathing habits, and possibly vomit.

"Morning, all," Jax calls dourly. His dark curls have grown too shaggy, hanging down into his eyes as he staggers onto the grounds. "Sparrow, you started without me?" He clutches a hand to his chest in mock agony. "I'm wounded."

Karston, who's got enough natural talent that I've asked him to give pointers to another sparring pair nearby, tilts his head toward Jax and shoots me a long-suffering look.

"I'm ready to bust some heads," Jax says, gripping my shoulder to steady himself as he sways on the spot. The whiskey smell is worse up close, making my eyes water. "Just point to where you need me."

I try my best to keep my face pleasant. I don't want to push him any further away than my leaving already did, but I also don't have time for this.

"Nipper!" I call to the dragon. She quickly found a use for herself during our training sessions: picking up fallen arrows for the archery students—when she isn't too busy playing chase with Lysander, of course.

The pink dragon, her mouth full of arrows clutched carefully between her pointy teeth, pricks her ears in my direction.

"Bring me my coffee beans, would you?"

After quickly depositing the gathered arrows at the students' feet, Nipper bounds off on my errand. She's surprisingly smart, at least for a creature who peed in the central courtyard fountain last night. Her tail swishes behind her as she runs, making me smile despite the pee incident. She's got my attitude, too.

As soon as Nipper has delivered the coffee beans—and received belly rubs as payment—I shove a fistful at Jax and murmur, "*Eat*. These should clear your head."

He nods, then shakes himself, as if trying to wake up further.

Somewhere on the grounds, a man cries out in pain.

"Make sure he doesn't endanger himself or others," I plead with Karston before rushing off to deal with the latest training injury.

Karston nods, guiding Jax to a spot where he can sit down while he eats the coffee beans. He's patient, even as Jax snaps at him and tries to shake him off—almost like he's had practice at this. I'm beginning to enjoy having Karston around. If I overlook his lack of experience, it's like having another necromancer in our midst.

Across the field, I find a man with a broken nose and his apologetic sparring partner who sneezes with every other breath. Most of the trainees still spend more time nursing injuries than they do learning, but then, they're trying to cram years of practice into a matter of days.

I wish I could trust even a single one with a blade yet. But that will come in time.

After balling up an old shirt to stanch the blood flow and sending the unhappy man off to Danial for some healing, I'm finally able to check on Jax again.

The trouble is, he's not where Karston left him.

My heartbeat quickens as I scan the grounds. He's nowhere in sight.

Not wanting to draw anyone's attention away from what they should be focused on—training—I wait until Karston's finished chatting with another sparring pair before pulling him aside. I don't want to go to the Rotten Rose alone, and that's the first place I intend to look for Jax. On second thought, I call Nipper over, too, and clip her leather lead to her collar.

Her tail thumps against Karston's legs as she waits to see where we're going, making the purring sound that means she's pleased with me. Between her barking, purring, tail wagging, and love of Lysander's fish meals, I don't think she knows what sort of animal she is.

"He's gone," I whisper to Karston as Nipper strains at the lead, ready for an adventure.

"What? No!" Karston looks wildly around, then mutters a Jax-worthy curse under his breath. "I'm so sorry. I was watching him until just a little while ago. If it wasn't for those two"—he pauses, pointing to the sparring partners he was just overseeing—"actually trying to kill each other, I wouldn't have had to look away at all. It's like there's a new problem around here every bleeding minute."

I can't help it—I grin. "Welcome to my life, my friend." Karston raises his brows at that, and I continue, "If you're serious about testing out this partnership, now's the time. What do you say? Are you up for helping me find Jax and bringing him back?" I cross my arms and glower at the empty space where I saw Jax last. "He needs us to save him from himself, no matter how much he protests." I have some experience with that, after all. And by the shadow that flits across Karston's gaze, he does, too.

"I'm in," he agrees without hesitation. "Partner." As I shoot him a look, he winces and asks, "What? Too much?"

I shake my head. "Don't push it. Hey, cover for me!" I call to Danial over my shoulder as Karston and I race off.

Given how slowly Jax was moving when he got here, I'm betting we can catch him before he enters the pub, if we're fast enough. And I'd rather not go in there.

On our way into the heart of the city, we hurry through a warren of twisting cobbled streets, once passing a smashed terra-cotta pot that has Jax written all over it.

"Have you been to the Ashes before?" I ask Karston between breaths.

I don't hear his answer. About a hundred feet to our right, on the third-story balcony of a tailor's shop, balancing precariously on the balcony railing's edge, is Jax.

Karston shouts his name as Jax leaps into the air.

I don't have the breath to say anything.

But instead of plummeting to the ground like a stone, Jax disappears. One moment he's there, then I blink and he's gone. Narrowing my eyes at the spot where he vanished, I see it: the faint blue outline of a gate to the spirit world.

After what we went through with Vane and his army of Shades—after how his mentor, Master Nicanor, died—I can't believe he'd break the necromancer's first rule: Never go into the Deadlands alone. I'm scared for him, not because of what's lurking in there, but because I don't know what he'll do.

Turning back to Karston and taking a shaky breath, I mutter, "I hope you're ready for this. Looks like we're going to the Deadlands."

XV

There are so many reasons why this is a bad idea. For starters, I don't have the usual necromancer's tools with me. My blade is back on the training grounds, and the small knives hidden in sheaths on my ankles won't do much against Shades. My vials of milk, blood, and honey, if someone hasn't thrown them out by now, are rotting in a closet somewhere within the palace, probably in my old room.

We won't need the milk or blood on this trip—it's the honey I'm worried about. I trust myself and my connection to this world to always guide me back, but Karston might be more easily led astray, tempted to remain in the Deadlands forever. I don't feel good about taking someone so inexperienced there while we're defenseless, but time isn't on our side.

At least we've got Nipper. The dragon eagerly claws the damp, fragrant earth of the tunnel after our precarious climb up the balcony and our huge leap through the gate, nearly pulling me off my feet in her apparent haste to get to the Deadlands. Not that she needs to. For me, the Deadlands have a pull all their own, calling to my blood and moving my feet forward even when my mind is reluctant.

I didn't think I'd be back here this soon, if ever. Especially not with a fledgling necromancer beside me, goggling at everything. And especially not when I don't feel ready to face Hadrien's spirit yet.

Who knows what trouble he's causing in the spirit world?

"Remember, stay close," I whisper to Karston for at least the tenth time since we jumped through the gate. It's a testament to our newly flourishing friendship that he hasn't started rolling his eyes at me yet. "Don't touch anything. For that matter, don't even look at any one thing for too long. Don't try to talk to the spirits, either."

Instead of frowning, Karston nods like he's committing my words to memory.

My shoulders relax a little as the tunnel slopes downward and the twilit glow at the end grows brighter. We're nearly there. The tunnel's dirt floor gives way to springy grass underfoot, and above, a rich lavender sky flecked with stars. Straight ahead, I spot a familiar garden, where elderflower wine pours from a grand marble fountain and huge flowers bloom, though they give off none of the sweet fragrance one would expect.

"How does it feel, losing half your senses?" I joke, keeping my voice pitched low. It's impossible to know who might be listening down here, though I don't see any spirits flitting between the maze of hedgerows as I scan them for signs of Jax.

"Cold," Karston says, giving me a hesitant smile and rubbing his bare arms. His deerskin vest was fine for practice, as was the old, thin shirt I borrowed from Simeon, but we'd be much more comfortable here if we had cloaks. "And everything looks so . . . pale. Washed out," he whispers. "I miss home already."

By the keen way he keeps turning his head to study everything from the distant mountains to the silver-white trees lining the path as we approach the garden, he's not really serious about that last part.

Still, it makes me wonder. "Where was home for you? Before the school, of course."

"My parents' dairy farm in Ethria Province." So that's where his slight accent comes from. Not wanting to pry, I lapse into silence as we walk, until he breaks it by adding, "I mostly miss the cows. And my mom's apricot-and-ginger custard. And our cat—she used to terrorize the barn. And this cute guy who helped with the milking sometimes. And all the cute girls who showed up when we hosted cheese tastings . . ."

"Sounds like a life a lot of people would kill for," I murmur, sneaking a glance at him as a muscle in his jaw tightens. "Myself included. Why leave it behind?"

He pauses on the path, turning to me. "Because my parents made being different a terrible thing. Because losing one family was worth the chance to gain a new one where I actually belong." Softer, he says, "I guess I'm still different—everyone at the school is. But we celebrate that, instead of trying to hide it."

I nod, satisfied with his answer, and we resume our hasty walk.

"What was it like for you, growing up?" he asks me a short while later, sounding slightly out of breath. I guess it's a fair question, seeing as I pried into his life. "You started your necromancer's training when you were really young, right?"

"Right. On my tenth birthday, to be exact. I'll never forget the day *my* mentor, Master Cymbre, showed up at the convent with this scrawny boy in tow. He needed a haircut so badly, I couldn't see his eyes, and he liked lizards, so I called him Evander Salamander for a whole year until he found a live one and put it on my head . . ."

As we make haste toward the garden, I find myself telling Karston things I don't often share, because I'm not often asked about them. It's nice, talking to someone who seems genuinely interested in hearing it all, who can offer an outsider's perspective.

At last, we reach the garden's edge, where I call softly, "Jax?" But my mind is elsewhere, turning over things I haven't thought about in years, like whether my parents were forced to give me up or couldn't wait to hand me off to the nuns at Death's convent. Still, whatever their reason, I don't think I much care. I'm happy with the family I was given: Master Cymbre, Evander, Simeon, and Jax.

Nipper suddenly makes a sound not unlike Lysander's battle roar—a deep, booming noise straight from her chest that rattles on its way up her throat. It's the first time I've ever heard her make a noise other than playful little growls and yips.

She lunges forward, tugging the lead so hard it feels like she's going to rip my shoulder out of its socket.

I grab the lead with both hands, wrapping the leather cord around my forearms and digging my heels into the ground. "What's gotten into you?" I gasp as she pulls me forward, off my feet and toward the garden's central courtyard.

She drags me over a bridge, past shiny fruit trees bearing apples and plums all year round, past a pale statue I've never seen before. The knees of my trousers are ripped, the skin undoubtedly scraped given how badly it's stinging, and my elbows aren't faring any better.

At least I haven't seen any sign of Hadrien yet.

"Karston!" I hiss, not wanting to yell and potentially attract any Shades in the area. "Are you still with me?"

Twisting as much as I can while being thrown around like a sack of flour, I search for Karston, hoping to find him running in our wake.

I don't see him anywhere. Shit.

"Bad dragon!" I splutter as Nipper finally stops dragging me. "Very bad! I thought we were friends, Nip."

Apparently she's reached the destination she was seeking with so much urgency: the big fountain. She slithers up the steep marble side and flicks her forked tongue into the bubbling stream of dark wine.

If she were human, tasting anything down here would trap her in this world forever. But as she keeps lapping, seemingly unchanged, I suppose our rules don't apply to her.

"You're the worst, you know that?" I groan as I push myself to my feet, wiping the biggest chunks of dirt and grass from my cuts. My heart thuds against my ribs with the speed of a jackrabbit as I call again, "Karston? Jax?" and get no answer.

What if Karston is lost? Surely he already knows that the Deadlands are constantly shifting, moving mountains from here to there in the span of a heartbeat. I'll just have to trust that he knows his best chances of being rescued are to stay put until I can find him—unless, of course, he spots a gate and rescues himself.

Hoping Nipper isn't about to go anywhere now that she has what she wants, I untangle her lead from my hands and take a few steps away from the fountain, peering through gaps in the trees and flowering bushes that surround this small courtyard area.

A flash of something white near the fruit trees catches my eye. Hoping it's a spirit who saw which way Karston went—any spirit other than Hadrien—I hurry over to investigate.

My heart sinks. It's only the statue Nipper dragged me past earlier, the one I didn't recognize despite having visited this garden hundreds of times before. It's a stately rendering of a woman gathering fruit and flowers in a basket. The detailing around her face and gown is exquisitely real, like nothing I've seen before.

The strangest part isn't the fine craftsmanship, though—it's how the entire statue is as transparent as an actual spirit. Usually sculptures around here are carved from solid marble, as spirits can touch and create things in their world.

I reach out to poke the statue's shoulder. It's like touching the surface of an icy lake, though I'm met with no resistance. My finger goes right through the woman's shoulder and comes out through her upper back.

That's when I realize what this is: not a statue at all, but a spirit that's been rendered motionless somehow.

I don't know who did this. I'd love to blame Hadrien, but it has to be some sort of magic, and mages lose their powers when they die. Whatever awful thing he's up to these days, it isn't this.

"Karston," I call softly again, hurrying away from the frozen spirit. I want to find Jax and get out of here. We can come back and check on the spirit another time, when Jax actually has his wits about him and I've got my blade.

My blade.

Without it, Nipper is my only real protection here. But when I run back to the fountain, there's no sign of her.

"Great!" I yell, dashing a hand through the fountain and spraying elderflower wine everywhere. "This is just great! Can anything else possibly go wrong?" I splash my hands in the wine again. "Everything..." I splash more wine onto the pale cobblestones at my feet, staining them crimson. "Sucks..." Again. "So much right now." And again.

"Sparrow?"

I draw a breath and turn toward the thin, distant sound. I think it came from the north end of the garden. Bounding past the fountain, I start down the narrow wooden path over another stream and call out, "Jax? Is that you?"

"Over here!" he answers, though it sounds like he's shouting to me from across a wide lake. I've got a ways to go.

As I run, I search both sides of the path for Karston with no luck. At least the cold air soothes the scrapes on my knees. They're numb by the time I spot Jax sitting in a floating gazebo in the middle of a small pond.

"What are you doing here?" Jax frowns, sitting up straighter. Nipper, that traitorous little beast, is curled innocently around his ankles.

Fish dart away from my feet as I leap across large, flat stones to the gazebo's entrance, cursing Jax and the dragon all the while.

Finally inside the gazebo, I grab Nipper's lead and wrap it around my wrist. "No more running off," I say sharply, dropping onto the bench beside a still-hungover-looking Jax. "But . . ." Something inside me softens as the dragon stares up at me with big eyes more luminous than the starry sky, and I pat her head. "Thanks for finding Jax for me."

I glare at the stubborn necromancer in question. "Well? Let's go."

There's no time to waste. We still have to find Karston, and the longer he's out there, the more he's at risk of touching something, tasting something, or becoming Shade bait. And now that I've heard his whole life story, some ridiculous part of my brain has decided that whether he's my partner or not, whatever happens to him is my responsibility.

Jax pushes his unruly hair off his forehead, and his frown deepens. He makes no move to leave the gazebo. "I figured you were here when I saw your weird new pet, but—" He leans closer, gazing into my face with eyes like oceans, like whole unknowable worlds that still take my breath away. "Why? Were you looking for me?"

It takes me a moment to find my voice. "Of course, you idiot."

Shaking his head, Jax growls, "I'm not an idiot. I'm honestly amazed you'd bother. Since when do you care where I go or what I do?"

Anger flares in the pit of my stomach, spreading through me like wildfire. "Since the day I met you, Jax of Lorness!"

His eyes narrow, though they don't leave mine. "You mean, since you got back from Death only knows where and decided it was convenient for you to care again? Like it was convenient for you to be in my bed one day and gone the next?"

"I needed to go away for a while. That doesn't mean I ever stopped caring about you. I'm pretty sure I could vanish from the world completely and my caring for you would still be here. That's how strong it is." I grip his wrists, my nails digging in perhaps a bit too hard, as he winces. "This isn't like you. You know I'd die for you. If that isn't caring… You've never questioned…" My voice trails away as I stop myself from bringing up the night we almost became more than friends.

Jax tilts his head at that. My racing heart fills the silence for several long moments, until he breaks it.

"Someone left me without a goodbye a long time ago, and they never came back," he says. It costs him something to hold my gaze, lines of pain cutting across his face as he continues, "My dad walked out on me when I was two. He was all I had, and he just left me on my own. I guess he thought I could fend for myself, even though I could barely say my name." He laughs, bitter as the favorite tea of the nuns who raised us. "I nearly starved to death before someone found me. A trapper, who kept me for a year before giving me to the Convent of Death." He rubs a hand over his left shoulder, where a tattoo of a wolf is currently hidden by his dark shirt. "He's the one who taught me to appreciate wolves. Only thing I remember about him. That, and he didn't hit me."

I wrap my arms around him and say nothing, stunned. I don't think there's anything I *can* say. There aren't words to shield him from the world, and the damage my friends and I had long suspected—but never knew about for sure—has already been done. I've always wondered about his past, but he never offered any details even when I gently prodded. Even when his best friend, Evander, asked him about his family over a stolen bottle of the king's prized whiskey, he said nothing. I hold Jax as close as I can, honored that he trusts me with this now and trying to form a barrier between him and his troubles, if only for a little while.

After a moment, his breathing slows.

"I'm sorry I repeated your father's mistake," I murmur. "I had no way of knowing."

"I understand." He kisses the top of my head. "I've never told anyone that stuff before, but I'm glad I shared it with you." He swallows. "For what it's worth, I'm sorry, too." Gesturing to the pond around us, he says, "My coming here isn't what you think. I've been looking for Hadrien. I haven't seen any sign of that bastard since you left, and I don't trust his absence. He's got to be up to something. The drinking is for strength," he adds sheepishly. "It makes coming down here after—after Evander—less painful."

"Jax, there are too many other, *real* threats to face right now. Look at what happened to Valoria's leg! We need you focused on those, not chasing phantoms." I take a deep breath, bracing for the protest that's sure to follow what I'm about to say. "Whatever this thing is—this vendetta against Hadrien—you've got to let it go."

"Do I?" Jax snarls. "You haven't been here. But *I* have. I've seen how much Hadrien hurt Valoria, and the pain goes so much deeper than her scars."

I wince, once again reminded that I was away when Valoria

needed me most. "Even so, after what happened to Evander and Master Nicanor, don't you think you could have asked someone to come here with you?" I press, still worried about him. "Maybe, you know, Simeon? Your partner? Or Karston? Or me?"

Jax shakes his head, dismissing the idea. "Si's busy with his students. He actually likes teaching. You saw how I get along with Karston. And now that you're back, you've got Meredy. I don't want you risking your happiness just to come here with me."

"And what about *your* happiness?" I demand. "Enough with the hero act, Jax! You're suddenly the only one who should be sacrificing himself so that Hadrien doesn't put us all in danger again?"

He doesn't seem to have an answer for that. "I've been careful, sober or not," he insists. "I'm always watching for Shades when I come here." He smiles grimly. "I haven't seen any, but I've got Valoria with me just in case."

I stare at him, utterly bewildered, as our friend is nowhere in sight. "You—*what*?"

Jax shakes his head, grinning slightly, and motions to the sword at his feet.

"Ohhh," I murmur as comprehension dawns. "You named your sword after a girl?"

"A really brave, really confusing girl."

Unable to fight my rising curiosity, I ask, "Does she know?" If so, I'll be hurt. I assume Valoria would tell me right away if she knew Jax's feelings toward her had changed.

"No. Didn't think it was important. It's just a name." Jax shrugs, completely missing the point, then touches the two smaller blades strapped to his forearms. "But since you're so interested in my blades, you might like to know I named all my knives Sparrow One, Two, Three, and Four. I wish Karston hadn't used my favorite one to—"

"We have to find him!" I gasp, a thrill of panic racing up my spine, spreading gooseflesh across all my limbs. I can't believe I got distracted. I meant what I said when I told Karston that hanging around me could get him killed, but I don't know how I'd live with myself if it happens this soon. He was just starting to grow on me.

Jax swears as he jumps to his feet and grabs his sword. "You brought him with you? What were you thinking?"

"I was following the ancient rules of necromancy," I snap as we leave the gazebo. Not giving Jax time to form a retort, I start describing everything from where I saw Karston last to the spirit frozen in place.

We rush across the pond and fly down the path that brought me here, Jax in the lead, both calling Karston's name all the while. Just as we reach a narrow part of the trail where rosebushes taller than Jax press in close on both sides, a crouching figure bursts through the thorny shrubs hardly more than a stone's throw ahead.

Snarling, it shambles onto the dirt path on all fours and turns to face us, blocking the way forward. Ribbons of drool hang thickly from its sharp mouth, and a rotten strip of flesh dangles from its cheek as it tosses its head and pierces our ears with a screech.

Even Nipper seems to shrink away from the sound.

I see these monstrosities all the time in my dreams, but nothing is as awful as the real thing. For one, there's no stench of baking rubbish in my dreams. For another, I never seem to remember just how awful the sound of a Shade's jaw clicking as it unhinges truly is. Or how dark the pits of its sightless eyes are as it seems to stare into my soul, toying with me, waiting for me to run or scream before making its move.

Jax draws his sword, muscles tensing. I grab his free arm, my own aching in protest from where Nipper nearly dislocated my shoulder earlier. I can't watch Jax die the same way Evander did. I can't.

"Wait!" I cry. "Let me try something first—damn!" I gasp as he breaks free of my hold. "Jax, no!"

He sprints ahead, rapidly closing the distance between himself and the Shade, raising his sword. Apparently he was already too focused on the coming fight to process my words.

If he gets any closer, Nipper won't be able to use her fire breath. I hope Azelie was right when she said necromancers in Sarral use dragons to kill Shades.

"Jax, get back!" I scream. "You have to trust me—*get back!*"

It's now or never.

Jax feints to the right, then dives into the prickly hedges on his left.

"Nipper, kill that thing!" I shout, dropping her lead and pointing at the Shade.

The dragon flicks her tail with what I can only guess is eagerness. She opens her mouth wide, sucking in air.

For a moment, nothing happens.

Jax groans from the bushes.

With a rumble more menacing than thunder, Nipper lunges forward, a cloud of mesmerizing blue-white fire erupting from her mouth. The Shade darts away at the same time, trying to throw itself into the bushes.

It might be quicker than humans, but it's not faster than fire.

Howling, the Shade claws at its skeletal face and collapses beside the hedgerow, rolling across the path as its body pops and sizzles. The heat of the dragon's flames must be more powerful than anything in the liquid fire potions we often carry, because it only takes a few blinks for the monster to be reduced to lumps of bones and a putrid dark liquid. Steam rises from the remains, the fire having burnt itself out. Nipper flicks her tongue at the puddle of Shade but quickly slithers away, apparently having no desire for a second taste.

And once again, the grandest garden in the Deadlands is quiet. Just the way the spirits like it.

"What was that you said about there not being Shades around here?" I ask as Jax crawls out of the rosebushes, scratched and bruised but really no worse for the wear. We exchange a shaky smile, and he accepts my help in standing.

After each giving Nipper a quick but thorough belly scratch, her favorite, we hurry away from the stink of blackened Shade goo.

"Good to know you still trust me," I murmur to Jax as we resume the search for Karston.

"Good to know there's a better way to kill Shades than what we've been taught all these years," Jax grunts, shaking his head as he studies Nipper. "Wonder what else King Wylding was keeping from us . . ."

I nod, not really listening because every time I push aside a branch or peer over a hedge, I half expect to see Karston's lifeless body sprawled in the grass. The Shade we just killed might have gotten to him before we did, and my muscles are tensed at the possibility. Or worse—what if we find Hadrien standing over our fallen companion, laughing?

But when we circle back to the fountain at the garden's center, Karston is sitting on its edge, swinging his legs and humming cheerfully as he takes in the sights, dutifully not tasting the flowing wine.

"Where were you?" I demand, rushing to his side with Nipper and Jax in tow. Without waiting for an answer, I throw my arms around him, giddy with relief that he hasn't become a pile of bones on my watch.

"I got lost trying to follow you and Nipper," Karston explains as I scrutinize him further. He looks completely unhurt, not even a scratch. "I guess I took a wrong turn somewhere. I passed this place"— he pats the fountain—"a couple times while I was looking for you, so

I decided to sit here and wait for you to find me. I didn't mind." He flashes me a warm smile, the kind that makes my lips twitch upward of their own accord. I have to admit, he's charming when he's excited about something. "I knew you'd come, and besides, it's *amazing* down here. Even more beautiful than I'd been told. Why . . . ?" His gaze darkens. "Something happened to you, didn't it?" He looks from me to Jax, his brows knitting in concern.

"Come on." I grab Karston's hand, pulling him down from his fountain perch. "You're holding on to me the whole way back. I'll explain while we walk."

The gentle pulse of a gate draws me toward home, toward the living world, but I pause to look sternly between Karston and Jax. "And no one—I mean it, *no one*—is going into the Deadlands by themselves again. Ever. Understand?"

Karston promises right away. I knew I could count on him. He might not make a bad partner someday, especially after managing to survive the Deadlands alone on his first visit.

But Jax's long pause before agreeing doesn't convince me.

XVI

Kasmira and her crew don't show up for the morning's training session.

Maybe they had a late night in the city. After all, the Festival of Oranges was last night, although Valoria didn't throw a party at the palace to celebrate—she's too busy preparing notes for her second talk with Devran. Or maybe Kasmira lost patience with the way the trainees' injuries still outnumber their victories. I'm barely hanging on to what little patience I have left myself. The only ones who seem to be making any notable progress are Meredy's archers, and even that isn't saying much—just that they've stopped hurting themselves and have started aiming toward the proper targets.

Still, it wouldn't hurt to pay Kasmira a visit. I'm worried about her hand, and maybe I can convince her to let Danial take a look at it.

As I hurry through the city toward the harbor where the *Paradise* is anchored, I notice several shops whose insides are dark, their signs hung and doors barred. It's enough to make me pause. After all, it's midmorning, a popular time to do business. And although the day is a little overcast, the wind a touch too biting, that's never been enough to keep people from going about their daily errands.

When I get to the docks, I'm relieved to find the *Paradise* swaying gently in the dark water as usual. But my pulse quickens when I don't spot any sign of any life on board.

I run up the gangway, my heart lodged somewhere in my throat at a sudden sense of wrongness. But before my boots touch the deck, Kasmira cries out in a choked voice, "Sparrow—stay back!"

She appears from the darkness of the stairwell, leaning against a side wall for support. There's a faint sheen of sweat coating her brow, and she shivers violently as she regards me. But what twists my insides into a hopelessly tangled knot is the coughing fit that suddenly grips her, rattling her chest until a blob of something thick and black leaves her lips.

That's where the black fever gets its name. Not from the fever itself, but the black gunk it creates deep in a person's lungs.

A few years ago, Jax barely survived it.

More often than not, it kills its victims—usually within a few days, but sometimes over a slow and painful process of weeks if the person is strong enough to fight it. Since no healer can cure it without dying themselves, and it's highly contagious, the sick are left to their own devices.

The black fever strikes every winter, and though this is early in the season, it's not unheard of. As it runs its course, it sweeps through the whole of Karthia, a dark time that used to keep us necromancers busy raising more Dead. Now that raisings are banned, this is bound to be the most tragic fever season in centuries.

Staring at Kasmira, I'm flooded with cold, but I somehow remember to cover my nose and mouth with my shirt. After watching Jax suffer with the fever, I never want to experience it firsthand.

"This can't be happening to you," I grit out, my throat tightening as Kasmira's coughing fit continues. "Not to any of you. Is anyone— have you lost anyone yet?"

Kasmira shakes her head. When she can, between coughs, she croaks, "Matter of time. Now do me a favor and get the blazes out of here."

Kasmira and her crew aren't the first to fall ill, but before the week is up the boatswain is the first to die, shortly followed by Dvora.

When the black fever rages, no one holds funerals for fear of spreading more sickness, so I don't get to say goodbye or properly mourn her passing. The bodies of black fever victims are collected and buried without ceremony, though sometimes the process takes days, especially when the masked guards charged with carrying out the grim task are already exhausted and spread thin.

Corpses pile up in the Ashes, dumped outside of homes not out of anger, but desperation to save those fighting for their lives inside.

Valoria is hardly to be seen except occasionally at mealtimes; she's constantly in meetings with her council and the palace healers. I've practically learned her schedule in my effort to see her, an effort that has yet to pay off.

Every day, when she receives the latest news over breakfast before her meetings, she asks the young messenger tonelessly, "Who died this time?" and listens, dry-eyed but shaking, to a list of names. The number of ravens she gets increases each day as the black fever begins to take hold outside of Grenwyr City, too, with scattered cases reported in villages from one of Karthia's coasts to the other.

The volunteer soldiers remain in the city, but since Valoria forbids all visitors from entering the palace to protect us while the fever rages, morning practices are temporarily suspended. So is patrolling the cemeteries for signs of Shade-baiters, and so is Valoria's next meeting with the rebel leader, Devran, though she writes him a long letter and frets when she doesn't hear back right away. She was so sure he'd love her suggestion of appointing citizens to her council to help approve new changes to the city.

There's not much to do now but sit and wait, and I've never been good at sitting still.

King Wylding used to throw even more parties than usual when the fever arrived, trying to keep people drunkenly distracted, but Valoria has decided against her council's wishes that there will be no festivals until the danger has passed in order to combat the spread of sickness. As a result, young nobles—Valoria's kin and those descended from long-dead friends of King Wylding—are more restless than usual, so they throw their own dances in the palace's roomier common spaces and drink late into the night.

Meredy and I try attending one, but neither of us has any fun, especially not after receiving the news that Elibeth has taken ill with the fever recently. We're much more comfortable passing the time in our room, though when we're there, all we do is obsess over each other's every sneeze and cough.

"This is kind of nice, in a way. Training being canceled," I mutter, flopping down in the middle of our shared bed, still in my party dress. "I mean, I know how important it is, but . . . we've been so busy ever since we got back to Karthia. I missed seeing you in the light, and right beside me, not all the way across the training grounds." I reach out a hand, beckoning Meredy to sit beside me.

She doesn't notice, too busy pacing the room. I frown. We could be making the most of the time we have to spend together, and instead, she's restless as a caged animal.

"Meredy, what's on your mind?" I ask a little louder, hoping to draw her gaze.

"Oh!" She blinks at me, apparently startled. "I'm worried about Elibeth. She's never had the strongest constitution . . ."

Of course. She's afraid for her sister, and here I am being a selfish jerk.

"I hope to Vaia the fever doesn't linger as long as usual," I say firmly, hopping off the bed and going to Meredy to put my arms around her. "I've had enough of death to last lifetimes already. We both have."

"I hope so, too," Meredy says softly. "Though whether the fever stays around or not, I don't think Vaia will have anything to do with it." When I shoot her a questioning look, her cheeks flush. "I don't think Vaia exists, or ever existed, for that matter," she explains. "I mean, I'd like to believe there's some powerful being looking out for all of us, but . . . if there really were a being as powerful as that, why wouldn't they stop the black fever from killing anyone in the first place? Why would they have allowed Hadrien to make monsters?"

I shake my head, unable to answer her. I don't usually think about Vaia as anything more than a vague idea, or ancient history. Definitely not as a part of our world. I shiver and rub my arms. What Meredy said makes sense. Too much sense, if I'm being honest. After all, it wasn't Vaia that stopped Hadrien. It was me. Still, I have to hope she's wrong, because if there was ever a time to have an all-powerful being on our side, it's now.

"At least we have Valoria," I say aloud. "With her brain, I bet she could outsmart Vaia. She'll think of some way to stop the fever. I'm sure of it."

Meredy smiles, absently rubbing her palms together. She winces slightly, her hands no doubt still sore from recent archery practices.

"You should tell *her* that, not me. I think she needs her friends right now, only . . ."

I nod. Meredy doesn't need to finish her sentence for me to understand. Valoria has never been the best at asking for help when she needs it. It's up to us to go to her.

I motion for Meredy to follow me.

"It's deadly late," she says, looking at me curiously as she pulls on a robe. "Where are we going at this hour?"

"To the kitchens." I smile as I shut our door, leaving Nipper and Lysander slumbering inside. I'm pleased with my own brilliance for once. "Then we're going up to Valoria's tower for some mandatory fun."

Meredy tilts her head in a way that's almost catlike, distracting me into wanting to kiss her before we've even started our mission. "Can fun ever be mandatory?" she asks.

"It is tonight. And violators will be punished severely."

Giggling, Meredy says near my ear, "Then don't make breaking the rules sound so fun."

Supplies in hand—a grapefruit chess pie, Valoria's favorite, and two bottles of the elderflower wine Meredy and I love—we ascend the stairs to Valoria's tall, lonely tower with the blessing of several guards who recognize us.

As I expected, there's light escaping from under her door.

Meredy knocks, and when Valoria's voice tells us to enter, we walk into a riot of colors, of drawings, diagrams, and heaps of wires and gears on workbenches.

I push aside the folded canvas top of an air balloon, something I've seen in this room before, to set down our offerings of wine and pie. Cursing, I realize I forgot to bring glasses.

Valoria, who has her back to us, raises her head at the sound but doesn't turn.

"I could fix all this, you know," she says wearily, by way of greeting. She's gazing down at a tiny, perfect model of Grenwyr City. "If I had more time to work on my Dream City and actually start changing some things, the black fever wouldn't have room to take hold the way it does now."

"There are a lot of things I wish I could fix, too," I tell her, though I know understanding can't ease her guilt. Taking her arms, I gently pull her away from the Dream City, and Meredy raises her chin so we can look into our friend's shadowed eyes.

"You saved me more than once when I was sick," I tell Valoria, my voice growing more unsteady by the moment. "And now I want to help you."

"I do, too," Meredy agrees. She and Valoria went through a lot together in curing me of the calming potions that I couldn't stop drinking after we lost Evander.

"I'm not sick, though." Valoria's gaze hardens. "And just because you feel you have some debt to repay doesn't mean—"

"That's not why we want to help you," I cut in. Remembering something she said to me when she tried to drag me from my bed, not that long ago, I add, "It's because that's what friends do."

Pulling off her glasses to wipe them on the sleeve of her gown— an old habit—she frowns at me and snaps, "Now you're using my own words against me? Great."

But her expression softens, and she allows Meredy and me to each take one of her hands and lead her over to the workbench where I set the wine and the pie. Grabbing our picnic supplies, the three of us sink down under the workbench like it's our hideaway.

We eat pie with our fingers, share wine from one bottle, then the next, and gossip about how various palace residents must be spending the time waiting for the fever to pass. We talk about everything from ideas for new hairstyles—even trying a few out on Meredy with hilarious results—to what gifts we most want this year for the Festival of Giving. We nearly render Valoria speechless by asking her about how she liked training for hand-to-hand combat with Jax, and she makes us giggle and give each other a private sort of smile when she asks what living together is like.

As we laugh at Valoria's story about one of her meaner cousins accidentally flashing everyone in the throne room recently, she lowers the bottle of wine she was finishing. Her eyes brighter than usual, she says, "I needed this more than I realized. Needed to unwind, I mean." She lets her head fall onto my shoulder and says in a small voice so unlike her own, "Don't ever run off again." She toys with a leather bracelet on Meredy's wrist, one I bought her in Sarral, adding, "I can't do this without you. Not that I need help. That's not it."

"Of course not," Meredy and I chorus together.

I lean my head against my queen's. "I love you, Valoria." The words roll easily off my tongue after all that wine. And I mean them. But as soon as I say it, I can't help but glance at Meredy, who gives another smile meant just for me. "We won't leave again," I add, refocusing my attention on Valoria. "Not unless you're on board whatever ship we take."

"That's good news," Valoria laughs, her breath warm against my hair. "We've been short on that lately. But who knows, maybe that's all about to change . . ."

Yet as another day dawns, chasing away the warmth of wine and shared laughter with news of more death, hope is hard to find.

XVII

Three ravens arrive for Valoria over breakfast the next morning. "Ooh, I hope there's something from Devran finally," she whispers as the young messenger places three tidy scrolls on the table. True to his word, Devran has been able to keep most of the destruction and harassment of guards at bay, although according to Kasmira, Valoria's last firepost was smashed to pieces and used in a bonfire the other night by those impatient for a tangible resolution.

I *could* wait to hear what news Valoria wishes to share as soon as she's finished reading. Instead, I lean closer to her and read over her shoulder.

The first scroll is indeed from Devran, offering Valoria a report on the fever in his part of the city. There's more to it than that, a whole second page that discusses the possibility of working citizens being selected for the royal council, but Valoria hastily sets it aside—to read later, I suppose—and opens the second scroll.

At this, she frowns right away.

"Who's Empress Evaria?" I ask, sounding out the name. "Never heard of her."

"She's the ruler of a large country north and west of here. We've written once or twice," Valoria answers quickly, her brow furrowing as she continues to stare at the parchment.

As I read on, I see why.

"The Ezorans have pulled out of Sarral and are now attacking her home," Valoria explains unnecessarily. "She wants Karthia to send aid. I—I'll think of something to tell her. She doesn't know Karthia doesn't have an army."

"*Yet*," I say firmly as gooseflesh spreads along my arms. I wonder what made the Ezorans tire of attacking Sarral. Were they driven back? Or have they found some vulnerable place that seems easier to conquer—someplace like Karthia? "Give us a little more time. We're working on it."

As Valoria opens the third scroll, I push my breakfast plate away, no longer hungry after hearing that the Ezorans are on the move.

"This one's from the school," Valoria tells me before I can peek over her shoulder again. Even though the old building is just a short walk away, she's ordered that we send outside communications by letter to avoid potentially exposing ourselves to the fever.

Judging by her animated expression as she reads, this scroll doesn't contain other deathly news.

"Simeon says something wonderful has happened!" She drops the scroll onto her toast crusts, elated. "We have to get to the school right away. Will you come with me?" Lowering her voice, she adds, "Just the two of us, and let's be really quiet about it. I don't want to make a scene."

No one in the palace would want her leaving with the fever still raging in the city. I probably should tell her no, to stay where she's safe, but I can never resist that light in her eyes when she looks at me like she needs something.

"Sure," I agree. "But give me a moment. We should at least bring Meredy with us."

Only Meredy is nowhere to be found. Panting from my run through the palace as I make my way back to Valoria, I remember Meredy saying something as we drifted off last night about trying to have supplies sent to Crowther Manor for her sick sister.

I'm glad my girlfriend has such a good heart. At least, that's what I tell myself as Valoria and I walk to the temple over ground damp with fallen leaves, forcing Valoria to lean hard on her cane and me to keep from slipping. But the truth is, I miss her.

"This had better be *really* important, Simeon!" I call as I push open the temple door and usher Valoria inside. "I hate risking our queen's safety!"

We're greeted by an empty library—aside from Noranna's three metal soldiers keeping guard over the bookcases—and a roaring fire in the room's modest hearth.

As we hurry past the soldiers toward the warmth of the flames, a metal arm shoots out, blocking our path.

"What the blazes?" I shout, pushing Valoria to safety as I gape at the metal soldier whose arm is now extended in front of us. I feel Valoria peeking over my shoulder, her breathing rapid from the scare.

Before I can think what to do next, the soldier's fingers bend in my direction, grabbing a fistful of my cloak.

I try to tug it from the soldier's grasp. It yanks on the cloak so fiercely in return, I'm forced to surrender it or be pulled into the sturdy embrace of metal arms. Given the choice, it can have my cloak. The soldier bows with a whine of hinges as I let go.

"Fascinating," Valoria breathes.

"Not really." I grab her arm, guiding her away from the soldier as it flicks my cloak over its shoulder like a butler and returns to its motionless state beside its fellows.

"Simeon!" I growl, my voice echoing down the corridors that spiral off from the library. There's no way Noranna invented metal brains for the soldiers' metal bodies since the last time we saw her, so this has to be a joke of Simeon's. He's gone too far this time, though, and I can feel my temper rising as my heartbeat refuses to slow down. "I don't know what kind of prank this is, but you should know better than to—"

"It's not a prank!" Simeon calls as he hurries into the room. "Trust me," he says, unable to keep from grinning despite shrinking back slightly when he sees the anger written across my face. "This is going to change *everything*."

The mage students, minus Karston, follow Simeon into the room with Noranna in the lead. I'm relieved not to hear any sniffles among them, only eager whispers. Mostly eager, anyway. Noranna bites her lip as she sees the soldier holding my cloak, and a faint crease cuts between her brows. Frowning, she whispers something to Azelie.

"Simeon," I say slowly, feeling like I'm missing something obvious. "What did you—?"

"It was my doing," Karston says proudly, appearing from behind the bookcase closest to the metal soldiers and tossing a cocky grin to the room at large. Suddenly, I realize why he and Jax don't get along: There's a bit of Jax's storm in him, and Jax is his own worst enemy.

"What in Death's name?" I demand, glowering at Karston as I gesture to the soldier holding my cloak.

"I finally figured out my gift, Master Odessa. Majesty." He glances between me and Valoria, and as he does so, the three soldiers turn as one to face us. "I can make things move without touching them. With just my thoughts."

The soldiers bow stiffly, then do a little shuffling dance across the library rug. Karston never touches them, though he moves his hands at his sides just slightly as the figures do whatever it is, I suppose, that he wills them to.

"Is that all they can do?" I manage, swallowing over a dry throat.

Karston shakes his head, a hint of pride in his voice as he replies, "Not half of it."

"How is this possible?" Valoria moves closer to Karston to study him with her glasses lowered, as though without them, her Sight will show her how Karston's mind works. Just like he's one of her inventions.

I glance at Simeon, trying to read his expression as Karston gives us an explanation of what he can do. None of what he's saying makes any sense, yet Simeon doesn't seem worried in the slightest. In fact, just the opposite. Guess that means I'll have to be the voice of reason here.

"You saw the gates to the Deadlands when we went to find Jax, didn't you?" I ask sharply, drawing Karston's gaze. When he nods, I continue, "Then you definitely have a necromancer's Sight. That makes you a *necromancer*. End of—"

"But his eyes aren't blue," Simeon answers for him. "We've been trying to figure out his gift since he came here, but given recent changes to the law . . ." He glances guiltily at Valoria, then back to me. "It's not like we could test his gift the old-fashioned way, by having him perform a raising."

"I'm sorry I startled you, Master Odessa," Karston adds, holding my gaze.

"There's nothing to apologize for," I grumble. Though we talked at length about our lives while looking for Jax in the Deadlands, how much I hate surprises wasn't something that came up. "And you really ought to quit using my title."

"All right." His excitement begins to return as he gestures to the soldiers. "I was hoping to impress you when you arrived. I can make them fight, not just dance. I was thinking . . ." He takes a deep breath. "I was thinking I could help by training with them, learning how to fight with them while you're training the, ah, human volunteers. And I can start right away, seeing as these soldiers can't get sick."

I may not understand his unusual gift—how can he have this other magic, when he has a necromancer's Sight?—but there's plenty about the world that baffles me, like the existence of dragons. A boy with a Sight that doesn't seem to match his gift is still far less strange than a fire-breathing lizard with poisonous teeth.

And there's no denying I like the determination glimmering in his eyes.

"Fine," I sigh, resigned to what I'm about to suggest. "Let's see how well these things can fight already, then. Three on one. Not exactly a fair fight . . ." As my voice trails away, Valoria meets my gaze, and we exchange a smile as I add, "For them."

The metal soldier who took my cloak clomps over to Karston, handing him the cloth bundle without anyone touching the pull cords on its back. Then all three metal figures turn to face me as everyone else clears away to give us room.

I draw my blade, raising it as though I'm about to cleave the head off the metal soldier nearest me.

Some of the students chuckle.

"Any time now," I murmur to Karston, waving my sword in the nearest soldier's blank face and trying to sound like there's not an army of ants crawling around in my stomach right now. It's not that

I don't trust my own skills so much as that I don't like the way the soldiers' dark eye holes remind me of Shades.

The closest soldier bangs its spear sharply against the ground, startling me into even greater alertness, then raises the weapon to attack.

I block its blows without much trouble, forcing it back toward the bookcase that it so recently toppled. I hope someone's thought to secure it to the wall.

I see one of the other soldiers spring into action out of the corner of my eye. While blocking another blow from the first, I kick the spear from the hands of the second, but it grabs on to my ankle, taking me down to the floor and forcing me to abandon my blade.

Its grip is, unsurprisingly, like bands of iron. Impossible to shake.

Valoria sucks in a breath as another soldier reaches for my fallen sword. I crawl toward it, the soldier who grabbed me still digging into my ankle.

I've just closed my fingers around the hilt of my blade, ready to jab the grabby soldier right in its empty eye socket, when a petite, curly-haired student—Noranna—takes a step forward and cries out, "Don't!"

"She can't hurt them," Simeon tells her quickly, in a low, reassuring voice.

As if to prove his point, the soldier abandons its grip on my leg and grabs hold of my blade with both hands. It starts to squeeze and bend my faithful weapon. I'm pretty sure it'll destroy the sword before its hands are in any way hurt.

"That's enough!" I whirl toward Karston, who mutters a hasty apology as the soldier returns my sword, offering me the hilt. "You've made your point," I mutter as I inspect my poor blade. Luckily, I don't think it's ruined. "I don't see how anyone could fight these things. They can't stab them, and they can't burn them."

"In other words, they'd make a pretty sweet army," Azelie chimes in.

I toss her a grin. "Exactly, Zee."

"You made them move like they do in my head," Noranna tells Karston, her fingers pressed to her full lips in quiet awe as she studies her now-motionless soldiers.

He nods, clearly trying hard not to look too pleased with himself. "Just glad I could help someone. Especially you, Nora."

"You're all right, then?" Valoria asks me breathlessly, hurrying to my side along with Simeon and Karston. The moment I nod, she turns to Karston and beams in a way I've only seen when she's worked out something for one of her inventions. "You're giving Karthia an incredible gift," she declares, grabbing one of his hands, then one of Noranna's. "Both of you are." She takes a deep breath. "How many more of these can you make?"

A smile blooms on Noranna's face, as big and beautiful as a Deadlands flower. "As many as you need, Majesty. I can start right away."

"I'd like that," Valoria agrees swiftly. "I've gotten word that the Ezorans have moved on to other targets, which means we could be next. So Karthia needs to continue building an army despite the fever, and I think we've found our solution. But . . ." Her eyes sweep over the little library and the narrow corridors leading to small workshops and bedrooms. "Not here. You'll need more space." She shifts her gaze to Karston. "Both to build *and* to practice. You two will have rooms provided for you at the palace, and you can use the last empty dungeon as a workshop—hopefully, I won't need it back to fill with more traitors. You'll find it's quite roomy. Oh, and there's one more thing." She pushes her glasses up, frowning slightly. "I think we should keep our new weapons between us for now. Until we need them."

I know what she's thinking. The people of Karthia are restless as it is, plagued with the fever and desperate to stop any changes to their city. Seeing a bunch of iron figures with spears probably wouldn't have the intended effect of making them feel safe and, worse, could seriously undermine the tentative conversations between Valoria and the rebel leader when she's promised a temporary halt to new projects.

"I can show you some more complicated moves for the soldiers. Some blocks and attacks, and even that kick I did," I add to Karston, slowly warming to the idea of these killing machines now standing so quiet and still beside us. "But they've got to keep their hands off my blade from now on, understand?"

Karston laughs and flashes me one of his dazzling grins. Shame he'll never be my necromancer brother-in-arms now. "Deal, Odessa."

After that, the rest of the students slowly trickle out of the library, heading back to their various studies, a buzz of excitement still flitting through them. Azelie heads off to clear the remaining vines from the building, Valoria and Noranna continue to talk in low voices beside the soldiers, Karston cracks open a big old book with a torn leather cover and starts reading at a table near the bookcases, and Simeon makes me a big cup of tea that I sip in front of the library fire without really tasting it.

Now that the thrill of our new defenders is wearing off, something that's been bothering me since we walked in pushes itself to the front of my mind.

"Where's Jax?" I ask, frowning at Simeon as he stares into the fire from the armchair opposite mine.

"Music lessons. He's taken up the harp," Simeon jokes, though he doesn't smile.

"He could get the black fever again," I mutter, shaking my head.

Just thinking about Jax venturing into the Ashes right now, turning to some pub for liquid courage before prowling the Deadlands, makes my tea taste bitter. "Would he really want to risk that?"

I'd trusted him not to go there alone again. He'd promised. But I wouldn't keep a promise like that, so I suppose I shouldn't expect him to.

Simeon doesn't answer for a while. The fire pops and hisses in the absence of words. At last he says, "I don't think either of us knows what he's willing to risk anymore, not when he's so determined to protect us in his way." He runs a hand through his hair and finally looks at me. "That's why I want you to be the Witness at our wedding—mine and Danial's. I was going to ask Jax, since Danial wanted you to be his, but . . . somehow, if you can fight three soldiers at once, I think you can handle double wedding duties."

I hastily set down my tea, searching for words. In the absence of finding any for such an honor—usually reserved for blood relatives only—I leap out of my chair and pull Simeon into a fierce hug.

"I probably should've waited to ask you in a better way," Simeon murmurs into my hair. "But we're trying to make this thing happen in a week or two. Valoria already agreed we can hold it at the palace. It'll be small, thanks to the fever, but Danial and I agree it's now or never, and neither of us is okay with the never. So, what do you say?"

I draw back to study his face. "Didn't the hug answer your question?"

Simeon grins. "In that case, here's the first important matter we need to discuss: How would you feel about a rosemary cake iced with lavender? Too plain?" Before I can reply, he adds, "Oh! The palace chefs have been working on some new frosting flavors. You'll love the pumpkin. They still haven't convinced me to try the sweet cheese or the seaweed, though . . ."

I purse my lips, imagining it. "Seaweed? In a cake?"

As we talk about frostings and fillings, my mind wanders to Meredy, wondering when we'll get back on the training ground— even from a distance, I like the way her practice clothes cling to her curves. Somehow, those thoughts turn to wondering which of her favorite frosting flavors she wants on her wedding cake someday. Persimmon, ginger, or both. I picture her wearing a crown of daisies, in a dress the color of the forest she loves so much. And the partner facing her, holding her hands and whispering something that makes her laugh, wearing a red dress far more suited to a bonfire night, is *me*.

My insides give a guilty twist as I think of the list of songs Evander made, ones he wanted the musicians to play at our wedding. His favorite songs for dancing. I still have the scrap of parchment in the inside pocket of my cloak, where it's been for months.

"Sparrow, what's wr—? Oh, you're out of tea! I'll fetch the kettle. Hold on." Simeon leaps up and hurries away. The fire is little more than glowing embers now, and Noranna and Valoria are talking in such soft voices that I might as well be alone in here.

In the quiet, Simeon's song echoes loudly through my head, drowning all my other thoughts in a welcome distraction. I start to hum it.

"What's that tune?" Valoria asks, startling me slightly. She drops into Simeon's vacant chair, her conversation with Noranna apparently finished. "I don't recognize it."

"Oh! Um, Simeon made it up." I give her a hesitant smile, and when she returns it, I decide to treat her to a few bars. Just as I belt out at my off-key best, "*Our bloody king for a day!*" Karston coughs loudly.

I don't bother looking up, but instead keep singing. He must have gotten dust up his nose from that moldering book.

"*With a head far too big,*" I continue, with Valoria looking more perplexed by the moment, "*To fit in his—*"

"For the love of Vaia, would you *please* sing something else, Odessa?" Karston asks in a strained voice, slamming his book shut.

I blink at him, surprised. "But you love that song."

"Sorry, I . . ." He straightens, scratching the back of his neck. "I've just heard it too often, being around Simeon all the time."

"Right," I murmur, giving Karston a thoughtful look. He must have been more nervous than he seemed about his demonstration with the soldiers. Or maybe he's worried that he doesn't have enough magic to control a whole army of them once Noranna builds more.

After all, that's a lot of weight on one person's shoulders, especially a mage who's just discovered what he can do. He probably doesn't even know the cost of his gift yet, though he'll find out soon enough with all the work that's ahead.

If any of the leaders Valoria's been writing to decides that Karthia seems ripe for plundering, we may need those soldiers sooner than anyone's expecting. Especially when, as Valoria is still quick to point out, there aren't many who'd fight under her banner.

"Get some rest today, all right?" I give Karston's shoulder a reassuring pat, then add, "And tell Simeon to save my extra cup of tea for later, if you would."

"We'll send a few guards to escort you and Noranna to the palace this afternoon with all your things," Valoria says kindly.

Wrapping our faces against the cold and the spreading sickness alike, she and I prepare for the hurried trip back to the palace. It's time to give our friends a taste of what we've all been short on lately: hope.

Valoria pauses, turning to me with her hand on the door. I can already feel a bitter wind slipping through its cracks.

"You know, now that I'm speaking with Devran, *and* we have the makings of a defense against potential invaders . . ." She presses her lips together, seeming torn about whether to say more. Taking a hard look at me, she continues, "You shouldn't feel like you have to stay here. If you and Meredy want to go back to Sarral, or anywhere else, you should feel free. Forget what I said the other night—that was just the wine and the pie talking. I'm not Eldest Grandfather. I won't keep anyone against their will." She tries to smile, but it falters.

"I'm not going anywhere." I want to hug her, or maybe hit her— how can she know so much, but not realize that I want to be right here, by her side? "There's Simeon and Danial's wedding coming up, and after that . . ." I shrug, not sure of the answer myself. All I see in my immediate future is Karthia. "I'll be here. With you, dummy."

Valoria laughs, and I start to grin, too, because we both know it's a funny thing to say to one of the smartest people in all of Karthia.

"I'll be here," I insist again as I follow her out into the chill.

"I know." She lets me slip my arm through hers as we set off, and we walk in perfect rhythm all the way up to the palace.

"See? Still here," I tease as we reach the gates, earning a reluctant smile.

But as soon as I've seen her safely inside, I slip my hands into gloves and wrap a thick blue scarf around the lower half of my face before taking off again, bounding down the great hill toward the Ashes in search of Jax.

XVIII

Shouts greet me as I draw near the edge of the palace grounds, coming within view of the seaside market on the lower cliffs that's mostly frequented by nobles and servants. Instinctively, I reach for my blade, ready to put a stop to whatever destruction of Valoria's brilliance and hard work Devran and his companions have under way now—when I realize one of the sounds I'm hearing is the distinct clap of wooden swords banging against one another.

The market itself seems deserted, but across from it, amidst tall golden grass and the husks of late-season flowers in an ill-used palace field, a small group of people practice their sword work.

Slinking through the grass toward them, I instantly recognize Freckles and Sunshine, Valoria's favorite ladies-in-waiting.

"Shouldn't you be with our queen, putting your new training to use by watching her back?" I call, announcing my approach, though the words are somewhat muffled by my scarf. There's no real anger behind the question. Valoria was with me all morning, and besides, she has plenty of guards at the palace, ones who actually know how to wield a blade.

Freckles frowns at me, which I guess I deserve. I haven't been very friendly to her or Sunshine, though it's not their fault that Valoria likes them well enough to call them friends. I can't even remember their real names.

"There wasn't much to do by way of hair dressing, gown fastening, or guard duty this morning," Freckles says coolly. "I expect you know more about that than we do." Pointing her wooden sword toward the ground, she adds, "We decided to take advantage of the quiet to practice."

Gazing around, I see that *we* means most of the volunteer army we've been assembling. They've come here to keep sharpening their skills, choosing not to leave the city, to keep fighting for their queen as long as they're healthy.

"Don't worry," Freckles adds as I scan the faces of those practicing for any signs of the fever. I don't like the lack of scarves over their mouths, though most are wearing gloves, at least. "No one here is sick. We're not letting anyone onto the palace grounds who doesn't belong, and neither are they." She motions to a swell of land on the horizon where several archers stand at attention.

"Good," I mutter. I turn to go. I shouldn't be here. I need to find Jax. Besides, there's probably no need for the volunteers to practice anymore now that we have metal soldiers with ten times their strength and Karston's magic to guide them if the need ever arises.

Yet something stops me in my tracks as I walk past people sparring on either side of me, sweat flying off their foreheads, their breathing labored. There's something here I didn't see among the volunteers before, perhaps because I wasn't looking hard enough:

potential. If they're this determined to learn to fight, I'll do my best to teach them.

Turning around, I hold out my hand to Freckles.

"Let me help you," I say over the wind rustling the grass around us. "I can meet you here every other morning, if you'd like. I'll teach you anything you want to know—but from now on, everyone needs to cover their mouth *and* bring gloves, all right? And don't tell Valoria," I add with a pang of guilt. Knowing how worried she is about the fever's spread and preventing more uprisings, she wouldn't consider this a good use of our time. She hasn't seen the determination here. "These meetings will have to be our secret."

"Agreed. And your guidance would be . . . appreciated." Freckles gives me a long, thoughtful look. Finally, she offers me her practice sword and inclines her head toward the rest of the group. "No time like the present."

I shake my head, my heart sinking as Freckles turns away. Even Sunshine's smile disappears as she follows her friend back toward the group. "We can start tomorrow!" I call after them. "It's just that I have to find my friend right now. It's urgent. I'm afraid he—"

"Looking for me?" Jax's voice, so close to my ear, startles me into whirling around.

Bracing myself for the stench of whiskey beneath the black scarf tied tightly over his nose and mouth, I lean in close to him and inhale. There's no scent but his own, clean and sweet with a musky hint of sweat underneath.

"Smell something you like?" Jax crooks a brow, his gaze skimming between me and the volunteers practicing.

My face warms as I step back. "I just thought you were . . ."

"Drinking away my problems? Getting my ass kicked by Hadrien in the Deadlands? Kicking asses? Breaking a promise to you?" Jax ticks off the possibilities on his fingers, and although I can't see his lips, I know he's grinning wolfishly as he watches me squirm.

All that and more is exactly what I thought and feared, and he knows it.

He has a leather bag slung over his shoulder, and from inside, he produces an empty soup crock and the cloth wrappings of a flaky pastry. "I was bringing a meal to Kasmira and the crew. That's all I've been doing lately," he sighs. "Kasmira still won't let me on board, but she allows me to toss her this bag." Sensing the unspoken question in my gaze, he adds, "She's better. Not cured, but I think she'd agree that she's on the mend."

The news makes me grab Jax's hands and spin around with him on the spot.

"So what are you doing out here? Giving dancing lessons?" he grumbles, letting go of my hands. Before I can answer, he says, "I want in."

Even though I'm exhausted from our secret practice, I have a surprise planned for Meredy, who promised to meet me in our room before sundown. Usually, we eat in the dining hall with Valoria and the others, but tonight I got permission to use the main palace kitchen to make a bunch of her favorite foods. I'm hoping the meal will take her mind off of her sister suffering with the black fever, at least for a little while—and if that fails, she'll surely be distracted from her worries when I tell her about the metal soldiers and Karston's magic.

I've set up a folding table that fits into our large room without trouble, and as the sky turns a fiery orange, I take a seat at one of the two chairs. Meredy should be here any moment, but I can't resist swiping a finger into a steaming bowl of buttery mashed turnips.

The taste reminds me of the convent, of suppers where Simeon and I begged to be allowed to bring our toy soldiers to the table to eat with us. We won the argument about half the time, and the memory brings a smile. Master Cymbre taught me almost everything I know, but it's the Sisters of Death who got me comfortable in the kitchen well before I ever learned the rules of necromancy.

The sun dips lower. I alternate between watching its progress out the window and keeping an eye on the door.

I wonder what's keeping Meredy. She must have Lysander with her, since he's not here, so I'm not too worried. I'm more annoyed that she didn't keep her promise. And—though I'd never admit it, not even to her—a little hurt.

Eventually, as the sky turns from soft lavender to indigo, and the food has turned Deadlands-cold, Nipper hauls herself into the chair opposite mine. With her stocky legs, long tail, and a body that lacks the muscles for a proper sitting position, her effort is one of the strangest things I've ever seen. Miserable as I am, I can't help laughing.

"You look ridiculous," I tell her fondly. "You know that, right?"

Nipper's tail pokes through a space in the back of the chair as she stands awkwardly on the seat, gazing expectantly at the food. Her big, liquid eyes shimmer as they catch mine, and she makes a soft, pleading sound.

"Oh, go on, then," I sigh. "Try everything. *Someone* ought to enjoy my cooking."

Nipper flicks her tongue over the turnips, but they don't seem to interest her much. Neither do the slices of roast boar, which is surprising given her love of fish jerky. But when she finds the spinach—something I'll never understand why Meredy likes—the dragon plunges her whole head into the bowl.

After Nipper has devoured most of the dishes, minus the turnips,

I make sure the door is unlocked for whenever Meredy deigns to arrive. Then I flop down on the bed I thought I'd be sharing with her tonight. "No point staying awake, is there?" I say to Nipper as she leaps onto the pillows beside me.

I put an arm around her, take a final look at the blackened sky, and close my eyes.

Nipper snuggles against my chest and burps in my ear.

"You're a rude date, but I think I'll keep you around," I tease her without bothering to open my eyes. They're suddenly heavy, and it takes no effort to fall into a deep, mercifully dreamless sleep.

That is, until a high, piercing wail fills my ears and startles me awake.

Breathing hard, I throw back the blankets and glance around the darkened room as the wailing continues, a haunting sound like wind forcing its way through narrow gaps in a stone wall. Nipper isn't in my arms anymore, but I'm not worried. She's developed a habit of kicking her cushion under the bed and sleeping there.

Trying my best to still my breath and quiet my heart, I focus on the wailing. It has a certain rhythm, I realize after a while. And though the pitch makes me shiver, it's much more like some person or creature trying to sing than, say, anyone being tortured.

Still, even if there's no danger, there's no way I'm getting any more sleep until that racket stops. I wish Meredy were here to listen, too, even though I'm still mad at her. Just so I can be sure I'm not imaging things.

Slowly, hesitantly, the bedroom door creaks open. As Meredy enters, a candle in her hands to light her and Lysander's way, the wailing doesn't seem to get any softer or louder. There's an unfamiliar shadow in Meredy's eyes as she sets the candle down on the bedside table and pulls off her cloak, and it stops me from asking her about

213

the sound. Figuring out what's wrong with her is far more important than some weird noise.

When her gaze roams over the remains of our supper, she winces and turns, finally seeming to notice me for the first time. "Dessa, I'm so sorry." She pulls off her trousers and climbs onto the bed with me. "I was visiting Lyda, and I lost track of the time."

"Yeah?" I mutter, feeling a sharp stab of resentment toward the baroness, which I'm sure has nothing to do with Meredy's lateness and everything to do with how Lyda Crowther once blinded me and left me for dead. "Did your mother make all your favorite dishes for supper, too? Did she even make extra and wrap it up so you can have meals delivered to Elibeth tomorrow?"

Okay, so maybe I'm resenting Meredy right now, too. She's been full of excuses for her absences lately, but she's never let me down like this before—never promised to be somewhere and then completely forgotten. And of all the things that could make her forget a promise, I didn't suspect the woman who helped Hadrien would be on the list.

"How much of your time have you been spending down there in the dark with that woman, anyway?" I ask in a much nastier voice than I intended. "All those times you said you were with Elibeth, were you really—?"

"Careful," Meredy says softly. She knows me too well—how I say things I don't mean when I'm angry. "I thought you cared when I told you about visiting Lyda. I thought you *understood*. But you only care about yourself and what you are or aren't getting, no?"

I didn't expect her to suddenly get angry, too. The shock of her bitter words instantly cools my temper.

"I'm so sorry, Mer." I reach for her hands, and when she puts them into mine, I realize she's shaking. But when I try to calm her by rubbing my thumb across her palm, she gasps and jerks her hands away.

Too late, though. I've already felt the burns—burns even worse than the ones the crystal gave me both times I used it. The crystal I thought Nipper had buried.

"Explain," I say softly, trying to keep the heat from returning to my voice. "I thought I asked Nipper to bury that thing. And I thought we both agreed it's just a trick. A bit of dangerous magic no one should have." I swallow hard, feeling sick as a thought occurs. "You haven't really been spending time with Elibeth, or even going to see Lyda, have you?"

She says nothing.

"Have you?" I ask again, almost shouting, my stomach twisting.

She flinches and holds up a hand as if in surrender.

"I did see Lyda, once," Meredy says at last, in a small voice. "That first time I told you about visiting her. But, Dessa, real or not, talking to Evander again—talking to Firiel—I couldn't just let you throw away the chance to be close to them again."

Firiel. Her girlfriend who died in a hunting accident.

I can't believe what I'm hearing. "You don't know what you're saying! Meredy, it isn't *real*. It repeated my thoughts back to me, just masked in Evander's voice. It's a trick, a nasty one. I thought you of all people would know never to mess with something like that. Remember when that potion made me see visions of Evander, and you and Valoria tried so hard to save me from the way it was destroying me? And now you're just—what?"

Her eyes have filled with tears, and she's shaking her head. "I've lost so much. I thought you'd understand. Evander does."

I leap off the bed to grab my cloak and boots, unable to listen to this any longer. "Meredy, it's *not him*! I'm sorry I ever bought the damn thing." Before I can consider the words coming out of my mouth, I add, "Evander, the real Evander, would *never* have fallen for a trick like that. And he would never have chosen a stupid rock over me."

Meredy crosses her arms as I pull on my boots. "Firiel warned me you'd react like this if you found out," she says softly. The words hit me like a slap to the face. "She told me your selfishness and your temper would be the end of us—that, or the way you look at Jax sometimes, or the way you're always comparing me to my brother. And I'm sure she's right. No one understands me like she does."

I take a deep breath, trying to clear my head, and let my cloak drop from my hands. I can't just storm out of here. Meredy needs me, the way I needed her when I wasn't sure what was real and what wasn't anymore. Until now, looking at her, I don't think I ever realized how close I'd come to losing my sanity because of those potions.

"Will you show me where the crystal is?" I ask gently, approaching the bed.

Her eyes harden, and she shakes her head. "No. I can't do that. I won't let you come between me and—"

Something bumps against our door, a dull, heavy thud that startles her into silence.

"Who's there?" Meredy asks sharply as she grabs a knife, and I grab my sword.

The doorknob rattles, and there's a shuffling of feet just outside. Someone wants in.

Together, Meredy and I tiptoe to the door. When I nod to give the go-ahead, she unbolts the lock with one hand, raising her knife with the other.

Tensed and ready to strike, I lunge forward as the door swings open to reveal Karston. He slumps to his knees across the threshold, his eyes closed, but he jolts awake just a moment later as I set my sword down.

"Karston?" I whisper, dropping to my knees on one side of him, Meredy on the other. "What in Death's name is going on?" Recoiling slightly at an unpleasant thought, and motioning for Meredy to do the same, I ask, "Do you have chills?" Maybe he contracted the fever during his move to the palace earlier today, though why he'd come to me, I have no idea.

Then I remember: He's a sleepwalker. One of the other students at the school was teasing him about it the day I met him.

It takes him a moment to orient himself, gazing around the unfamiliar lantern-lit room. Finally, he pushes himself to a sitting position and rubs the sleep from his eyes, murmuring, "I'm sorry, Odessa. I guess I should've warned everyone about my sleepwalking." He shakes his head, plainly annoyed at himself. "It never got me into much trouble at home, because I couldn't figure out how to get past the cows' paddock in my sleep."

"One of the nuns who raised me used to sleepwalk," I share as I climb to my feet and then help Karston to his. "Don't worry, you can't die of embarrassment. But you should try to get some more rest." I point him toward the open door with a sympathetic smile. "You've got a lot of work ahead of you, from the sound of things."

"Can we get you anything before you go?" Meredy adds, carefully avoiding my gaze. "A glass of water?"

Karston shakes his head. "Thank you, but I'll be fine. I'm just lucky that out of all the doors in this place, I wound up at yours." Grimacing, he adds, "Jax would've been so pissed if I'd woken him up instead!"

XIX

The bed is cold in the morning, the sun too bright and intrusive, with Meredy no longer curled against my back.

Remembering the fight we had last night—a fight that would've gotten worse if Karston hadn't showed up—a wave of dread washes over me, anchoring me to the bed. I'd like nothing more than to hide in here all day, but I'm supposed to have another secret sparring session with Jax and some of the other volunteers. More importantly, I have to help Meredy. I doubt she'll willingly show me where the crystal is, but if I can somehow prove to her that it's fake, maybe I can convince her to destroy it herself.

The trouble is, I don't have any idea how to do that. But I know someone who might. Someone who always has an answer for everything: Valoria.

As I climb out of bed, something clatters against the wood floor, followed by a thump. Leaning over the side of the bed, I realize Nipper's trying to get something from underneath. The basket of food I'd planned to send to Elibeth by way of the guards tending to the sick. The dragon closes her teeth around the handle, picking up the basket, and I smile.

"Think you can deliver that for me, girl?" I ask hopefully.

Nipper chirps once, tugs open the unlocked door by wrapping her long tail around the handle, and bounds away.

I hurry out after her. If I'm quick enough, I should be able to get Valoria's advice on what to do to help Meredy before it's time to meet Jax, Freckles, and Sunshine for training.

Bryn and Sarika, I correct myself, pretty sure I've finally gotten their names right.

After rushing past the warmth of the already-bustling kitchen, I jog up a spiral staircase that leads into a long hallway full of windows, with a beautiful view of the palace gardens. I've gotten to know this path well, because at the end of the hallway is another staircase, this one even taller and twistier, leading to Valoria's private tower room.

As I near the steps, where a group of guards awaits—meaning Valoria is surely up there right now—I slow my pace. There's a familiar figure standing on the opposite side of the guards, lingering in the shadows like he's not quite sure how to approach them.

"Karston! Hey!" I wave him over.

He raises his head, giving me a hesitant smile but not coming any closer—and who could blame him, after last night's incident? I'd be beyond embarrassed if I stumbled into someone else's bedroom in my sleep.

Finally, he seems to decide I'm not about to tease him and strides past the guards to join me by the windows overlooking the garden. "I . . . I'm so sorry about last night," he says as he reaches me. "I hope I didn't interrupt—"

I throw my arms around him and pull him against me for a hug, shocking the rest of his words right out of him. "Honestly? I'm glad you did. Let's just say you saved me from saying a lot of things I would've regretted this morning. I owe you, big time."

He studies me with mild concern—and, perhaps, understanding—as we break apart. "Girl trouble?" he asks. Judging by his tone, he knows something about that.

"Girl trouble," I confirm, pressing my lips together in a firm line to keep from frowning when I think of the way Meredy and I went to bed after Karston left last night—with neither of us saying a word to the other, only curling up against each other for warmth at some point during the quietest hours of the morning. "That's why I'm here," I add, gesturing up the stairs that lead to Valoria's tower room. "For some advice. What about you?"

Karston scuffs the toe of his boot against the floor. "I . . . well . . ." Forcing his gaze up to meet mine, he confesses, "Girl trouble, too, believe it or not."

Having seen the way he looks at Noranna, I sure can.

"She tells Valoria everything," Karston continues, as if he's certain I already know who the *she* in question is. "I figure Her Majesty might have some advice for me on how to get Noranna to finally notice me. *Really* notice me, I mean. But it can wait. I still can't decide what I'm going to say, and your situation sounds more pressing, besides. You should go up there first." He gestures to the stairs.

"I haven't even told you what happened!" I say, shaking my head but smiling. "Thanks, though. I promise I won't take up too much of our queen's time. I'm in a hurry this morning. Oh, and Karston?"

He meets my eyes again as I turn back to him. "You can talk to me about your girl trouble, too. Not that I'm in any position to give advice, but . . ." I shrug. "I'm always happy to listen."

"You know, I just might take you up on that. Thanks, Odessa. It's too bad we can't be partners. You make me wish I'd turned out to be a necromancer after all." He gives me a smile so bright and unexpected that I can't help returning the gesture.

"You should have supper with us tonight," I call as I hurry on my way. "All of us. Me, Jax, Simeon, Danial, Meredy, Valoria . . . think about it, at least."

"I'll be there!" His voice follows me up the stairs.

Even though it's fairly early, I find Valoria already dressed for the day in a gown of rose gold, her hair pinned up in a braided crown and decorated with sprigs of dried lavender. Her head is bent over a piece of parchment on her workbench, but she quickly looks up as I enter.

"The flowers were Bryn's idea. She's always thinking of things like that," Valoria says when she notices my gaze traveling over her braids. She swipes at her cheek, leaving a smear of grease across her pale skin. "Now, what brings you up here this morning? Not that I'm complaining."

"Here." I pull a handkerchief from my cloak pocket and offer it to her so she can wipe her face clean. It's one that Meredy gave me, with colorful leaves sewn on the edges. As Valoria uses it, I feel something tighten in my chest.

"Oh, Sparrow . . ." Valoria frowns, her bright brown eyes telling her more than I could convey in a single sentence as they sweep over my face. "Tell me everything."

We sit together on a rug near the pile of wires and gears Valoria is always intending to sort through, and she takes my hands as she listens. I don't spare her any detail—not even the nasty things I said. Confessing them to anyone else, my face would be burning by now, but with Valoria I always feel safe to be honest.

"So your current theory is that this crystal takes a person's private thoughts and somehow plays them aloud to a room in the voices of dead loved ones?" she asks thoughtfully when I've finished. There's a darkness in her gaze as she adds, "I'd like to meet the person who invented such a thing and ask them what they were thinking, deliberately tampering with people's minds! They should be forbidden from ever using magic again."

I shake my head. "I don't know who invented it—I doubt it was the man who sold it to me, though." Gently gripping Valoria's forearm, I ask, "What should we do? I'm so worried about her. And not just her burns."

"Me too. But all we can do right now is try to find the crystal," Valoria says. "Once I have it, I can study it, see how it works, and hopefully come up with a cure for Meredy. She needs a clear head—we all do—if we're going to survive the challenges to come. There are so many dangers in Karthia now, and I'm afraid this unknown magic could—sort of like when you were taking the potions—"

"I know," I cut in as Valoria's lower lip trembles. "I'm afraid for her, too."

"While we're trying to find out where she's hidden the crystal, we can at least do something for her burns. Ask Danial for his orange salve. It really helped my leg—as much as anything could, anyway." Valoria gives me a weak smile, and when I return it, she seems to take heart and casts a quick glance at the parchment she was reading when I arrived. "I should get back to work now, but you'll come see me again soon, won't you? And let me know how Meredy's doing?"

Stepping up behind Valoria, I wrap my arms around her and assure her, "Not even a pack of hungry wolves could keep me from you, Majesty."

"Don't call me—" She whirls around to see my teasing look and relaxes. "Say, I have an idea. Why don't you and Meredy help me test out my air balloon some night soon? I'm going to ask Devran to come along as well, to show him how exciting some of my inventions can be, and on the slim chance he agrees . . . I know I shouldn't be alone with him." When I nod fervently at that last part, Valoria beams, taking it as agreement that I'll get in her balloon. "Maybe that'll take your mind off the crystal for a while—yours and Meredy's."

"I don't doubt it," I mutter dryly, thinking of how much I *don't* want to be off the ground in a basket held up by a canvas sail and a fickle flame. I especially don't want to go anywhere with a man I don't know, a man who's already caused so many problems for Valoria with his rebellion—even if he swears he and his people aren't the ones who've been trying to have her killed.

"Say—any more news from Empress Evaria?" I ask, as I now do every time I see Valoria. She shakes her head regretfully. At least Valoria has contacts willing to report on the Ezorans' activities, even if news travels slowly and sparsely.

As I head back down the stairs, visions of plummeting into the sea in a wicker basket have me so preoccupied that I don't notice Azelie striding urgently through the hall until we collide.

The protective eye goggles perched in her hair fall down over her eyes as we bump heads.

"Whoa!" I grab her shoulders to steady her. "Zee, what are you doing here?"

Azelie blinks, jarred from her own thoughts. The small army of several different herbs and plants following behind her like a herd of ducklings chasing after their mother all stop and fall over, no longer able to move without her magic guiding them. I spot a few of the spirit orchids she loves so much, cushioned by a leafy green I don't recognize.

"Oh. Hi, Odessa!" She gives me her usual warm smile, but there's a hint of exhaustion lingering beneath it—and something else, too, some emotion I can't quite place. She runs her hands over her earth-stained apron, trying to brush some of the dirt off it. "I'm just on my way to . . . I mean, I wish I could talk, but there's something I've got to—"

"Girl trouble?" I guess automatically. I don't even know if she likes girls, but after my chat with Karston earlier, it seems everyone has these problems lately.

Azelie shakes her head. "Er, no. There's something important I've got to do, but I can't say more just yet . . ." She falls silent, looking uncomfortable. Before I can reply, she adds, "I'll see you later, all right?"

"All right, but—is everything okay, Zee? You do like this place, don't you?" After all, if she doesn't, it's my responsibility to make it right. I brought her here.

She smiles broadly, and I'm immediately relieved, even before she exclaims, "Are you kidding? I'm going to have my own greenhouse soon! This place is *amazing*!"

"Have you had any word from Sarral?" I ask quickly, knowing she's in a hurry. "Valoria told you the Ezorans retreated from the border, right?"

"She did. I haven't heard anything myself, though I did send a letter to Uncle Halmar a few days ago." Grinning slightly, she adds, "I had a dream the other night that the Ezorans all drowned. Hopefully it'll come true!"

With that, she hurries down the hall toward Valoria's staircase, her plants following dutifully in her wake again.

Practice is already under way at the unofficial training grounds across from the deserted market by the time I show up. The dull clash of wooden swords and the occasional curse or excited shout fills the cool salt air, doing little in the way of keeping this meeting *secret*.

As I slog through the sea of waist-high golden grass that surrounds the practice area, I try to leave behind every troubling thought: the black fever, the rebellion and Valoria's many enemies, all the bad things that could happen to Meredy if she keeps using the crystal. I still don't know how I'm going to make things right between us, but hopefully sparring will help clear my head and give me an idea.

Jax is already here, practicing with Bryn and Sarika at the same time. I'm pleased to note that all three of them are wearing their scarves and gloves today. With a sword in each hand, Jax is working up a sweat blocking every one of their attacks. That is, until Sarika sneaks in a low jab and taps him on the thigh.

"That's a point for me!" She bounces on her heels, unable to contain her excitement.

Jax puts his wooden blade to her throat as she celebrates.

"What—?" she splutters, her eyes widening.

"If this were a real fight, I'd have all your points now, because you'd be dead," Jax says matter-of-factly. Then he winks. "Never let your guard down, even when you think you've got the upper hand."

Bryn notices me watching first and waves. Her long raven hair is tied back for practice, revealing the tips of her very pointed ears— catlike ears. I quickly avert my gaze, not wanting to be rude, but fascinated by what must be the price of her magic.

"Mind if I cut in?" I ask Jax, bumping his shoulder in greeting. He's so sweaty that his black shirt clings to him like a second skin. "Go get some water," I urge, gently pushing him away. "And lose the shirt. I can handle these two for a bit."

Gazing between Bryn and Sarika, I muster a grin before realizing they can't see it through my scarf. Still, they must sense it, because Sarika's eyes crinkle as though she's smiling back. Bryn, always more guarded, just nods and raises her sword.

A girl of few words. I like that.

"Let's go, Freckles," I call, issuing a challenge. She doesn't need to know I've stopped using her nickname in my head.

Bryn and I face each other and raise our swords. She gains a little ground on me, so I don't hold back with any of my swings. As we spar, Sarika watches from the sidelines, turning her hair from brown to blue and commenting on everything from the weather to shirtless Jax to the new metal soldiers.

"Who told you about them?" I pant, blocking a jab to my right side from Bryn.

She blocks one of my blows with such strength that my arm protests. "Noranna. She's really excited about what Karston can do with them," she says between rapid breaths. "Of course, it's no secret that he wishes she'd be excited about him for a different reason."

A shiver of amusement races through Sarika's voice as she adds, "I don't know why Noranna doesn't go for him. He's *cute*."

"He is," Bryn agrees, breathing harder as I hit her with a flurry of quick attacks. "But it's complicated." To my surprise—and hers, judging by her blink—she blocks most of them. After that, she lowers her sword, signaling the need for a break. "They've known each other since they were little, apparently. They came here together from the countryside and everything."

"Noranna just likes him as a friend, though," Sarika says, stepping up to take her turn with me. "But maybe her loss will be *my* gain." Still giggling, she raises her sword, but her stance is all wrong.

Motioning with my free hand to correct her, I keep lashing out with my blade, challenging her to block my blows. Talking to the two of them, even while sparring, is almost effortless. And kind of fun. I can see why Valoria likes them so much.

"What brought you two to Grenwyr City?" I ask as we all take a water break.

"Family stuff," Bryn answers, a slight edge to her voice.

"As in, we both left ours when we heard about Valoria wanting to meet mages with unusual abilities," Sarika adds, sounding wistful. "I was going to visit my parents soon, but they want me to stay put until the fever dies down."

"How about you?" I ask Bryn, passing her a waterskin. "Any plans to visit home?"

She shakes her head as she lifts her scarf to take a drink, her mouth forming a thin line, and I catch her eye to let her know she doesn't need to say more. I understand. For some of us, the family we choose seems to stick better than the family we were given.

Sarika breaks the slight note of tension in the air with a sudden chorus of "King for a Day," and everyone laughs.

Even me.

Jax strides toward us, his stomach muscles rippling with each step in the absence of his shirt, having just finished checking on the other sparring pairs. "I'd ask if you'd like a little one-on-one," he says, meeting my gaze and grinning slightly beneath his scarf so that his eyes gleam, "but it looks like you have other plans already."

He points across the field, to a familiar red-haired figure striding through the long grass.

I break into a run and meet her halfway.

Her hair is pinned in a braided crown on top of her head, much like Valoria's, and instead of her usual fur-lined tunic, she's wearing what looks like one of my old necromancer's uniforms for sparring clothes. Lysander lumbers in her wake, flattening the grass wherever he steps.

There are so many words fighting to leave my lips first that none of them manage to find their way out. I'm so scared for the brilliant girl running to meet me. I'm so sorry for shouting last night instead of trying to help her. I'm so angry—not at her, but at the crystal and whatever false promises it's made her.

I start to tell her about getting some of Danial's orange salve for her burns, but all it takes for her to render me momentarily speechless is a hesitant smile as she lifts a pale pink scarf away from her mouth. I can't quite bring myself to return the gesture.

"Training in a new secret spot, I see," she murmurs, arching her dark brows and letting the scarf fall back into place. "I take it Valoria doesn't know about this?" Before I can respond, she draws a deep breath and adds, "I'm sorry about last night. You were right to worry. That crystal could drive a person mad, but I got rid of it—threw it in the kitchen rubbish heap on my way here."

"You did?" I ask. "I mean—that's great, Meredy." It *is* great. So why don't I feel like sweeping her off her feet in celebration? "You promise it's really gone?" I watch her face fall as I say it, hating myself for every word. But I had to ask, to try to silence my nagging doubt.

"I just said it is. Don't you trust me, Odessa?" she counters, a frown in her voice.

"Of course," I answer, perhaps a little too loudly, trying to drown out the doubt once and for all. I'm still worried about her, but she doesn't need to know that. Besides, there are other things I need to say. "I'm sorry I compared you to Evander. That was wrong."

"And I shouldn't have said what I did about Firiel." Meredy bows her head.

"I shouldn't have shouted."

"I shouldn't have missed that delicious supper you made," she sighs. "Elibeth already sent me a raven to say that Nipper delivered it all safely. Thank you so much for looking after my sister even better than I am."

I nod, wishing I felt even cautiously hopeful that she was back to her old self. Instead, I have to stop myself from searching her face for signs that she's distracted, her thoughts still with the crystal. "Anytime."

She takes a long, guarded look at me, then gestures to the field where others are still sparring. "Shall we settle our remaining differences with some hand-to-hand combat?"

I hesitate. If I don't try to take her at her word and act like things are getting better, will I be giving her a fair chance to show me that they really are?

Finally, I pull her against me without a word in answer. I've never felt a longing this intense, not even with Evander, I realize now—I want to be as close as possible to her, the essence of her, not just her beautiful skin. It's like my spirit wants to grab hold of hers and never let go, but since that's impossible, I settle for tugging down our scarves and kissing her in front of all the volunteers.

Jax wolf-whistles.

Feeling slightly better than I would have expected upon waking this morning, I point to an open spot in the shorter grass. When we reach it, Meredy faces me and spreads her arms wide. "Ready when you are, *Master Necromancer*." She gives me a long look as the words leave her lips, like she's afraid a bit of teasing might damage our relationship even further. She doesn't seem to realize that it's not *us* I'm worried for—it's *her*. And right now, it seems like what she needs is me.

"Now you've done it." I mock-growl as I charge toward her, tackling her to the ground.

Just like that, she momentarily banishes every worry to the

darkest corners of my mind. As we spar—or what passes for sparring when no one is landing any blows—we both glance up at the sound of Lysander's roar.

He leaps out of the grass nearby, colliding in midair with a large dappled cat. Bryn, in her animal form.

"Think we can spar like that?" Meredy teases as she pins down one of my wrists.

Using my foot as leverage, I flip her off of me, knocking the wind out of her. That only makes her laugh, once she has the breath. "Oh," I whisper, pushing down another stab of worry, "I think we can do better."

XX

The Ezorans are getting closer.

We learn as much on a gray day the following week, when Valoria receives a message from another leader, King Andris, delivered by one of her own mechanical birds. The Ezorans are attacking the king's home, Bravinia, a land located slightly east of Empress Evaria's domain of Ocren and north of Lyris. Valoria shows me each place on a moldy old map she found in the Temple of Change, and I don't need to ask why she looks worried to the point of sickness.

Unnerved, Valoria assigns several people to assist Noranna in making more metal soldiers. With help, she's able to complete several new ones each day, and Karston spends his time learning how to command them to do different moves at once.

I watch him practice once or twice, impressed by the strength of his gift and his focus and dedication to his magic as the soldiers march and fight with deadly precision.

Each night, whenever we can, we all gather at the palace for supper—me, Meredy, Valoria, Jax, Simeon, Danial, and Karston, who fits in effortlessly from the first time he decides to eat with us. Like Meredy, he loves animals. Like me, he finds himself drawn to anyone attractive, regardless of gender. Like Jax, he can be surly and withdrawn. Like Simeon, he loves to tell outlandish stories. He could never replace Evander, of course, but our group feels almost whole again. Especially after one of Valoria's aunts, upon seeing Jax with potatoes in his hair and Karston and me dueling with breadsticks, sharply declares that we have the manners of a pack of wolves and are unfit to dine with our queen.

"To the wolf pack!" I shout as the noblewoman retreats, raising my glass of mead.

Grinning, Simeon adds, "We'll eat your heart out—literally!"

Jax and Karston chime in with a chorus of howls. Danial, shaking his head at them, lends his voice to the cause a moment later after Simeon elbows him in the ribs.

Bryn and Sarika, sitting at the opposite end of the table, catch on and join in, too. At last, so does Meredy, followed by Valoria, who raises her wolf-headed cane with a laugh.

This is the most at home I've felt since we returned from Sarral. Though for how long, I don't know. Not when the Ezorans are inching ever closer to Karthia and, despite what Devran promised, there's no end to the protests in sight. Valoria still isn't sure he'll accept her invitation to an air balloon ride tomorrow at sunset.

Reports of the black fever continue to arrive every morning by raven, though Meredy's sister, Elibeth, like Kasmira, seems to be making a tenuous recovery. We wrap ourselves in scarves and gloves to bring food and other supplies to them both, as well as other fever-afflicted families, helping Jax with his meal delivery routes. That is, when we're not training the volunteers or helping Simeon and Danial with wedding preparations.

We're needed so often lately, in so many places, that I only get one chance to sift through the kitchen rubbish heap for the crystal Meredy claims to have thrown away. I don't find it. I help heal her hands with Danial's orange salve and don't notice any new burns. Still, a cruel voice in the back of my mind won't stop wondering if she's lying to me whenever she has an errand to run.

Valoria's searches for the crystal prove equally pointless—not that she has much time to look, either. Carts of supplies intended for the sick, particularly those carrying the new, stronger cough potion Valoria invented herself, keep being waylaid on their route or completely overturned. Guards attempting to clear the streets of bodies find themselves surrounded by people who won't let them do their job until they put on the older, less secure masks that King Wylding had them wear during fever seasons past. The culprits? Devran's rebels. They may not be able to burn anything else on the palace lawn during the quarantine, but they're still giving Valoria plenty of headaches as she tries to care for them. They pass around their own version of a coughing potion, an older, less effective one, and seem to believe they're actually *helping* the sick more than Valoria could.

Thoughts of the dangers we face from inside and out trouble me every night, but I'm so exhausted that I somehow manage to fall asleep almost the moment my head hits the pillow.

"Dessa." Meredy's voice drifts through the blackness of my dreamless sleep. "Do you hear that?" She gently shakes my shoulder.

Now alert, I realize what's bothering her before I even open my eyes to the darkened bedroom. The mysterious wailing is back, the sound I heard the night of our argument.

"It's giving me a headache!" Meredy whispers sharply. "What is it?"

"I don't know, but I've heard it once before," I murmur. "When we . . . you know . . ."

She crinkles her nose, reluctant as I am to mention our fight. "I must've been pretty out of it not to notice," she says at last—the closest she's come to mentioning the crystal in days. I try to take her hand, but she hesitates, as she usually does now when we're not wearing gloves. She thinks I don't trust her, that I check her palms for burns when she's sleeping.

She's not wrong.

"You're a girl of many talents," I joke, but only half-heartedly, trying to stay focused on the eerie sound. It's almost like when someone wets their finger and runs it along the rim of a wine glass. But it can't be that, because it has a distinct and varied melody despite its ear-bleeding qualities.

"Well, it's definitely not *human*," Meredy says after a while, rubbing her temples. The noise hurts my head, too. "What could it be, though? One of Valoria's inventions?"

I shake my head. Valoria would have noticed and silenced it by now. Plus, it sounds too close to be issuing all the way from her tower.

"What about some sort of bird?" she suggests next. "A peacock being strangled?"

"Maybe," I mutter, not quite convinced.

Meredy leans against me and yawns. "Maybe it's Jax, rehearsing in secret so he can serenade Valoria," she suggests, making us both laugh.

From down the hall comes a crash, a curse, and the sound of hurried footsteps.

I exchange a look with Meredy, then leap out of bed and pull on my cloak and slippers as Meredy does the same.

Sword in hand, I lead the way down the hall, tiptoeing past the kitchen.

"Sparrow!" someone hisses. "Over here!"

I turn to find Jax standing in the kitchen doorway, his dark hair messy from sleep, though his eyes are bright and alert. He motions Meredy and me forward, into the kitchen itself, where he's lit a candle. Ten of Noranna's metal soldiers stand in various positions around the room. There's one with its hands on a large stove and another posed as though peering into a pantry. Shivering, I notice that one of them has its hands placed on either side of a knife block where the butcher keeps some of his smaller tools. The soldier nearest us is in a heap on the floor, making me think this is the one that made the crash we heard.

Not yet lowering my blade, I whisper, "What in Death's name is going on?"

Jax points to the soldier on the floor and, as I expected, whispers, "I tripped over this bastard on my way to get a snack. All the training's been making me extra hungry. Who put these in here?"

He looks ready to hit someone, while I'd like nothing more than to run out of the room.

"Karston could've done it," I say slowly, thinking aloud. "But only if he's awake, right? I've never heard of anyone using their magic in their sleep, and it is awfully late."

"It could be someone's idea of a joke," Jax suggests. "I can name five people who would find this entertaining and have the strength to move these things without any magic. Of course, none of them live at the palace, so . . ." He frowns at the soldiers again. "All I know is, when we find whoever did this, I'm going to have a chat with them that they'll find absolutely hilarious. At least, *I* will."

I shake my head at him as he makes a fist and slaps his other hand against it.

"Well, we should go find Karston, anyway," Meredy says thoughtfully. "Even if he had nothing to do with this, he can move the soldiers back to their proper place a lot faster than the three of us."

As we linger in the doorway, talking in low voices about who within the palace would have the strength and sense of humor to pull off this prank, Jax moves deeper into the kitchen. The soldiers creak as he moves one behind another, bending them both over the stove in a back-to-front position that leaves no room for questions as to what they're up to.

"Jax?" Meredy asks warily. "What in the world are you doing?"

"Making them look less creepy," he grumbles, arranging three more figures in a curious position I wouldn't have imagined.

I shake my head. I don't think anything could make the soldiers look less eerie, short of covering up their eye holes. "Come on." I take Meredy's hand, pulling her away from the door, and Jax follows a moment later. "Let's go see Karston."

We hurry toward his room, leaving a scene worthy of *The Baroness's Secret Heartache* in our wake.

Despite Jax banging on his door, it takes Karston a long moment to get up and undo the lock. His violet eyes are half-closed, as if sleep hasn't quite shaken its hold on him. He clearly hasn't been sleepwalking tonight, or using his magic.

As I hastily explain what happened, confusion and surprise twist Karston's smooth, even features. "What? Someone moved our soldiers? They're pretty heavy . . . that would've taken someone the better part of the evening, carrying them without magic. Why bother?"

"To scare one of the cooks, or someone else who frequents the kitchens, I expect," Jax growls.

"And they wound up scaring you instead," Karston says, catching on. He looks slightly more awake with each passing moment. "I can see how they wouldn't be fun to run into in the dark. Are you all right?"

Jax frowns hard, leaning in toward Karston until they're close enough to kiss. "I don't get scared. Of anything. Ever. And don't you forget it."

"Sure." Karston's lips twitch as he fights to keep from smiling. "Understood."

My shoulders shake a little with the effort of not laughing outwardly at the pair of them. "Listen, Karston, would you mind coming with us to the kitchens and moving the soldiers back where they belong? You'd be saving us a lot of time."

"Of course," he agrees, pulling on his boots.

"Thank you. And, Karston—you're doing an amazing job with them," I say, giving him what I hope is an encouraging smile. "Seeing as you've been working so hard, you should really take tomorrow off. Valoria won't mind. We have somewhere to be with her anyway, and she'll need all her focus on making sure our little adventure goes well—in fact, you should join us. If you dare."

Meredy meets my gaze and grins. Unlike me, she's not dreading the ride in the air balloon. The twisted girl I adore so much is actually looking forward to it.

And judging by the grin Karston gives Meredy as she describes what we're planning to do, she's not the only one excited about hovering Vaia only knows how high off the ground in a flimsy basket, possibly accompanied by a man who rebels against change.

We talk in whispers about our plans to meet with Valoria the next day at sunset as we all head back to the kitchen, Jax in the lead and not paying attention to anything we're saying. Meredy and I get so caught up in talking about Valoria's inventions that neither of us remembers to breathe a word of warning to him about the soldiers' curious positions, courtesy of Jax.

His laughter spreads swiftly among us when he sees them, first catching on to Meredy, then me, and finally a reluctant Jax, until we're all doubled over gasping for breath.

I decide I like the prankster, or at least the soldiers. Eerie as they look, they're certainly good for something besides fighting. For making Meredy laugh, for making Karston look less exhausted and Jax less surly, I could practically kiss a metal cheek in thanks. That is, until I remember what awaits me tomorrow: the dreaded air balloon.

XXI

"That's it, Odessa," Valoria says soothingly as I put one foot into the air balloon's basket the next day. "Come on. Now the other one."

"You can do this," Karston urges, extending a hand to me.

"I'll give you a kiss if you hurry up," Meredy offers, clearly afraid we're going to be standing on the beach until well after dawn at the rate I'm going—and it's not yet suppertime.

Devran yawns from inside the basket, looking bored, and turns away from me to gaze out over the crashing waves. I'm surprised he showed up. Valoria really didn't think he would, yet by the time we dragged the bulky basket-and-balloon combination onto the beach, he was there waiting. I narrow my eyes at him. From the back, with his generous height and choppy blond hair, he reminds me too much of Hadrien.

"I just don't understand why we have to do this so close to the water," I grumble, knowing I sound like a child as I reluctantly tug my other foot out of the beach's warm sand and put it, along with the rest of myself, into the huge basket.

Karston thumps me on the back and cheers.

"I feel like an apple waiting to be taken to market in this thing," I sigh, now trapped inside the narrow confines of a basket that so resembles a farmer's fruit-selling one. I glare at Devran, daring him to make fun of me for being afraid, but he keeps his gaze trained on the sky, watching the sun drip down a canvas of red and pink threaded with amber.

Meredy grins and pulls me closer to give me that promised kiss, taking my attention away from Devran, while Valoria—beaming at our display of affection—asks with a snicker, "And are you a sweet or sour apple?"

"Oh, she's sweet enough, trust me." Meredy laughs as she draws back slightly to watch Valoria light the flame. She must be able to feel me shaking from head to toe, because she keeps a protective arm around my shoulders.

"So, how is this supposed to work?" Karston asks eagerly, gazing upward into the colorful canvas balloon over our heads.

"I was wondering the same thing," Devran remarks. There's a dryness to his voice, as if he's bored to tears, but a slight twitch at the corner of his mouth betrays the real reason he'll barely look at any of us: He's scared, too.

Unable to keep from smirking slightly, I try to listen as Valoria explains how the flame will cause the basket's canvas top to inflate and carry us upward, and how she'll control it. But when we begin to hover above the sand, I get too nervous to focus on a word of her scientific ramblings.

"I know you hate not being in control of everything for once,"

Valoria says near my ear a moment later. "But you trust me, don't you?"

"If anyone else said that to me, they'd be sailing out of this basket about now," I answer sweetly, casting a glance at Devran. I hope I haven't given him any ideas about tossing any of us out once we're high in the air.

Grinning, Valoria tells me, "You're in good shape if you're making jokes already." Gazing between me and Meredy, she adds with a gleam in her eyes, "Let's take flight."

As we begin to climb slowly, gently toward the few clouds in the watercolor sky, I realize I've left my stomach somewhere on the ground. I swallow hard to keep from being sick, but once Meredy guides me to sit on the narrow floor of the basket and put my head between my legs, I feel a little better.

For his part, Devran stands motionless, his back to us, silent as the water below even as Valoria leans in to speak to him. My shoulders tense. He could try to push her out of the basket when she's that close. I don't know that he would, but that's the problem—I don't know him. Valoria, seemingly oblivious to our sudden worry on her behalf, continues to chat away to him as the rest of us watch closely, ready to react at a moment's notice.

She babbles away about some of her other inventions as Devran nods stiffly. She's too fixed on tonight's mission of getting him to find something positive in the new and unexpected to actually read his body language, but I'm not. I don't think he's buying a word she's saying.

Our balloon climbs higher still, making my world feel so unsteady that I give up on watching Devran like a hawk. I don't know how much time passes before Valoria says, "Odessa . . . you've got to see this. Please. If you can."

"Come on. This is incredible," Karston says, flashing me a reassuring smile. Excitement shines in his dark eyes, which look more brown than violet in the shadows cast by the sinking sun. Tipping his head back, he does his best wolf howl.

"You and Jax would be the best of friends if you'd realize how much alike you are," I mutter, more to myself than Karston.

"What was that?" he asks.

"Nothing," I say, grinning guiltily.

"All right. That's enough stalling." Meredy locks eyes with me and smiles. "You really shouldn't miss this—if you're up for it, of course." She and Valoria both offer me a hand, while Karston steadies me with a hand on one of my elbows. Carefully, with no small amount of shivering, I stand and grip the basket's edge.

We're floating high above a flat, glassy sea. It's like a mirror to the sky, reflecting each and every swirl of color, and it makes my breath catch in my throat.

Meredy, who by now is attuned to even the slightest change in my breathing, whispers just for me to hear, "That's how I feel every time I see you."

I don't know how I got so lucky, or what she sees in me, but I'm sure that I need to stop worrying so much.

With effort, I pry the fingers of one hand from the basket in order to put an arm around Meredy's waist. Meredy pulls Valoria away from Devran and into our embrace, I pull Karston against my other side, and together, the four of us take in Karthia as we've never seen it before: the sun-washed cliffs, huge and jagged, and the marble palace sparkling like a red jewel, like a crown for the hill it tops.

Giddy beyond reason, beyond remembering that we don't want to draw too much attention to our adventure, we all start howling at the sky. Up here, floating above the world like no one ever has, we're untouchable. Invincible.

Up here, with fire reflected in her eyes and warm light threaded through her hair, Meredy steals another piece of my heart with a simple gesture—pulling me back from the edge of the basket, into her embrace, the moment I start to shiver. I just hope my trust isn't misplaced. That by leaning into her, I'm not letting her steer us—and more importantly, her health—into disaster.

"Devran?" Valoria breaks away from us at last to touch his arm.

Stiffly, he turns to her, his expression stony.

"Well?" she prompts, spreading her arms to indicate the stunning scenery. "What do you think?"

He takes a deep breath. "It's incredible. Forgive my not saying so until now, but I've been too busy trying to get my body to catch up with my brain and stop craving solid ground."

I think the poor man just wants to sit down until his knees quit shaking, but Valoria has a certain spark in her eyes now: She's encouraged. "Imagine what we could do with more of these! Imagine not being bound by the limits of what ground a horse can cover in a day! Imagine no seasickness. I mean . . ." She leans closer, peering up at him through her glasses. "You have to admit, this is pretty fun."

Devran shakes his head, and I tense. Once again, he's too close to Valoria.

"I don't know about fun," he says at last. "But fascinating."

"It could change people's lives," she adds proudly. "And *not* for the worse."

"Perhaps," he says slowly, finally yielding to the desire to sit in the cramped bottom of the basket, "you could."

Valoria's cheeks glow pink as she hands us her spyglass to pass around. It's not one of her inventions, but one she made from an old book she found at the school.

Devran clears his throat. "I've been thinking about what you proposed, and I'd like to offer this—if you'll allow us to elect ten citizens to your council, one for each noble, and hold off on bringing any more inventions into the city"—he pauses, warily eyeing the flickering flame that powers the air balloon—"until our council members have been installed, we'll cease all protests. What do you say? Of course, we expect you to start raising the Dead again, too." He extends a hand.

Valoria's face is a mask, revealing nothing of her thoughts as she gazes at Devran's outstretched hand.

He sighs and finally drops his hand, apparently sensing that Valoria isn't about to budge on that issue. "Don't you have someone you miss, too? The palace used to be twice as full!"

"They're always with me," Valoria says firmly.

Devran lapses into silence.

After that, Valoria turns her attention to guiding us along Grenwyr's coast as Meredy, Karston, and I comment on the sights. Even the Ashes look beautiful from up here, somehow softened by the dying light, the old buildings there made new from our incredible viewing spot. When it's my turn again, I look along a path that brings me out of the Ashes and through Market Square, taking in the shadows of trees and the glow of fires—like tiny embers from here—flickering in the homes of those who must be busy preparing supper.

"So, what do you think, Sparrow?" Valoria asks as I twist the spyglass. "*This*," she adds, spreading her arms to encompass the balloon and the view, "is the future I want to give our people. If they want to fly, I want the wings—or rather, basket—to be there for them."

"It's certainly not your worst invention," I grudgingly admit. She asks me something else, but I'm distracted by what I see through the glass—what starts as a small fire, growing bigger by the moment. A fire coming from the Temple of Change.

The school is ablaze.

The flames dance and multiply in the reflection of Valoria's glasses as her eyes widen and all the warmth and excitement of our ride drains from her face. She seems to be fighting back tears, perhaps unwilling to cry or shout in front of her esteemed guest.

Unlike her, I don't care about niceties.

"Did your people do this?" I demand of Devran, rounding on him.

He stares through the spyglass, his lips a thin line. "Honestly, I don't know. If they did, it wasn't on my orders."

"Yeah?" Karston asks, crossing his arms. "We'll see soon enough."

It seems to take an agonizingly long time for Valoria to steer the air balloon over the temple. Before we've even reached a landing spot, though, we see that the fire isn't coming from the building itself, but from the gardens behind it. Still, it'll reach the school soon if we don't act quickly.

Mouth dry, heart racing, I'm half-tempted to jump the rest of the way to the ground so I can help the students, Simeon, and Jax as they rush to throw buckets of water on the flames. It seems no one among them is a weather mage.

But I've got Devran to worry about, so I stay put. After exchanging a glance with Karston, I keep my gaze trained on the rebel leader as our basket finally touches down, ready to tackle Devran to the ground. If he really did plan this, and he's about to do something stupid to make the situation worse, Karston and I will be on him like a Shade on raw meat.

As we leap from the basket, someone cries out. I follow the sound to a large old tree, one that must have been weakened before the fire.

The way it's leaning, it's going to fall any moment—right on top of the school.

Before I can think of what to do—before we've done more than start to run toward our friends, Devran on our heels—the tree groans, pulling itself upright. It crumbles in on itself as the flames eat away at its core, sparks flying in every direction, but it doesn't hit anything.

"Good job, Zee!" I call. I don't see her amidst the chaos of leaping flames and people running in all directions, but I know she's there. No one else could have made that tree move away after it had started falling. She's even better at moving things with her magic than Karston—but then, she's been practicing longer.

"It was nothing," she answers wearily from somewhere to my right.

As I start passing buckets of water with the others, Devran to my right and Meredy on my left, I hear Azelie sob, "My poor garden." I toss water onto the blaze as fast as I can, wishing I could do something more to ease the pain I know will grip her when night descends on a fragrant, unruly garden turned to ash.

Karston, who seems to be thinking along the same lines, whispers, "I'll go see how I can help her," before hurrying off in the direction of Azelie's voice.

"I'm going to find and kill whoever did this," I growl as the flames begin to die down.

"Not if I get there first," Devran snaps from beside me in the water line. He shakes his head, his eyes on Valoria. "Burning a statue on the palace lawn to get your attention is one thing, but setting a fire meant to burn a bunch of students alive? And for what, exploring the magic that exists inside us all? That's different. Darker. My people didn't do this, but I wish I knew who did. All I know is that there are always those who will kill to get their way, and they clearly don't realize the consequences. Without a Wylding on the throne, we'd drift even further from the Karthia we love."

"Down with the queen!" someone shouts over Valoria's reply to Devran, well out of view and out of reach. "Death to change!" Their words are followed by whoops and rough laughter.

"Cowards!" I shout back, only to be answered with silence and the hiss of water putting out more of the blaze.

"I just don't know what to do," Valoria sighs, wiping sweat from her brow. Passing another bucket of water down the chain we've formed, she adds, "I can't go down Hadrien's path. I don't want to hurt my own people. But if I can't end these attacks . . ."

She swallows, unable to finish, and I nudge her with my shoulder to let her know she doesn't have to.

"Are you all right?" Devran asks tersely, frowning as Valoria's complexion turns paler despite the heat. "Majesty?"

That last word alone is enough to startle Valoria back to the present. "Yes, I—I'm sorry. I was just thinking about how we're going to handle this new threat," she whispers, looking stricken.

It's more than that, though: She hasn't told Devran about the Ezorans' movements, at least not to my knowledge, but I understand her dilemma. Should she focus all her attention on her people—their welfare and happiness? Or on the outside forces that could draw nearer at any time to destroy everything and everyone here, regardless of what they stand for? Because if her attention is split, something is bound to slip through the cracks.

Valoria seems to have opened Devran's mind tonight—that remains to be seen—but somewhere out there is a group of people desperate enough to attack more than just their queen. We'll have even more death on our hands if someone doesn't find and stop them soon. Looks like I have a long night ahead of me.

* * *

My body aches from lack of sleep when Meredy kisses me awake in the morning.

"What are you doing?" I groan, sitting up and glancing across the room at Lysander and Nipper, both still asleep. They've got the right idea. We didn't get back from the temple until well after midnight, meaning we've only had a few hours' rest, but the whole building survived with minimal damage to the wall nearest the garden. There was plenty for the healers to mend, with many burns sustained and one bad case of smoke inhalation, but everyone survived. Everyone, that is, but Azelie's plants.

I made a long, pointless search for the arsonists, following broken branches and other evidence of their path away from the school, before I lost their trail near a creek and was forced to return to the palace angry and empty-handed.

"Getting you up and dressed." Meredy tosses a shirt at me, then a pair of trousers. "I've been awake for hours already, thanks to our mystery singer, so I figured we might as well deliver some more food parcels to the sick—they still need our help, no matter the danger."

"You realize I don't feel nearly as charitable as you before breakfast, right?" Pulling my usual black shirt over my head muffles the words. The arsonists yesterday didn't care if a bunch of students died, which means they probably wouldn't hesitate to kill the queen's friends if we were recognized outside the palace. But Meredy is right. The sick are counting on us for food and supplies.

She prods me until I'm awake enough to slip on my gloves and scarf. "Come on! We can eat breakfast while we walk."

On our way through the palace, we bump into Valoria. She has a notebook in one hand and a cup of tea in the other, and looks as if she never went to bed. "Morning, you two," she says absently, scrutinizing a page of scribbles in her notebook. Then, as if just realizing who she's talking to, she tucks the notebook under her arm and pushes her glasses up. "Where are you going? You won't be gone long, will you?" she asks, looking between us.

"We'll be back in a few hours, if you need us. We're just off to deliver more food," Meredy says, holding up some wrapped parcels and frowning. "Why? Did something else happen?"

A flush creeps into Valoria's cheeks as she says, "After yesterday's attack, the council thinks it's time I show everyone that I'm made of stronger stuff than anyone believes. This afternoon, they want me to show all the nobles living here—in *my* family's palace—that I have an army at my command to keep them safe." She seems pleased, though privately I don't know how a bunch of nobles will react to the creepy, eyeless suits of armor. They take a bit of getting used to. "Once I've given them a little demonstration, I'll be off to meet with Devran again first thing. If we could just get past our disagreement about the Dead, we'd really be getting somewhere." She sighs. "Besides, the only way to deter new attacks is by making our people feel heard and understood— and by searching for those responsible for yesterday's fire."

"You need us to search some more—?" I begin, ready to temporarily abandon our food delivery for this even more pressing issue.

"No. Thank you, though," Valoria says wearily, though her voice is warm with gratitude. "Devran and a few of his people are assisting my guards in an attempt to find the culprits as we speak, so that's something. If the search goes well, the Shade-baiters in the dungeons will have new company tonight."

We're interrupted for a moment as Azelie passes by, but she doesn't stop to chat. There are fewer plants trailing her this time, and she looks exhausted, though that's no wonder after the fire last night.

"Speaking of the soldiers, are they still coming along well?" I ask Valoria, scrutinizing her for signs that she's working herself too hard, using too much of her inventor's magic. "Did you ever find the prankster who put them all in the kitchen the other night?"

"The soldiers are coming along splendidly, but I haven't had time to look into the prank in the kitchen, I'm afraid." Valoria holds up her free hand, revealing grease-blackened fingertips. To my relief, I don't notice any gaps in her memory, no slurring of her words or a vacant stare, all signs that would mean she's pushing her magic too far. "When I'm not writing letters or in meetings with the council and the guards, I've been helping Noranna and the others with construction while Karston rehearses with them. Did you know we've made over a hundred already?"

Meredy and I exchange surprised glances. That's more than I thought. Way more. Of course, given how the Ezorans have been moving through kingdoms lately, I'm hardly surprised she'd want to hurry production.

"Just make sure you don't work Karston and Noranna too hard," I say carefully, not wanting to discourage the tenuous hope Valoria is placing in this metal army.

"Never," she assures me, her eyes widening with sincerity. "I'll just need Karston to work his magic for a little while this afternoon, when I call all the noble families to see their new protectors on display," she adds, looking from me to Meredy with a tired smile. "Will you return in time for the demonstration, then?"

After agreeing, we wrap our faces with our scarves and set off for the palace stables, bound for the aviary outside Grenwyr where those afflicted who live farther from the city have been going to pick up food and other supplies.

Once we cross through a dense section of forest and guide our horses up a gradual slope, I spot our destination at the top of the next hill: a massive structure made entirely of glass, big enough to rival the ever-expanding palace, bursting with plants and flowers that press against its sides like they're longing for escape. Lilting music wafts toward us, beckoning us closer to Grenwyr Aviary.

A few hundred yards from the glass building, there's a large canvas tent set up, its cloth siding dyed a bright red to make it unmissable. There, two guards outfitted in Valoria's latest anti-sickness masks wait to collect donations of food and other supplies that they'll later redistribute to those in need.

"Elibeth showed me this place years ago," Meredy says as we make our horses comfortable in the aviary stable and deposit our heavy parcels with the guards. "Since the horses need a break anyway, suppose we should take a peek inside?"

I nod. With the mysterious group of arsonists still loose in the city, no doubt already plotting their next move, who knows when I'll have another moment like this with Meredy? She grins like she's sucking on something sweet as we walk arm in arm toward the aviary doors. "Speaking of Elibeth . . . Kasmira heard my sister is slowly recovering, too, and she's volunteered to bring her supper tonight." Her grin widening, she adds, "For the third time this week."

I shake my head, imagining Kasmira being mobbed by Elibeth's overexcited greyhounds upon arriving at the Crowthers' manor house with any kind of food in hand. But before I can say that I hope there's something there, between two people I've known for so long, we step inside the aviary and the heady mix of hundreds of flowers steals my breath. The scent is a welcome relief from the sour smells of death permeating the city.

We're so enchanted that we remove our scarves and gloves, wanting to let this place fully engage our senses.

Overhead, birds flit from tree to flower to the small ponds scattered throughout the building, flashing feathers of every color in their wings and tails. On the path, birds like peacocks and even a fancy rooster strut past our feet as if they know they're something special to look at. Given the recent fever outbreak keeping everyone indoors, they must not have had many visitors lately. The only people I see moving between the plants are the aviary attendants themselves, green-eyed beast masters like Meredy.

"You probably want to put your hood up," Meredy says, drawing the hood of her own cloak over her neatly braided hair. She wipes a smear of something white from her shoulder to demonstrate her meaning, and I follow suit at once, laughing under my breath.

"So now what?" I ask her.

She grabs both my hands. Her bare palms are cool and smooth against mine, with no hint of roughness or warmth that would let me know she's been using the crystal again. I rub my callused thumbs across her perfectly healed skin and, for the first time in a while, let myself imagine what our future could hold.

"Now we listen," she whispers. She arches a brow as I keep rubbing my thumbs over the soft skin of her hands, but I can't seem to stop, I'm so relieved. Shaking her head at my behavior, all she says is "Maybe we'll hear our mystery singer!"

"Maybe," I agree, pulling her closer without hesitation.

But I forget what we're supposed to be listening for as we stand there among the birds and flowers. When we're bound like this, I don't know where she ends and I begin. And while it's usually impossible not to think of the fever, of the unrest in the city, of how I miss my old job, all those troubles feel as distant as someone else's nightmare, trapped outside the aviary's glass walls. Not even memories of Evander seem able to reach me in here, in this other world I've entered with Meredy, and, strangely, I don't mind. I don't want to know anything but her touch, her laughter, the spark when her eyes meet mine. Whatever the future brings, however many days I have left, I know I want to spend them all with her.

I know this thing rising up inside me, almost impossible for my skin to contain. This is love. I know it because I've loved before, and I remember how it felt, though this isn't quite the same. The soaring feeling I get when I'm around Meredy is familiar and different all at once. It's sudden and swift and deep as the endless sea. And I want to be swept away.

XXII

M eredy and I are among the last to arrive for the demonstration. I want to tell her how I feel, but the moment doesn't seem right, not when we're racing against time to be there for Valoria.

As we return our horses to the stable and hurry to the farthest garden, where Valoria asked us to meet her, I wonder if Devran and the guards caught any of the arsonists, and whether Karston will be pleased or embarrassed by the attention his unusual gift is sure to bring from all the nobles. I just hope it's the right kind of attention, the praising kind, and not the same fear we've seen from unhappy Karthians so far.

A small crowd of finely dressed nobles are gathered in a semicircle around Valoria and five of the metal soldiers. It's good to see that she's not overwhelming them with the full set.

Karston stands before the crowd, his uniform crisp and pressed, his posture the relaxed stance of someone who has the world at their fingertips and knows just what to do with it. He must be waiting for Valoria's signal to make the soldiers move.

Spotting Jax, Simeon, Azelie, and Noranna near the front of the crowd, as close to Karston as they could manage to get, I elbow my way through a cloud of perfume and silks, making space for myself and Meredy to join our friends. When Valoria spots us coming through, her eyes light up. She must have already given a speech about them, because there's a whisper winding its way among the crowd that buzzes with anticipation.

Seeming to take new strength from our arrival, Valoria faces the soldiers and spreads her arms as though embracing them and the crowd together. "For more than two hundred years, Karthia has shut out the world. But not anymore," she says in the ringing voice I remember her using in the throne room when we returned. "Rejoining the world will mean new discoveries. New friends. But it also means new dangers, and as such, we need to have an army ready to defend our beloved shores. *This* is what awaits anyone who dares to challenge us!"

She drops her arms, which is apparently Karston's signal. The soldiers turn, forming a single-file line, and bang their spears against the ground before performing some impressive twirling and marching stunts with them.

Just like he has been every time I've seen him practice, Karston looks alert, not the least bit worn down from using his magic so often. He's in total control of the soldiers, their every movement coinciding with every bend of his fingers and turn of his wrist.

His gift is so strong—his power so impressive. He must pay a terrible price, though I haven't seen a sign of it yet.

The whispers of the crowd intensify. Someone stumbles over my toes as they take a hurried step back, a woman wearing boots instead of the usual silk slippers. I wince. Noranna, seeing my distress, offers me her arm for support. Unlike Valoria, she doesn't smile when she sees her soldiers. Her brown eyes are thoughtful as she watches them clash spears in midair during a leap. Perhaps she's regretting them not being used for their original purpose—really creepy butlers. I think I'd prefer them without their spears.

Finally, after each making a bow to Valoria, Karston has the metal creations resume their original positions, standing in a neat row facing the crowd.

As Valoria begins another speech, Karston looks around until he finds me, Noranna, and the others and starts to make his way over. His part of the show is apparently finished, and his relief is only evident when he wipes a layer of sweat from his brow with the back of his hand.

"I'll take questions now," Valoria says, catching my attention as she skims her gaze over the crowd and points to a young duchess. "Yes?"

"Why do they have those horrible eyes?" the duchess asks, eliciting giggles from a few of her friends. "Why bother giving them faces at all?"

Valoria frowns. Before she can answer, however, Noranna pipes up from beside me. "Because I wanted them to look friendly rather than faceless!" Her eyes blaze with a typical Karthian temper as she glances in the duchess's direction. "What, should I have stuck some roses on them for you?"

The duchess and her friends have a lot to say about that, and Karston has a lot to say about them insulting Noranna's creations. Valoria tries to restore order, but a telltale creaking sound draws her gaze, and mine, away from the bickering nobles.

One of the metal soldiers, the one closest to Valoria, now has its spear angled forward in an attack position. It definitely wasn't like that when I saw it moments ago.

I shift my gaze back to Karston as he growls a colorful name for the duchess, and toss him a wink in approval. She deserved that one.

Valoria gasps. I turn in time to see the soldier with the pointed spear fall forward onto her, bringing her swiftly to the ground.

She manages to dodge the spear, at least. The soldier's hand glances off the side of her neck, likely not giving her more than a scratch, though her face is tight with pain as she tries to lift the heavy iron body off of her own.

Karston gives an anguished cry. Several nobles scream, too, a sound like angry geese. Of course, that might be in part because Jax and I push several of them out of our way in our haste to reach Valoria in the first moments after the collision.

"I'm getting Danial," Simeon announces over the clamor of creaking metal.

Nearby, Karston raises his hands, using his gift to move the heavy iron figure off of Valoria as tears roll down his face.

Breathless, Jax and I kneel beside Valoria amidst the unhelpful flappings of the nobles, trying to assess her condition.

"Hurry!" I call after Simeon.

The spear didn't miss Valoria after all. A long gash in the side of her neck is bleeding heavily, like a red mouth yawning against her pale skin. The stiff white collar of her new inventor's jacket is already stained a gory mix of black and crimson. Valoria breathes rapidly, but she seems to be aware of her surroundings. At least, she winces when Jax climbs to his feet and starts kicking the fallen metal soldier over and over.

Trying to shield Valoria from the stares of the crowd with my cloak, I lean over and squeeze her hand. My mouth goes dry in the tense moments that I wait for her to squeeze back. If she does, it's only faintly, or I'm shaking too much to notice.

"How . . . bad . . . ?" she coughs.

"You'll be fine," I say firmly, while inside I'm screaming. "I've survived worse." It's true, but only because my friends got me to Danial before I bled out.

Valoria has to be fine. There could be no replacing my best friend. And for Karthia, there could be no replacing the queen they've tried so hard to reject. No doubt people would be even more restless with her twelve-year-old brother, next in line to the throne, guiding Karthia into an uncertain future.

"Let me see her," Danial says tersely, dropping to his knees beside me. Exhaling at last, I back up slightly to let the master healer work, but continue using my cloak to hide Valoria from all the prying eyes.

As I try to rein in my galloping heart, Karston catches my gaze as he attempts to peer around my cloak.

"Is she going to live?" he asks hoarsely.

"Karston, what happened? Did you—?" I begin hesitantly, trying to keep the accusation from my voice.

"Of course not! I'd *never* make that soldier—" He breaks off, scrubbing a hand over his face and breathing hard like he's going to be sick. "Odessa, you saw me. My hands weren't even raised. I was talking to Duchess Aventine, and—"

"I know," I say through gritted teeth, desperate to placate him. "I *know* you didn't do it. But right now, we need to let Danial work in peace."

I try not to let my doubt show on my face as Karston bites back a bitter curse, his hands balled into fists at his sides. I don't know who exactly he wants to punch. Perhaps, given the way his shoulders hunch inward, the person he wants to beat bloody is himself.

Still, I have to wonder: If he wasn't trying to kill Valoria—and it doesn't seem that way—could this attack be related to the cost of using his magic? Or perhaps this is a strange effect of Azelie's animation magic. After all, those soldiers can't move on their own.

Yet, who's to say there wasn't someone else in the crowd today who knows how to magically move things? Someone from the city who wants Valoria dead, perhaps? Guilt needles me as I realize that should've been my first thought, not accusing my friends.

"Jax," Valoria murmurs a few times before going oddly still.

"Right here." Jax hastily abandons his beating of the metal soldier and drops to the ground beside Danial. He grabs Valoria's limp hand, cradling it like he's afraid that if he holds on too tightly, he'll shatter her.

Danial, ignoring him, lightly touches the wound on Valoria's neck as lines of concentration crease his brow.

I turn away, unable to watch any more. I've seen someone I love die before, and I don't think I'll ever shake the nightmares.

The soldier Jax was kicking is just a few feet away. I frown at the metal figure, replaying the moment it attacked over in my mind, but it's hard to remember details with a nervous crowd surrounding me. It's hard to think at all when I don't know yet if I'll have my best friend an hour from now.

I'm startled from my thoughts when Danial collapses in Simeon's arms. His body is in the grip of the temporary paralysis that always follows a difficult healing.

Forgetting the crowd, I drop my cloak and anxiously study Danial, then Valoria. There's still blood everywhere, but no wound gapes on her neck, and her eyes have their shine back. Jax helps Valoria to sit up while Meredy collects her crown and blood-spattered glasses. After polishing both on the edge of her cloak as best she can, she returns them to the queen.

I sink down to my knees and throw my arms around Valoria,

knocking her crown askew. After taking a close look at our friend, as if to assure herself Valoria isn't about to collapse again, Meredy joins the embrace. I'm reminded of the picture Valoria drew of us once, before she had any idea she'd ever be queen.

"You really scared me," I murmur into my friend's blond hair.

"I'm sorry," she whispers in reply. A bit of color reappears in her cheeks. "Did you happen to watch the healing process?" she asks, drawing back to look between me and Meredy. When we both shake our heads, she frowns. "Really? Neither of you? I was hoping someone could describe it for me."

It's so typical of Valoria that in another time, in another place, I'd laugh. But the metal soldiers are still on my mind, and Valoria's blood is soaking into my shirt from where I hugged her, making laughter impossible. Even Karston gazes distrustfully at the fallen metal soldier, his shoulders hunched, his body tensed with the pain of invisible wounds.

A sob makes me look toward the edge of the garden just in time to see Noranna's brown curls disappearing as she bolts away from the palace.

Azelie hurries after, her face unreadable.

After helping Valoria to her feet, my gaze returns once again to the soldiers. That night in the kitchen, they seemed almost comical, but there's nothing funny about them now.

"Lock them up," Danial says to the attending palace guards, those made of flesh and bone, nodding at the metal soldiers. "Put them in the empty dungeon and chain them to the floor. They're to be kept under lock and key, the doors always guarded, until further notice."

"Will you help me over there?" Valoria asks Meredy and me in a low voice, nodding subtly toward the horrified crowd. "I've got to show them I'm all right, or they'll never trust me."

"Damage control," Meredy murmurs sympathetically. "Right."

We try our best to make it look like Valoria is walking unassisted toward the nobles, like we're just worried friends sticking close to her side when really, we're helping to keep her upright. Her voice is calm and commanding as she reassures everyone that she's going to be just fine, and that there are clearly flaws in the soldiers' design. She's apologetic and somehow still authoritative—that is, until the crowd finally disperses.

That's when she wilts and leans on us as much as she can to stay upright.

"Help me get her to the garden?" I ask Meredy, who nods at once. As we march deeper into the garden, away from the few lingering nobles and the servants already scrubbing blood off the flagstones, I call over my shoulder, "Jax. Karston. Simeon. Danial. Group meeting, *now*!"

Karston doesn't seem to hear me like the others. He stumbles toward a row of bushes closer to the palace walls, looking like he's going to be sick. Can't say I blame him.

When the rest of us are far enough away from the crowd that the sigh of the sea drowns out the babble of distant voices, I find a bench where Valoria can stretch out and recover from almost dying. Danial, whose limbs are still painfully stiff, joins Valoria on the bench while everyone else sits beside me on a bed of ivy.

"We need to talk about what happened with those soldiers," I say in a low voice—just in case. "Could there be something wrong—some flaw in their design?"

"It's possible," Valoria says at last, rubbing a flake of dried blood off her cheek. "I got so swept up in their potential—you know how I am—but the truth is, we need a real, operational army that doesn't rely on magic. It's too risky. We can and will keep training our human volunteers. That's a promise. In fact, once the fever dies down, the council and I have a plan to bolster our recruitment efforts. I can't share it yet, but it's a good one. I should know." She allows herself a small smile. "I helped think of it, along with Danial. Today's display with the soldiers was really intended to placate the nobles closest to my family, nothing more—though they failed spectacularly at even that."

"So you have a plan. Good," Jax says, carefully avoiding my gaze. I'm sure he's thinking of the plan we've put in place, continuing to train the volunteers. "What about the soldiers you've already built, though?" He frowns. "If we don't dismantle them, what's to keep them from trying to hurt you again?"

"They're just objects. From my understanding, they can't do anything without a mage to move them," Simeon cuts in, looking unusually grim. "What we should do next is make a list of everyone we know who has a magical gift that causes things to move. If we stop the mage, we stop any chance of this happening again."

"We can add their names to the list of people Valoria has her guards investigating for the fire at the school," Meredy adds thoughtfully. "Maybe we'll find a connection between the arsonists and today's attack."

"Good thinking," I say softly, directing the best smile I can manage in Meredy's direction. She answers me with a softening of her gaze, a blink of affection. Louder, I add, "It's going to be a long list, though, when it could be any number of people. A rogue mage, even, like Vane. We might have stopped a lot of deaths if we'd known about him and his power sooner. That's why I think we need to take action now, too—with our swords, not a quill."

"Still, a list is worth trying," Danial says softly, weary from the earlier healing. "Now, as for the soldiers themselves—I say we burn them. The metal can be used again, but since we have a plan to build a real army, they aren't needed."

"Very well," Valoria agrees after some thought. "I'll make a list of potential enemies at today's demonstration and check them against those being investigated for the fire. And as soon as we can, Noranna and I will take a few of the soldiers apart to see if there's a flaw in their design. Just in case they can be salvaged. If we don't find anything, I'll make arrangements to have them melted down." As I expected, she makes no mention of taking a night off to rest after her brush with death.

"You really think any further tinkering with these murderous piles of junk is safe?" Jax asks, frowning at Valoria. "Let me be there when you do it, at least."

"Why? Because I can't take care of myself?" Valoria's eyes narrow. Combined with her crimson-stained jacket, the effect is chilling, but Jax doesn't shrink back from her as she leans in until they're nose-to-nose. "You forget, Jax of Lorness, I'm not a damsel. I'm not even your equal. I'm your *leader*, and it's my job to protect *you*—" She takes a deep breath, drawing back from him to gaze at each of us in turn. "All of you. It's my job to protect all of you, and that's what I'm going to do now."

With that, she rises from the bench and strides toward the palace without looking back. I watch her go, reluctant to take my eyes off her after coming so close to losing her yet again.

"I'll make sure she gets some rest before going anywhere near the dungeons," Meredy declares, getting to her feet and offering Danial a hand. "Come on, I'll take you back to your room on my way. You need rest more than anything."

Leaning heavily on Meredy's shoulders for support, Danial limps off, leaving me, Jax, and Simeon alone.

"I have another theory," I say quickly, before the others decide to go their separate ways, too. "About the soldiers."

It's an idea so wild that Danial, Meredy, and Valoria, in their various well-intentioned trappings of practicality, would have rolled their eyes if they'd heard it. But my fellow necromancers, the two boys sitting on either side of me, have never laughed at even my wildest thoughts before. I suppose this will be a test of our friendship.

Glancing between them, I get the words out quickly before I lose my nerve. "What if the reason we didn't see a rogue mage working their magic on the soldiers at the demonstration is because that mage wasn't there in the flesh?"

Simeon arches a brow. "You mean . . . a mage who can use their power from a great distance? I guess it's possible. Many things are possible—the students at the temple remind me of that every day."

I shake my head. "I mean . . . I know it's a long shot—the longest—but what if a spirit from the Deadlands was loose in our world?"

"The Dead never came back with their powers when we raised them, though," Jax says gruffly. He crosses his arms, looking confused, but not dismissive.

"I'm not talking about one of the Dead. I'm talking about a spirit who hasn't been brought back by a necromancer. What if a spirit left the Deadlands on their own and came back here to seek revenge on Valoria for banishing them from their cozy life in Karthia?"

"You mean, the spirit of one of the Dead she had us take back after the battle?" Simeon asks, frowning. "They all seemed at peace with leaving on the night we said goodbye."

"But that doesn't mean they were okay with it after they had some time to think it over," I argue. "Valoria made that decision pretty quickly after the battle. And last time I was in the Deadlands"—I pause, exchanging a look with Jax—"the spirits seemed to be avoiding us. Except for the one who looked frozen, like she'd been turned into a statue."

My fellow necromancers are quiet, neither looking directly at me.

Face burning, I mutter, "Forget it." I must sound ridiculous. "It's not a practical theory, I was just thinking of how many enemies Valoria must have among the spirits. There's Hadrien, for one, but there's bound to be a host of others. Think of how many of his supporters we buried, and how many we locked up—some of them must have relatives in the Deadlands."

I turn away from my friends, toward the cliffs. In the distance, at the point where the garden ends and a cliff overlooking the sea begins, there's a faint blue haze that won't begin to really glow until nightfall. Looking at it, I can't help but worry about what's been happening in the Deadlands since my last trip there.

"I think we should go," Simeon says at last.

"Sparrow, I don't know if what you're suggesting is even possible, but there's no better way to find out than asking the spirits themselves," Jax agrees.

"Wait here, then," I tell them, pointing toward the distant gate. "I just have to get Nipper, and then we're going on a little trip." I start to walk away, but turn back to add, "And nobody breathes a word of this to Valoria, in case it turns out to be for nothing. Deal?"

While our queen searches for answers her way, making lists and picking at gears, I'm going to seek them the only way *I* know how, even if it's all for nothing. I'm going to probe the darkness of the Deadlands on the chance that something sinister might step into the light.

XXIII

The weight of my necromancer's belt is like an old friend's embrace, comforting and familiar. When I went to fetch Nipper, I couldn't help putting it on. I even took a few extra moments to visit the kitchen and refill the glass vials of milk, honey, and blood that are supposed to accompany me to the Deadlands, and knowing they're by my side makes me stand a little taller. I have my armor back.

"Looking good, Master Necromancer," someone calls as I hurry down the hall, giving a soft, musical whistle. Meredy. We exchange a smile as I head outside.

With Nipper straining against her lead, I'm about to leap into the faint blue light of the gate after Jax and Simeon when movement out of the corner of my eye makes me pause. I turn back toward the palace, shielding my eyes against the dying sun.

It's Azelie, standing near the edge of the gardens with a long pair of shears in hand, taking some clippings from the rows of herbs. "Be careful in there!" she calls after us, frowning uncertainly at the gate.

"We will," I answer, wincing at how loud my voice sounds as it carries across the otherwise empty grounds. "And Zee . . ." I give her my best pleading face. "If she asks, tell Valoria we're just taking a peek in one of the cemeteries. Please?"

When she nods, I turn back to the gate and shift my focus to the task at hand.

Simeon and Jax are waiting for me on the other side of the gate, in a dank and dim tunnel. "Nice belt," Jax tells me as we make our way down the long, dark path that eventually opens into the Deadlands.

"But where's your pin?" Simeon asks, touching the sapphires above his heart.

I shrug. It still didn't feel right to put it on even though I chose to wear my belt. That pin stands for something. It makes what we're doing here seem too official, when really, we're just breaking the law.

Pulling my cloak tighter around my shoulders—the chill in this world seeps all the way into my marrow—I guide Nipper through a pale, luminous garden, careful to keep both hands on her lead this time.

Jax makes Simeon walk in the middle of our procession, slightly behind me, but ahead of himself. He keeps his sword drawn, guarding Simeon's back with a muttered, "Don't try anything stupid down here. You're going to be a married man soon."

Usually, Simeon would punch Jax and have a joking response at the ready, but today he just nods and sticks close behind me and the dragon.

"Look," Simeon gasps a little while later, pointing to something in the distance. "Some friendly faces we can ask. You'll do the talking, right, Sparrow?"

Up ahead, many spirits flit like butterflies around the garden's edges, their toes just skimming the grass. We try approaching some of them, but any time we come within reach, the spirits scatter like minnows darting away from a child's careless foot in a lake. I don't like it. The spirits know us. They usually don't avoid us unless they're hiding from something else—like a Shade. But when I came here last time, looking for Jax, they gave me this same strange treatment.

Even spilling a little blood from the vial on my belt doesn't bring any of the spirits a single step closer to us, and it's usually irresistible.

By the time we've crossed the garden, looking for a friendly spirit, the scenery beyond its hedges has changed from a star-flecked mountain range to a dense forest of pines. It's one of the things that still amazes me here—how the Deadlands never rests, constantly fitting its pieces together in new ways like a patchwork quilt that, no matter how it changes, always makes sense when it's done.

"Shall we?" I ask my companions, gesturing to a yawning black gap between two pines where I sense movement.

"Looks dangerous," Jax mutters, raising his sword and grinning. "Why not?"

Simeon looks less thrilled, but follows close behind me as we step into the deeper darkness. "There had better be a talkative spirit waiting on the other side of this murder forest," he grumbles resentfully, pushing a branch out of his face.

Once our eyes have adjusted, we can at least see the shadows of tree trunks to avoid bumping into them, though it's strange being deprived of both smell *and* most of my sight. It reminds me of how Lyda left me for dead here, bleeding and blinded. Suddenly freezing, I wish I could reach for Simeon's hands, but I can't let go of Nipper's lead for even a moment after what happened last time.

As if to confirm my worst suspicions, Nipper barks, a sharp sound almost as high-pitched as the wailing Meredy and I have been hearing at night—though without the beautiful melody to accompany the ear pain.

"I really want a dragon of my own now," Simeon remarks. "Think your friends in Sarral would send me—?"

He stops talking as I'm thrown forward onto my knees. Nipper bounds through the trees, barking again, and this time I decide to let go of the lead rather than being dragged over fallen branches and probably getting some new scars.

Jax and Simeon help me to my feet, and we take off running after her through the dark, silent forest that looks and smells like nothing from our world.

Cold air stings my nose and eyes as I chase after the sound of Nipper's lead rustling among a bed of dry pine needles on the forest floor. My lungs and throat are burning by the time the dragon leads us to a break in the trees, to a glen where spirits sit on either side of a small stream, but I don't stop until my eyes are back on my dragon. I can't lose her. She's one of the best things about Karthia changing.

Nipper coos at me and charges toward the stream where a few spirits are standing knee-deep, letting the current wash over them.

As we make our noisy arrival, a shadow darker than the trees themselves flees into the blackness of the forest on the other side of the glen. It looks vaguely human.

"Did you see that?" I gasp.

Jax shakes his head but takes a step toward the spot where I'm pointing. Simeon grabs his shirt, holding him back before he can break into a run.

"Could be a Shade. You're so not going after it," Simeon declares, staring disbelievingly at Jax. "We'll just keep an eye out from here, where we can actually see what's creeping up on us, all right?"

Jax and I both nod as I finally grab Nipper's lead.

"Sorry if we startled you, by the way," I tell the spirits, pleased to finally find some that aren't running away from us on sight. Spirits might not be able to speak, but there's nothing wrong with their hearing, so it's strange when none of them turn to acknowledge me.

Simeon pokes the nearest spirit in the shoulder. It's a young boy, the dark stains around his mouth suggesting he died from the black fever.

Nothing happens. The boy doesn't run away or even blink. I don't think he can.

Gazing around at the ten or so spirits gathered here, I don't think any of them can move. They're frozen, just like the one I found before. Even the ones standing in the stream, already stripped of most of their memories, usually sway slightly with the current. But now, they stand as rigid as the metal soldiers.

"This is just like what I saw last time," I whisper. I don't know why, but whispering feels like the thing to do here. Gooseflesh runs along my arms, and it isn't from the cold. Whatever this is, I don't like it. I don't even understand it.

Jax starts pacing, scowling at nothing, as Simeon and I sink to our knees on the stream bank between a few of the spirits.

"Did Master Cymbre ever teach you about anything like this?" Simeon asks, gesturing to the immobile spirits.

I shake my head. "I take it Master Nicanor didn't, either."

"Maybe something is wrong with the Deadlands itself," Simeon muses in an unsteady voice. "Maybe now that we're not raising the dead—"

"Something is off balance here?" I jump in, warming to the idea. It makes sense. Nothing has felt right here since I came with Karston, searching for Jax. And Master Cymbre was always talking about balance between the living world and the spirit one. "I think you're right. Maybe this could've been avoided if there were still necromancers coming to the Deadlands regularly."

"We should be doing that anyway," Jax cuts in. "The spirits here may not be welcome in our world anymore, but we owe it to our loved ones to keep them safe in their own world by coming down here sometimes, making sure all is well in their new lives."

Simeon and I nod our agreement, and after a moment I ask, "But how do we fix this now, short of performing a bunch of raisings to see if anything changes?"

"I don't think there's anything we can do," Simeon says after studying the frozen spirits for a while.

Nipper rubs her head against my legs and coos as if agreeing with him.

"Agreed. Unless . . ." Jax stands taller, gripping his blade with more confidence. "I think we should talk to Valoria, whenever she has time. Tell her what's going on down here and see if she and her council will give permission for necromancers to at least start patrolling the Deadlands more often."

I don't know how Valoria's council will react when presented with our disturbing findings, but there's one thing I'm sure of as we pick our way deeper into the dark heart of the forest: Necromancers are still needed, even if we're not raising the dead. I'm still needed. Me, the Sparrow. Valoria will understand. She'll help us make this right.

We can't turn our backs on the spirit world any longer.

"What was that?" Simeon yelps, interrupting my thoughts. I see him pointing to his left, but this forest is the kind of dark that makes a torch just give up.

It's only when we emerge from the trees altogether, into a small valley split by a fast-moving river, that I see her: Firiel, dipping her toes into the rapid, icy current.

Her death wound, the arrow that used to pierce her middle, has vanished. She looks much as she must have in life, only paler, but a hint of her brown hair can be seen when the clouds overhead roll back to reveal the moon. There's a certain peace in her eyes, too, as she watches us approach, without a hint of surprise or any other emotion.

She bears all the signs of a spirit ready to move on to whatever mysterious place awaits them after the Deadlands. The place where, if it really does exist, Evander might be. I still don't understand how Master Cymbre, when she was alive, was always so sure of what comes after we're gone.

"Firiel," I say quickly, reaching out a hand. My fingers close over the icy coldness of her forearm. "Stay with us a moment. We won't keep you long, I promise."

Jax holds out his vial of blood, fresh as mine, in offering.

Firiel shakes her head but takes a step back from the stream bank and faces us to show she's listening.

"I'm a friend of Meredy's," I say by way of introduction, hoping to stir up a memory. I study Firiel's face for signs of recognition, but it's clear she doesn't know who I am, or even who Meredy is anymore. The absence of connection to everything she was, everything she loved, chills me worse than thoughts of anything Valoria's worst enemies might be planning next.

She clearly hasn't been talking to Meredy through a crystal, or in any other way. I hope that crystal is at the bottom of the ocean right now, where it can't trouble anyone's mind ever again.

"We came to ask you something strange," Jax prompts, reminding me of our purpose. "But we hope you'll hear us out."

"Most of the spirits here are avoiding us—are they angry?" I jump in, watching her hopefully for signs that she understands.

Her face remains blank, but finally, she reaches for the vial of blood Jax offered earlier. He hands it over, and she drinks every drop, licking the glass clean. Simeon offers up his vial, too, and she drains that one as well while we repeat our question a few times.

Slowly, her brows knit together and a gleam of understanding enters her soft eyes. She nods, seemingly in answer to our question, then lowers the second vial and points to something at our backs.

I whirl around, half expecting to see a Shade looming behind me, but we're alone on this mountain except for the trees and the moon.

Turning back to Firiel, taking a deep breath to keep my patience, I press on with my questions. "Have any spirits left the Deadlands recently? Is that even possible?"

Again, she points toward something behind us. As I exchange a glance with Jax and Simeon, who seem as lost as I am, Firiel strides forward, beckoning for us to follow. We only have to walk a little ways along the border of the dark forest, making our way up a tree-covered hill with Nipper following at Firiel's heels, before we see what she wanted to show us: a gate at the bottom of the hill, opposite the side that we climbed.

"This is getting ridiculous," Jax grumbles. "She doesn't understand anything."

But Firiel, crossing her arms and bristling at his words, points again toward the gate.

A trickle of cold slides down my spine. "So there *is* a spirit in our world—in Karthia?" When Firiel nods, I demand, "Who is it?"

Firiel shrugs, looking apologetic.

"How is that even possible—a spirit in our world without a body?" Jax cuts in. "Do you know if they want to hurt Valoria?"

Poor Firiel shakes her head, unable to answer him.

"You were right, sister," Simeon says softly to me. He's still processing things, and I understand—it's a lot to take in. "Got any other incredible theories you want to run past us?"

As I shake my head, Jax mutters, "At least part of this makes sense. I can see how a spirit newer than Firiel would still be drawn to our world. Bet a lot of them are wondering what's been happening without King Wylding around."

"But how are we going to find this wandering spirit?" Simeon asks worriedly. "Or send them back here without running a sword through some decaying body?"

Jax and I exchange a glance. Neither of us has an answer, so I refocus my attention on Firiel. I have one last question for her.

"Do you know why some of the spirits here can't move?" I stand still as a statue for a moment myself, but that only causes Firiel to blink politely.

She's told us all she knows. I start to thank her for the help she was able to give us, but she's already slipping away, back toward the river. There seems to be no resisting the pull of the world after the Deadlands, not once someone has lingered here long enough. Even the blood wasn't enough to tempt her back to life, toward warmth and light and laughter. "Tell Evander I say hello, if you find him," I call after Firiel, a familiar lump forming in my throat despite all the thoughts racing through my mind. Then I start down the hillside toward the gate with Simeon and Nipper beside me, and Jax slightly ahead.

With my wild suspicion confirmed, it's time to head home. Time to remind the dead and the living where each belongs.

We barely get in a few steps, picking our way carefully through the trees, before a shrill cry splits the Deadlands' still air. I know that sound. "Shade," I mouth to Simeon. One so close that its hunting call reverberates painfully in my ears and makes my shoulders tense in anticipation of a fight.

The three of us draw our swords.

I scan the dark border of the forest to our right, ready to give Nipper the command to use her fire breath the moment the monster bursts from between the trees.

Something silver bounds through the shadows alongside us, making my every muscle tense, but it looks more like a spirit than a Shade.

The Shade howls again.

Nipper growls and tenses, flicking her tail.

The silvery creature darts past us toward the forest's edge, and I get a close enough look to see that it's Firiel.

As she crashes into the forest, her movements becoming harder to track with each passing moment, the Shade's cries diminish. She's drawing the monster away from us, giving us time to get safely into the tunnel that will take us home.

We were chosen for this job because we had no loved ones in the Deadlands. We were taught that it was dangerous to feel something, anything for a spirit here, because our hearts could trap us here forever. But after what we just witnessed, I think somehow, a long time ago, some other necromancer got things wrong. I'm grateful for my friends here, but not even Firiel's selflessness is enough to make me want to stay a moment longer than necessary. Not when there are people who need me back in our world.

Not when a spirit with a score to settle might be lurking unseen within the palace.

XXIV

We emerge in our world not by the cliffs near the palace gardens where we started, but in the sunlit graveyard behind Noble Park, maybe two miles away. Time can move inexplicably in the Deadlands, and though we left at sunset and were gone for what felt like only a few hours, it appears to be bright and early the next morning.

Wrapping my arms around myself to stave off a chill, I take in the sights. This is the best graveyard in the city, the only one with a sea view. It's also the graveyard full of headstones that now bear many familiar names: Cymbre. Evander. Even Hadrien. In some cases, we had no body, so all we buried were memories.

The last time I came here, patrolling for Shade-baiters, the grass grew thickly, as if the headstones and the memories they hold rarely had visitors. Which is probably true. The grass still looks healthy, growing unchecked, only now flowers decorate the green everywhere we step.

Simeon plucks one from beside a white marble headstone and

cradles it in his palm. The yellow pheasant's eye in his hand, a type of buttercup, is a symbol of bitterness.

I spot a few more just like it, scattered throughout the headstones, but they're far outnumbered by the tiny bright pink blossoms dotting almost every grave. "Oleanders," I announce when the others struggle to come up with the name. These flowers aren't in season right now, yet they look as fresh as if they'd opened their petals yesterday. There's no reason the colorful blossoms would be growing here unless they came from the spirits of those buried beneath them, now residing in the Deadlands.

Meredy would know what the oleanders stood for right away— she's got a good memory for flowers, as Lyda always liked them. But since Meredy isn't here, I search my mind until I find the oleanders' meaning. And when I do, I'm more uneasy than I was in the Deadlands, being stalked by a Shade.

I draw Nipper closer to me, unable to stop her from nibbling on the blossoms.

Beware, the oleanders warn as I look around.

With so many of them surrounding us, they seem to shout it.

But what good is their warning when they don't tell us how to fight an enemy we can't name or see?

As we stride down a sunny but deserted street on our way back to the palace, we argue over what to tell Valoria, if anything.

"Why add to her troubles until we see this spirit ourselves and have proof there's something to this?" Jax asks, the words muffled slightly by the cloth he's wrapped over his mouth to protect against the fever. "Firiel could still have been mistaken, and even if she wasn't, the soldiers are locked up and about to be melted down for scraps. The spirit can't use them to hurt her again."

"I'm worried about other ways they might try," I insist. "And the flowers were proof enough to me that something's up."

"I don't know . . . I'm with Jax on this one, Sparrow." Simeon shakes his head. "Once Valoria makes peace with her people, *then* we can tell her what we saw today and ask her permission to start visiting the Deadlands regularly again. But she's got enough to handle at the moment as is, and she's already constantly under guard."

I can't argue with that. As we come within sight of the palace, we go our separate ways—Jax and Simeon to the temple, and Nipper and me to the palace to find Meredy. She'll definitely appreciate hearing what we learned in the Deadlands.

Approaching the door to our room, I hear voices issuing from the gap beneath it. No—make that just one voice, though it changes its tone every time it speaks. Sometimes, it sounds like Meredy, and sometimes, it sounds higher than her usual voice.

Quieting my breath, I put my ear to the door and listen until the words become clear.

"Firi, why can't you just tell me where you are? I could come to you. Wouldn't you rather talk face-to-face?" Meredy pleads. "No one has to know. Odessa doesn't even realize we're still talking—that orange salve she gave me works wonders. My burns are completely healed, see?"

Reeling, I lean against the wall beside the door, feeling like I've just been punched. Meredy hasn't stopped using the crystal after all. Just when I thought she was doing better, when things were finally normal between us again, whatever normal means—it turns out she was lying to me this whole time. My stomach twists as I force myself to keep breathing, to keep listening.

"We've been over this," Meredy sighs in a high voice so unlike her own.

I shudder as a mix of revulsion and shame course through me. Apparently the crystal relies on the user's own voice and tricks the mind into thinking that someone else is speaking by drawing from memories. That explains why neither of us realized how it worked before—we were using it at the same time, both being fooled by its illusion.

"I can't tell you," Meredy continues in an imitation of Firiel's voice, drawing my attention once more. "I'm sorry. Isn't talking like this enough? Aren't *I* enough?"

"No," she answers as herself. "Firi, you know how I feel about Odessa, but I still love you, too. Come back to me. Please!"

How she feels about me? My heartbeat quickens for the briefest moment before the longing in her voice, longing for someone else, brings tears to my eyes. I'm scared for her. Scared of what will happen if I don't help her break the crystal's sway—and soon.

There's no denying that she betrayed me and lied to me repeatedly, but I'd still do anything to help Meredy. I'll pull her back from the brink of this madness even if she's unwilling, even if our relationship doesn't survive it. Just like she would—like she already has done—for me.

Her safety comes first.

Turning away from the door, unable to listen any longer, I rub my temples and try to think. How can I prove to Meredy that it isn't really connecting her to anyone? She certainly won't take my word for it, or it would be long gone by now. What I really need is some way to capture voices and then hear them aloud. If she could listen to herself imitating Firiel, she would surely come back to her senses.

But where would I find such a strange thing? Something that doesn't yet exist?

Keep talking, I silently plead to Meredy as I run half the length of the palace to Valoria's room, stopping only to get permission to sprint past the blockade of guards set up around the base of the tower stairs.

By the time I reach her, my breathing is ragged, and I drip sweat on her clean-swept floor. She doesn't seem to care, though.

Taking one look at my stricken face, Valoria drops the tangle of wires in her hands and demands, "What's wrong? Is it—Meredy? The crystal?"

I nod. I don't want to waste time explaining how the magic in the crystal works, so instead I blurt, "I need something that captures voices. Something that lets you hear words after they've been said. Do you . . . ?"

I let my voice trail away as Valoria's eyes light up with the fierce pride of an inventor.

"You need my recorder. One moment." She grabs a stool and moves toward a high shelf piled with junk. I recognize some of the objects as former mechanical bird designs as I hover beside Valoria, ready to catch her if she falls.

At last, she hops down from the stool with a clunky black box about the size of my head tucked under her arm. She points to a few buttons, explaining how to use them to capture voices and then replay them.

"I've only tested it with my sisters once or twice, and it's been a while, but it should work." She frowns as I take the recorder from her. "Odessa, I know you're in a hurry, but can you just tell me if she's in any immediate danger?"

"I don't think so."

"But she's not all right?" Valoria twists her clasped hands, smearing grease across the skirt of her gown.

"She will be," I say firmly, a promise to Meredy and Valoria both.

I give the buttons on the recorder another glance. "This is just what I needed. Thank you."

By the time I return to our room, recorder still in hand, there's no way to disguise the fact that I'm panting from all the running. I just have to hope Meredy is still too involved in her conversation with "Firiel" to notice.

I push the biggest black button on the side of the box like Valoria showed me, and quietly as I can manage, I shove it against the bottom of the door and put my fingers in my ears. I can't stand the thought of hearing her tell someone else—the idea of someone else—that she loves them again. Especially not when I was about to speak those same words to her at the aviary.

Precious time slips away as the babble of voices from Meredy's room continues. My leg cramps up, forcing me to stand and stretch instead of kneeling beside the box. A guard passes by on some urgent errand, boots tapping against the floor.

At last, the voices stop. I pound on the door, and at first, no one answers.

Then Meredy clears her throat and says brightly, "Come in, Odessa!"

As I open the door and step inside, followed by Nipper, I ask, "How'd you know—?"

"I recognized your knock, of course," Meredy grins at me from the bed where she sits, the crystal tucked away somewhere out of sight. "What happened in the Deadlands?" she asks, patting the space beside her in invitation, as if she hadn't just told someone else she loved them. When I don't say anything or make a move to join her, she points to the recorder in my hands and gives me a questioning look. "Did you find that box in the spirit world? It looks like something of Valoria's."

"It is," I say, hating the way my mouth goes dry and sudden tears prick my eyes. I have a bad feeling about what's going to happen when I turn the recorder on, but I have to do it. Nothing matters more than Meredy's sanity. I take a deep breath and release it shakily. "You're going to hate me, but you need to hear this."

My stomach writhes as I set the box on the table and fiddle with one of the knobs, hoping I'm doing exactly what Valoria showed me.

As Meredy's voice crackles from the box, thick with static, the real Meredy asks quietly, "You've been spying on me? Eavesdropping with this—this *thing*?" She rubs her temples, looking as ill as I feel. No, not ill—furious, angrier than I've ever seen her. "I'm not a child. I don't need you looking over my shoulder. I make my own choices and mistakes—and clearly, trusting you was one of them."

The venom in her words sinks into me, making me sicker, but I have to keep fighting the crystal's influence if there's any chance of bringing her back to her senses.

"Death be damned, Meredy, would you just *listen*? Firiel isn't in some rock! She's in the Deadlands. I saw her there the time I came to rescue you from those Shade-baiters—those rogue necromancers. And I saw her again last night, with Jax and Simeon. She doesn't even remember her own name." I can barely bring myself to look at her as tears splash my cheeks.

"You're jealous, and a liar." Eyes flashing, Meredy leaps off our bed and grabs a bag, hastily filling it with her things. Lysander, sensing her agitation, shakes himself fully awake and crosses the small room to nuzzle her flushed cheek.

"You know whose voice I hear in that recorder?" I force myself to ask over the sounds of Meredy imitating Firiel as the conversation continues to replay. "Yours, and no one else's. It's all in your head, Meredy. And when Evander was in my head, remember what you did? You tied me down, and you let me curse at you and be completely horrible until I could see clearly again."

"Shut up." Meredy's voice is quiet but still somehow harsh. "Just shut up. I don't trust you anymore, not after this, and since you clearly don't trust me"—she pauses, gesturing angrily at the recorder—"we clearly have nothing left to say to each other. It's over, Odessa. *We're over.*"

It's hard to speak around the lump in my throat, hard to do anything at all when she's in the midst of walking out. This is exactly what I was afraid of, but if there's any chance that hearing this recording could save her, even if she hates me as a result, having Meredy back to herself will have been worth the pain.

She starts toward the door, her overstuffed bag in hand, followed by Lysander. For the first time in a long time—if ever—the grizzly growls at me, his eyes glowing an ethereal green. I know he's only sharing her quiet fury, but it makes my chest tighten all the same.

"Meredy—"

"No!" she growls, her face suddenly draining of color as the recorder keeps blaring out the conversation she thought she had with Firiel. "Don't talk to me. I'm going to be sick."

"Please, don't go," I beg as she reaches for the doorknob. I know I can't stop her. But part of me refuses to give up hope for us. "I want to help you get better. I'd do anything for—"

I'm stunned into silence as the door slams, rattling in its frame.

A soft sob echoes from the hallway, then footsteps fade into silence.

I turn off the recorder and collapse on the bed, curling up in the still-warm spot where Meredy was waiting for me when I came in.

I want a calming potion more than I have in a long time. My fingertips itch to curl around a vial of vivid blue. I don't want to feel anything. I don't want to hurt again. I don't want to lose the person I love again. But it seems I have no choice, all because of the same sort of illusion that nearly broke me once. I know I hurt plenty of people, her included, while I was under the sway of those potions. I don't think I realized how much until now.

I'd hoped Meredy could learn from my mistakes, but then, she's not me. She has to learn for herself. Hopefully what she just heard through the recorder will begin to help soon.

Wishing I could sink through the bed and disappear, I call Nipper's name, and the dragon climbs up beside me. She starts shaking—or maybe that's me—as I cling to her back and try to shut out the world.

"I love her," I mumble to Nipper, who gently chirps. "I don't know what to do. I still want to be with—"

From somewhere down the hall, Meredy screams. And even though she just broke up with me, even though she destroyed my heart in the span of a few moments, I do what I always have and always will when Meredy is in trouble—I run to her.

XXV

Even though it's still morning, the palace hallways are darker than usual as I race through them, heart beating out of control, in the direction of that awful scream.

I find Meredy sprawled at the bottom of a staircase just past the kitchens, looking stunned but otherwise unhurt. Gasping for breath, she struggles to sit up. She must have had the wind knocked out of her by a fall.

Lysander worriedly licks her face, but after realizing his master is going to be just fine, he bounds up the stairs in pursuit of something. A flash of pink darts past the spot where I kneel beside Meredy—Nipper, dashing after the bear.

"Someone pushed me down those stairs," Meredy wheezes when she can finally take a breath. I'm relieved that she doesn't seem to need a healer, as she shrugs off my attempt to help her up. "Two men—I've never seen them before. There might be more. Come on."

We start up the stairs, but we're only halfway when Lysander's loudest roar fills the halls, sending the whole palace into chaos.

Meredy and I are the first to arrive at the scene in the upper hall-way, a windowless place with few torches along the walls. This par-ticular path isn't often used, I suppose. In the dimness, we're greeted by the strangest sight I've ever witnessed.

A fair-haired man whimpers and writhes, lying prone on the floor with Lysander's front paws pinning him down. Every time the man moves too much, Lysander opens his mouth and drips thick, fishy drool onto the man's face. For a heart-stopping moment, I think the man is Devran—they have the same haircut, the same narrow face—but this man's eyes are a pale blue, not hazel, and he doesn't have Devran's traces of a beard, either.

I still trust Devran about as much as I trust this stranger, but for Valoria's sake, I'm relieved it isn't the rebel leader under Lysander's paws.

Several feet away, a second man struggles against Nipper, who's wrapped her tail around the man's neck like a scarf. His trousers are filthy and ripped, and I'm pretty sure I recognize the bite mark in his left leg. He'll be starting to sweat any moment now, if I'm right.

The whole situation would be almost comical, if not for the vials of liquid fire potions stashed inside the baskets the men brought in— no doubt posing as farmers making a delivery. I check the vials for cracks, then carefully put the baskets in a corner where no one will trip over them until the potions inside can be properly stored.

They were going to set the palace on fire.

"Who let you in?" I demand of the criminal watched over by Lysander. The other is about to be rendered useless by Nipper's poi-son unless someone intervenes, and I don't make a point of saving people who want to kill me and my friends—at least, not saving them from a little pain. "Are you one of Devran's men? Or do you work for someone else—the group that tried to set fire to the school?" I press, though I doubt I'll get answers without a little help from my grizzly friend.

As if on cue, Meredy says calmly, "Lysander, you have my permission to bite his arm. Just a little one. Go ahead."

The man shrieks, not unlike a Shade, as the bear opens his mouth obligingly.

Meredy stops Lysander with a quick motion of her hand. "Got something to say to us after all?" she asks as Valoria, flanked by Bryn, Sarika, and a host of guards, comes running into the hall.

What little color there was in Valoria's face when she found us quickly drains away as she spots the baskets of liquid fire.

"Explain," she says frostily to the men, ignoring the discomfort of the one in Nipper's grasp even as sweat rolls down his face and soaks through his shirt. She nudges one man's leg with her cane impatiently—the leg Nipper bit—and it's enough to make him start talking. Or at least babbling somewhat coherently.

Our suspicions are quickly confirmed: They're some of the arsonists who tried setting fire to the temple. They tell us repeatedly that Devran's demonstrations are too docile, pathetic, and that the person who let them in was one of Valoria's maids. But they won't tell us what else they were planning, or whom they were working for. Valoria's face regains color as she listens—too much color, even, until the red in her cheeks looks downright dangerous.

"Are there more of you here? Anyone else lurking about?" the queen demands.

The men shake their heads, but she seems unconvinced, and rightfully so.

"I could have Lysander take a couple nibbles out of them," Meredy suggests sweetly. "That's what got them feeling chatty in the first place."

No one but me seems to notice the worried look Valoria gives Meredy, not even Meredy herself. Valoria finally shakes her head in answer, though disgust for these intruders is evident in her gaze as she directs her guards to free the men from our beasts' hold. "Let them rot in the dungeons until they're ready to talk."

She nudges one of the men with her cane again, this time out of spite.

Danial steps forward to direct the guards. "After a few days in solitary, seeing nothing and hearing nothing, they'll be ready to talk . . . even to me." He frowns, lingering near Valoria as if debating saying something more.

"What is it?" she asks, adjusting her glasses and looking at him with concern.

"My wedding is a few days from now. Or it's supposed to be. But now . . ." He spreads his hands in a helpless gesture. "Maybe we should wait. Maybe this isn't the right time."

"If you don't have your wedding when you planned it, you're just letting them win," I cut in, thinking of how crushed Simeon would be if his big day doesn't happen when he's expecting it to. "Right, Valoria?"

"Right. General, you'll recruit extra security for the wedding—guards you hand-select, ones you trust, and I'll do the same with the cooks and the serving staff. This celebration *will* happen on time, as you deserve," Valoria says, although a bit wearily, as she watches the two would-be arsonists get dragged away. "I haven't even had a chance to take the soldiers apart with Noranna, or else I might suggest using them for—"

"Majesty," a woman in a courier's uniform calls, sounding slightly winded. "I've been looking for you everywhere. I bring news from Lyris."

The woman holds out a wrinkled scroll, which Valoria hastily reads.

Once again, all the color recedes from her face as she whispers, "Ezoran ships have been spotted on their way to Lyris. There's no denying it—they've been making their way east for some time now, and if they stay on their current course, their next stop will be Karthia."

Meredy and I are shocked into exchanging a look.

"I've got to go now. I—I've got to summon the council and see how quickly we can put together our army. We'll have to resume training despite the quarantine. I have to ask Devran if he can convince his people to fight for me when we haven't even reached an agreement. I . . ." Valoria swallows, wearing an expression I've rarely seen on her: uncertainty. "I've got to protect my people, even the ones who are trying so hard to kill me."

Before she can go anywhere, I grip her shoulders and hold her gaze for a long moment. "I'd say *be careful*, but there's no point pretending we're not terrible at that." Right now, with the new scar on her neck and her skin so pale she almost glows, she doesn't look like a queen. She looks like a beautiful, breakable creature, and I'm afraid to let her go when it seems danger lurks down every corridor in this place lately.

"I will be," she assures me as Bryn and Sarika hurry to her side. "I may not be Karthia's favorite leader, but I'm our only leader. I have no intention of coming that close to a spear ever again." She steps back, squaring her shoulders and looking regal once more, all traces of vulnerability hidden behind her sharp gaze.

When I first met them, I never thought I'd be saying this, but I'm glad Valoria found Bryn and Sarika. With their newly acquired swords drawn, they lead her ever-growing escort down the hallway, and I find I can breathe easier knowing they're beside her.

As Valoria leaves, I sneak another glance at Meredy while she checks Lysander and Nipper over for any signs of injury. She's so tender with them. Getting over her seems impossible to contemplate, as impossible as a spirit somehow entering our world.

Standing in front of a floor-length mirror in Valoria's rarely used formal suite of rooms, I hold up a red gown while she and Meredy look on.

Meredy shakes her head. After frowning thoughtfully at a rainbow of gowns spread across her enormous bed, Valoria passes me another, this one in shades of blue. Meredy's eyes light up as I hold it against myself.

I wish she wouldn't look at me like that. Not anymore. It makes being around her that much harder, especially when we've hardly spoken since the breakup.

Still, Simeon and Danial's wedding is tomorrow, and Valoria insisted that we all take a quick break from training with the volunteers so the two of them can help me choose the right gown for my first time serving as Witness in a wedding ceremony. "You've got to help me keep an eye on her, no matter how much you two would rather avoid each other," a grim-but-determined Valoria reminded me when she showed up at my door earlier.

Ever since Meredy moved to another wing of the palace, Valoria and I have taken turns randomly passing outside her room. We haven't heard any voices from within, even when we stop by in the middle of the night. Still, until I know the crystal has been destroyed, I'll find it hard to believe Meredy is herself again. All we can do for now is watch her closely.

Three days have passed since Valoria began sending word of the Ezorans' impending attack to other parts of Karthia, and we officially resumed our training with the volunteers despite the threat of the black fever; three days since the intruders were locked in the dungeons; three days since their companions, still free, retaliated by burning one of the still-boarded-up Temples of Change, destroying precious knowledge that might have been inside.

Three days since my heart was shattered.

As I hold up a peacock-green confection of a gown with a feathered skirt, Valoria grimaces. "Definitely not that one."

I reach for the one in shades of blue again, this time to properly try it on. Valoria *oohs* and Meredy nods stiffly in approval. At that, Bryn and Sarika peer into the room from their posts outside the door and flash smiles of approval as they inspect the gown.

"See any new colors you'd like for your hair, Sarika?" I tease, mostly to take my mind off of Meredy.

The deepest of the hues in the gown's full skirt reminds me of the Deadlands' icy lakes, a sight I never expected to see again after we put the Dead to rest. Jax, Simeon, and I have been tempted to go back every day since we saw the frozen spirits, but with the Ezorans on their way, we have other, more pressing issues to attend to—like training the new volunteers arriving from the farthest reaches of Karthia.

"I hear Kasmira wrote to Simeon this morning," Valoria says, grabbing a strand of pearls from one of her dressers and slipping it over my head. After scrutinizing them from a distance, she frowns and declares, "You need more sparkle. How about—?"

"What about Kasmira?" I demand. From the letters she's written me and the things I've gleaned from writing to Meredy's sister, Elibeth, Kasmira is slowly making a full recovery. Still, having seen the vicious effects of the black fever, my heartbeat quickens every time I hear her name.

"She might come to the wedding!" Valoria gushes, tossing a cluster of sapphire and diamond pendants over my head. She seems extra determined to make conversation since Meredy and I are barely capable of exchanging two words these days. "Now if Elibeth is well enough, and we can just pull Zee away from her research, we'll have everyone together to celebrate!"

"What research?" I pull the heavy gemstones from around my neck and pile them on Valoria's instead, to everyone's amusement, as I wait for her answer.

"I'm not sure yet. She won't say." Valoria's lips twitch in a rare grin. "But researching something, whether you're an inventor or not, is a touchy business. We tend to build up the reveal in our minds, so . . ." She shrugs. "I haven't pushed her. She only told me about it because I caught her snooping in one of the healer's storerooms, taking a pinch of this and that." Winking, she adds, "Knowing her, she's probably concocting some potion for growing giant vegetables or making flowers sing."

"She hasn't seen a single Karthian festival since she got here, thanks to the black fever," Meredy adds thoughtfully. "Tell her she can't miss this."

"I'll be sure to pass that along," Valoria says. "I don't see how anyone could refuse an invitation to eat cream swans and drink until there are too many moons in the sky."

I laugh, but the sound quickly dies. Evander loved cream swans. So does Meredy, when they're served floating in a sea of berry sauce. Of course, we won't be sharing any dessert at tomorrow's wedding like I'd hoped. No dances. No laughter. No long conversations that last until even the stars are tired.

More than anything, more even than her words, I miss her presence. Her soft touch on my shoulder, the scent of vanilla in my room, the warm feeling that let me know she was nearby. I miss being close to the one who made me want to be a better version of myself—who knows what I'll become now?

At least I have training to keep my mind off my misery. It's been taking up every hour lately, so much that my body has begun to protest it. Valoria seems to enjoy the near-constant time on the grounds instead of being cooped up in the throne room, too—she's become quite skilled in wielding her cane like a weapon thanks to Jax, which makes sparring against her a real pain.

With Meredy and Valoria nodding their approval, I decide on the blue gown and add enough strands of sparkling necklaces and bangles to rival the stars. Maybe all the glitter will keep anyone from noticing there's no light in my eyes anymore.

Tomorrow, we'll celebrate Simeon and Danial's love while I mourn for mine—the old and the new, the never-to-be.

XXVI

The wedding ceremony itself is a brief declaration of love, as usual. It's really the following party that matters to any Karthian. That's always the part everyone talks about for months after, sometimes even years, so much that certain wedding celebrations become legend right along with people's favorite festivals. Of course, this wedding could be legendary for a different reason altogether—if the wandering spirit that escaped the Deadlands decides to make an appearance.

As we leave the ceremony site—a cliff near the palace overlooking the sea—I scan the crowd of guests and guards for Kasmira again, hoping I've somehow missed her.

"Kas took a turn for the worse last night," Valoria tells me gravely. "Unlike me." She walks beside me, her left arm looped through my right, while Meredy holds her other arm. Danial had a breakthrough with her healing sessions last night, and she's finally able to walk without her cane—though not without a slight limp. Somehow, we all manage to stay in step as we head into the palace's largest courtyard, even while surrounded by guards.

"What happened to Kas?" I demand, my throat tight.

"Just the fever being vicious. But don't you worry. She's with Azelie now, and—" Valoria breaks off, her brows drawing together. "And the other students."

"What?" I glance up sharply and accidentally meet Meredy's eyes. She shares my look of alarm. "And you're fine with that? What if they all get infected?"

"Azelie needs her help," Valoria answers vaguely. "Sarika escorted Kasmira from the *Paradise* to the school for me and is staying to ensure they take every precaution against the fever spreading while Kas is there."

That seems like an odd task to hand Sarika as part of her lady-in-waiting duties. I listen expectantly for Valoria to say more as we reach the courtyard, where musicians are already playing in anticipation of our arrival.

But instead of explaining further, Valoria spots Bryn hovering near the seven-tier masterpiece of a cake and waves to her, saying under her breath, "I'd better try the cake before Jax gets his hands on it." Her cheeks turn pink as she hurries off, a squad of Danial's favorite guards trailing her as closely as loyal hounds.

For a moment, I watch her, then turn my attention to the roaming guards whom I assigned to search for the loose spirit. Before the ceremony, I described to a trusted few of them what a spirit looks like in the Deadlands: gossamer-pale, almost transparent, and usually sporting their death wounds. All evening, they'll be combing the courtyard and palace grounds to ensure there's no such uninvited guest among the partygoers.

"I can't believe Azelie couldn't put aside whatever she's researching for one night." Meredy shakes her head, drawing my gaze back to her. I wonder if she realizes this is the most she's spoken to me, just me, in days. I lower my eyes so she won't know how much I've missed this. "But I suppose we can forgive her, since she hasn't known Simeon and Danial nearly as long as the rest of us. Oh—hello, Kat! Hello, Shealea!"

Brightening, she waves at a pair of passing baronesses who are new to Valoria's council, but not to the palace. Stray flower petals fleck Kat's long red-brown hair, remnants of the wedding ceremony, and Shealea looks equally festive with a white flower purposefully tucked into her black hair, just behind her ear, and a sparkly silver gown that hugs her willowy frame.

"Fancy seeing you two here!" Baroness Katerina jokes, her pale blue eyes warming as she returns the wave. A white cat with one tabby ear and tail prances jauntily at her heels.

"She should've been born a beast master," Meredy comments in a low voice to me before calling after them, "Care to join us?"

Shealea's small, dark brown eyes meet mine for a moment, glimmering with regret. As she inclines her head at something—or rather, *someone*—behind her, I realize the baronesses are on the move to avoid being swept up in conversation with the overbearing young count who appears to be trailing them.

With a strained silence settling over us, Meredy and I watch as the happy couple races arm in arm into the courtyard, both wearing the customary crowns of dried flowers whose blossoms symbolize every aspect of love: lilac for new love, red roses for pure love, pale honeysuckle for the bonds of love, violets for faithful love, and several more besides. While they couldn't look more opposite—Simeon so blond and tan, Danial with his raven hair and stark white skin—the smiles and glances they keep giving each other let everyone know they belong together. That, and they're wearing matching dress robes for the occasion, white trimmed with interlocking silver and gold threads.

I can't help looking at Meredy and wondering if that could've been us someday.

"Time for the crown toss!" Jax calls from across the courtyard. A bright flash meets my eyes as the last shred of daylight glints off the silver flask in his hand. He snags Valoria around the waist with his other hand.

At first, she looks startled. But after a moment, she seems to decide she doesn't mind and puts her arms around his neck, leaning in to kiss him.

I blink. She chose quite the moment for what I have to imagine is their first kiss. I didn't even think they were together.

To keep from staring, I focus on the crown toss. Danial and Simeon stand in the center of the courtyard and, on Jax's shouted signal, throw their crowns at the rest of us gathered behind them. I snag Simeon's crown out of the air as it soars just above my head and turn to grin at Meredy in the thrill of victory.

Her smile is suddenly a little uncertain, and my face burns as I realize why.

Whoever catches the crown is supposed to be close to finding a love of their own.

As she carefully avoids my gaze, I nestle the crown in her wine-red hair and then drop my shaking hands to my sides as the party becomes a blur of torchlights and stars. "There. Now you'll find your true love soon."

"Sparrow," a little girl's voice says as someone tugs on my skirt. "Why are you crying?"

Glancing down, I meet the doe-brown eyes of Valoria's youngest sister, Ruthenia, who can't be more than six years old. I'll bet anything that her other two siblings, a boy and girl in their early teens, are supposed to be keeping an eye on the littlest Wylding, but the two of them appear to have their hands full with glasses of punch and too many treats—much to the irritation of the guards assigned to shadow them. I doubt they'll get a moment's rest tonight.

My insides writhing, I answer the young girl with "Weddings tend to do that to people. You'll see one day, Ruthie. Love hurts." Hastily grabbing a glass of honeysuckle wine from a passing tray, I drain it in one long gulp. Blinking hard to clear my gaze, I focus on the small blond girl still clutching my skirt. "Let's dance, shall we?"

As Ruthie nods enthusiastically, I sweep her off her feet and into the wide space left open for dancing. As the wind shifts, a wave of heat washes over us, and we turn in time to see Simeon and Danial tossing the first handfuls of colored powder into the evening's bonfire.

Ruthie giggles and claps as I spin her around some more and waves at the guard nearest to us. Being at a party where the guards nearly outnumber the guests, and where there could well be a spirit on the loose, doesn't seem troubling to her young mind, so I try not to let it completely kill my mood, either.

"Fireworks. We need fireworks!" Karston rubs his hands together as he passes us, weaving through the dancers and guards with a purpose. He caught the other flower crown, but instead of giving it away, he's stuck it on his own head, wearing it with a swagger in his step. I nudge his shoulder and grin as he passes by. His eyes always look darker at night, but as the torchlight catches them, they shift from brown to their true violet—making even me, in all my misery, a little bit breathless.

The music changes, the melody becoming faster, and Karston pauses his fireworks mission long enough to entertain everyone with some spectacular dance moves. People clap and whistle. He's the life of the party tonight. I have to imagine he's relieved that the metal soldiers have been locked up ever since the almost-deadly demonstration.

As I twirl Ruthie around, I catch sight of Meredy in her flower crown, standing off to the side to watch the dancing. Somehow, knowing she's not dancing with anyone else only makes me feel worse. I want at least one of us to be happy after all we've suffered, but it seems we're equally miserable. I just hope the reason she hasn't snuck off to use the crystal yet is because the recordings finally got through to her. Then all this unhappiness will have been worth it.

"Sparrow," Ruthie whines. "You're all frowny again."

"Sorry. I'm just—hungry," I murmur in reply. It's true that I haven't eaten much today, and supper won't be served until everyone's exhausted from dancing and light-headed from all the wine. But right now, light-headed sounds good. "And thirsty," I add.

After returning Ruthie to the care of her brother and sister, I grab a flute of wine and find a seat on a bench near the musicians, well away from Meredy. I watch Valoria force Jax to do a twirl in the middle of the dance floor. I drain my glass. The dancers become a blur, one face indistinguishable from the next.

A short while later, my stomach growls. I guess I really do need to eat something.

As I make my way to the food, a low rumbling like thunder shakes the sky—the first firework exploding. Usually, there would be a swarm of Dead around the sweets and cheeses, trying but never managing to sate themselves. I think of them longingly as I reach for a plate, but a tap on my shoulder makes me turn.

"Here, try this," Karston says, holding out a thick slice of strawberry and rhubarb cream cake cradled in a napkin. He grins. "I managed to steal a piece before someone took the whole thing away to carve it up for after supper."

I shake my head. "You stole it, you eat it," I tell him, almost smiling.

"No, I owe you," he says quickly, shoving the cake into my hands before I can protest. "Aside from Noranna, you're the first real friend I've made since coming here. Don't get me wrong, the others are great—but you're the one who let me in. Besides, I need to save my appetite for supper." Grinning again, he gives me a wave and dashes off.

Shrugging, I stuff the cake in my mouth as I work my way back toward the benches. The sweet frosting reminds me of Simeon, as it's his favorite, and I search the crowd until I find him. He and Danial are setting off the fireworks together, and he can't seem to stop laughing.

For the first time all night, I smile. There's nothing like seeing my almost-brother happy, truly happy, after everything we've endured.

I polish off the cake and, after stashing its cloth wrapping on the edge of a table, spot Meredy again. Now she's dancing with Lysander, Elibeth, and Elibeth's growing pack of greyhounds—which, for all their graceful stature, can't easily move to the music. I take a deep breath and try to stop shaking inside as I watch her having fun.

More wine helps.

This is what I wanted: Meredy, healthy and herself again without the crystal. But then why do I feel so terrible? I wish she could be happy with *me*, but even if I watched her throw the crystal into the ocean tonight—could I ever trust her again, after all the times she's lied?

I stride toward Ruthie and the other two Wylding siblings, intent on joining them to have some fun myself, but a voice stops me in my tracks. "Sparrow! Where are you headed?"

Jax and Valoria have been inseparable tonight. So when I turn and see Jax sitting alone on a bench near the start of the pathway leading into the garden, frowning at his flask, I hurry over to see what's wrong.

"Where's Valoria?" I ask, slightly out of breath. I blame the wine. "You two looked like you were . . . having fun."

"We were. At least, she was," Jax says slowly as I drop down beside him. He shrugs. "Something just didn't feel right. I can't really explain it."

Glancing over at Meredy, still dancing with her sister in the distance, I mutter, "I know the feeling." I'm not sure how much he knows, or has guessed, about my breakup with Meredy. I have to imagine Valoria told him everything, though.

"Well," Jax says a moment later, slurring his words slightly. "We could talk about it, I guess. Or . . ." He holds the flask under my nose. "Drink with me like we used to, Sparrow."

I have a hard time saying no to Jax. Especially when those crystal-blue eyes are staring so deeply into mine, like he knows all my secrets.

In the end, I don't say anything. I just grab the flask, take a long drink from whatever foul liquid is inside, and try not to wince as it burns its way down my throat, where it mingles with the wine and cake. My stomach does a flip, but I ignore it and lean against Jax.

"You ever wonder," he murmurs as he takes a sip, "if we're destined to never be happy? I mean, look at Simeon and Danial. You think if we found that, we'd recognize what it was? I don't know if I'd be capable of feeling it."

"Maybe you can't. Maybe I can't, either," I say, accepting the flask again.

"At least the whiskey's all right," Jax concludes.

We fall silent, sharing the flask back and forth as the music becomes more subdued. Soon I can't tell much difference between the fireworks and the shimmering stars appearing in the deepening night sky. Once or twice, I think I spot a shooting star, only to blink and lose track of where it fell.

I'm not sure how much time passes before Danial rushes toward us, his eyeliner smudged at the corners.

"Come on, you two," he murmurs, putting a hand on each of our shoulders. "We were worried about you. And you're making everyone else wait on their supper."

Startled, I glance around and realize the courtyard is empty save for those tending the bonfire and cleaning up spilled wine. Everyone else has already moved to their seats at the long tables set up in the gardens for a late supper. Still, it makes no sense that someone would send Danial to find us. This is supposed to be the best night of his life.

But the moment I feel a familiar sensation of warmth spreading from my shoulder through the rest of my body, I realize why he must have insisted on looking for us himself. Danial's healing touch sobers us up just enough for us to head to the gardens unassisted, and for my face to burn with embarrassment as I begin the long walk to the table where an empty seat beside Meredy has my name on it.

I curse myself for not telling Simeon about the breakup. I'm sure he would have made alternate seating arrangements for me, even at the last minute.

Hardly anyone is looking at me or Jax as we sit—instead, their gazes are trained on Simeon as he finishes giving a toast I assume was meant to occupy the guests while Danial fetched us. A cheer rises into the night air.

Meredy doesn't even look my way as I slide into my seat.

"Now it's a party!" Simeon calls, flashing Jax and me teasing grins to show he's not upset. He gestures to the first course, already laid out in front of each of us. "Dig in!"

I poke at my slices of cold boar smothered in some sort of light brown sauce, moving them around on my plate so it looks like I'm enjoying the food. Despite the healing from Danial and only eating a slice of cake so far tonight, I'm no longer hungry. Something smells the slightest bit off, a whiff of an odor that reminds me of parsnips. I've never liked them.

From the look of things, Jax doesn't have any appetite, either. He's already back to sneaking sips from his flask when Valoria, seated beside him and hungrily tucking into her meal, isn't looking. At least he's put his fork in his hand to feign interest, though.

Gazing toward the head of the table, I watch the happy couple while Meredy alternates between eating slices of her meat and sneaking some into the napkin on her lap to give to Lysander later. I don't understand how she can carry on like nothing's wrong. I guess she really isn't hurting over being apart.

Like Jax and me, Danial hasn't touched his food yet, too busy kissing his new husband's neck as Simeon tries to chew and swallow his latest bite while laughing.

Suddenly, Simeon drops his fork. It clatters against his plate, and instead of picking it up, his hands fly to his throat.

Beside me, Meredy coughs violently, gripping the edge of the table for support.

Strange, those two choking at the same time.

A moment later, Valoria falls forward into her plate, wheezing and clutching at her throat like Simeon. She can't even seem to sit up.

Something in the air shifts as people begin to murmur worriedly to one another.

On Valoria's other side, her twelve-year-old brother and her middle sister start foaming at the mouth, coughing and spluttering. A few seats down, Baroness Shealea's lightly tanned complexion drains of color as she, too, struggles to breathe. Beside her, Katerina spits a mouthful of meat into a napkin, all sense of decorum abandoned.

And it's not just them. The sounds of people gasping all around disrupt the still night air.

I don't understand.

I grab Meredy's shoulders to help her stay upright through a fit of coughing, my heart pounding in my ears. There has to be something more I can do. Her face reddens as she struggles for breath against whatever is ailing her.

Slowly, the horrible realization takes hold: There was something in that sauce that shouldn't have been.

"It's lady's lace!" Danial shouts hoarsely above all the choking. He's already trying to heal Simeon, so his Sight must have revealed the type of poison coursing through his husband's veins. "Don't touch the food!"

Lady's lace is a dark green plant with tiny white flowers. As kids, Evander and I called it break-your-mother's-heart until Master Cymbre taught us its proper name. Everyone knows that it kills by forcing your airways to constrict, which means no one would be stupid enough to put it in a sauce. Unless they were hoping to kill us all.

I can tell by the way Danial looks wildly around as he heals Simeon that he wants to do more, but he can only help one person at a time, and there's no way he'll get to everyone before they die. There's no way he'll get to everyone, period. He'll be paralyzed long before that from using his magic too much in one night.

Even with the aid of the other healers in attendance at the party—two of whom converge on Valoria at once—there's no way all the guests will make it out of here alive. Guards run around the long tables, helpless to do anything but try to hold people up and direct the healers toward them.

Meredy collapses in my arms. Somehow, through a haze of tears, I manage to lay her on the grass a few feet away from our chairs. I lean over her and exhale into her mouth, trying to breathe for her. Her coughs become more pitiful with each passing moment.

"You can't do this," I murmur, patting her cheek as her eyes drift closed. She doesn't open them again, even when I shake her. "You can't go. I love you too much." I stroke her hair and cradle her head in my lap. "Please, Meredy, I love you."

I can't sense the rise and fall of her chest anymore.

"Please, don't leave me," I beg through a sob, staring at a patch of grass. It hurts to look at her. It hurts to breathe. Everything hurts.

Finished healing Simeon, Danial swoops down beside me, and I scramble out of the way as he puts his hands on Meredy's throat. His face is expressionless, as though it went numb from healing his new husband.

A dull thud nearby manages to make me tear my gaze from Meredy for the briefest moment. Noranna has fallen out of her seat. The white foam on her chin and the way she's not moving tell me she's past the point of help, even as I shout for a healer to go to her. Of course, they're all busy already.

Karston rushes to Noranna's side at once. The scream that tears from his throat when he sees her face is so full of anguish that he sounds more like a Shade than a human. No, worse—like a Shade that's been set on fire and knows the end is near.

The littlest Wylding girl, Ruthie, sobs as she tugs on her middle sister's skirt, then her brother's arm, unable to get a response from either of them. Abandoning her seat, she rushes to Valoria's side, gasping terrified breaths.

But just like her other two siblings, Valoria is past the point of comforting Ruthie. I can't even tell from here if my friend is still breathing.

A few seats down from Valoria, Baroness Shealea slumps in her chair, the white flower now missing from her dark hair, her arms around two smaller figures beside her. None of them move. All are too pale. I hope Shealea's spirit finds the children's in the Deadlands so they can continue to comfort each other in the next life. Nearby, Baroness Katerina lies equally still and silent, her forehead touching the table. Her white cat won't stop nuzzling her cheek, not understanding that her owner, pale in life but now paler than the moon, will never respond again.

I turn my head to the side, stricken with a sudden urge to heave up the meager contents of my stomach into the cold grass. Twice. Three times. In between, I glance skyward. The stars sure are bright tonight. They twinkle sweetly, like thousands of grains of scattered sugar, like they don't understand what they're witnessing in the slightest.

As I wipe my mouth, Danial leaps to his feet and rushes to aid someone else.

I glance down at Meredy as I take her in my arms again, scrutinizing her face. She's breathing, a little wheezily, but sounding no worse than if she were getting over a cold.

Wearily, she rests her head on my shoulder and closes her eyes. "I love you, too," she mumbles, drawing another heavy breath. As I hold her, I study the lantern light reflecting off her hair, unable to look at her anymore.

She probably thinks you're Firiel. She doesn't know what she's saying.

Shaking my head to chase away the thought, I force myself to gaze through the tables. The few other healers among the partygoers are still busy assisting Danial in healing whomever they can. Good thing, too, as Danial himself seems unable to walk anymore. He rests on an empty chair, looking as though the sheer effort of sitting up is almost too much for him.

Simeon drags a figure through the grass, headed toward Danial. It's Valoria, her crown missing, her chin slick with white foam. There's no color left in her face.

I sob harder, holding more tightly to Meredy as she stirs weakly in my arms.

Valoria is dead. The whole world is falling apart, and I can't do a damn thing about it. Raising the dead is forbidden now. I can't bring back anyone here, not even Valoria, thanks to her new law. And for good reason. I remember all too well how easily the Dead can become Shades, and how a single one of those monsters can cause waves of death in the space of a few heartbeats. Still, I hate knowing I have the power to ease a little of the hurt that this tragedy will bring to so many families, yet not being able to use it.

I could.

But I shouldn't.

I can't. I have to honor the law. The Dead belong in their world, the living in ours.

I hate this.

When Danial sees Valoria's body, he shakes his head sadly. "Bring me someone I can actually help," he tells Simeon, his voice breaking over the words.

Simeon nods, biting his lip, and embraces Valoria as her hair slowly changes from blond to a deep brown before my blurry gaze.

"Sarika is *gone*, Si," Danial croaks. "You have to let her go."

Baffled, I blink away tears and look closer at Valoria's body to see that Danial is right. Sarika must have been wearing Valoria's face all evening. It's her we've lost, and I can't help but feel the briefest surge of relief, followed by a stab of pain for Sarika, a girl whom I'd also come to call a friend. The garden shimmers beneath my gaze as I try to take a breath.

As Elibeth hurries toward me, I reluctantly give Meredy over to her care. I need to help Simeon find those who are fighting the poison long enough to be healed.

"Where's Valoria?" I demand as Simeon and I kneel near several fallen forms in the grass to check for a pulse. I'm afraid that wherever she is, she might have eaten the poisoned boar, too.

"She couldn't make it," Simeon says hollowly. "She's at the temple with Azelie. She said it was urgent, but she promised to make it up to us later. She sent Sarika in her place so it wouldn't look suspicious that she was away from the palace on 'such an important occasion,' as she put it."

Someone cries out—Elibeth—as Danial falls to his knees, exhausted already from using so much of his magic. Simeon stumbles toward him, tripping over something in the grass in his haste to help his husband despite feeling sick himself.

I grip the back of a nearby chair to stay standing, gazing around at everyone we've lost.

There's Sarika, still bravely wearing Valoria's face, though her hair has returned to its natural brown.

Bryn, who died while comforting Valoria's middle sister during her last moments. From a distance, both of them could be sleeping, but neither is.

Noranna, the brilliant inventor who tried so hard to help us form defenses for Karthia, whose body Karston clings to as he makes a constant low, moaning sound.

Valoria's brother, the boy with the nice laugh, next in line for the throne.

Valoria's middle sister, an innocent girl who's scared of the dark.

Baronesses Katerina and Shealea, friendly faces around the palace, with whom I've shared a laugh or dance at countless parties.

Several of Valoria's cousins have left us, too.

Even Duchess Aventine, the noblewoman who laughed at Noranna, who Valoria was sure had tried to kill her before, is blameless in this slaughter. She, too, lies among the dead.

And now we could lose Danial.

I knew the oleanders signaled something was coming—something terrible—but this is beyond my worst nightmares.

As my gaze travels back over Sarika, realizing how close we've come for a second time to losing Valoria, I'm tempted to add my screams to those of the frightened and grieving partygoers around me. Thinking of how close I came to almost losing Meredy, to watching her die just like Evander, I could scream until my throat is raw and my voice is gone.

But I've faced death before. I won't let it render me helpless again.

Between us, Elibeth and I move Meredy inside, carrying her and many others up to the healer's wing of the palace. Yet long after we've left the area, long after the dead have gasped their last breaths and the healers have collapsed from their efforts, the partygoers' screams still fill my ears.

I claw at my head, wishing I could pull them out of my scalp, but they refuse to be silenced. Maybe I don't want them to stop. Those screams are all I have left of Bryn, Sarika, and Noranna. All I have left of my friends.

Those screams beg me to make sure no one else meets their fate.

Someone has to pay for this. Someone has to suffer. The men who broke into the palace intending to start a fire—was this the work of their friends, seeking revenge? Or the work of an angry spirit? I want to watch the guilty one die—better yet, I want them to die by my hand. That way, I can make sure it's nice and slow.

XXVII

The spacious waiting room in the healer's wing has never felt so stifling.

Jax and I share an oversized armchair that's lumpy from years of use, giving Simeon the other chair to himself. He won't look at either of us, having gone silent after expressing his guilt at being the first one saved and, therefore, the person to suffer fewest effects from the poison. Now he keeps his head bowed as he thumbs through a messy, age-stained book with the cover missing. When I asked him what it was about, he mumbled that it had something to do with heartache. I wonder if Meredy gave him the book we used to read together, but I don't get any more out of him.

I'm sick of silence.

Behind the tall white doors on the other side of this room, Danial's fellow healers are trying to save him from succumbing to the price of his magic. Usually, healing only paralyzes a small part of him for a short while, but he saved so many lives tonight that the paralysis went deeper. They're worried it might stop his heart.

Also behind those doors somewhere are Meredy and everyone else whom Danial and the other healers saved. They'll need sleep and a few days of extra care to fully recover, and until then, all the rest of us can do is wait.

I'm sick of waiting, too.

Behind those doors somewhere, Valoria is being given a potion for shock, a potion so painfully familiar that my teeth ache at the thought of it sliding down her throat. But she needs it to get through the night. Her brother and one of her sisters are gone, and she lost Hadrien and her mother just months ago. Little Ruthie is with Elibeth, playing with her hounds and trying to forget the horrors she just witnessed. She's all Valoria has left now.

Well, unless Jax and I, and the rest of the wolf pack, count for something.

He shifts restlessly beside me, toying with the empty flask in his hands. I'm sure he's itching to refill it, because that's what he does when he can't change things and he's angry at his own powerlessness.

When I can't change things, I usually go swing my sword around, but I can't leave Simeon here. I won't. Still, I don't know what I can do for him. I know that worrying solves nothing and helps no one, and yet, it washes over me in waves.

More than anything, I'm sick of feeling helpless.

Suddenly, Jax leaps to his feet and sucks in a breath as though stung by something. He swipes his hand across a small table holding a tray of drinking glasses, seemingly for no other reason than to watch them shatter on the tile floor.

Simeon doesn't even flinch, but I have to admit, the sound is oddly satisfying.

Abandoning the chair, I knock over the tall ceramic water pitcher resting beside the now-empty spot where the tray of glasses was.

Water soaks the fancy slippers I forgot to remove earlier, so I rip them off, standing carelessly among the pieces of shattered glass and clay.

Jax grabs the vase beside the entryway and hurls it at the closed doors behind which we can only guess at how our friends are faring.

I put my fist through a painting of a rose garden.

Jax puts his fist through the wall.

I rip the curtains off the room's only window and shred them with my bare hands, tearing my fingernails in the process until they're bloody.

Jax snaps the legs off the table that held the drinking glasses and uses those to make more holes in the wall, showering us in chunks of plaster and wood that make me cough as I breathe in some tiny pieces.

I kick over a potted plant, grabbing heaping fistfuls of dirt from the shattered vase and throwing them everywhere.

Jax shreds the plant itself, the dark juice in its stems running thickly down his hands.

A healer emerges from behind the white doors, poking her head out to see what all the commotion is. She quickly retreats, gasping at something. Maybe it's the sight of my bloody hands, or the bloody footprints all over the tile where I've stepped in glass, or the crimson knuckle-prints all over the walls from Jax's fists.

Whichever the reason for her startled look, it only fuels our rage as Simeon continues to read without glancing up once. I wish he'd join us.

It feels good, breaking things. Destroying a little bit of the world that seems bent on destroying us.

* * *

The next day, with guards stationed outside every occupied bedroom in the palace, we pretend to sleep. With guards watching closely over our breakfast, we chew tasteless food that's been tested for poison first by some poor soul.

With guards breathing down our necks, we mourn.

Still reeling from the previous night's tragedy, Valoria returns to the throne room to ponder how to prepare her unhappy people for an invasion that now seems inevitable. At least she has Devran to communicate some of her subjects' wants and needs and pass messages between the palace and the city. Just yesterday, before the wedding ceremony, he came back around to having citizens join her council and agreed at last that the subject of the Dead could wait for now.

Simeon won't leave Danial's side, and Jax won't leave Valoria's even when she's in meetings, which means it's up to the guards to search the palace for the poisoner and interrogate the arsonists in the dungeon to see how much they know about lady's lace. I wander the palace halls alone in a daze, looking for the escaped spirit around every darkened corner, and only visit Meredy's bedside once before she's back on her feet. She's so determined to find the culprit behind the poisoning and stick them full of arrows like a giant pincushion that she comes to my room to talk through potential suspects just five days after the wedding that broke so many hearts.

"Is it possible Devran could have done something like this, and his cozying up to Valoria, compromise-is-the-way routine was all an act?" Meredy asks as she sits on the rug covering part of my floor. Already, there's hardly any scratchiness left in her voice thanks to Danial's quick actions a few nights ago. "Who do we know who would have access to a plant like lady's lace? It's not in season right now."

Lysander, guarding the door along with Nipper, growls at the distress in her tone.

"Too hard to say," I sigh. "For all we know, it could be an Ezoran assassin who managed to sneak into the palace somehow. But more than likely, it's a friend of those scumbags in the dungeon, someone with a background in smuggling, perhaps." Or another faction that wants to see someone other than Valoria in power. It's certainly *not* the loose spirit—how would they be able to find and pick up that plant if they aren't back in their body? And yet, the possibility lingers in the back of my mind.

I know Jax and Simeon didn't want to trouble Valoria with the fact that we went to the spirits' world recently, or what we found there, but I'm sick of keeping a secret from her and it's only been a few days. I need to get it off my chest.

Excusing myself from Meredy, I head for the throne room—the most likely place to find Valoria these days. Nipper's claws skitter across the palace's tiled hallways as she follows at my heels, startling a few people along our path by swatting them with her long, pointed tail.

Somewhere between the kitchens and his room, I cross paths with Karston, who seems to be sleepwalking, he's wandering so aimlessly, and I don't have to wonder why: Noranna.

"Hey." I almost reach out to touch his shoulder but think better of it. Startling him won't do him any good. When he blinks and meets my eyes, his are damp, wide with a mixture of sorrow and fear. I know something about that. "I've been where you are," I tell him softly, over the sound of Nipper cooing in concern. "If you need to talk, or even if you need to sit in total silence and throw shit at the wall, I'm here. If you need to punch someone, I can take it. Just don't . . ." I hesitate, not sure *don't make the same mistakes I did* is the right thing to say when his grief is eating him from the inside. "Just know you're not alone. Not at all," I finish lamely. He still hasn't said anything. "I'm on my way to see Valoria—want to come?"

Karston shakes his head. "Thanks, though," he rasps. It's only when he nudges my shoulder and says, "Wolf pack forever, right?" with a shadow of the grin I've come to recognize that I feel like he'll be all right, eventually.

"You're coming to training this afternoon, right?" I press. "It's more important now—"

"I'll be there," he promises dully.

"Good." I shoot him a look. "If you're not, I'm going to let Nipper drag you to the grounds, and trust me, you won't enjoy it."

Karston blinks at Nipper as if just seeing her for the first time. He's really out of it. He's played fetch with her more times than I can count. After making him swear on Vaia that he'll show up to training, we finally go our separate ways.

The guards recognize me when I reach the throne room doors and step aside to let me through, but something stops me from pushing the door open more than a crack. Valoria's been in meetings with her council almost constantly in between planning her siblings' funerals, but now, there's hardly any sound coming from the room.

When I peer inside, Valoria is alone except for Jax and several guards who gaze dutifully at the floor while my friends whisper to one another.

"You should get some sleep. You never do anymore, and my studies indicate that's not good for anyone," Valoria murmurs to him as they sit on the wide velvet cushion of the new throne, faces turned toward each other. She lifts one of his hands, inspecting knuckles that must still be bloody from our destruction of the healer's waiting room.

"I'm not leaving you," Jax insists. "Not for a second. I can rest when I'm dead, but you can't save the kingdom if you're in the spirit world."

Valoria frowns, raising her chin a fraction. "Fine. But so we're clear, I'm not a damsel. I'm simply smart enough to recognize when someone is better than me at something, and you happen to have skills with a sword that would have made Eldest Grandfather shake in his boots. You can do things with a blade I'll probably never understand."

"That the only reason you like having me around?" Jax murmurs, and something in his tone makes my face grow hot. I have the feeling I shouldn't be hearing this, but if I don't try to talk to Valoria soon, she'll get swept up in another meeting and then who knows when I'll get the chance.

Valoria leans closer to Jax, putting a hand on his chest. He grabs both sides of her waist, drawing her to him.

"I'm still your leader," she whispers, a hitch in her voice. "You're my subject. Nothing that happens between us will ever change that—you won't suddenly be able to order me to make the safe choice over the *right* choice, just because you don't like seeing me get hurt."

Jax nods his understanding, his eyes burning as they hold her gaze. I know that look. He never gave it to me, but it's the way he stares at his blade when he's polishing it. It's a different version of the look he used to give his best friend, Evander, before spending any time apart.

"And in case anyone hasn't told you this," she continues to ramble, "you drink too much. You don't think before you act. And you're terribly uncouth."

"Call me anything you want," Jax growls, "if you'll just tell me I can kiss you for real now."

"I—what do you mean? For real?" Valoria's eyes widen as Jax groans softly at his mistake. "Explain."

"At the wedding," he says gruffly, like he wants to get this over with in a hurry, "you kissed me—at least, I thought you did. Then I realized you'd never been there." Valoria starts to pull away from him as he adds, "It didn't feel right, that kiss. Not anything like I've been imagining."

"You idiot," Valoria whispers, her eyes shimmering.

"I know," Jax says, frowning at himself.

"You . . . think about kissing me often?"

"All the time, lately."

"Suppose we should try it, then? Just an experiment—to see how it lives up to your imagination?" Before Jax can answer, she leans in to close the remaining distance between their lips, wraps her arms around his neck, and kisses him slowly.

I hastily drop my gaze to my feet, my face burning. But hearing the sounds of two people I know kissing, imagining how it looks, is somehow worse than actually watching it happen.

Someone bumps my shoulder as they fling open the throne room doors. I was so distracted by the scene inside, I didn't hear her approach. The woman wears the plain skirt and blouse of someone from one of the poorer coastal villages, but judging by the scroll curled in her hand that appears to be damp with sweat, she's also a messenger.

"Your Majesty," she says briskly to Valoria as I follow her into the room. "I bring grim news from Lullin." She holds out the scroll.

Valoria unfolds it and quickly scans it. "The Ezoran army is here at last," she says calmly—too calmly, like she's come to expect the worst.

A chill washes over me. They're here. And of all the places they could have landed, the tiny coastal village of Lullin to the west wouldn't take them long to conquer.

"According to this, they didn't kill anyone, though," Valoria adds quickly, looking between me and Jax as she finally notices me standing behind the messenger. "They merely caused some damage and stole a great many things before returning to their ships." She checks the parchment again, slower this time. "Apparently almost everyone in Lullin has the black fever. They need supplies to sustain their few caregivers, since the Ezorans took most everything of value—fresh water, furs, and meat."

"Maybe they're just resupplying before heading back to sea," Jax suggests lamely, though given the dark look on his face, he doesn't believe it.

Valoria shakes her head. "The enemy ships were spotted sailing east as Baron Stryker was finishing this letter. It seems they're headed toward Grenwyr City, which should only take them a day's sailing from where their ships would be right now." She calls for one of the guards outside the door. "Summon the council and, if he's able, Danial," she says without a trace of weariness. "This is what we've been planning for."

I don't know how she can keep going after everything that's happened to her lately. But there's no way I can trouble her about strange happenings in the Deadlands and the oleanders' warning now. I'll have to take care of it on my own.

"Odessa, were you looking for me?" Valoria asks, meeting my gaze. "What is it?"

I shake my head. "Nothing that can't wait." I turn to go, but add quickly, "I'll send Nipper with a message to Simeon to let him know what we just learned." It's a good thing Simeon returned to the school this morning, since Danial woke up well enough to walk unassisted. Now Valoria will have one less thing to worry about—warning the students.

"Thank you." Valoria looks past me and waves to someone. The first council members are arriving. Returning her attention to me for the briefest moment, she says, "Once you've sent the message, get your weapons ready. And then . . . wait for sunset. That's when we'll assemble on the grounds with all the soldiers we can muster." She leans forward. "And, Odessa? Don't you dare do anything risky in this fight. That's an order from your queen. Remember, I know how you think."

"Majesty." I acknowledge the command with a bow.

"Valoria," she corrects me at almost the same time.

We exchange the briefest smile. "Valoria. I'll try my best." That's all any of us can do when it seems the whole world is against us.

XXVIII

The palace buzzes with activity as I send Nipper off to the school, a message for Simeon tucked in her collar. News of the Ezorans' imminent arrival must be spreading through these halls faster than a wildfire.

In just a few hours, Valoria and Danial will have finalized their battle plan. Danial wasn't in a state to do much of anything last time I saw him, but that was five days ago, and he doesn't have a choice. He'll have to manage somehow. Just like I'll soon have to go join the volunteer army making its way toward the palace grounds by sunset.

As I turn a corner on my way to my room, wanting to pick up a few things before going to check on Karston, a familiar voice stops me.

"Odessa," Meredy calls as she hurries toward me, holding something in her cupped hands. Lysander follows her, lagging slightly behind. "Do you have a moment?"

For her? Always. Especially now that we're talking again, almost like old times, even if it's mostly about the dangers we're facing. But

I don't say any of that. Instead, I tell her what I just learned in the throne room. That we're going to war with the Ezorans. Tonight.

"This is a lot to take in," Meredy says after a moment, tightening her hands around whatever she's clutching. "Do you mind if I—?"

Before she can finish, I open the door for her and usher her into the room we used to share. Lysander, upon peering inside and realizing Nipper isn't with me, grumbles his displeasure as he settles down in the hallway to wait for his master.

Meredy sits on the rug near the hearth, which I haven't used to build a fire since before we broke up, and takes a deep breath. Finally, as I settle myself across from her, she opens her hands to reveal what she's brought. "I thought you should see this," she says quietly as I stare at the glittering blue powder in her cupped hands.

The crystal.

She's holding proof that she fought a hard battle and finally returned to herself.

At first, it's hard to form words. "When—?"

"The day after you played the recording for me," she says swiftly, dropping her gaze to the powder. "I couldn't sleep that night, thinking I was going mad. I was scared, I was angry at the crystal—more at myself, though—and then after I destroyed the damned thing, I was embarrassed at just how right you were. I hurt you because of a stupid magic trick. I hurt the person I care about most in this life." Tears gather in her eyes as she continues, "I could barely look at you, let alone speak to you after that."

"You could've told me—" I begin, even as my throat tightens.

"After the way I betrayed you? After lying to you and hurting you all that time, you think I should have burdened you with more of my problems?" Meredy demands, shaking her head.

"Always," I say firmly. "You can always come to me." I wondered before if I could ever trust her again after the way she lied, but she never had any problem trusting me after working through my potion cravings. She deserves another chance, just like the one she gave me.

"No. I had to work through this alone," Meredy insists, biting down on her lower lip to keep it from trembling. A moment later, she adds, "I had to clear my head—something I've had plenty of time for in the healer's wing. I had to make sure I could take care of myself, without the crystal, before I even thought about being with someone else again. Not that I expect you to take me back," she says quickly. "That's not why I'm here. I came to say I'm so sorry."

She leans forward and tosses the blue powder into the hearth and dusts off her palms. "There. Now you have a little extra something to burn the next time you want a fire."

As I tear my gaze away from the glittering fragments of a lie now coating the hearth, I say softly, "I'm sorry, too, by the way. For eavesdropping. I know it was wrong, but what else could I do? I didn't want you to lose your mind, and I didn't want to lose *you*. Though I did anyway," I continue, my voice breaking. "I hate being apart from you. I hate it because there's so much we haven't done together yet. I hate it because I love you so much it hurts, Meredy."

Watching her tears fall harder creates a lump in my throat too painful to swallow around.

She reaches out, inviting me into an embrace, but I hesitate. She hurt me. Betrayed me. She's sorry, and she's better now, but there are so many *what if*s that scare me. So many other ways she could break my heart all over again. Still, she keeps her arms open, beckoning. "Thank you," she whispers. "For saving me again."

I shake my head. "You did that on your own. You destroyed the crystal."

She gives me a shaky smile. "Just so you know, despite thinking

I was talking to her, I still fell in love with you. The crystal made me confused, made me say things I didn't mean. The truth is, I *do* love you—only you, Dessa. I've loved you for a while now."

"That night at the wedding—?" I ask, remembering what she whispered to me there.

"I knew who I was talking to," Meredy says swiftly. "I knew who was holding me. I said I loved you then, and I meant it. I love you now. I'll love you every day for the rest of my life. I know I don't deserve you after all the damage I've done, but I'd like the chance to become someone who does."

Finally, I sink into her embrace.

"You make it sound like I'm perfect," I murmur against her ear. "Before you decide who you want to be with, I should remind you that I'm petty, I'm reckless, and don't forget *selfish*—"

"And beautiful, and impossible," Meredy adds, now smiling slightly through her tears. "And I love every inch of you." There's a hitch in her voice as she draws back farther to meet my eyes. "I know you'll always have your memories of Evander, like I'll always have mine of Firiel—and I'd like to share them, if you're willing. I'd like to build a future with you. I want that more than anything. If you'll be my girlfriend again . . . ?"

"Of course I will," I promise against her lips.

"You're willing to trust me again, after . . . everything?"

"With my life."

The girl with the scarred cheek and wine-red hair who's kissing my neck, turning my thoughts into a warm, blissful nothing, is everything to me now. She has been for a while, and this—this is what I missed and was afraid I'd lost forever. This closeness with her. How she challenges me to be a better friend, a better necromancer—a better person.

"And from now on," she adds, her voice still a little unsteady, "no more keeping secrets. Not from each other."

"Done," I agree as she finally, hungrily kisses me.

She stops only to whisper a question, and at my firm "Yes," she pulls off my blouse, accidentally popping off one of the buttons in her haste as she pushes me against the bed.

She gasps when I start kissing every bit of her exposed skin in return, which only encourages me. I slide a hand up her leg, trailing my fingers higher until they're slick and Meredy's knees are threatening to give out. My necromancer's belt drops to the floor with my trousers, helped along by Meredy, who seems determined to make me fall over before she does. The light, quick movements of her skilled fingers have me gasping at her every touch. I push her down onto the blankets on her back, where she spreads her legs at once. It seems we want the same thing, then.

I take my sweet time getting there though, wanting to memorize every part of her: The scent of her hair. The perfect arch of her spine as her body gives in to my touch. The way she makes things better—makes *me* better—seemingly without effort.

As I'm kissing up her thighs, she puts a gentle hand on my head and stops me from getting any closer to my goal.

"We shouldn't—we don't have time for this," she says breathily, as if startled by some sudden realization. "What you said about the Ezorans . . ."

"It's midafternoon, and we don't meet the others until sunset," I assure her, pushing her hand away and kissing her in just the right spot to make her cry out and give in to her desire. "This is *our* time."

After all, with the invaders nearly on our doorstep, this could be the last chance we ever have to be together like this. And if my spirit doesn't just blink out of existence, the way all necromancers' supposedly do, I want to remember the blazing white light that is the essence of Meredy long after I've forgotten my own name.

When it's my turn, and Meredy and I have traded places, her lips and fingers alone make me forget a great many things.

It's only later, when our sweat has finally dried and we're wrapped in each other's arms, that tendrils of dread sink their hooks into me once more. There's so much that can and will go wrong once I leave this bed. And judging by the reds and golds appearing in the sky for a fiery sunset, it's nearly time to meet the soldiers and go over our plan.

But first, before I fight any battles, I need to find a bathroom.

Giving Meredy a quick kiss, I pull on a robe and open the door just enough to slip through, since she hasn't bothered to put on any blankets or clothes. Not that I mind. I hastily shut the door behind me.

Hurrying down the hall to the nearest bathroom, the floor cold against my feet, I find myself humming Simeon's song. It hasn't drifted through my head in a while, but the cheerful melody suits my mood just now.

Thinking of a really good thing Meredy did earlier, I bump into someone as I round a corner. Their hands close around my throat and squeeze, hard, before I have time to make sense of who's choking me.

Blinking tears from my eyes as I gasp for air, the identity of my attacker finally registers: Karston.

"I told you to quit singing that damn song," he hisses, a malicious gleam in his eyes. "It makes me sound like such an idiot."

"What? Why?" I cough, scrabbling at the hands digging harder at my throat. Gazing into his face, I see no hint of the boy I've come to call a friend. There's a hard glint to his eyes, a mean curve to his lips that I've seen before, only not on him. I can't quite place it. It's hard to think with the air being squeezed out of me.

"Oh, come on, Sparrow." Karston scoffs, his voice calm and cold as he continues choking me. "You were never this stupid."

I know that expression. I know that tone. I know who Karston reminds me of just now.

This must be the spirit Firiel warned us about. The spirit I most feared was free.

"H-Hadrien?" My vision goes fuzzy at the edges. Not a good sign. I try to reach for my sword, but it's not there. My fingers close uselessly over the cloth belt of my robe, and Karston—Hadrien—shoves me hard against the wall at my back.

"No blade to stick me with this time, I see." He smirks.

"How?" I wheeze. I don't want to believe it—I'd call it a fever dream, except I'm in too much pain to be asleep. Somehow, I'm talking to Hadrien's spirit inside Karston's body. As I pry desperately at his fingers, he tightens his grip.

Hadrien tried to choke me to death once before. It makes sense, in some twisted way, that he'd want to do it again. Of course, last time I had a dagger, and his hands weren't Karston's broader, stronger, work-hardened ones.

My only hope of surviving this time is that Meredy somehow hears us struggling from down the hall and comes running.

"Surprised to see me?" he asks, his breath washing over me and making me shudder as I fight for air. He leans closer, pressing his whole body against me and forcing my robe open in the process, like choking me is some kind of lover's act. "And to think . . ." He laughs lightly, his gaze roaming slowly over the gap in my robe as his eyes slowly darken from violet to deep brown. "I used to fear you were smarter than me. Too smart for your own good. But you've gotten soft while I was away. You're making this *too* easy." His grip tightens.

Much as I'd love to spit in his face, all I can do is wheeze.

There's no sign of Meredy, and I can't hold on to what little air is left in my lungs for much longer.

"I'm sure you'd like to know how I got inside this pathetic boy's body," he continues calmly, as though we're talking over tea. "But I'm afraid that has to remain my secret for now." He smiles, and although he's using Karston's mouth, the shape it takes on—just like the shade of his eyes—is unmistakably Hadrien's. "How lucky that I returned to this world in time to lead *my* army against these invaders. They won't stand a chance. I thought you might like to know that before you die."

Thinking of Meredy, holding her light in my mind, I claw back against the edges of the darkness that's beginning to cover everything.

I can't go like this. I have to get back to her, but my arms don't seem to understand. My efforts to break Karston's fingers are becoming weaker. More than ever, I want to *live*. I just need one breath . . . then I can fight . . .

Down the hallway, a door opens, a sound as distant as the sea far below the palace.

Something with claws gives a deafening roar as it bounds down the hallway, forcing Karston—Hadrien, I remind my foggy brain—to release me and flee.

I crumple to the ground, too light-headed to stand.

Coughing and rubbing my throat, I glance up through streaming eyes in time to see the blurry shape of Lysander tearing after Karston, and Meredy running toward me.

"No, no, no," Meredy sobs, dropping to her knees beside me. "We'll get you a healer, just hang on—"

"I'm all right," I insist, though the words don't come out too clearly. "But Karston isn't. Hadrien's spirit is inside him somehow."

"*What?* How is that possible?" Meredy demands.

I shake my head, unable to explain. I know nothing of whatever magic let Hadrien's spirit inhabit a living person's skin. When necromancers bring back a spirit from the Deadlands, we return them to their own shrouded bodies. Always. I don't understand how a spirit could inhabit a living body with another soul already inside it.

Still, I can't believe I didn't see it before, now that so many things make sense: the time Karston snapped at me for singing his favorite song, the brief moments at night when his eyes would turn a deep brown instead of their usual violet, how out of it he seemed when I met him in the hallway earlier with Nipper. What if the poisoning at the wedding wasn't the work of unhappy citizens, but Hadrien, acting through Karston somehow?

Meredy wraps her arms around me and helps me sit up, drawing me from my thoughts.

Together, we gently inspect my throat. I'm sure I'll have a garden of bruises blooming there within hours, but I don't care. I'm just glad to be drawing breath after greedy breath, filling my lungs so the burning in my chest will subside.

"I don't know. A living person with another spirit inside them—it's never happened before, but I'm sure it was him," I say, my voice rough, but stronger. "Karston might still be in there, too, though." If he is, I have to try to save him. "We have to go after him before he hurts someone else—or himself."

Climbing to my feet is harder than I anticipated when I'm still light-headed, but I manage with Meredy's help.

"Wait." Meredy tightens her grip on my hand, as if afraid I'll rush off without her.

I squeeze hers to let her know I won't do any such thing.

"Let me check on Lysander first. He should have caught him for us by now." As she frowns in concentration, her eyes flash a brighter, iridescent shade of green that means she's magically joined her mind with the grizzly's. She's seeing through his eyes now. "He got away. Lysander's coming back," she says in the dreamy voice that seems to come with looking into another's mind.

She blinks, and the ethereal green light fades from her eyes.

"We'd better hurry then. I don't want Karston—*Hadrien*," I correct myself yet again, "going anywhere near Valoria. He said something about an army, too," I add, shaking off another wave of dread as we run back to our rooms for proper clothes and weapons.

My necromancer's uniform and belt donned, my sword and daggers at my side, I'm about to rush out the door when I spot the double sapphire pin that's been sitting on a table since we returned to Karthia.

Meredy smiles softly in approval as I pause just long enough to fasten it on my tunic.

It finally feels like it belongs there, not weighing me down in the slightest as it clings to the fabric over my heart. Maybe that's because Hadrien somehow found his way back to our world, and while I can't explain it, there's one thing I'm sure of when it comes to spirits: I'm Odessa of Grenwyr, and the dead answer to me.

XXIX

A commotion echoes sharply from some other part of the palace, drawing my gaze.

Hadrien, I can't help but think right away.

It sounds like someone banging pots and pans together in the kitchen, only the noise is coming from much farther away—the dungeons, I realize as we race toward the sound. We're joined on one of the lower staircases by Lysander.

"Where's Nipper?" Meredy asks as we run.

"With Simeon," I pant. I'm glad I left him and the students with some scaly protection after what we've just discovered.

The three of us dash into the dark, windowless part of the palace belowground to find the doors of the metal soldiers' prison unchained and flung wide open. Valoria and several guards, Danial and Jax among them, stand with their weapons drawn, gazing disbelievingly at something inside the open chamber.

The metal soldiers may not have their spears anymore, but that isn't stopping them from fighting each other. Having somehow broken free of their bindings, they use the chains formerly wrapped around their hands and feet as a means to choke one another. Some don't have chains, but that doesn't stop them from trying to rip off one another's heads and limbs. None of the humans in the room make a move to intervene while the soldiers pummel a few of their kin into useless, dented scraps of iron.

Valoria watches with one hand over her mouth, the other flung out as a barrier between Jax and the soldiers, as if that could keep him from charging forward to aid in the soldiers' self-destruction.

Lysander seems particularly terrified of the soldiers. It's the first time I've seen him show fear at anything, and he's fought Shades and gnawed on the bones of vicious rogue mages. He hides his bulk behind Meredy and me, keeping to the shadows as if he wants to be sure he can make a quick exit.

Neither Karston nor Hadrien—whichever has control of Karston's body right now—is anywhere to be seen, and we just ran down the only staircase leading to the dungeons. Yet somehow, the soldiers continue to fight as we all look on, until ten of the iron figures are completely out of commission.

The rest toss their broken companions into a heap in a corner of their cell.

How they could be moving without the aid of Karston's magic, I have no idea.

"I—I must be dreaming," Valoria murmurs, apparently sharing my thoughts. "The soldiers—do they have minds of their own?" Her brow furrows. "I don't understand. I took two of them apart and found nothing but the gears Noranna and I put there . . ."

"That's because your weak Sight doesn't let you see the spirits inside." Hadrien's voice issues from Karston's mouth somewhere behind us.

There's a clanking sound as the hundred or so remaining metal soldiers turn to face him as well, standing at attention as if awaiting orders. Whirling around, I watch Karston bound partway down the staircase. I draw my sword, not the least bit worried about the short sword in his hand, and start to rush toward him.

Hurrying after me, Meredy quickly grabs the back of my tunic, holding me in place as she whispers, "Remember, you said Karston might be in there, too!" That said, she releases me.

After all, I have no idea how Hadrien's spirit got in there, but I'm willing to bet that putting a blade through Karston would force the mad king out. That's how we cast spirits out of their bodies and send them back to the Deadlands.

"Oh, no," Hadrien murmurs as I watch him warily for any sign of movement. I'll fight to save Karston, but I'm not letting Hadrien leave my sights again. "I see a few of my subjects got cold feet and decided not to stand with me after all. Shame." I follow his gaze to the handful of crumpled metal soldiers now piled in a corner of the dungeon, the ones that the larger group turned on. The spirits must still be trapped inside the mangled metal bodies, but now those few who might have been persuaded to help us will be of no use. Their bodies aren't in any shape to fight, let alone stand.

"Subjects? Explain," I demand, my heart thudding madly as I gesture to the metal soldiers standing at attention.

"Sparrow." Hadrien's gaze locks with mine. "Still alive, I see. Another shame." He smiles, his eyes turning a darker shade of brown, shifting further away from violet. He's taking over Karston more completely the longer his spirit is inside him. He looks to Valoria next. "And you, dear sister. You pathetic, wretched little thing. I used to think you had so much potential, yet here you are, letting an orphan from the Ashes fight your battles for you. But no matter," he adds cheerfully. "You'll both be dead soon, anyway. You all will. Just like this silly boy whose body I took."

That's it. He may be wearing Karston's face, but if Karston isn't in there anymore, I'm going to beat Hadrien to within an inch of his life before I kill him for a second time. But what if Hadrien's spirit just leaps into another body once Karston's is dead? After all, we're dealing with strange, unknown magic here. But I still have to try.

I charge forward, growling a challenge as Hadrien raises his weapon. He's not fleeing up the stairs. Good. Time to remind him once again that I'm the better swordsperson. My blade sings as it clashes against his.

"Last time I fought you, you didn't even bother picking up your sword." I push against his weapon with all my strength, letting my anger at his casual mention of Karston's death fuel my movements. Though I have far more training than him, Hadrien is a more formidable opponent in Karston's muscular body. "Looks like you're learning."

Behind me come the sounds of Danial and the other guards moving closer, ready to assist me at a moment's notice.

The metal soldiers, I see briefly out of the corner of my eye, watch us with their blank faces, seemingly awaiting Hadrien's orders.

Suddenly, Hadrien's eyes roll back in his head. He sinks onto the stairs, and I lower my sword, breathing hard.

"Odessa," Karston grits out, sounding like he's in pain. His eyes are pure violet again and wide with shock. "Your Majesty," he adds to Valoria, trying to bow while slumped over and almost toppling off the stairs. "Please, forgive me. All I wanted to do was help Karthia."

His eyes start to roll again. Keeping my blade safely out of his reach, I lean forward to grip his shoulder, giving him a sharp shake. We need to keep him talking while he's still in there. We need answers.

"Stay with us, Karston," I urge him. "It's good to see you again." I hope the warmth in my voice tells him that I mean it.

"Hadrien said there are spirits inside the soldiers," Valoria says quickly, gesturing to the line of iron figures still standing at attention, still waiting for their master to command them. "How is that possible?"

Pain twists Karston's handsome features. "I— It started when we went to look for Jax in the Deadlands," he says quickly, as though he knows he's running out of time. "Odessa and I got separated, and I met him. Hadrien. I didn't know who he was—how would I recognize a prince I'd never seen? I'd never even been to Grenwyr City until the school opened, and besides, he used another name." He gives a short, bitter laugh. "He asked me to come back to see him again. He said he'd keep me safe in the Deadlands—so I kept visiting. He was funny and kind, and he made me feel special. He understood me. And even though you all welcomed me into the pack, Hadrien made more time for me than anyone else. He's—he was—a good friend, I thought."

I dab my damp face with the bottom of my tunic and nod for him to continue as waves of nausea roll through me. The thought of someone feeling anything but revulsion toward Hadrien after what he did makes me sick, even if the mad king was hiding his true identity.

"He helped me figure out what my gift really is—raising the dead in a different way," Karston says softly. "See, I can take spirits and carry them inside myself from the Deadlands to our world. I can put them in anything I choose," he continues, a faint sheen of sweat coating his brow. "I told Hadrien about training with our volunteers, and how we didn't stand a chance against a real army yet. So when Noranna started making those metal soldiers, Hadrien and I came up with a plan. He found me spirit volunteers who didn't mind the idea of iron bodies, and I put them in the soldiers."

"Did you ever see any frozen spirits while you were in the spirit world? Is that part of your magic, too?" I can't help but ask, though it hardly matters now that all the danger is here, in our world.

Karston shakes his head, looking as confused as I feel when I think of the temporarily immobile spirits.

As we fall silent, Valoria steps forward, her gaze trained on Karston. She studies him for a moment before speaking.

"Why didn't you tell me this on any of my visits to the temple? You couldn't have told Odessa, or Simeon, or *anyone*?" Valoria asks, her voice thick with a mixture of pain and shock. "I trusted you, Karston. My friends and I, we accepted you as one of us. Welcomed you into the pack, as you said. And still, you lied to us about your gift. You're no better than Ha—"

"You think I don't know that?" he bursts out, cutting her off. "But you needed an *army*, Majesty, and you'd forbidden raising the dead. I wanted to be invaluable to you, so I could stay in Grenwyr for good—the one place where I finally fit in. The only way I knew how to give you what you needed was by lying about my gift. I didn't think it could do any harm. Hadrien promised me he'd be one of the first into the soldiers, and that the other spirits would listen to him. I . . ." He raises his chin a fraction, but he struggles to meet Valoria's piercing gaze. "I was going to tell you, once I was sure it worked. But every time I tried, every time the soldiers did something strange, *he* took over. I guess he doesn't mind me telling you now—now that he's shown himself. I started losing hours here and there. Anything he didn't want me to know, he'd try to wipe from my mind." He bows his head, clearly ashamed.

"Spirits being able to take over your body—that must be the cost of your magic," Valoria says shrilly. I think she's in shock. "After pulling a spirit from the Deadlands, your body is open to other spirits as a vessel they can occupy—just like the ones you put them in. I could have helped you figure that out, if you'd just come to me and been honest! I also could have told you that my brother never cared for you. He's never cared for anyone but himself."

"Why would I have come to you, Majesty?" Karston's voice breaks in his anguish. "I didn't know what was happening! I thought something was off after the soldiers attacked you at the demonstration, but I wasn't entirely sure. Hadrien kept messing with my memory, leaving me in the dark with fragments to piece together. But I finally figured it out after he used me to kill Noranna and everyone else at the wedding." He shakes his head, his shoulders quaking under waves of grief. "I was on my way to put a stop to this—to end things for good—when he took over and used me to strangle Odessa and free his army. I don't want to hurt anyone ever again. I don't—I can't take the pain. Mine, theirs—it's too much."

I wish there was something I could say to ease his suffering. But I don't have words for my friend crouching on the stairs, looking like he's about to be sick. Because I failed him. Maybe Valoria did, too. From the sound of things, a lot of us did. I should have spent more time with him. I should have—

"Hadrien," Karston says sharply, interrupting my thoughts. I wonder if he's yelling at the other voice in his head. But as his eyes begin to shift from violet to brown, I realize it's a warning and raise my blade.

XXX

Holding his short sword carefully, Karston staggers to his feet. I hesitate. What if there's some other way to get Hadrien's spirit out of him, one that won't kill him?

Karston blinks, pressing his mouth into a grimace, and when he refocuses his gaze on me, his eyes are violet again. "He's too strong," he murmurs as sweat drips from his forehead. "He has too much control now. I can't fight him anymore, but I have one last thing to try." He gives me a shaky smile. "Odessa, if this doesn't work, promise me you'll save the kingdom. Again."

"Karston, what—? No!" I shout as he quickly turns the blade on himself and shoves it through his chest. Other shouts join mine, almost drowning out the sound of Karston gasping at the impact, at the pain. He sinks to his knees. "His . . . hatred has no place here," he grits out, the last words soft as a breath.

The most striking eyes I've ever seen quickly close.

I rush up the few stairs between us, kneeling at his side as his head falls forward and blood gushes from around the wound. I call for a healer, for Danial. He hurries to join us on the narrow staircase.

Right behind him comes Jax, somehow making room for himself between me and Danial. "Don't do this. Don't go. I'm sorry I was such a jerk," he says, gripping Karston's shoulders as if trying to shake him awake. "I just . . . you're a fighter." He swallows, gazing into Karston's now-peaceful face. "You're me." He shakes his head, his eyes shining, unable to say more. But I know what he means. The person Jax is hardest on is himself.

"Hang on, Karston," I choke out, grabbing his broad, warm hand. "We can fix this. We'll find a way to send Hadrien back to the Deadlands without hurting you."

Danial gently nudges me in the ribs, shaking his head. "There's nothing I can do."

Karston is gone.

For a moment, I can't hear anything but the sound of my heart beating, cruelly reminding me that Karston's *isn't* anymore. I sink against Jax, who crumples against me at almost the same time. Howling with grief, we cling to each other.

Even knowing that Karston must have taken Hadrien with him doesn't make me feel any better. Another friend is missing from our world now, and there's an army mere hours away that will take full advantage of our weakness. Worse, we're standing in a room full of powerful figures with spirits inside them, spirits who seem to still be awaiting orders—for now.

All the time and effort we put into the metal soldiers, and we were creating a weapon for the enemy all along.

All Karston's efforts to help his kingdom were turned against him, thanks to Hadrien.

"It's my fault," Valoria says darkly. "I should have been paying closer attention to the students. Besides, I banned raising the dead, and—"

Karston's head snaps up. His hands grip the sword hilt and begin to slowly draw it from his chest as his rich brown eyes survey the dungeon.

Hadrien casually drops the sword. He smiles as Danial, Jax, and I stagger back, nearly falling down the remaining stairs in our haste to retreat. Karston's body dying should have meant Hadrien's spirit leaving, too, just like when we would run a blade through a person's body to send their spirit back to the Deadlands.

But this is unfamiliar magic. Dangerous magic.

Already, the blood is drying on Karston's necromancer's uniform. And though the wound in his chest still gapes, it doesn't seem to be slowing his body down in the slightest with Hadrien pulling the strings from inside.

He leaps over the stairs, soaring past us as Danial, Jax, and I try to stop him with our blades. He bumps into a stunned Valoria, knocking the crown from her head, and hurries into the embrace of his metal soldiers—those spirits from the Deadlands apparently loyal to him. They close ranks around him, shielding him from view.

"Go," he booms out from behind his wall of iron. "Flee. I'm not stopping you. In fact, you've all become so boring and pathetic, I'll give you a head start before my army gets to work. Sound like fun?"

Already, Danial and Jax are ushering Valoria up the stairs still slick with Karston's blood. Her crown rests on the floor near one of the metal soldiers' feet, apparently forgotten.

We can't fight Hadrien's iron army. Not with our hands. Not with our weapons. Not with fire. I've experienced what it's like to fight the metal soldiers firsthand, back when I thought Karston was in control of their every move, and even that would have proven fatal had he really wanted to hurt me. They're too strong.

Much as I want to stand my ground and stab things, our only chance for survival right now—our only chance to save Valoria—is to flee as fast and far as we can.

"There's nowhere in Karthia you can run," he calls after them, as if sensing my thoughts. "Whatever you do, however far you go, it won't matter. The kingdom is finally mine again." A few of the soldiers shift creakily at that, as if in protest, and he hastily adds, "Ours. Karthia is *ours*. You tried to banish the Dead, Valoria, but we're here to take this world back! This is our rightful home, and now it's *you* who will have to suffer a dull eternity in the Deadlands. Death to the living!"

The soldiers applaud stiffly before beginning to march forward. Lysander leaps between them and us, and though he's trembling all the while, he guards our backs as I grab Meredy's hand and we race up the stairs together.

"Lysander!" she screams, turning back to check on him as I try to keep her moving after the others.

The grizzly bounds up the stairs close behind us as another light, metallic sound begins to fill the dungeon. But the soldiers aren't following us, I realize as the eerie sounds of their movements pursue us. They're collecting their spears, preparing to march.

We tear through the palace, alerting everyone we can along the way, and finally emerge into a cold, misty night.

In the gardens, I listen for the clanking sounds of Hadrien's soldiers and try to catch my breath as Valoria explains what just happened to the remains of our volunteer army, those who gathered here and have been waiting since sunset on her orders.

Someone produces a lantern—Danial.

As he raises it toward the sky, shining light across our faces and the cliffs, I glance warily at the horizon. There aren't any ships cutting through the night yet, but there will be soon. I hope Hadrien won't have as easy a time dealing with them as he seems to anticipate. That would buy everyone in the city a chance to escape.

Jax whistles, getting everyone's attention so Valoria can address the group. She has to shout to be heard over the sounds of terrified nobles in their robes and dressing gowns fleeing down the hillside, shrieking about metal monsters.

"We need to get to the school," Valoria says quickly.

"Majesty, you need to go to the harbor. Get on the *Paradise*, and get out of Karthia," Danial says, his voice low and urgent.

Valoria shakes her head. "I'll go, but only after we fetch the students. They have to come with us. They're Karthia's future as much as I am."

"Fine," Danial agrees. "I'll raise the alarm in the city and meet you at the *Paradise* after." He stands tall despite having barely recovered from all the healing he did, despite the screams now issuing from the palace windows. Apparently not everyone heeded our warning when we fled the palace. Casting his gaze over the volunteers, he asks, "Who's with me?"

Almost all the new soldiers, young and old alike, follow him down the hill, toward the city. I can't help but wonder if and when we'll see them again as their retreating figures grow smaller.

"I'll head to the rookery," one of the remaining volunteers offers, her expression grim. I think she was a friend of Bryn's and Sarika's. "Someone has to warn the other provinces."

"You'll never make it out of there," I say quickly. "You heard what they want—that *death to the living* nonsense."

"But someone has to do it," she insists. "I'll send as many messages as I can before they reach me."

I shake my head, looking to Valoria, expecting her to talk some sense into this brave girl. But Valoria merely bows to the guard, then embraces her. As they pull apart, and the girl dashes back into the palace, the crownless queen echoes softly, "Someone has to do it."

The few remaining guards accompany Valoria, her little sister Ruthie, Jax, Meredy, and me as we begin the brief journey to the temple. Lysander brings up the rear.

There's no time to wrap our faces against the wind that spreads the black fever.

Hoping for the best, we run, chased by the sounds of the metal soldiers streaming out of the palace and making their way toward the city. Following the path of Danial and his army. I hope Hadrien's soldiers can't run as fast as real people.

But as we near the temple, distant screams tell me everything I need to know, and everything I feared: Hadrien's army caught up with Danial's. And once he's done with them, no doubt, he'll use his soldiers to murder the living in their beds. Not because he wants to convince them of anything this time, but because he's grown even more twisted in the Deadlands.

I don't know what I'll tell Simeon when I see him.

Valoria leads the way inside the temple, flinging open the door to find Simeon and Nipper in the library with a few of the students, all pulling on cloaks as if preparing to leave.

The moment she spots me, the dragon bounds over and wraps herself happily around my legs. I pat her head absently as I listen to Simeon.

"We heard the screams," he says by way of greeting, glancing from face to face. "We figured it was bad." Softly—almost unconcernedly, someone might say if they didn't know Simeon—he adds, "I see Danial's off doing something stupid."

Valoria quickly explains everything that happened at the palace, and the students' eyes grow wide with shock.

"Where's Zee? And the captain?" a dark-haired girl only as tall as my waist asks Simeon. She glances around the shadowy library, illuminated on this cloudy night only by the dying fire in the great hearth, her eyes shimmering with worry.

Despite all that's happening, my heart gives a leap. Captain. Kasmira must be here.

"Coming!" Azelie's voice bounces down the hallway. She sounds slightly out of breath. She appears a moment later, several vials and notebooks in her hands, followed by—

"Kasmira!" I shout.

Heedless of the black fever, I meet her partway down a hall leading off the library and rush into her open arms. She chuckles softly as she embraces me, clearly not yet aware of the extent of the danger—and to my amazement, there's not a hint of strain in her breathing.

"So you finally conquered the fever," I say, drawing back to see that her gray eyes are as clear and alert as ever.

"Only thanks to my friend here," Kasmira says, nodding to Azelie. "I'm *cured*."

Azelie lifts her chin proudly as she holds up the vials and notebooks. "I was able to recreate Hadrien's research on a cure for the fever. It was a lot of work—a *lot*—since I could only find a few scraps of his notes that weren't destroyed. Still, it was enough. I would've told you sooner, but I didn't want to get anyone's hopes up until it was ready to test."

For a moment, all I can do is stare, amazed by the power Azelie holds in her hands: an end to so much death and agony. A cure for the black fever. Finally. I'm so grateful for all she's done for Karthia in her short time living here.

The three of us hurry to rejoin the others in the library, only to find them all standing by the doors, tense but ready to leave. Simeon and Jax hold some of the youngest students' hands.

"We'll take the *Paradise*, of course," Kasmira says. "We'll fit as many people as we can . . ." Her voice trails away as she scans the faces gathered by the doors. "Wait. Where's Elibeth?" she demands.

"Danial and the others will warn her when they reach Noble Park," Valoria explains.

"That's right," Jax says brusquely. "Now, we need to get the queen out of here—"

"Danial and the others might not make it to warn anyone," I interrupt, unable to look at Simeon as I say it. "They were being attacked by Hadrien's army, last we heard."

"You're right. I have to go to her. I have to make sure she's safe," Meredy says softly. Meeting my gaze, she adds, "She's the only family I've got left. I'll meet you all at the ship, if I'm able, but don't wait for me." She closes the distance between us, and the others step back slightly to give us room.

"I don't like it, but . . . I understand," I murmur. "At least let me come with you," I add, though I see the answer in her gaze before I've even finished speaking.

Meredy shakes her head, her eyes shimmering slightly. "There's no guarantee I'll make it back. And besides, Valoria needs you." She pushes a finger against the sapphire pin on my chest. "Trouble with the Dead has your name all over it, Master Necromancer. I know it seems impossible right now, but you'll figure this out. You always do."

"I could still come," I press, even knowing she's right. "You can't stop me."

"Of course not," she agrees, leaning closer, our lips almost touching. "But you'll do the right thing—getting our queen as far from here as you can—no matter how much you grumble about it. That's part of why I love you."

"I hate this so much," I whisper as her face begins to blur.

"I know," she murmurs against my mouth. "But we've survived worse."

She kisses me, long and slow. Usually, her kiss tastes like strawberries, but this time there's nothing lingering on my tongue but the ashen aftertaste of a goodbye.

"I'll be safe. I have Lysander," she says as we draw apart.

In the absence of her touch, I struggle for breath. The ending in that kiss hit me like a blow to the stomach.

"Protect our queen, love. Protect our friends. And the cure." She gives me one final embrace before climbing atop Lysander's back. He sometimes grumbles about being treated like a horse, but today, he seems to understand the gravity of the situation and accepts his rider without so much as a growl. "See you on the ship!" she calls over her shoulder as Lysander dashes out the temple doors.

Simeon grabs my hand, and I hold on tightly. Both our hearts are in other parts of the city now, out of our bodies, out of our protection, and out of our control.

With everyone else ready to leave at last, our small group of soldiers and mages—and one dragon—charges into the night, leaving behind the shelter of their new home.

There's nowhere in Karthia you can run, Hadrien said.

So we flee to the harbor. To the sea.

With only occasional moonlight to guide us when there's a break in the clouds—a lantern would attract too much unwanted attention—it's easy to pretend that the dark forms slumped on the ground here and there are just shadows. Not people.

But we can't ignore or imagine away the screams as we run through the mists of the Ashes toward the harbor.

Despite the late hour, the whole city is awake and terrified. People hurry by us in every direction, some carrying belongings, others clutching small children, all fleeing Hadrien's army as it marches through the streets. All around us, metal soldiers lash out with their spears, spreading chaos and destruction as they stab anyone unlucky enough to stumble across them. Sometimes, they use their hands to snap a neck or toss someone out of their way.

Fury at Hadrien tries to claw its way out of my chest as a metal soldier breaks down the door of a darkened shop and saunters inside, carelessly scattering glass. A woman, who must have been hiding there, cries out and is quickly silenced.

The spirits inside those iron bodies, the ones doing the killing, are no better than Shades. They're just as violent. Just as senseless. I suppose listening to Hadrien long enough would be enough to turn anyone's mind into something almost as twisted as his.

A crash draws my gaze straight ahead. Two metal soldiers have toppled a clothing stall in our path, forcing us to change direction as they march toward us.

Valoria gasps and Jax curses, shielding her, as we nearly collide with a group of frightened-looking women in charcoal-gray habits. It's the Sisters of Cloud, the nuns who maintain the temples of Vaia's gray-eyed face. We follow them through a gap between two dark, seemingly deserted buildings. The one on our right, I realize after a brief glance, is the tailor's shop where Karston and I found a gate for our trip to the Deadlands.

Simeon trips over a piece of a shattered door that's been wrenched from a shop and thrown into the street. Still holding my hand, he nearly pulls me down with him. We stumble for a moment, then quicken our pace to catch up to the others.

There are more hazards like the broken door in our way—chunks of glass, pieces of wood, dropped belongings.

Grenwyr City hadn't even begun to rebuild in the wake of its last battle against Hadrien. I have a feeling it will take even longer before recovery begins now, with hopes and funds already so low.

"Any sign of him?" Simeon asks me once in a while, in the same would-be-casual tone he used back at the temple.

Each time, I shake my head. I've been searching for Danial and the volunteers in every alleyway we pass, no easy task in the deep darkness. But the only bodies I've glimpsed among the rubbish have been unrecognizable.

As Simeon shivers and squeezes my hand, I resolve not to dwell on the possibilities. I have to hope Danial is still out there somewhere, still fighting. Just like Meredy.

Somewhere along our flight through the city, we lose the Sisters of Cloud. I stop noting which twists and turns we take, mindlessly following Kasmira. As we splash through a dark substance that stains the pale tiles of Merchant Square, Azelie coughs and gags. Moments later, the smell of carnage overwhelms me, and I swallow hard to keep from retching.

"Almost there!" Kasmira whispers over her shoulder, careful not to attract the attention of the few metal soldiers nearby.

Lucky for us, they don't seem to take notice of our little group, too busy storming into buildings and throwing bodies out of windows.

We quicken our pace. Nipper bounds along at Azelie's heels, for once not straying off on a whim. As the clouds roll back, I get my first glimpse of the harbor, moonlight glinting off ripples in the water.

There are a few other ships hastily drawing up their anchors and setting sail, ships full of panicked people who most definitely aren't the captains and crew of the vessels they've commandeered.

But the *Paradise* stays anchored, what remains of her crew standing proudly on the deck, their blades drawn. No one goes aboard without Kasmira's permission, like always.

I never really understood how she could love that patched, scarred, hopelessly waterlogged ship more than any living creature—until now. The *Paradise*, whispering of escape every time she creaks in the wind, is the most beautiful thing I've ever seen.

We're almost to the ship when someone behind me cries out.

It takes me a moment to realize who's made the sound, because it comes from a voice I've rarely, if ever, heard raised in pain.

Jax.

I was so focused on reaching the ship, I didn't see the three metal soldiers breaking away from their companions. One leaps in front of Valoria, blocking our path to the ship's gangway. Another positions itself at our backs, spear raised, hindering any hope of retreat toward the city. The third soldier pins Jax to the ground with a spear shoved into his chest.

I draw my blade. Just as I told him the day I followed him into the Deadlands, I'm prepared to die for him. Valoria pushes her way through her guards toward the back of our group, trying to reach us.

My heart drowns out every other sound as the metal soldier pulls its spear unceremoniously from Jax's chest, leaving him for dead.

Valoria beats on the metal soldier's chest with her fists, but it remains unmoved. "Why are you doing this?" she screams. The crew on the ship are shouting something to us, but I can't make out the words over Valoria's continued screams. "You don't belong in this world! I won't let you have it! If you want to kill someone, take—"

Her words are replaced by a choking sound as the soldier wraps its free hand around her throat and squeezes.

I lunge at the soldier throttling Valoria. I may not be able to wound the blasted thing, but I can at least distract it by jabbing my sword into its eye holes while both its hands are occupied, and hopefully allow Valoria to break free.

As the tip of my blade nears the soldier's face, strong hands pull my arms back so hard and so quickly that I think they might have dislocated my shoulders. Another soldier has me in its grasp, making me drop my blade and pinning me against its chest. It holds me like shackles, impassive as I kick its iron shins and scream every curse I can think of.

I don't know why it's not just snapping my neck. The other metal soldiers seem to be trying to kill everyone else while I'm forced to watch.

As Valoria's guards attack the soldier who has her by the throat, its companion picks the human soldiers off one by one, knocking them unconscious and throwing them into the harbor. There's a flurry of movement and more shouting as the *Paradise* crew tries to assist, saving whomever they can.

Of course, I realize with a blinding burst of rage, bruising myself as I continue to thrash in my captor's hold. These must be Hadrien's orders to the spirit soldiers: To leave me alive long enough to watch my friends die. To bring me to him, so he can kill me himself.

After helping Azelie escape a soldier, Kasmira manages to reach Jax and drops to her knees beside him, trying to stanch his bleeding by putting a hand over his wound and pressing down. As I watch, furious at my own helplessness, I try to remember if there's a healer among the *Paradise*'s crew. Since Dvora died, there may not be, and Kasmira's efforts won't be enough to keep Jax alive for long.

The whole world seems to narrow in the space of a few heartbeats, shrinking to nothing but a burst of violent sound: Valoria's choking, Ruthie's cries as she bangs on the shins of her older sister's attacker, people screaming as they're thrown into the water, soldiers' creaking limbs, Jax's delirious groans, and Kasmira's cursing.

Above it all, an eerie, wordless melody begins to echo in my ears. The song Meredy and I have been hearing at night.

I look everywhere for the source of the sound. It seems to be coming from somewhere to my right, where Nipper stands gazing up at something on the *Paradise*, mesmerized. Is someone on board our mystery singer?

Suddenly, the soldiers freeze—just like the spirits in the Deadlands, the three figures seem unable to move. Simeon frees himself from a soldier's grasp and hurries to my side, though I manage to break free of my captor on my own. Together, we drop down beside

Jax as everyone else relieves the metal soldiers of their weapons by tossing the spears into the water.

"Who was singing just now?" I demand. But no one is listening.

Freeing her neck from the grip of iron fingers, Valoria staggers over to embrace Ruthie, looking dazed from lack of air.

The remaining guards kneel at the water's edge, searching for survivors, while Azelie examines the precious glass vials in her hands, checking them for cracks before another cloud obscures the moon. Shards of glass glitter near her feet like fallen stars, the result of her struggle against one of the soldiers.

Gazing down at Jax, I take over for Kasmira, holding the life inside him for who knows how much longer. I can barely feel him breathing.

I'm not aware of how much time passes before Simeon gives a startled shout and runs toward something behind me. I tense at his cry, reaching for my fallen blade with my free hand, wondering if more metal soldiers are headed our way. But it's Danial who appears and swoops down beside me without a word, his white healer's robes stained black and crimson.

The *Paradise* isn't the most beautiful thing I've seen, after all. Danial is, even when he's covered in other people's blood, looking like the face of Death.

After a few hurried minutes of Danial's careful ministrations, Jax gasps and sits up, clutching the spot where the spear pierced his chest. Valoria trips over the dock's uneven boards in her haste to embrace him, and as Kasmira helps our queen up, she says firmly, "There will be time for reunions on the ship, Majesty." Glancing back toward the city, where the ruddy glow of a fire is beginning to spread, and then to the soldiers as still and civilized as statues, she adds, "We need to hurry."

Already, Azelie is running up the gangway with her remaining vials of potion, giving a wide berth to the three unarmed metal soldiers who are still frozen in place. Of course, even without their spears, they can be deadly, and I don't know how long this mysterious reprieve will last.

I grab Valoria's arm and start to follow Azelie, but turn back at the sound of a huge splash. Jax has thrown one of the heavy iron figures into the water.

Letting the others run ahead of me, I hurry back to help him.

He leans on me for support—just a little, not enough that he'd ever admit he accepted help from someone—as we watch Noranna's creations sink. Water bubbles out of their empty eye holes as they go down.

"Come on, you two!" Kasmira calls tersely.

We dash aboard, and as the crew prepares to depart, most everyone else heads belowdecks to give the sailors room to work.

I can't bring myself to leave the railing, though. My skin prickles with heat as I watch the city burn, hoping to hear a grizzly's roar amidst the human screams. Hoping for Meredy and Elibeth to emerge from the blaze and run toward the ship.

Several times, I think of leaping over the rail to go find Meredy. After all, Valoria is safe now, and so is the black fever cure. I've done what I promised Meredy I would: I've gotten our queen to safety. Still, Meredy would want me to stay by Valoria's side and help her come up with a plan to stop Hadrien's army. I'm as sure of that as I am of my own name.

As we begin moving slowly seaward, my knees grow weak, and I lean harder against the rail. Meredy and I had barely gotten back together, and now we might never see each other again. I just want to hold her one more time.

"Hey, Sparrow." Someone wraps their arms around me from behind. "Just because she's not here doesn't mean . . ." Valoria whispers in my ear, but she can't even finish the sentence. "I'm here," she says instead, holding me tighter. "I'm here, and so are you, and we're going to figure out how to fight this together."

I shake my head. "Things just keep getting worse. Every time I think we've solved one problem, there's a bigger one right behind it. It's never going to stop."

"That's life," Valoria says softly. "But there are good parts, too. Like this." She leans against me. "This is why we keep fighting."

Trying not to think about the girl who stood beside me the last time I watched Karthia's shore grow smaller, I will myself into numbness and let Valoria lead me belowdecks. We step into a crowded cabin where Nipper greets me with an enthusiastic bark, and Simeon makes space for me on the cot I once shared with Meredy.

As I sit between Simeon and Valoria, I somehow manage to keep my grief buried down deep. Hopefully, it won't resurface until something reminds me of *her* too strongly to be ignored.

"To business, then," Simeon says, casting a look around at the handful of mage students, the few surviving volunteer soldiers, his husband, and his friends. "We need to get the spirits out of those metal bodies. Without a physical home to anchor them here, they should be sucked right back to the Deadlands through the nearest gate. We already know we can't burn them, beat them, or stab them. So . . . who has another idea?"

"The singing," I say at once. "You all heard that wailing sound right before the soldiers froze, didn't you?"

Most of the students nod. Even Valoria, who was being choked at the time, says she heard it.

"Well, when it was happening, Nipper here"—I pause, giving my little dragon an appreciative smile—"was looking up at the *Paradise*. I think someone on board knows a song that stuns the soldiers. We just have to find out who."

A wiry young man with eyes of deep sea blue, one of the mage students, turns toward the door. "I heard the wailing, too. I'll go ask around."

"You'll need help!" a green-eyed little girl declares, hurrying after him.

But as she reaches the door, she pauses, coughing so hard that her whole body rattles with the force of it. Something dark spatters her hands as she lowers them from her mouth.

It's only then that I notice the droplets of sweat clinging to her forehead.

"It's all right. No one panic," Azelie says from the back of the narrow cabin where she's tearing strips off her colorful skirt, carefully wrapping her potion vials in cloth. "I've still got these, no thanks to those brutes that made me drop some outside."

Her hair has come partially loose from its two knots on either side of her head, and I spot the beginnings of a large bruise on her cheek from our fight with the metal soldiers, giving her a wild—and fierce—look. I wonder if she's realized yet how many lives she's going to save. She did us all a huge favor in coming to Karthia.

Some of the students head up the stairs to help search for the mystery singer, while others watch Azelie give a few drops of her antidote to the little girl with the bad cough. Danial falls asleep with his head in Simeon's lap, his body rebelling against him for saving Jax's life. Jax leans back against the wall, holding Valoria in his arms. He holds her like she's all that's anchoring him to this world, like there's no tomorrow. And for all we know, there may not be.

I try to keep my mind on the trouble at hand, worried about what thoughts will creep in the moment I'm not focused. This is a problem with spirits, a problem for a necromancer—*me*—yet I don't have any idea how to stop the soldiers if I can't sink my blade into their flesh. That's how we've always sent spirits back to their world. That's all I was taught, all I know.

My eyes begin to drift closed of their own accord, lulled into drowsiness by the steady breath of the sea. But when I'm almost at the point of slipping under, images of Meredy flash across my darkened eyelids—visions of her lying in an alleyway somewhere, of her broken body cradled in the embrace of a metal soldier. Somehow, even though she appears to be dead, she's screaming for me. Screaming my name.

I sit upright on the cot, soaked in sweat, breathing hard. At first, I think it's the pain in my shoulders that woke me—I couldn't bring myself to make Danial do any more healing—but then I hear Meredy's voice still echoing in my ears, calling for me.

Someone *is* calling me, I realize as the haze of sleep rolls back.

Only it's not Meredy.

I rush up the cabin stairs, Nipper at my heels, apparently excited that someone is awake for her to play with. Valoria untangles herself from a slumbering Jax and hurries after us.

Kasmira stands at the top of the steps, silhouetted by a glorious golden dawn, her expression grim. "There are ships," she pants. She must have run to us from the helm. "Strange ships on the horizon."

XXXII

Within minutes of Kasmira's sighting, everyone gathers on deck to watch the ships draw nearer. The Ezorans have found us.

This is it, then. Valoria would have died if she'd stayed in Karthia, but now it seems she's going to die in the one place we thought she'd be safe. Along with the rest of us.

Heat surges through me, rising with my temper. I don't want to die like this. If this is really the end, I want Meredy beside me. But she's not here, which means that somehow, I'm going to have to fight the Ezorans.

"I could conjure up the worst storm they've ever been through," Kasmira offers, glancing at Valoria, but the queen shakes her head. She knows about the tremors in Kasmira's hands, having seen it firsthand while sparring with her during one of our early training sessions.

Not one to admit defeat so easily, Kasmira says, "I could turn the ship around. Try to lose them somewhere."

Again, Valoria shakes her head and frowns. "Given how quickly they're moving, they'll catch up to us no matter which direction we choose. And I doubt they'll just let us sail away, now they've spotted us."

Indeed, the ships have altered their course since Kasmira first saw them, now heading directly into our path.

"I know," Kasmira agrees softly. "But if we don't try running, we'll really be—"

"Out of options," I finish for her, gooseflesh spreading across my arms and neck. I count the enemy ships as they get close enough to be distinguished from one another, surprised to find there are only ten. Even more surprising is that, while their ships' cannons could easily reach us from here, they've yet to open fire on our lone vessel.

"That hardly looks like an army," Danial says, sharing my thoughts.

Simeon glances sideways at him. "Ten to one? I like their odds better than ours. Maybe not against Karthia, but out here . . ."

"You're right," Danial muses. "They could finish us off here and now if they wanted. Wonder why they haven't fired yet."

As I watch the Ezorans' tattered flags billow in the wind, I remember the raven Valoria received from Baron Stryker in Lullin, where the warriors first landed. They didn't kill anyone there, according to the baron's message. They just stole things. And while I can only guess at their reasons, having witnessed the devastation they caused in Sarral, an idea is beginning to take shape in my mind.

"We could try talking to them," I blurt, raising several eyebrows among the group as I explain my thinking. "Valoria, you could send a coalition aboard to find out what they want with us. Or at least one person. I'll go."

Valoria is quiet, looking across the water at the ships as she considers my idea. "It seems rather risky, even given their behavior in Lullin . . ." she says at last.

"It's not a risk," I say at once. That raises even more eyebrows. "We don't have any risks left to take. The ships will be on top of us before we know it, and we don't have enough people or weapons to challenge them in a fight. There's no running, and there's no winning." I glance toward the horizon, where the ships loom larger with each passing moment. "Trying to reason with them is our only move."

"All right," Valoria agrees, her shoulders slumping in defeat. "We'll try it. But I'm coming with—"

"No!" several people say in unison, shouting her down.

"Fine," she bristles, her eyes bright.

"I'm going with you, sweet sister," Simeon says firmly, glancing between me and Danial. "But our general should stay here, to protect the queen."

"Agreed. But I'm coming, too," Jax jumps in, hurrying to my side. "And, Majesty, if this doesn't go as planned . . ." He meets Valoria's gaze and, drawing his favorite sword, hands it hilt-first to her. "Kill every last one of these bastards for us."

"You have my word," Valoria says, accepting the blade. "But you'll be back at my side before you can miss me."

Jax pulls Valoria's hood up over her head, concealing her face so she won't be such an easy target, though there's really no need in the absence of her crown. "I don't think that's possible."

I turn away from them, my stomach in knots as doubt and hope war within me. They both sound sure the other will survive. It's the kind of certainty I should have had all this time about Meredy. Surely she found her sister. Surely she, Elibeth, and Lysander are well away from the city now. Meredy's smart. Smarter than me, and more cunning, less reckless. She'll know places where they can hide.

Suddenly, I'm anxious to get back to shore. I'll see her again. I *will* find her, if she doesn't find me first.

One of the sailors hands me a piece of torn sail, drawing me from my thoughts. Reluctantly, I push Meredy to the back of my mind and inspect the frayed cloth. The fabric is weathered and stained, but still white enough not to be mistaken for anything but the peace it's meant to represent.

Once it's been hoisted, there's nothing to do but wait for the Ezorans to kill us or join us.

To my surprise, the Ezorans don't have the heads of their victims decorating the bows of even a single ship. It feels more like years ago than months when Azelie told me that gory detail. She also assured me they have a penchant for experimenting with dark magic, and if that's true, our blades won't be much use if they decide to wield their mysterious powers against us.

Still, as the first of their ships draws alongside us, I absently put a hand on the hilt of my sword. Simeon gently elbows me in the ribs as he, Jax, and I wait for the gangway to be lowered, and I drop my hand to my side.

They could have fired on us or used their powers long before now, I remind myself as I study the faces of the warriors on the Ezorans' ship. Their pale skin—paler than I remember, even—seems almost ashen beneath the charcoal-dark tattoos of intricate dots and swirls that grace their faces and arms. Many are sweating profusely, too, no doubt miserable in their rich furs and leather even with the cool sea breeze providing some relief.

A woman who looks to be in her twenties, her white-blond hair half in braids, breaks away from the rest, surveying us imperiously.

"Come. We must speak," she commands in Kanon. "We will keep our swords from your throats. For now." Silver rings set with gems flash in the morning sun as she beckons us with a curl of her fingers.

As I prepare to cross the makeshift bridge laid down between the ships, Kasmira struggles to hold Nipper's lead. The dragon seems eager to accompany me, Jax, and Simeon, completely unaware of the curious—and, in some cases, hungry—stares that the Ezorans are giving her.

My knees seem to dissolve as I make my way slowly over the bridge. It's not the warriors and their extensive collection of pointy objects that worry me, but the precariousness of walking a thin line where the ocean waits on either side to swallow me up if I make a single misstep.

I meet the blond woman's eyes in a challenge as I walk. She's clearly their leader, and I want her to know I'm not afraid. At least, not of her.

As I step onto their ship, I feel the weight of my necromancer's pin against my chest. It makes me square my shoulders and stand taller. I don't reach for my sword. Instead, I face the blond woman and offer her my hand.

"I'm Odessa of Grenwyr. Master necromancer. And these are my companions." Turning, I gesture to Simeon and Jax on either side of me and continue the introductions. "We're here to speak on behalf of Her Majesty, Queen Valoria Juline Wylding. Ruler of Karthia."

For a moment, the Ezoran leader regards me in silence. I leave my hand out in offering. I don't think I've ever had so many people stare at me quite this intensely, even when I killed my first Shade.

At last, after exchanging a glance with her companions, she nods and says, "Well met, Odessa of Grenwyr. I am Orsa, the Exalted One of Ezora."

"Is that like . . . a queen? Or more like a nun or a priest?" I'm not sure if I should be asking that, but then, I'm not sure of anything in this situation.

Orsa frowns. Her pearly blue eyes, which I have to admit are quite beautiful, narrow as she regards me. "I am," she says at last, "more like a queen." I think I see a hint of a smile cross her face, but the moment I blink, it vanishes.

She reaches toward me, apparently willing to take my hand at last. But before our fingers can touch, her eyes widen and she brings her hand to her mouth instead. A violent coughing fit shakes her, and when she's finally able to stand tall and face me again, her fingers are covered in black goo.

Cold washes over me as I realize I almost touched the hand of someone sick with the black fever. I cross my arms, resolving not to touch anything on this ship. Of course, being this close to the sickness and breathing the foul air means we're probably already infected.

If not for Azelie and her cure waiting back on the *Paradise*, I wouldn't be nearly so calm at the thought of getting sick.

"They've all got the fever." Jax's voice is a low rumble in my ear. "Look around."

The telltale blackberry-colored stains adorn the Ezorans' shirtsleeves, their hands, and the few handkerchiefs I spot poking out of pockets. All thirty or so people on this boat appear to be infected, and I can only assume the others in the small fleet have fared similarly.

Orsa doesn't try to shake my hand again, but she clears her throat to get my attention and manages to suppress another cough long enough to grit out, "Karthia's plague is swift and vicious. It is nothing like the one that devastated our home, but I fear it may kill us before we see our shores again."

"We cannot go home, Exalted One," another Ezoran adds. His

Kanon is stiff and formal, every word carefully pronounced. "If we bring this plague to our people, it will be the end of us. We *will* get aid from Karthia for the suffering they have caused us with their filthy cloth and goods." He glares at me and my friends as he takes a wheezing breath. "Or we will take as many of you with us as we can when we die."

"Why should we care if you're sick?" I blurt, directing my question to Orsa, who still stands closest to me. "Weren't you coming here to murder us all anyway?"

Beside me, Simeon sucks in a breath.

I definitely don't have a future as a diplomat.

Orsa's eyes flash in the intense morning sun. "Perhaps our war in Sarral confused you. We fight Queen Jasira and her people to take back part of her kingdom only, land that was once ours in ancient times. We made our way to Karthia seeking only to raid as we have in other lands along the way, for supplies to fuel our war. Sometimes, death is an unfortunate side effect of taking the things one badly needs. But we aren't murderers by trade—no matter what rumors would have you think."

I open my mouth to point out the obvious, but Simeon silences me with a look of alarm and another well-placed elbow to the ribs.

"So," I say as politely as I can manage with Orsa's entire crew staring me down, "you need supplies. Even if you're not on great terms with Queen Jasira, why not ask leaders like Empress Evaria and Queen Wylding for aid before stealing and leaving so many de—so many *unfortunate side effects* in your wake?"

Orsa leans closer. We're almost nose-to-nose, and the sourness of infection on her breath is enough to make my toes curl in my boots.

"Don't you think we tried?" she growls. "Our homeland has been blighted. The soil doesn't nourish our crops the way it used to, and the animals we rely on for meat have been dying off as a result. There's less of everything, yet babies continue to be born, and sicknesses take hold more easily than they used to because we're always hungry, always tired, always weak. I despise weakness—we all do—yet that's what we've become. So we wage war against Sarral in hopes of having a place to send our people, and in turn they spread rumors about us, making other leaders fear and hate us. There's no help to be found."

She draws back slightly, gesturing to the other nine ships flanking this one. "This is all we have left of the once-great Ezoran army. My best warriors have been reduced to the paltry number you see on these ships." Once again, she closes the distance between us. There's a bit of black goo staining her lower lip, and I try not to breathe. "Back when there were more of us, we pleaded our case before every leader we could find. None of them would aid us. The rumors some of them started, just to keep us away . . ." She shakes her head, bitterness deepening her voice. "Eventually, we had to start trying to take back our land in Sarral."

"Well, if it's food and supplies you're after, Karthia has plenty to share, as I think you've already seen." Eyeing the curved sword on her belt, I add sharply, "Plenty to share with those who don't threaten us with their blades, anyway."

"Maybe you should consult Valoria first . . ." Simeon whispers to me as the Ezoran leader turns to her companions. "She might not want you—"

The rest of his words are drowned by shouts coming from behind us. From the *Paradise*. Several people gather around Valoria, trying to hold her back, but she pushes her way through them and begins the precarious walk across to the Ezorans' ship.

Jax opens his mouth to say something, but one look into Valoria's hardened eyes is enough to stun him into silence.

In this moment, head held high as she strides confidently across the beam, she's every bit the queen I knew she could be.

"Exalted One, I'll gladly offer you food and supplies for peace!" Valoria says as she moves onto the ship, stepping nimbly between me and Orsa. "What do you say? If you agree not to attack us or steal, we will open trade with Ezora. Trades in your favor."

When Orsa says nothing, merely tilting her head, Valoria continues, "There's land here for the taking, too, good land your people can farm and live on, should they wish to submit to Karthia's laws and my authority. We will welcome them. Perhaps you'd rather continue your war with Queen Jasira though, burning through what few supplies you can manage to steal in other battles along the way . . . ?"

I shoot Valoria a grin, impressed.

The Ezorans' expressions are guarded as they listen. Orsa drops her gaze to the ship's deck, keeping her face unreadable as she considers the offer.

"I don't think they believe her," Simeon murmurs. "Not sure I would in their position, either. Can she really give them all those things?"

I nod, confident that she can. With the Dead gone, our farms have been producing more food than the living can handle, resulting in tons of extra waste in the rubbish heaps. Karthia has plenty to give if this is a matter of life and death.

At last, Orsa looks up, though her blue eyes still reveal nothing. "No one has ever offered us such a thing," she says coolly, "and we've journeyed to kingdoms from Sarral to ones so far away, they speak nothing like our language and have never heard of Karthia."

"Well, you've finally come to the right place," Valoria says firmly, standing taller. If she's uneasy, her voice doesn't betray it. "There's just one problem we'll have to deal with before you send your people to Karthia."

As she describes our trouble with Hadrien and the metal soldiers, the Ezorans' expressions turn feral in their anger. Some shake their heads or scoff, and a few even draw their blades.

"They're mocking us!" a man hisses to Orsa, glaring at the four of us. "I say we slit their queen from throat to belly and see what she's made of. Then maybe her friends will start speaking the truth!"

A chorus of agreement rises among the crew. Slowly, we edge backward toward the makeshift bridge that will carry us to the *Paradise*. I try to get Valoria to cross first, but she resists with more strength than I remember her having. I struggle to get a good grip on my sword's hilt with my sweaty hand sliding across the metal. But before we can make our escape, Orsa raises a fist in the air.

The restless warriors fall silent at once.

"How can we trust you when you tell such fantastical stories, queenling?" Orsa demands, staring pointedly at Valoria.

She holds Orsa's gaze, keeping a gentle smile on her face despite the insult. "It shouldn't be too hard. I've already given you my trust." She nods to me, Jax, and Simeon. "I sent three of my best friends onto your ship. And I'm here. You could slit my throat right now if you chose."

Orsa's lip curls. "So? All my warriors would gladly die for me on an enemy ship as well. And I would be there, too, fighting beside them. Now, give me a real reason to trust you, or you'll have to watch—watch your friends die before I kill . . ." She doubles over as another coughing fit squeezes all the air from her chest.

A murmur of concern ripples through Orsa's warriors as she chokes and gasps, dropping to her knees. Someone rushes forward to assist her, offering a handkerchief that quickly turns from ivory to a deep purple when held to Orsa's mouth.

"We have a cure for the sickness that ails you," Valoria says coolly, unruffled by the threats. "We don't have enough for everyone yet, but if you give us time to take back Karthia from my brother's army, we'll be able to make plenty. And as a token of our goodwill, we'll give this ship what little we have of the cure right now."

"You have my attention, queenling," Orsa chokes out, still breathing heavily from the coughing spell.

Valoria turns back to the *Paradise* and signals to Azelie, who begins making her way across the bridge between ships with a dancer's grace, several glass vials clutched in her fingers. If she's nervous, it doesn't show. It's only when she's standing beside me that I notice the liquid inside the vials sloshing around slightly thanks to her hands shaking.

I can't imagine what it must be costing her, facing the warriors who've been battling her people and not being able to retaliate. I don't think I could stand as still as she is, or offer to save their lives if they'd already wounded Karthia the way they have Sarral.

Orsa nods to the fair-haired woman on her left, who appears to be some sort of commander, judging by the sun-shaped pin on her leather vest and the extra array of tattoos on her face and hands. She steps forward to accept the vials from Azelie, who takes care not to let her skin brush the Ezoran woman's in the slightest. Once the cure is out of her hands, Azelie releases a breath and balls her hands into fists at her sides.

I put a hand on her back, lending my silent support. I just hope she's saved at least one vial back on the *Paradise* for all of us who might have been exposed here.

"Now, who's going to test this for me?" Orsa demands.

Several of her warriors volunteer at once, but Orsa's gaze remains leveled at me and my friends. "All five of you will drink it at once, while we watch," she says firmly.

The commander uncorks a vial and wafts it under our noses, surveying us calmly.

"If this is poison, we're going to kill every last Karthian and take the whole kingdom for ourselves," Orsa snarls, returning her gaze to Valoria as she drinks deeply.

"I've already told you," Valoria replies steadily, wiping her mouth on the back of her hand, "that there's an army of spirits inside metal bodies murdering my subjects. We don't need any more enemies. There was a time when it might have been in my best interest to poison you, but what we need now are allies." Nodding toward a warrior with black goo on his hands, she adds, "And since you're all sick, and your only hope of survival is our cure, it would seem we need each other."

Azelie gives me an encouraging nod as the commander presses the vial to my lips. I take a small, hesitant sip, remembering the bitterness of other potions. This one, despite the liquid's grayish appearance, tastes surprisingly sweet.

"This unique combination of herbs and flowers purifies the blood," Azelie says before it's her turn to drink. "There's nothing to be afraid of."

Orsa falls victim to another coughing fit as Jax and Simeon take their sips from the vial.

"They should show signs of any type of poisoning within a few hours," the commander tells Orsa, tossing the empty vial aside. It shatters on the deck, glittering like diamonds. "I'll monitor them, and if they still look healthy at the end of the third hour, we'll try this cure."

So we wait, the silence on the ship broken only by the occasional cough, listening to the wind rippling in the sails overhead. The commander walks back and forth in front of the five of us, peering closely at our faces for signs that we're taking ill.

My thoughts wander back to Meredy, to home, and to all the lives we could be losing at this very moment thanks to Hadrien.

A drop of sweat beads on my neck and trickles partway down my spine.

Somewhere in the distance, gulls cry, having strayed too far from home.

Finally, the commander nods, satisfied, and begins distributing the cure among her people, saving an entire vial for Orsa alone.

The Exalted One lifts the glass to her blackened lips, tosses her head back, and downs the liquid inside in one long gulp. "I don't feel any different," she mutters, narrowing her beautiful eyes at Azelie.

"That's because it doesn't work instantly," she huffs, crossing her arms. "This is medicine, not magic."

Orsa considers her for a moment, then nods and returns her gaze to Valoria. "If your cure works, we'll have a deal. Food and land for peace," she grits out, her words ending with a cough. "And if not, we'll board your pathetic excuse for a ship at sundown . . ." She pauses for a labored breath, during which I swear I can hear Kasmira spitting a curse at her. ". . . and kill every last one of you. Slowly."

XXXIII

With the threat hanging over us, we're free to return to the *Paradise*.

"How long will it take for Orsa to realize she's getting better?" I ask as Nipper bounds over to me, jumping up and colliding with my chest so hard that I nearly fall over. I run my hands over her smooth scales, and she nuzzles my cheek like she's forgotten once again that she's a dragon, not a kitten.

"A few hours, at the very least," Azelie admits reluctantly. "But certainly before sundown. She won't get her chance to order a murdering spree, if that's what you're asking."

I nod and gaze around the ship, determined to make the most of the wait. After all, even if Orsa were cured instantly, going back to Karthia still wouldn't be possible—we haven't gotten any closer to figuring out how to stop the metal soldiers.

As the sun climbs higher in the sky, I talk with the mage students who searched the ship for our mystery singer. They had no luck. I call Simeon and the rest of the students over to one side of the deck, where we toss out ideas for stopping the metal monstrosities: luring them all to a cliff and shoving them into the sea is the only plan we all agree could work. Under water, they wouldn't be dead, but they wouldn't be able to do any more harm.

While we try to come up with a way to draw the soldiers to the cliffs, Azelie plays fetch with Nipper, to the irritation of several of Kasmira's crew bustling about on duty. Some of the Ezorans gather at the rail of their ship to watch, many with smiles or envious looks, and I get the sense that they'd love nothing more than to raid a dragon farm and have their own scaly companions. I wonder if they know about the dragons' poisonous bites.

Valoria stays at the rail of the *Paradise*, too, watching and waiting for some sign that Azelie's cure is taking effect on the other ship. Jax tries to draw Valoria away several times, but eventually he gives up, brings her something to eat, and joins her at her post.

Raised voices on the Ezorans' ship cut short our conversation about whether the metal soldiers would eventually be able to crawl out of the sea.

The sun has half disappeared below the horizon, I realize with a start, putting a hand on my blade as my heart begins to race. Others around me do the same. I thought the Ezorans would wait until evening to attack if our cure didn't work for them, but maybe they get bored if they haven't stabbed something for a few hours.

When I glance over to their ship, however, I don't see anyone with weapons drawn.

Orsa mounts the bridge and quickly walks across to our ship. Alone. I don't know whether to call that brave or stupid, but I guess I have to admit it makes me respect her. Just a little, though.

Most people on our side lower their blades as Valoria rushes to meet her. She offers the other leader a hand as Orsa steps onto the deck of the *Paradise*.

But Azelie, it seems, wants nothing to do with this meeting. She disappears belowdecks, looking sickened.

"I've come to thank the people who saved my life," Orsa says stiffly, as though admitting our help was worthwhile causes her pain. "I didn't believe it was possible, but I'm not coughing nearly as much. And so, perhaps, your story about the metal soldiers is as true as your promise of a cure for the fever."

"We have a deal, then?" Valoria asks cautiously, clasping Orsa's hand.

Everyone gathers around them to hear the answer. I have to hold Nipper back by her collar so she doesn't charge in between them, demanding attention.

"We do. As of today, Karthia and Ezora are allies. We won't attack or raid, so long as you fulfill your end of the bargain." Orsa shakes Valoria's hand, and some of the Ezorans watching from the other ship applaud.

"There's one other thing I wanted to ask you," Valoria says hopefully. "Do you suppose your people could help train Karthians to fight?" She glances at me, then back to Orsa, and smiles. "A friend of mine has informed me that your warriors' skills are without equal, and the things they could show my people would be useful in keeping future threats at bay."

"We'll see," Orsa says. "Once you've begun to welcome us into Karthia, perhaps protecting its shores will be in our best interest, too." She sweeps her gaze over the rest of us, her eyes lingering on Nipper. "Ah. This must be one of the famed Sarralan dragons," she murmurs, excitement evident in her tone as she moves closer to me. "May I see her?"

"Go right ahead." I smile grimly. "But I have to warn you, she bites."

"I've heard dragons have incredible magical abilities," Orsa says as she kneels and pets Nipper's scales without a moment's hesitation. There's a warmth to her eyes that wasn't there before. "Has yours demonstrated any powers yet? She looks old enough."

"Not that I've noticed." I shrug. "Unless you count the poisonous bites, the fire breathing, and general trouble-causing?" I shake my head fondly at the dragon, who rolls over shamelessly for more petting.

The Ezoran leader arches her brows. "You haven't heard her sing yet, then?"

"What?" I wince, not having meant to shout.

Orsa smiles—more of a smirk, really. "In Ezora, we collect knowledge of the world's most arcane and interesting forms of magic," she says, raising her voice so others on the ship can hear. "Dragons may be scarce now, but it wasn't always so. We in Ezora, while we have no dragons of our own, hold the only known scroll ever written on dragonsong."

Valoria and Jax hurry over to join us. So do Simeon and his students, everyone crowding around us to listen. With Nipper demanding more belly rubs from her, Orsa obliges and continues, "Dragonsong, while often mistaken for the cries of angry spirits, does have one notable use: It may be used to aid a necromancer by momentarily stunning a troublesome spirit, so long as that spirit isn't already housed in flesh."

As she goes on to describe different types of sounds dragons can make, including a high, wailing melody, Jax, Simeon, and I exchange stunned glances.

That explains the spirits frozen in place in the Deadlands when I went there with Nipper. It also explains the song Meredy and I kept hearing at night. Nipper must have been trying to protect us when the metal soldiers tried to roam the palace halls.

I shudder. That also means those things were walking around more often than we realized.

Kneeling beside Nipper, I let her put her claws on my shoulders and lick my face, something I rarely do. She coos happily. Just like with Karston, I should have paid more attention to her. Maybe then I would have seen what she could do without the Ezorans telling me. She swishes her tail, whacking me in the head with it and almost making me laugh despite everything.

As I glance up, I catch Valoria beaming at Orsa, clearly grateful for her knowledge. I can't bring myself to give her any thanks, though. She is, after all, still a murderer, no matter how helpful or pleasant she's choosing to be right now. Plus, I'm not sure I buy the Ezorans' claims about once having owned land in Sarral. For all we know, that might be an excuse they made up to try to sweep in and take all the dragons there.

Of course, none of that prevents me from swallowing my pride and locking eyes with Orsa to ask her a question. "In all of Ezora's experimenting with dark magic—that's right," I say as she frowns at me, "I've heard about that. Anyway, in all your experimenting, have you ever figured out a way to rid an object of a spirit trapped inside it?"

Orsa continues to stare me down for a moment before nodding curtly. "I'll let Commander Ilyra explain. She's the only one among us to have done so."

The commander nimbly crosses between our ships, coming to stand beside her leader. When Orsa nods, Ilyra looks between me, Jax, and Simeon and says, "Pay attention. What you speak of is possible, but challenging at best. It's going to take hours, and it's going to bring you what may well be the worst pain of your life."

We listen in silence as Ilyra explains the process of drawing a spirit from an object. Every muscle in my body tenses as I realize what we're going to have to do. It sounds terrible. Still, some tiny part of me rejoices, renewed energy singing through my veins and waking me more thoroughly than a sunrise. Finally, we have a way to defeat Hadrien's soldiers that's far more permanent than tossing them into the sea.

"Let me make sure I heard right," Simeon says, his voice a shade higher than usual. "We"—he gestures to me and Jax, then himself—"have to be wounded to the brink of death so *our* spirits can reach through the metal husks and pull out the spirits inside? Then they'll be forced back to the Deadlands, never to trouble us again? Or at least, not until the next violet-eyed mage comes along?" When Ilyra nods, he laughs weakly and mutters, "Sounds like fun."

Simeon's words bring the awful reality of what we have to do crashing down over my head, snuffing out my momentary spark of joy. If Meredy were in my place, she'd be determined to stop the spirits regardless of the consequences. Knowing that, I resign myself to the fact that I'm going to have to deliberately bleed out when we return to shore.

But there isn't time for another plan, not with so many lives at stake. With Karthia itself at stake. It may not be exactly like the place I knew and loved for so long, and it may have taken Hadrien threatening to raze the place to the ground for me to realize it, but Karthia is still my home. It's still the place that smells of bergamot and the salty sea. Though we've both rearranged our contours in the last few months, we've found new ways to fit together, Karthia and me.

"How can we be sure you're telling us the truth?" Valoria demands suddenly, crossing her arms. She stands on her tiptoes, giving her a boost in height that still doesn't quite allow her to tower over Orsa and Ilyra the way I think she's intending. "All we have is your word, which means for all I know, you're trying to send my friends to their deaths. Can't we simply take the soldiers apart with tools and have our necromancers pull the spirits out without any of the bloodshed?"

Ilyra shakes her head. "That's not how the ritual works. There is no other way."

Orsa frowns as Valoria questions the Ezoran mage. "Do you forget your own words so quickly, queenling?"

Valoria frowns at the term. "I'm not a queenling. You're not that much older than me!"

"Yet you have so much to learn," Orsa says solemnly. "As you said earlier, it would seem we need each other. Our war in Sarral is not going well, and we found no allies in the places we raided on the way to Karthia. My people need new land, and you need help taking back that land before you can bestow it on us. It's in our best interest, as you say, to give you whatever assistance we can in this matter, be it knowledge, blades, or . . . both."

"Wait," I blurt, deliberately avoiding the gazes of Valoria and the others. "What are you saying? You're going to fight alongside us, when you could stay safe on your ship?"

Orsa just smiles, like the thought of a battle warms her heart, and says, "Perhaps it's difficult for you to see, young necromancer, but magic is limited. Fists, however, have infinite uses so long as one is alive. Why be a mage when you can be a warrior? And why turn down a chance to win a fight?"

I shake my head at her words. Still, I'm glad we'll have the extra swords when we return to Karthia.

Orsa offers Valoria her hand again. "I trusted you with my life when I was about to lose it, and you didn't disappoint me. But trust is a double-edged blade. I wouldn't risk the lives of your necromancers when I need them, too, unless it were absolutely necessary. Besides, our only practicing necromancer, Ilyra, will work with them. My wife."

"I will?" Ilyra says, her eyes widening as she turns to Orsa.

"You will," Orsa says to her before meeting Valoria's gaze again. "We must trust each other for this alliance to work."

"Trust," Valoria echoes, a note of doubt in her voice.

"That's right. I'm sure you're familiar with the concept." Orsa draws a small knife from her pocket, and my hand immediately flies to my blade. But she offers it hilt-first to Valoria. "Let's make an oath here and now, deeper than our words. Be my sister in blood, so that we'll never betray each other."

Valoria accepts the knife. She glances my way, but I'm careful to keep my face blank. I can't help her decide whether to make a blood oath with a leader who, while she doesn't seem as bad as the rumors made her out to be, is practically a stranger. The unknown can be dangerous, as we've learned all too well.

Gritting her teeth, Valoria draws the knife across her palm and hastily hands it back to Orsa, who does the same. It's a good thing Azelie's cure is flowing through their veins, purifying any lingering traces of the fever.

The Ezorans watching from the other ship applaud, howl, and whistle as Orsa's commander and wife, Ilyra, binds their hands together with a scrap of fabric. Valoria doesn't flinch once, not even when they have to squeeze their hands, mixing their blood further, or when they break apart and Danial sees to their wounds.

Just like that, it's done.

From the doorway, a small voice says, "Well, then. If our new allies can spare a few of the supplies they stole in Lullin, I'll get started on making more of the cure right away. There must be many sick people on the other ships in their fleet."

I glance toward the stairway leading down to the sleeping cabins, trying to gauge Azelie's expression, but her face is thrown into shadow by the lantern light. I hurry to her side and drop my voice to a whisper. "You don't have to do this. You've already helped Valoria by gaining their trust. Why—?"

"I've been listening, and they aren't as bad as they seemed," Azelie explains quietly. "They've done some terrible things, it's true, but they aren't the monsters everyone in Sarral believed them to be. I had no idea they once lived on part of our land." Softer, she adds, "When you think about it, most everyone here has probably done something terrible at one point or another. Even me. It's how we survive."

I squeeze her shoulder. She's right about that. Still, I won't lose any sleep over killing Hadrien this time around. Things have changed— I've changed—and I'm ready to do whatever it takes to stop him a second time. For good. "Give me a list of supplies," I say quickly, "and I'll bring it to Orsa before we set sail."

As Azelie scurries off to find parchment, I turn away from the stairs to see my friends waiting for me. Valoria, Kasmira, Jax, Simeon, Danial, and even Nipper form a circle around me, drawing me into their midst. I try not to think about the fact that we might be the only living members of the wolf pack.

"Are you sure you're up for this, you three?" Valoria asks, glancing between me, Simeon, and Jax. "As your friend, I really don't want you to, and as your queen, I'd rather you tell me *no* when I ask this, but..."

"But we're going to do it, no matter how much it hurts, because we have to," Jax says firmly. "Karthia is depending on us."

Simeon nods his agreement.

They're right. It's time to do the job I was born for. The job that's so much a part of me that I want to keep doing it, even if it kills me.

Putting an arm around each of them, I catch Kasmira's deep gray eyes and say, "Take us home, Captain."

XXXIV

A shroud of smoke and silence hangs over the seemingly abandoned depths of Grenwyr City. The only other ships in the harbor are two ancient vessels that clearly aren't seaworthy, and the only other people we see are unmoving corpses on the harbor walkway.

The haze of smoke lingering over the Ashes, the markets, and the taverns has turned everything gray and lifeless despite the presence of the morning sun. Stepping around both broken glass and bodies is a challenge, though the dead we spot can't possibly account for more than a fraction of the city's population.

Either everyone is hiding or most of them managed to escape.

"There's no telling where the soldiers are now," I say to Valoria and Orsa in the barest whisper, walking with them near the back of our group. Even though there's no gleam of anything metal in sight, I'd rather not risk drawing attention.

"They'll be at the palace, guarding Hadrien," Valoria whispers back. "If I know his twisted mind at all, he'll be there, polishing my crown."

Since our ranks have swollen considerably with the addition of the Ezoran volunteers from Orsa's ship—the rest of the fleet remained offshore—there's no stealthy approach to climbing the palace hill.

The group keeps relatively quiet as we follow Danial and his few remaining volunteer soldiers through the long grass toward the wrought-iron gates.

Sure enough, as Valoria predicted, there are six metal soldiers standing guard behind the gates—which means Hadrien, wearing Karston's skin, is somewhere inside his former home. My hands curl into fists at the sight.

"I see my trust wasn't misplaced, queenling," Orsa says softly to Valoria.

As they spot us, one of the metal soldiers breaks away from its companions and stomps into the palace, no doubt to warn Hadrien.

There's no way the other five will let us inside without a fight.

Danial pauses, turning and scanning faces until his eyes find Simeon's. "You ready for this?" he asks shakily.

Simeon hurries toward him, taking the general in his arms. "Not exactly, but this is what we do every day, right? One of us does something stupid, the other saves his life, then we make out." Faking a grin, he adds, "Besides, I risk death every time you give me one of your heart-stopping kisses. I'm used to it by now."

I kneel beside Nipper as they continue talking in low voices. "I need you to sing, girl," I murmur, hoping her uncanny ability to understand what I've asked her in the past wasn't wishful thinking.

Pointing to the metal soldiers who watch us impassively, with no idea what's coming, I pet Nipper's scales and whisper, "Sing for us. Please."

Nipper raises her head skyward. Not seeming to open her mouth at all—it's no wonder I never noticed she was our mystery singer—she begins to fill the air with dragonsong. The soft, eerie wailing swirls around us, drifting toward the palace and the soldiers at the gates. Nipper continues to sing as Valoria hurries forward, a set of ancient, rusted keys in her hand. Danial guards her with his sword as she unlocks the gates.

Only when she's a safe distance away does he draw them open with the help of an Ezoran warrior.

The metal soldiers remain frozen in place as Nipper's song echoes through the still morning air. They don't creak or move even the slightest bit when Jax shoves one to the ground and spits on its prone body.

"We're good," he declares. "Let's do this."

"I'm ready," affirms Ilyra, the Ezoran necromancer. If it weren't for her willingness to bleed out alongside us, I'm not sure I'd have agreed to try this at all.

With a last look at Nipper, I join Jax and Simeon in shoving the rest of the soldiers down into the grass, next to their companion.

Turning back to our friends, I look first to Danial, then Valoria, then Kasmira. "Well? Who's going to do this?" I spread my arms wide. "Somebody hurry up and stab me." After all, we don't know where Hadrien is hiding, or just how long the spirits in these bodies will stay frozen thanks to the dragonsong.

Valoria steps forward, Jax's blade in her hand, a determined glint in her eyes. But as she presses the blade against my side, her hands shake so much that all she does is nick my skin. The sword falls to the grass.

The three of us look to Danial, who shakes his head. "I'll be on hand to heal you, if this goes too far," he murmurs. "But don't ask me to do *that*." He mimes stabbing us in the ribs, looking unusually pale.

"I'll do it," an unexpected voice says. Orsa, the Exalted One, steps forward with her blade drawn.

I'm about to thank her for volunteering when she jabs her sword into me.

I fall to my knees in the grass beside the metal soldiers, trying to think of Meredy. She always gives me the strength to keep fighting. But all I can think of is how much everything hurts. As I writhe in the grass, I realize I'm on my back now, not my knees. Small gaps of time seem to pass without me noticing as my heart picks up speed, pumping blood out of me faster and faster with each beat like it's working against me. I touch a hand to my side, and it comes away slick with red. I wonder if I'm about to see Evander again. That, I wouldn't mind.

"Sparrow, the spirits!" Valoria's voice echoes dimly in the swirling darkness of my mind. "Grab the spirits!"

Oh, right. We have a job to do. I have to stop trying to stanch the life leaking from my skin if this is going to work.

Gritting my teeth, I take a deep breath and push back the dark and the pain. I manage to crawl on my knees toward the nearest soldier. Either this is getting easier or shock is dulling the worst of the agonizing burn in my side now.

I've never willingly let my spirit leave my body before. But I have to try, for the sake of all the blurry faces gazing worriedly down at me.

Putting my hand on the metal soldier's chest, I test the limits of my skin, trying to feel past it. Light-headedness overcomes me, and instead of taking a deep breath to clear my head, I welcome it, letting the feeling lift me up and carry me out of my body.

My hand—or rather, the filmy fingers of my spirit's hand—reaches with ease through the metal confines of the soldier and draws out the spirit of a wiry, angry-looking man. Count Rykiel. I don't like him any more in death than I did in life.

His spirit sneers at me for a moment before he's whisked away, toward a faint blue spot near the cliffs overlooking the sea—a gate.

I release a shaky breath and move to the next soldier, resolving not to look at how much of my blood is staining the grass around me.

As I place my hand on another metal shell, now understanding exactly how to reach past it, I catch a glimpse of Jax, Simeon, and Commander Ilyra. They're pale, but they're still here, just like me. I'm not sure whether they've figured out what to do yet.

Everything's so blurry.

Everything but my spirit's hand, that is, which I push out of my skin and plunge into the metal body before me to draw out another spirit.

The distant sound of creaking joints tells me more of Hadrien's soldiers are rushing out of the palace, but they're all stopped by a loud burst of Nipper's song before they reach us. As I tear my gaze away from the spirit of a tall woman I've just removed from her metal husk, I see the new batch of soldiers got stopped somewhere between the palace's front entrance and where their fallen companions lie. I wonder if they realize the metal bodies piled on the ground are now nothing more than scraps, as they'll soon be.

I'm not sure how many spirits the four of us necromancers pull from their metal hosts—not enough, or someone would have told us to stop, and Danial would be healing us. But I don't mind. I hardly feel anything now, except a nagging urge to follow the spirits I'm freeing toward the hazy blue glow.

My spirit pushes against the walls of my skin, restless in its cage.

I don't think I can hold it in much longer.

I'm about to call for Danial. But before I can shout his name, Valoria screams.

Glancing up, my eyes find the palace doors, but no one new emerges.

It's only when I glance at Valoria that I realize her scream was one of rage, not fright. And only when I follow her gaze do I realize that Hadrien is running along the cliffs in Karston's body, Valoria's crown on his head sparkling in the sun as he flees down toward the city.

Someone has to stop him.

A *necromancer* has to stop him.

Dragonsong won't work on him any more than blades will, not when he's inside flesh and blood. But I can't stand the thought of him wearing Karston's skin for another moment. I'm going to draw him out like poison from a snake bite.

I stagger to my feet, fighting now to stay inside my body, to keep myself standing. With one hand, I apply pressure to the stab wound Orsa created. With the other, I cast aside my useless blade. It'll only slow me down, and I don't want him to use it against me.

"Go get him, Sparrow!" Simeon calls weakly as he pulls another spirit from a fallen metal soldier with Ilyra's help. "We're almost done here!"

Valoria grabs my wrist, but I shake her off. "I have to do this," I grit out, already stumbling after Hadrien. I don't know if she can hear me or not. "It has to be me."

I take a path he won't expect, one where he won't see me coming until I'm right in front of him. I think the bleeding from my wound is slowing on its own, but I hope it doesn't slow *too* much. I don't want to have to reopen it again to let my spirit grab hold of Hadrien's.

I trip over something in my path as I hurry down the hillside—a body, I think. There's no time to check, no time to lament. As what little life I have left seeps from between my fingers, I run as fast as my weakened legs can manage to get to Hadrien.

We meet on one of the lower cliffs, just out of view of the palace itself.

Stars dance before my eyes as I try to focus. I had to outrun him and circle back, to surprise him like this.

He doesn't retrace his steps, or try to push past me, even though I'm clearly weak. Instead, he blinks calmly at me with deep brown eyes—brown, though they should be violet—and bounds to the very edge of the cliff, where a strong gust of a sea breeze tugs the cloak from his shoulders.

I may be out of it, but I know what this is. He's daring me to join him out there, where he can murder me with his bare hands. A choke, a punch, a push.

But the moment his hands are on me, I'll be able to draw his spirit out.

I take the bait.

"You don't look well, Sparrow." Hadrien's mouth twists in a sort of grin as I stagger my way to the cliff's edge, my head spinning more with every step. "Missing Evander too much to go on living?"

I shake my head, not in answer, but at the way he calmly closes the distance between us. But then, I shouldn't be too surprised—pride is what killed him the last time, too.

He swipes a hand toward me, and I let him, trying to feel the boundaries of my skin again and push past them like I did to reach inside the metal soldiers. Something clatters to the ground, blue stones that glitter in the sun. My necromancer's pin. He's ripped it from my tunic, and as he follows my gaze, he stomps the pin into the ground.

"You won't need that where you're going—or rather, not going," he murmurs.

I gasp as he grabs me by the shoulders and pushes me to the very edge of the cliff. I dig in with my heels, as the toes of my boots are over the open air, still trying to make my spirit grab hold of his.

"Enjoy your last breath," he hisses, using my friend's face to sneer at me. "After this moment, you'll be nothing. You are nothing."

There was a time when I believed that, too, I realize as we struggle on the cliff's edge, each trying to push the other over. But it's not the pin that makes me who I am. I've always been, always will be, a necromancer. Even when I ran off to sea, even when I turned my back on everything I am—I could never outrun myself. Without the pin, without even my name, I'd still be a fighter. I'd still be a commander of the dead. I'd still be a girl too in love with life to commit to death, even when it's calling to me more strongly than ever before.

Laughing, Hadrien breaks our strange embrace to land a blow to my side, right where Orsa stabbed me.

He has no idea he's given me just what I need.

A shove closer to death.

I latch on to his forearm. My flesh-and-blood hands dig their nails into him while I plunge my spirit's hands through layers of cloth and skin to reach his stubborn spirit.

The spirit tenses, jerking in my grasp as I try to pull Hadrien from Karston's body.

He's figured out what I'm trying to do. He's fighting me with all his strength, clinging to Karston's skin.

Suddenly, he sucks in a breath as Karston's body begins to fall backward off the cliff, an arrow sprouting from his chest. Hadrien's spirit, momentarily confused, clings to my hands, and I rip him out of his shell as Karston's body tumbles into the sea far below, crown and all.

I fight back a sob, even though I know Karston is long past caring.

Hadrien's spirit thrashes in my hold, but getting him out of my friend's body has momentarily renewed my strength, and I hold him in place as I try to figure out what to do with him. I don't want him returning to the Deadlands, poisoning more spirits against necromancers. I don't want him to hurt anyone ever again.

Blackness crowds the corners of my eyes, but I take a deep breath, willing myself to stay conscious just a little while longer.

Hadrien's blow to my wound caused it to bleed again, and this time, it's not slowing.

If it's the last thing I do, I have to put his spirit someplace where he can't do any more harm. Holding fast to him with one hand, I grab a large rock with the other. I must be delirious for even thinking it's possible, but what if I can do with this ordinary rock what Karston did with the metal soldiers? What if necromancers are capable of far more than I ever dreamed was possible?

Tightening my grip on Hadrien's thrashing spirit with one hand, I wipe some of my blood on the rock with the other. Spirits can't resist a taste of life. I guide his filmy hand toward the rock, prepared to watch his spirit simply drift toward the Deadlands gate nearby. But instead, he vanishes into the unremarkable grayish-brown stone.

Briefly, I consider kicking the rock into the sea. It's what he deserves, all things considered. But I still my foot. Better to let him sit here and watch the world pass him by until these cliffs fall into the sea, under guard and utterly helpless.

For the rest of time, he'll be trapped in silence, bound to something so ordinary, he would never have deigned to so much as glance at it.

"There now," I mumble at the rock, slurring my words. Not a good sign. "You've gotten what you wanted most—eternity in the living world."

My head spins again, bringing me to my knees. As the cliffs and distant palace begin to fade before my eyes, I'm able to catch a glimpse of Meredy running toward me from several hundred paces away, her bow still in hand, with Lysander and Elibeth at her back.

I smile.

I can go now. I can slip out of this skin and be free. This is how I wanted it to end, when it was my turn. Seeing Meredy's face one last time.

But death doesn't come quickly. Too tired to speak, I watch Danial and another healer sprint onto the cliff and work together to heal me as though I'm a spectator, not a part of this moment at all. Meredy sobs into Lysander's fur while her sister, Elibeth, keeps a hand on her arm as if to prevent her from rushing to my side and interrupting the healing. Simeon and Jax hurry onto the cliff next, their wounds already mended judging by their speed.

Warmth envelopes me as Danial and the other healer work. I'm going to make it through this, but I'm still too tired to move or talk.

Valoria, seemingly unable to watch, walks to the edge of the cliff and looks down. I wonder if she can see anything—a body? Her crown?—but it isn't until Kasmira arrives and lets Nipper off-lead to lick me in the face that I find my voice.

"What do you see?" I call weakly to Valoria as the healers work.

"Sea foam," she calls back, walking slowly to my side and kneeling.

"All right," Danial relents, raising his hands in defeat and rising with the other healer. "You're good as new, Sparrow. But rest here a moment. It might take a while before you feel up to walking around again."

I barely get a chance to thank him before Lysander and Meredy are on top of me, vying with Nipper and Valoria for a chance to embrace me. Still a little numb, I smile to reassure them, keeping them all as close as I can while having enough room to breathe.

"Maybe Devran and the others were right, and I wanted too much change too fast," Valoria says suddenly, glancing between me and Meredy. "I suppose . . . new magical gifts like Karston's will require a lot more guidance and research before they're unleashed on Karthia. I'll have to close the school, at least for a while."

I nod my agreement as Meredy helps me sit up straighter. I lean against her and squeeze her hand in thanks. "I'm sure you'll have to introduce some new things," I tell Valoria, "but what if you brought back some old ones, too? Festival days were so much fun—at least, when Hadrien wasn't asking me to dance . . ."

My voice trails away as I catch sight of Hadrien's rock. The plain chunk of stone is just out of my reach, but I point to it and begin to explain what I did and how I did it.

The look of astonishment on Simeon's face would usually make me laugh, but nothing seems very funny when my body still feels like Lysander stomped all over it.

Slowly, Valoria moves toward the rock and nudges it with the toe of her boot. After covering her hand with part of her cloak, she reaches down to grab it, hesitating before closing her fingers around it as though it might bite. Once it's in her grasp, she strides toward the edge of the cliff and raises her arm to hurl it into the sea.

"Wait!" I call. As everyone looks a question at me, I start to grin. I can't help it. I'm that pleased with my own cleverness. "I have a better idea," I explain.

XXXV

Hadrien's rock now sits on top of the highest hill in Grenwyr City, overlooking the palace and its surrounds, a perfect vantage point from which he watched us give the metal soldiers' empty husks to the sea. From on high, he'll even have a view of tonight's fireworks as Valoria hosts her first public festival since the one at which we bid farewell to the Dead.

And festivals aren't the only thing she's reinstated in the two months since we stopped Hadrien a second time.

After I had a long talk with her about it, Valoria came to understand that while we necromancers are willing to respect her ban on raising the dead, she has to respect us traveling to the spirit world regularly to make sure all is well. She even has us training some young and eager necromancers who we rarely let out of our sights. I'm afraid one of them, a girl of about eight with a vocabulary far beyond her years, looks at me the way I used to look at Master Cymbre. If I'm right, I'm in for eight or nine years of trouble—especially since the trainees don't have much to do other than follow us around until Valoria reopens the mage school.

For now, she's turned the Temple of Change into a library where all are welcome. I even helped her place the metal plaque naming it after Karston.

He's on my mind now, as evening creeps over the palace and we prepare for a festival he certainly would have enjoyed. But soon my attention turns to Meredy, who helps me into my party gown in the privacy of our shared room. As she does up the laces on the sides of my dress, her fingers slip between the fabric and my skin, lightly grazing the scar Orsa's blade left despite Danial's best efforts to heal me. Meredy, on the other hand, came away unscathed thanks to all the training she did with Lysander in Sarral.

I don't mind my new scar, though. It tells me that I fought and won another hard battle. It tells me that nothing is impossible, no matter how dire things may seem.

Turning in Meredy's hold, I grab her hands and kiss her fingers, then her lips. "I have to tell you something," she murmurs, drawing back to look at me. Her new insistence on never keeping secrets seems smarter than ever, given all the suffering that could have been avoided if people had been more open with one another.

"I asked Valoria for a favor this afternoon," she says, watching my face carefully. "She's going to set my mother free tomorrow and banish her from Grenwyr Province for good."

I squeeze her shoulders, letting her know I support her decision. "What brought that about?" I ask gently.

"Hadrien's rock. It got me thinking about prisons," she says, grabbing a brush from a nearby table and starting to fix my hair. "The ones we choose. The ones we create. Don't get me wrong, I think

Hadrien is right where he belongs—he more than earned his place."
She strokes the brush through my hair with a tenderness I've never
known from anyone else. "But my mother isn't any unhappier in her
cell than she was in her mansion. She'll still suffer when she's free, and
perhaps more so. Wherever she goes, she'll be reminded of everything
her cruelty cost her."

As she pins tiny, glittering butterflies in my hair, we talk about
who might be at the party tonight. Already, Azelie's black fever cure
is being made by every apothecary from here to the Idrany Islands.
That's definitely something everyone should want to celebrate,
though Azelie herself won't be around to enjoy the festivities.

She left this morning with Kasmira, bound for Sarral as Valoria's
newly appointed ambassador to the dragon kingdom, to help reforge
our old alliance and broach the subject of peace talks with the
Ezorans. Of course, she only took the job with the understanding
that a greenhouse will still be built near the Temple of Change in her
absence, and a promise she'll have plenty of time to tend the plants
between diplomatic trips.

"Suppose Kasmira is giving her trainees a hard time already?"
Meredy asks, sticking the last pin in place. She holds up a small mirror so I can admire her handiwork.

Nipper coos her approval from the spot she's claimed in the
middle of the bed.

"No doubt in my mind," I answer after a moment, grinning at
her. "I'm sure she torments them daily—when Elibeth isn't keeping
her busy."

Valoria insisted that Kasmira take two gray-eyed apprentice
weather mages to guide the winds on their voyage to Sarral. Partly to
give her hands a break, and partly to allow Kasmira to focus on her
new role as royal explorer and cartographer for Karthia. Naturally,

Elibeth insisted on accompanying the captain as her new girlfriend, bringing a familiar leather-bound book of maps and notes with her. One I've known in Evander's hands, then Meredy's. There's no question that Evander's dream of seeing the world is still alive and well—and through it, so is he.

"Oh! Let me fix one thing . . ." Meredy murmurs, stepping forward to adjust a pin in my hair.

I grab her around the waist as she does so, stealing a kiss. Several, in fact. Not just on her lips, but down the side of her neck, too.

Someone clears their throat in the doorway.

Turning, I meet Valoria's gaze as she smiles at us. Beside her, Jax has a hand over his eyes. "Are you two decent?" he grumbles.

Valoria rolls her eyes and pulls his hand away from his face. She's wearing a new crown, I realize. It's the first time she's put one on since the old five-jeweled one fell into the sea with Karston's body. At first, I think tonight's crown might be a relic from before King Wylding's time, but the metal looks too shiny-new for that.

Following my gaze, she smiles and pats the crown. "What do you think?"

It's simpler than her old one. Instead of five gems set into the silver filigree, one for each of Vaia's faces, there's only one enormous stone. At first glance, it appears to be milky-white, but as she tilts her head, hundreds of flecks of every color imaginable dazzle my eyes where the stone catches the lantern light from our room.

"I thought this was more fitting," Valoria says uncertainly, reaching up to run a finger over the smooth stone, "seeing as the old one didn't really represent *every* eye color." Sure enough, as she turns, I catch a flash of violet and think of Karston. I see amber, too, and remember Bryn. Light reddish-brown reminds me of Noranna, and the swirls of color bring to mind Sarika's ever-changing eyes. There's even a blue so dark, it makes me think of Evander. The members of our wolf pack may be scattered now, and in some cases gone altogether, but every mage is represented forever in this new crown.

"I love it," I say truthfully.

Valoria beams as Meredy and I join her and Jax in the hallway, beginning the walk to the palace courtyard. "Don't want to be late for my own party," she says lightly, though there's a quiver in her voice. "Though I wonder if anyone will bother showing up besides us."

I arch a brow. She invited not just the denizens of the palace, but the whole city and then some—even sending ravens to the nobles from other provinces who ignored her requests for meetings, who never bothered to send aid when she needed to start building an army. Surely some of them are bound to come, whether she's well-liked among her subjects or not, given the number of wine barrels she's emptied from her ancestors' generous cellar.

Today is the Festival of Grapes, a perfect time to celebrate with friends and enemies alike.

Of course, Simeon, Jax, and I can only stay until midnight, when we'll need to slip away with our new trainees and Nipper to have a quick peek around the Deadlands. Simeon and Jax spent the entire week leading up to Azelie's departure begging and bribing her to bring them back dragons of their own.

We enter a courtyard resplendent with all the usual party fare. Strings of sparkling lights—one of Valoria's inventions, surely—try their best to outshine the torches and bonfires spewing clouds of multicolored smoke into the starry sky. But more shocking than the dragon-shaped fireworks that greet us outside and make Nipper bark—more shocking, too, than the ten-tier white cake whose every layer is adorned with grapes and flowers—is the crowd that welcomes us to the party.

There are people everywhere. So many, in fact, that the courtyard can't contain them all, and several have taken the festivities to the garden as a result. Orsa's wife and commander, Ilyra, and a group of Ezoran warriors stand near the wine barrels closest to us. Some have kept their furs, while others have donned gowns or robes. I'm sure Orsa would have enjoyed the party, too, but she needed to accompany the first boat of settlers to Karthia from Ezora in person.

The more we learn about them, the more I realize the importance of never judging by rumor alone.

Sweeping my gaze past the Ezorans, I spot Simeon and Danial near the musicians, spinning each other around in a fast-paced and impressively complicated dance. Danial lifts a laughing Simeon over his head, then lowers him for a kiss as a group of onlookers, mostly children, whistle and applaud. The show-offs. They'll have to teach me the steps so I can try that one with Meredy at next week's Festival of String Instruments.

Near Si and Danial, fishermen dance with nobles I only vaguely recognize from portraits in the palace gallery. Barmen dance with other barmen, with apple-sellers, with barons and baronesses, with liars and lovers and overly perfumed people from all over Karthia.

"I can't believe it," Valoria whispers, drawing my gaze back to her. As she surveys the crowd, she grabs my hand. "There's the new Duchess Aventine! And there's the latest Countess Rykiel! And isn't that the young Duke Bevan?" She glances from me to Jax to Meredy, as if hopeful one of us can confirm her guess.

We all shrug. She gives a quick, nervous laugh in response.

"Oh, I don't know! I've never even *seen* half these people!" Valoria bites the nails of her free hand, something I don't think she's ever done. "These nobles . . . they wouldn't even answer my letters, and now they're here? Drinking my wine and eating my—oh, stars!"

She squeezes my hand in alarm. "I don't think there's enough food! It looks like half the city is here! And I *know* that duke over there came all the way from the Idrany Islands."

"Breathe," Meredy advises her gently. "I don't think they came for the food."

She barely gets the words out before a young woman with her auburn hair in a braided crown calls, "Time for a toast!" She's the new Duchess Aventine Valoria pointed out earlier, taking the place of her aunt who died at Simeon and Danial's wedding. She raises her glass of elderflower wine toward the sky. "To Her Majesty, Queen Valoria!"

A blond man in a handsome set of red robes raises his tankard— Devran, rebel leader turned ambassador to the people of Grenwyr, and Valoria's critic turned friend. "To the queen who made our enemies into allies! The queen who saved us from war!"

"To Queen Valoria!" everyone echoes—Jax's shout the loudest of all.

He hooks an arm around Valoria's waist and kisses her in front of the crowd. As they draw apart, he flashes her his wolfish grin, and her face glows like embers in the torchlight. I have a feeling they'll be leaving the party together tonight, just like they leave all our gatherings a few minutes early, hand in hand.

After that, Jax is in such high spirits that he demonstrates his uncanny ability to procure drinks in the blink of an eye, pressing a glass into Meredy's hand, then mine. We join in the toasting, and I'm about to drink my first sip of honeysuckle wine when a voice beside me shouts to the night, "To our Sparrow, who twice defeated the mad king!"

Valoria winks at me as she finishes her toast.

"To Queen Valoria and her Sparrow!"

"To Meredy Crowther, who fired the shot that finished him!" I raise my glass.

The toasts go on and on. The wine is still flowing when our small group of necromancers goes to make our usual rounds in the Deadlands.

It's still flowing when we return.

Meredy sweeps me into a dance, and we don't stop even when it's light.

After all, we Karthians love a good party.

There are flowers blooming on Evander's grave. Long, purplish stalks of budding sage cover the earth under which his body is concealed, though they sprout no farther than the boundaries of the graves beside his—his father's and his grandmother's.

"Look at all those," I tell Meredy with a yawn, still exhausted from the Festival of Grapes yesterday. Maybe it was two days ago. Everything's a bit hazy thanks to Valoria's wine.

"That's a lot of sage. Pretty, though," Meredy says, squeezing my hand as the late afternoon sun disappears behind a bank of clouds. She's been coming here with me every day since Hadrien's defeat.

Softer, she adds a moment later, "Sage flowers mean eternal life, if memory serves."

I nod, grateful for Meredy's steadying presence as we kneel together among the out-of-season blossoms. I begin to pluck the stalks around me, weaving them into a crown as I think. Flowers, real flowers, only bloom on someone's grave when their spirit has a message for someone in the living world. But the spirits that send those flowers are in the Deadlands—or so we've always believed.

Maybe Evander really is gone for good, but I don't think there's any mistaking why these flowers are here, with him. Maybe his spirit is wherever the spirits from the Deadlands go after the water there carries them away. Maybe there are worlds upon worlds we can't and won't know until we're done with this life. Maybe we have forever to learn and love and exist—or perhaps, like I've always thought, we only have the now.

But if the past few months have shown me anything, it's that the world is so much more than what I've been taught, so I'll have to side with forever.

Tying off the ends of my flower crown, I nestle it gently in Meredy's wine-red hair as Nipper and Lysander chase each other among the surrounding headstones.

"Want to talk about anything?" Meredy offers, lacing her fingers through mine. Her emerald eyes skim the sea of sage flowers before returning to my face.

There's no shortage of things to discuss. How the necromancer trainees swear they saw their first Shade today; how the provinces with the richest farmland are preparing for the arrival of the first Ezoran families; how Simeon and Danial are about to have the time of their lives on a much-needed quiet getaway to Dargany's warm southern coast; how Jax managed to buy the Rotten Rose with his savings and move his things into Valoria's chambers in the same day, no doubt the best day of his life; how Grenwyr City will be rebuilt with Valoria's designs; how so many citizens have been hired to do the job; how they'll be building air balloons next.

But what spills from my lips as I hold Meredy's gaze is "You. I want to talk about you and me, and what we're going to do with this gorgeous afternoon."

"Suppose we should take a romantic trip to Dargany, like Si and Danial?" she asks, snapping off a flower stalk and blowing the petals into the wind.

"Why not take a tour of every province?" I counter, pulling her into my arms. "We can start now, if you like. But honestly, I'm not in a hurry..."

I kiss her carefully, slowly, until the stars come out. There's no real rush to go anywhere, because we're already home. Better still, we're alive. And if the flowers in my love's hair are any indication, no matter what darkness may be lurking on the path ahead, we have all the time in the world—and then some.

ACKNOWLEDGMENTS

Like Odessa, I am lucky to have a fierce team of people in my corner whom I'd be glad to have by my side during a zombie apocalypse—and without whom this book wouldn't have been possible:

Lucy Carson, my agent, to whom this book is dedicated. I appreciate your wit, warmth, and expert guidance on a daily basis.

Julie Rosenberg, my editor, who constantly taught and inspired me throughout the editorial process with her keen eye for detail and her great ideas.

Everyone else at Razorbill and Penguin Teen (hi, Elyse, Ben, Casey, Alex, Felicity, Elora, Kara, and Friya!), who are so hardworking and who have been in Odessa's corner from day one. You all deserve an unlimited supply of coffee beans.

The Sparrows, my street team, and other wonderful folks who tirelessly helped to spread the word about all things *Reign*: Brittany from *Brittany's Book Rambles*, Mana from *The Book Voyagers*, Becky G from *Life of a BookNerd Addict*, Katie from *Mundie Moms*, Rae from

A New Look on Books, Amanda from *Nocturnal Reading*, Kelly from *BookCrushin*, Becca from *Becca's Book Realm*, Kat Kennedy, Bethany Pullen, Christy Jane, Katherine Moore, Diana Dworak, Melanie Parker, Destiny Barber, Melanie Parker (TBR and Beyond), Shealea I., Julie (DailyJulianne), Heather Cilley, Heather Lane, and many more! I'm convinced that some, if not all, of you are actually magic.

The dedicated staff at Chop Suey Books and One More Page Books, two of my favorite indies. You all make being an author an absolute joy with your support and enthusiasm.

Jessica Khoury, who brought my vision of the world of *Reign* to life in beautiful map form. You're an awesome friend and artist.

Jo Painter, who once again created stunning versions of my characters. You make such great art.

Gwen Cole, who over the course of writing this book has laughed with me, listened to my worries, celebrated with me, and shared many tasty breakfasts at our favorite places.

Erin Cashman, KT Bucklein, Eve Castellan, Jessica Spotswood, Jodi Meadows, M Evan Matyas, Meagan Spooner, Alexandra Christo, Atia Abawi, Anna Schafer, Rachel Pudelek, Chelsea Bobulski, Dee Romito, Heidi Lang, Carolee Noury, Brian Schwarz, and the ladies of 16 to Read, who are my fellow authors and also amazing listeners, readers, editors, and friends.

Erin Oliva, Lenore Bajare-Dukes, Joe Sparks, Megan Placona, and my PoGo family, who all raised my spirits throughout the process of writing this book, whether it was through visits, texts, meals, or sighing/cheering with me when I had news to share. Thank you for liking me enough to help with the big move this year *and* listen to my stories!

Erica Kellar Brown, whose kindness and compassion are boundless.

Chris, who is always pushing me to dream bigger, who is my

partner in all things. I love you more than words on a page can contain.

Mom, Dad, my sister Lindsey, and the rest of my family, who support me in everything I do. You've shown your love in so many ways this year (and always!). Thank you.

Last but certainly not least, my readers, who have made me smile more often than they know. I am deeply grateful for you all.

This book is also dedicated in the loving memory of Kiowa Josephine (aka Khaleesi), who left us on April 2nd, 2018, to race among the moon and stars. Rest easy, my Roo.

RISE
of the
SPARROW

Before *Reign of the Fallen*, Odessa, Evander, Jax, and Simeon weren't masters—they were still training in the Deadlands. Turn the page and step back to the fateful night before Odessa killed King Wylding . . . for the first time.

It isn't like Prince Hadrien to miss a party. Sure, the Festival of Cloud happens each year, and everything from the outfits to the arrangement of the stuffed figs is always the same, but wherever there's dance and drink and laughter, that's where you'll find Hadrien. I may have only met him a year ago, but we've spent enough time together for me to tell when something's up. Even if he isn't in the mood to party, he'd never miss an opportunity to tell me how good I look in my new black dress and matching diamond-studded slippers.

Abandoning my search of the crowd, I weave around several Dead flocking to the banquet tables and a group of gray-eyed nobles performing a storm-summoning dance I swear I've seen a thousand times before. They lack the training of weather workers, and if they're able to make a single raindrop fall in Cloud's honor tonight, I'll drink a whole bottle of champagne to toast them.

If Master Cymbre lets me, that is. Apparently being fifteen means I'm too young for more than a sip of wine or cider, even though I'm old enough to go to the Deadlands to retrieve spirits and give them new life.

"Wielding magic doesn't mean you're responsible enough to drink yet—trust me, this job will make you do plenty of that in time, anyway," she says whenever I press the issue. Awesome.

The wind pushing through the palace courtyard blows my hair back from my sweaty forehead, cool but not cold, promising autumn. I fill my lungs with crisp, smoky air and hold it in for a moment, savoring the clamor of musicians, the heat of the bonfires, the beauty of the ever-changing flames.

It's a good night to be alive.

My fellow trainees wave me over to the bench they share, just out of reach of the trailing smoke. Simeon is tapping his foot in time with the music, watching the dancers with a slight frown. Evander seems to stare right through me, lost in thought. Jax looks bored, as he always does on festival nights. He has a leather lead wrapped around one wrist that's attached to the collar of a wolf with rust-red fur and amber eyes. The beast watches me warily as I approach, but doesn't curl its lip up or flatten its ears. I guess it likes what it smells.

"Jax, what are you doing?" I ask, nodding to the wolf.

"Babysitting," he answers with a shrug.

"I don't think you know the meaning of the word." I grin.

Jax crosses his arms, looking a little defensive. "Sure I do." He glances at the wolf. "This is Ash. I'm feeding him, walking him, and making sure he doesn't get any ouchies."

"Ouchies?" I arch a brow, grinning harder. "Whatever. I just hope you're getting paid for this." The amused gleam in his eyes tells me I haven't guessed right. "Well, then, you're doing it for some hot girl."

"Take a seat," he suggests, "and I'll tell you all about her."

I shake my head at him and gesture helplessly at the bench. There's no way I can fit on the wooden seat with my three friends taking up every inch of space, but they try their best to make a sliver of room between Jax and Evander.

The seams of my dress groan in protest as I squish between the boys, half on their laps. Jax laughs and elbows me into Evander, who barely cracks a smile as I grab his arm to steady myself, heat flooding my cheeks. His eyes meet mine for a moment, and it's not fair to him that I know him as well as I do, because it's easy to read the look he's trying to conceal: longing.

It steals my breath, both thrilling and terrifying. What could be better than getting even closer with the person who knows me best? And what could be a worse mistake than ruining my greatest friendship if it doesn't work out? Just imagining all the awkward trips to the Deadlands in our post-breakup future is enough to make me shove my wonderings away.

"So what's with you three tonight?" I tease, trying to lighten the mood. "Si? Van? You're quieter than the dead."

"Simeon misses his new boyfriend already, even though Danial's visiting the city with his parents again next month," Jax explains. "The Dead ate everything Ash and I wanted, so we're still hungry. And Van . . ." He narrows his eyes slightly at Evander, then shrugs. "He's nervous about tomorrow. If we screw this up, they might end our training on the spot. Replace us with someone who actually studies. We'll have to become Shade-baiters or learn how to farm carrots. Or I'll have to make this pet-sitting thing legit. You're not bad with a quill—maybe you can help design the flyers."

I follow Jax's gaze toward our teachers, Masters Cymbre and Nicanor, who are deep in conversation with one of the Dead. Tomorrow, for the first time, they'll watch as we kill King Wylding and bring him back to life. It's a ritual we've practiced many times since we began training, but never on the most important person in Karthia. His Majesty has seen many necromancers come and go in his centuries—no wonder Evander is worried about not measuring up. We've still got two years before we earn the title of Master.

Assuming we survive that long. The pay might be great, but the job hazards are more bountiful than the gold.

As I turn slightly to face Evander, he catches my gaze again—I don't know how long he's been watching me, but suddenly I'm much too aware of my leg draped over his.

He opens his mouth to say something, then hesitates, seeming to rethink his words. As he starts again, another voice cuts over his. "Trainees! Corpse-wranglers!"

That gets everyone's attention, even the wolf's. We all turn toward a person in a stiff-shouldered green messenger's coat with a mostly empty bottle of wine in one hand. They sway slightly on their feet as they sashay toward us in time with the lively song playing from the courtyard. "King Wylding re . . . requeries . . . requires your presence in the throne room to discuss tomorrow's ritual."

"When?" Evander says sharply.

"Sundown," the messenger answers, glancing at the velvet sky sprinkled with stars. Even through their drunken haze, they seem to realize their mistake. But all they say is, "Best be off, then! Good luck!"

"What's the point in hurrying when we're already this late?" Jax asks lazily, slowly unfolding his long legs as I untangle myself from the others and leap to my feet.

Simeon and Evander stand, too, seemingly without thinking. After five years, they're so used to being our partners that their bodies have adapted to sharing our space even when their minds haven't quite caught up.

Jax tugs on the wolf's lead, and with eager eyes and ears pricked forward, the beast trots at his heels. Together, we all rush into the palace.

King Wylding isn't in the throne room. He isn't in any of his usual haunts, either: The great hall and the rookery are empty but for a few guards on duty and one of the Dead quietly writing out a message for a bird to carry.

We're about to search the kitchen when an anguished scream from somewhere above sends us all running for the stairs—quietly. Spending time in the Deadlands has made us experts in stealth. We don't know who or what cried out just now, and while we have rooms here with beds and desks inside, we all know this isn't our home. It isn't our place to intrude on whatever might be happening. Not unless there's stabbing to do, which there very well might be, if the wolf's excited panting is any indication.

"Valoria," someone says urgently as we approach several doors concealing the royal family's chambers, "Breathe. She's still with us." I recognize the voice as a healer's, one who helped me when I broke my arm in combat practice last year.

A flurry of motion at the corner of my vision makes me turn and glance behind us. Hadrien emerges from another staircase into the hallway, cradling a glass container of smoking, emerald-green liquid, not seeming to see our group as he nudges open the door across from us with his shoulder and enters in a hurry.

"That's the fastest I've ever seen him move when he's not chasing a girl." Jax tilts his head in the prince's direction.

We creep closer to the door Hadrien left open. Evander's fingers rest lightly on my back as we walk, the way they have hundreds of times before. In the Deadlands, that touch has always reassured me. Tonight, it makes me misstep, catching my foot as we approach the door Hadrien disappeared through.

"Careful. You don't want to repeat my mistake." Evander grins as he steadies me, no doubt remembering the fall he took in the Deadlands last year. Of course, he wouldn't be grinning if *he* had been the one to drag someone almost two miles to the nearest gate, but I have to admit, the memory gets funnier over time

My laugh comes out breathy, forced, and I wonder if he notices. It's not like I haven't thought about kissing him before. What's bothering me is that tonight, I can't seem to get the idea out of my head, even though I know it would change everything. Every time we touch, he erases another bit of my resolve.

"Odessa. Van. What are you two doing? *Look*," Simeon whispers. I follow his gaze through the open door we're practically invading now, and what I see inside makes me forget everything around me.

King Wylding and an array of his guards stand toe to toe with Hadrien, blocking the prince's way forward to a bed where a small woman lies very still, her eyes closed—Hadrien's mother, one of the living Wylding princesses. I'd know her anywhere, sick or not. At a whisper from one of the guards, the king turns his masked face to me and my friends.

"Trainees," he says as warmly as his ancient vocal cords will allow, "I was worried you didn't get my message. Wait there, and I'll be with you shortly."

"Eldest Grandfather, you must let me through!" Hadrien's voice is higher than normal, tight with panic as he cradles his potion jar and looks toward his mother.

I study the sleeping woman on the bed, whose blond hair forms a halo against her many pillows. I've spoken with her several times, though Hadrien is by far the most social of the bunch, the public face of the Wylding heirs. I knew the princess had fallen ill with the black fever recently, but I hadn't realized how close she was to the end—the family must have been keeping it a secret to avoid worrying anyone before the festival. After all, the party must always go on, per King Wylding's command. He says it's the best way to keep the public from becoming consumed by fear and panic about the sickness that's bound to claim someone they love before the year is up.

I pull my shirt up to cover my mouth, and my friends do the same. The black fever is highly contagious. Hadrien's mother was the first case this year, and while none of the healers tending to her have fallen ill yet, it's only a matter of time.

Death's pallor and scent cling to the woman on the bed, the smell distinct even through the mask of my shirt. Pressed against the woman's side, their backs to the door, are two girls with long, blond hair and real masks on their faces: Hadrien's sisters.

One of the girls, the one with glasses, half turns to the king. "Hadrien's right!" she says, her voice wobbly at first, though she quickly controls it. "If he thinks he has a cure, let him try it. What can it hurt? She won't live out the hour—"

"Enough! You will not poison the blood of my blood with this . . . this foolishness!" King Wylding snarls from behind a porcelain mask delicately painted to resemble the Face of Cloud. The girl shrinks back against her mother's pillows as the king rounds on her, the points of his crown gleaming sharply in the torchlight. "Is that . . . a *new* hairstyle?" he asks the girl, his voice lower, more menacing.

We all know the rules: No new anything. No changing ourselves or our routines.

Beside me, Simeon sucks in a breath.

"N-no, Eldest, it's an approved style," the girl answers meekly, though she seems to force herself to sit taller. "I arranged it this way for the festival, just like last year."

The king growls again, studying the girl's head from every angle.

He doesn't scare me. Not in this form. But he's growling at the young princess like the Shade he'll become if we don't repeat the ritual tomorrow as planned, and that's enough to cover me in gooseflesh. It would be stupid not to be afraid of those monsters. No matter how hard I train, no matter how skilled I am, I'll never be a physical match for their speed or strength.

Hadrien makes a sudden move to throw the potion to one of his sisters while the king is distracted. The guards react almost instantly, but teetering on the verge of monsterhood, King Wylding is faster. He grabs the potion and shatters the glass with a squeeze of his heavy fist as the guards restrain Hadrien.

"Find the rest of this and destroy it," the king snaps at two of the guards.

The oldest of Hadrien's sisters takes advantage of the chaos to escape the room, pushing roughly through us, her hands covering her face. Tears leak from between her fingers, splashing her dress collar. She stops trying to fight the flow and drops her hands to her sides as she passes us, and something clatters softly to the floor.

Jax picks up the lost object—her glasses—and folds them before setting them on a small table just inside the door.

I doubt she's brave or foolish enough to try to outrun the guards and preserve the remains of Hadrien's potion—his black fever cure— but what if she were? There would be a lot less death in Karthia if the emerald-green liquid actually worked. Less death would mean less work for us necromancers, so I guess I should be grateful to the king, but instead, nausea twists my stomach.

Hadrien's mother struggles for breath in her sleep. The prince makes a strangled sound, anger, fear, and desperation fighting in his throat, and it draws my gaze back to him.

I hadn't realized Hadrien was researching anything on his many forays to the library. I thought he was reading adventure stories to pass the time or brushing up on law or looking for tips on how to charm girls. Maybe I don't know him as well as I thought.

"At least let us raise her," Hadrien pleads as he stands in the guards' hold, staring deep into King Wylding's shroud. The pain of loss is already etching lines into the prince's face. "I'll make the sacrifice myself—"

"You will not!" the king hisses, the words punctuated with a pop like cracking bones. "It was her wish not to be raised. She'll lie beneath the palace forever, in a beautiful tomb of white marble, just like the others who made her choice." His dry voice changes, softens, sounding more like the man I know. "I'm sorry, Hadrien. But you can still make your sacrifice tomorrow. You can go to the Deadlands to raise *me*."

If Hadrien is still angry—either at the king for ruining his cure, or at his mother for making such a choice without telling him—his face doesn't betray it. He merely bows his head with the weight of the words. "Of course, Eldest. It will be my honor." He draws his shirt up to cover his mouth. "Now, if I may, I'd like to spend a few minutes with my mother, as they're the last ones I'll ever have with her."

The guards release him at King Wylding's nod. Hadrien trudges forward as if fighting a swiftly moving current, not reacting as his polished boot scrapes through the spilled potion, hardly blinking as his young sister throws her arms around him.

Hadrien turns away from his mother just once, searching the

doorway where the four of us are gathered until his eyes meet mine. As he starts to say something, his mom stirs.

Silence strikes the room like a lash, sudden and deep.

The wolf at our backs whines sharply at the change in atmosphere, a reminder that we shouldn't be here. Even the king seems to realize it.

"Trainees, we'll talk in the morning. You're dismissed. Go, enjoy the party," he croaks, settling down on the end of the princess's bed opposite Hadrien.

Relieved, the four of us hurry away as quietly as we came, the chatter of drunk partygoers as soothing as warm mulled cider after what we witnessed.

Evander takes my hand, or I take his. Our hands find their way to each other. However it happens, I'm just glad it does. Maybe some mistakes are worth making. Maybe this won't be a mistake at all.

We follow Simeon and Jax to the table where Cymbre and Nicanor are finally eating supper, both resplendent in glittering face paint to celebrate the Face of Cloud. The artist who worked on Nicanor's adornments took advantage of his lack of hair, transforming the extra canvas space into thunderheads and lightning.

Before we can say a word, we're set upon by servants shoving the best of everything under our noses on golden platters: Fruits, cheeses, and dense, sweet-smelling pies. Once we've made our selections, they bow and retreat.

One of them tucked a little gold skull ring into the top of my berry pie. It doesn't look expensive, but surely it cost a portion of the giver's wages. I slip it onto my right index finger, but even the unexpected gift doesn't make me smile.

"You four look like you've seen a Shade," Cymbre observes. When none of us says anything, she prods, "You know the deal: no secrets. So, spill."

Jax, absently rubbing the wolf between its ears, starts telling our teachers what happened as we pull out seats and slump into them.

"Lower your voice," Nicanor says swiftly to Jax at mention of Hadrien's potion. "The prince is lucky His Majesty didn't want to try him for treason." Concern wrinkles his forehead. "We'll mention it no further—for everyone's sake."

"What's dead will always rise," Cymbre reminds him gently, flipping her long braid over her shoulder, away from her plate. "But this once, I think you're right." She takes a sip of her wine before narrowing her cool blue eyes at us. "You should all be in bed already. You've got an important day tomorrow."

Simeon nods, but instead of standing, he pulls a plate of sausages closer and starts tossing small pieces to the wolf, who catches them in midair. When Simeon shows the beast the now-empty plate, the wolf licks his muzzle and sits politely on his haunches. He must be a beast master's companion, which reminds me—after we're finished with the king tomorrow, I really have to find out who this girl is.

"Bedtime," Cymbre says again, the glow in her cheeks suggesting she enjoyed the wolf's display as much as the rest of us.

When none of us moves to get up, Cymbre clears her throat and nudges Nicanor. He tries to look stern, but his face paint totally ruins the effect. Anyone wearing that much glitter loves fun more than sleep.

Using my hair to hide my face from Cymbre, I roll my eyes so only Evander can see. I'm never going to ruin *my* trainees' fun when I'm a master. Of course, that means I'll have to earn my title. And that starts with having my wits about me tomorrow.

"You love my rules," Cymbre teases as I finally, reluctantly, get up to hug her goodnight. "Oh, and Odessa—we've chosen *you* to kill the king tomorrow. You're going to do great." I scowl as she kisses my forehead, trying not to let my mix of nerves and pride show, but Cymbre's smile doesn't dim in the slightest at my reaction. She knows she's the closest thing to a mother I've got.

I wonder who's going to hug Hadrien goodnight from now on.

The thought makes me want to go find him. I'm almost to one of the servants' side doors when a voice calls to me from the darkness. "Odessa. Wait."

Evander draws me into an alcove that hugs the palace wall. It's a cozy spot sheltered by flowering vines and shrubs. From here, we can see the partygoers, but they can't see us.

"Cymbre's right," I say as I sit. I like that I never have to tailor my thoughts around him. I can just let them flow, whether he likes them or not, and he accepts them. "We need sleep. We can't mess this up. It's our biggest test yet."

Evander nods, and I can't help smiling—I love when he admits I'm right. But he makes no move to rise.

"You know you're going to have to tell me what's on your mind sooner or later, and it might as well be now." I lean my forehead against his, inviting him in, but still he says nothing. "You're our best swordsman, Van. We need you tomorrow, all of you, fully focused. The king needs you. *I* need you. Did you hear what Cymbre said about me being the one to kill him? What if I miss his heart the first time? What if—"

"You won't," Evander cuts in swiftly, his eyes full of hope and something like wonder as he looks at me. The confidence in his smile silences my doubts. "You're an expert at finding hearts.

Whether or not you realize it, you've got mine in your hands right now."

I blink, my brain trying to process that this is really happening. "What?"

"I wanted to talk to you earlier tonight—before our big day—but I kept freezing," he confesses, shaking his head—I'm sure he's annoyed at his own lack of daring. "Believe it or not, even I get nervous. Especially with something this important."

"Lies," I murmur, my brain and heart finally catching up. "If you had any sense of self-preservation, you'd have picked a different job. Or at least picked Simeon as your partner. He listens to instructions and always follows the rules . . ."

It's strange, but I've never noticed just how dark a shade of blue Evander's eyes are. Darker than the deep ocean. Indigo feels like a better word—blue is too ordinary. Blue doesn't take my breath away. How have I looked into those eyes so many times and only recently realized that they make me feel like I'm flying without leaving the ground? I know he can see gateways to the Deadlands all around us, their glow outshining the fireflies, but he's only looking at me.

Evander rests a hand on my back, keeping me close, the longing in his gaze now undisguised, inviting me to dive in. He's never been afraid to take a risk, always looking for our next adventure. Surely he can feel my heart pounding like it wants to burst out of my skin, pummeling away the last of my doubts.

Maybe, like the first time I leapt off a cliff and dived through a gate into the Deadlands, I'll land somewhere soft.

I run a hand through his hair; he drops his hand to my waist. Everything that used to feel so familiar feels so new, but as always, we anticipate each other's movements better than the dancers around the bonfire.

We close the sliver of distance between us, kissing the salt and smoke of the night from each other's lips. For the space of a heartbeat, I don't know where he ends and where I begin. And when we pull apart, my head is still spinning.

We're partners. That used to seem like *everything*. But now I realize there's so much more. Now I feel more alive than I ever thought possible. Just like that first trip into the Deadlands, I'm glad I took the leap.

I thought he liked Jax. I know he sees the world the same way I do—beautiful people come in all genders—but I didn't think he saw us. Not like this. But as usual, even without talking it through, we've wound up on the same page.

"We'll get through tomorrow like we get through anything else: Together," he says. "You'll kill the king, and then we'll guide Hadrien through his first and only trip to the Deadlands with nothing to show for it but the spirit we came for."

"You make it sound so easy," I protest. When I think about what the new day will bring, my stomach clenches with a warning I can't quite understand.

Evander kisses my cheek. It's a sweet gesture, not hot like the kisses we just shared, but sweet is what I need right now. Sweet steadies my nerves. "Fine. Tomorrow will be hard, and will feel endless. We might come out of the Deadlands with a few broken bones, and we might see a Shade, but we'll survive. Just like always."

"Like always," I repeat.

Even knowing the danger that waits with every step I take into the spirit world, I wouldn't trade this life for anything. Whatever

I want, I can buy for myself. Everyone knows my name. Everyone respects what I'll become. Most orphans like me, they get none of that. Besides, if I didn't spend so much time around death, I doubt I'd truly appreciate the jump of my pulse beneath my skin, the rustle of bird wings in the bushes, the smells of food and sweat and nerves mingling in the air, the dizzying feast of senses that is the living world.

As Evander and I finally go our separate ways, I to my small palace quarter and he to his mother's beautiful manor house, the sweet-tart taste of possibility lingers on my tongue.

It's a good night to be alive, no matter what pain or sorrow it brings. The pain means we'll live to fight another day.

As I turn a corner toward my room, an oil portrait of the living royal heirs draws my gaze, and I linger a moment on a younger version of a familiar face. Poor Hadrien. No matter what crime he committed by making that potion, he didn't deserve to lose his mother like that. He's not quite an orphan like me, but he's close enough for me to understand. Instead of heading straight for bed, I look for him, but he's not in his mother's now-empty chambers or any of his favorite places.

Maybe tonight, he needed to disappear. Maybe he needed a way out of the cage King Wylding seems to have him in. Maybe right now, he wishes he were nowhere at all.

I leave a handful of honeysuckle blossoms on his bed, ones I plucked from the shrubs around the alcove where Evander kissed me. It's hardly a festival gift, let alone one fit for a prince, but I hope their beauty and sweetness will be enough to ward off a little of the darkness that surrounds him.

When I reach my room at last, I shuck off my dress and pick up my sword, practicing my stabbing poses. I yawn and stumble a little before quickly putting down the blade. Cymbre was right about needing sleep.

Tomorrow, I kill the king.

Tomorrow, I'll find his spirit and soar through the Deadlands back to the life I love.

As Evander's kiss reminded me, anything can happen if I'm willing to take the leap.